HELLO NEIGHBOR™

A GRAPHIC NOVEL

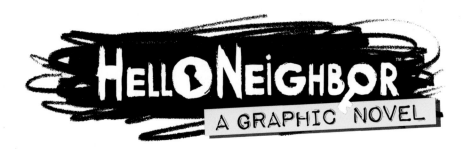

THE SECRET OF BOSCO BAY

BY ZAC GORMAN

ILLUSTRATED BY CHRIS FENOGLIO

SCHOLASTIC INC.

All rights reserved. Published by Graphix, an imprint of Scholastic Inc., *Publishers since 1920.* SCHOLASTIC, GRAPHIX, and associated logos are trademarks and/or registered trademarks of Scholastic Inc.

The publisher does not have any control over and does not assume any responsibility for author or third-party websites or their content.

Library of Congress Control Number Available

ISBN: 978-1-338-66202-3 (hardcover)
ISBN: 978-1-338-59648-9 (paperback)

10 9 8 7 6 5 4 3 2 1   20 21 22 23 24

Printed in the U.S.A.   40
First edition, October 2020
Edited by Michael Petranek and Chloe Fraboni
Art by Chris Fenoglio
Lettering by Bryan Senka
Book design by Heather Daugherty

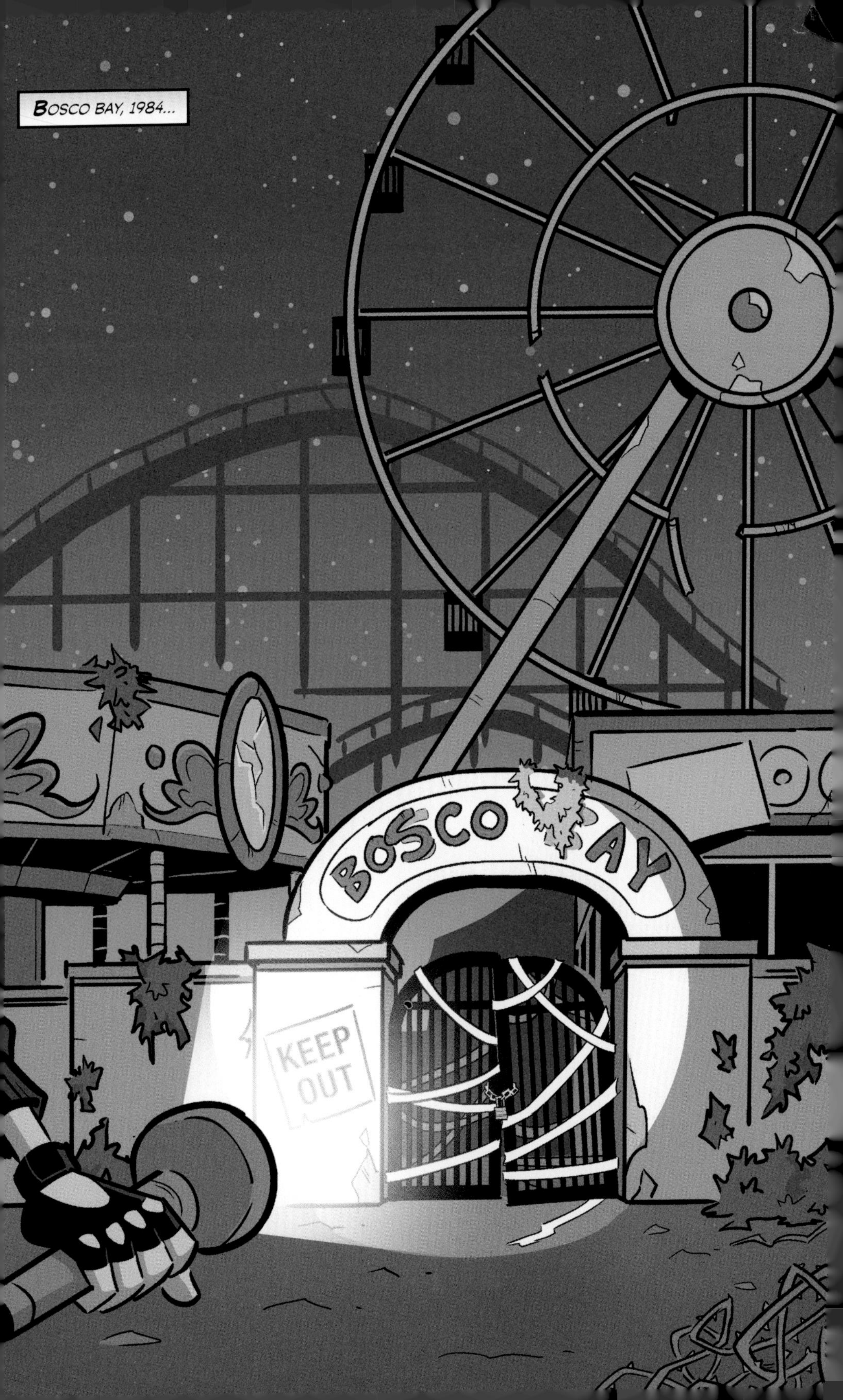
BOSCO BAY, 1984...
BOSCO AY
KEEP OUT

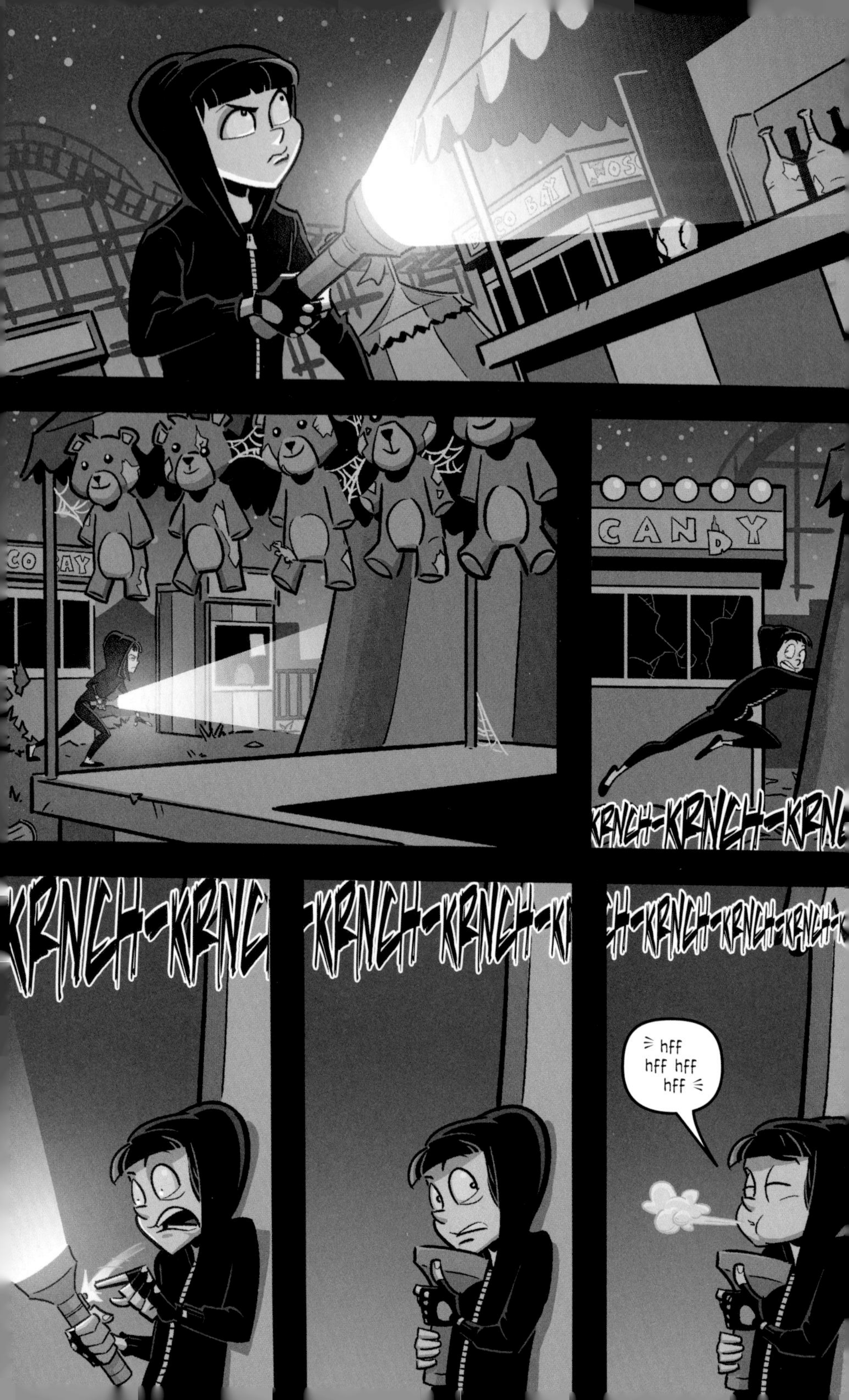
CO BAY
CANDY
KRNCH-KRNCH-KRN
KRNCH-KRNCH
KRNCH-KRNCH-KR
CH-KRNCH-KRNCH-KRNCH
hff hff hff hff

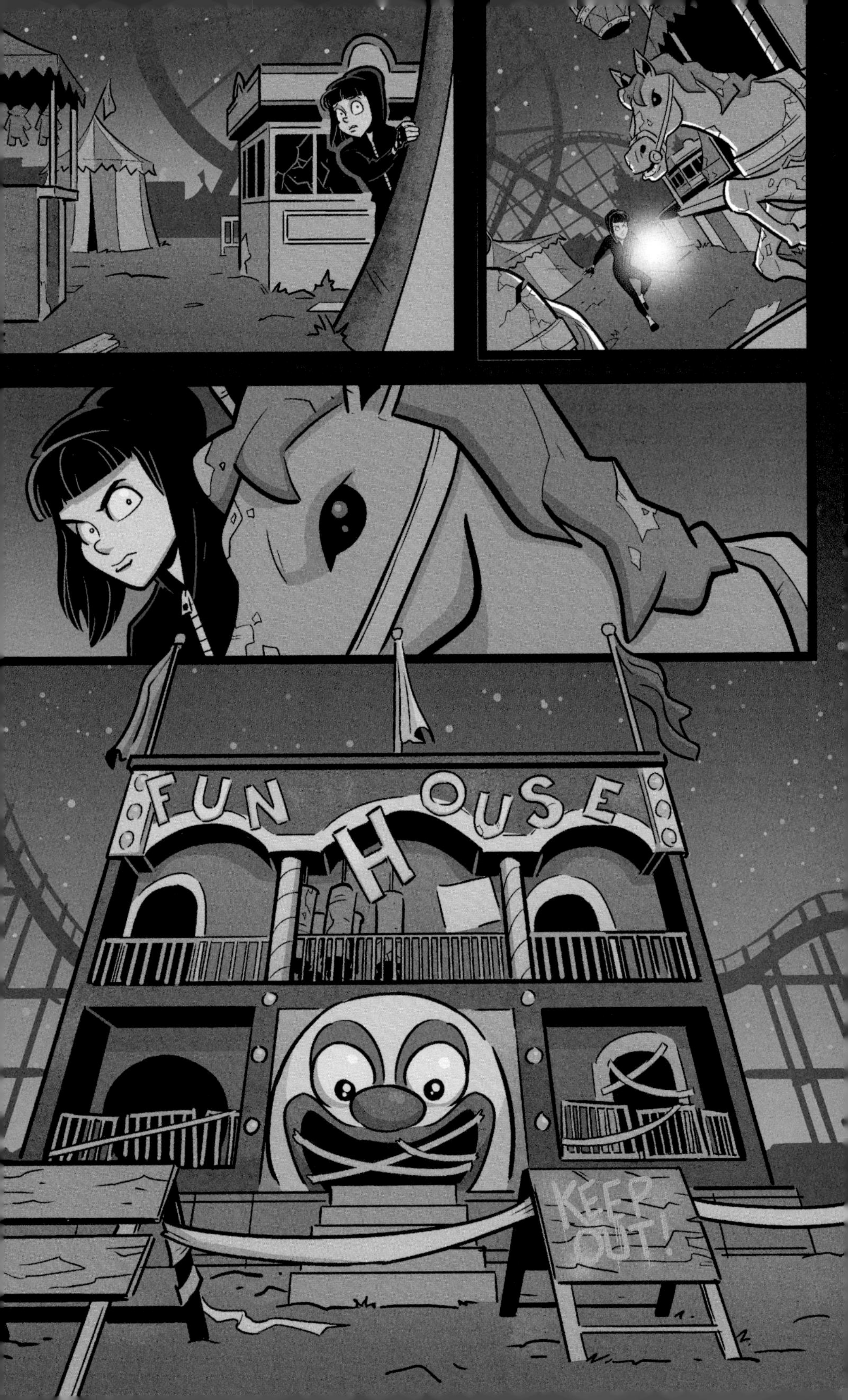
FUN HOUSE
KEEP OUT!

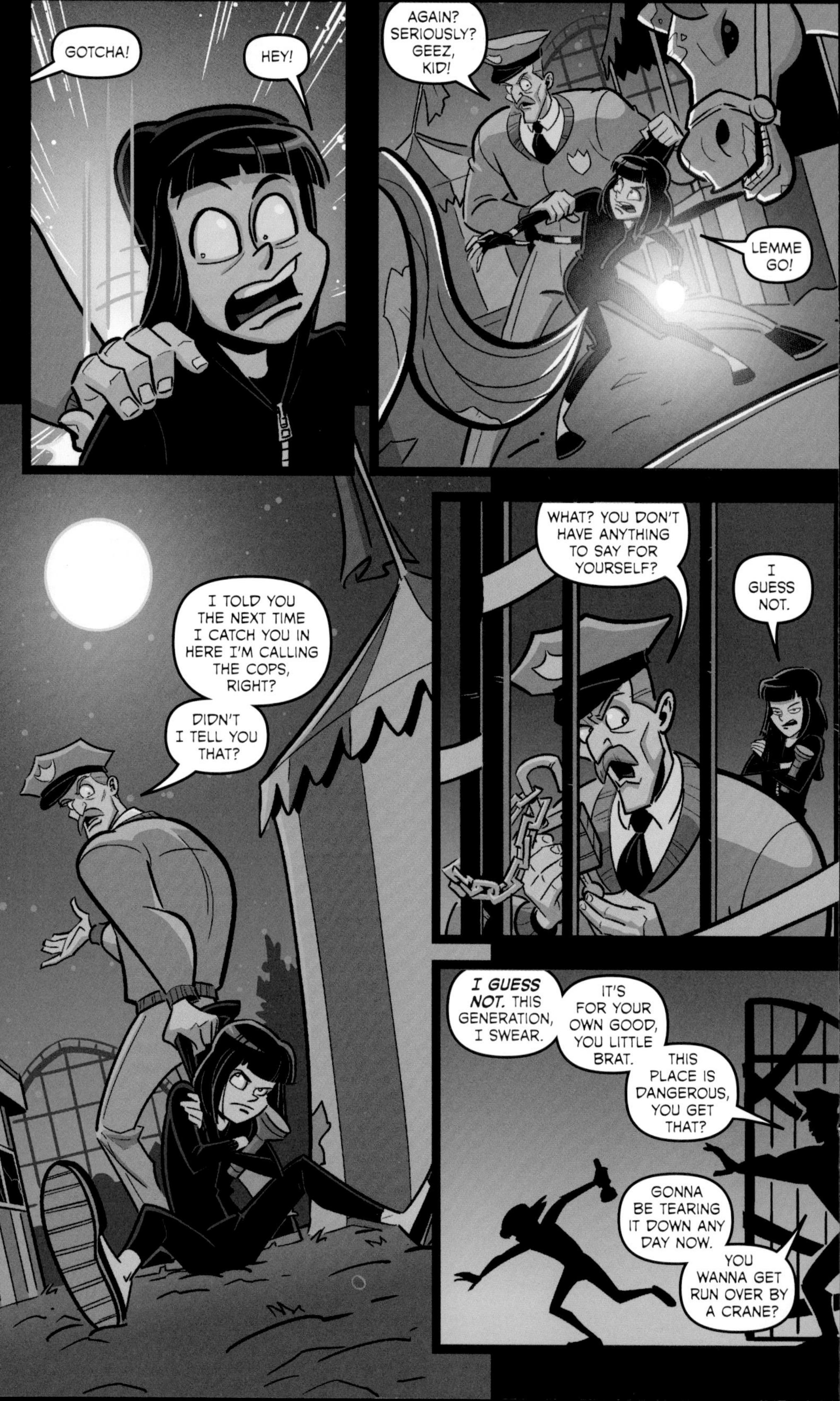
GOTCHA!
HEY!
AGAIN? SERIOUSLY? GEEZ, KID!
LEMME GO!
I TOLD YOU THE NEXT TIME I CATCH YOU IN HERE I'M CALLING THE COPS, RIGHT?
DIDN'T I TELL YOU THAT?
WHAT? YOU DON'T HAVE ANYTHING TO SAY FOR YOURSELF?
I GUESS NOT.
I GUESS NOT. THIS GENERATION, I SWEAR.
IT'S FOR YOUR OWN GOOD, YOU LITTLE BRAT.
THIS PLACE IS DANGEROUS, YOU GET THAT?
GONNA BE TEARING IT DOWN ANY DAY NOW.
YOU WANNA GET RUN OVER BY A CRANE?

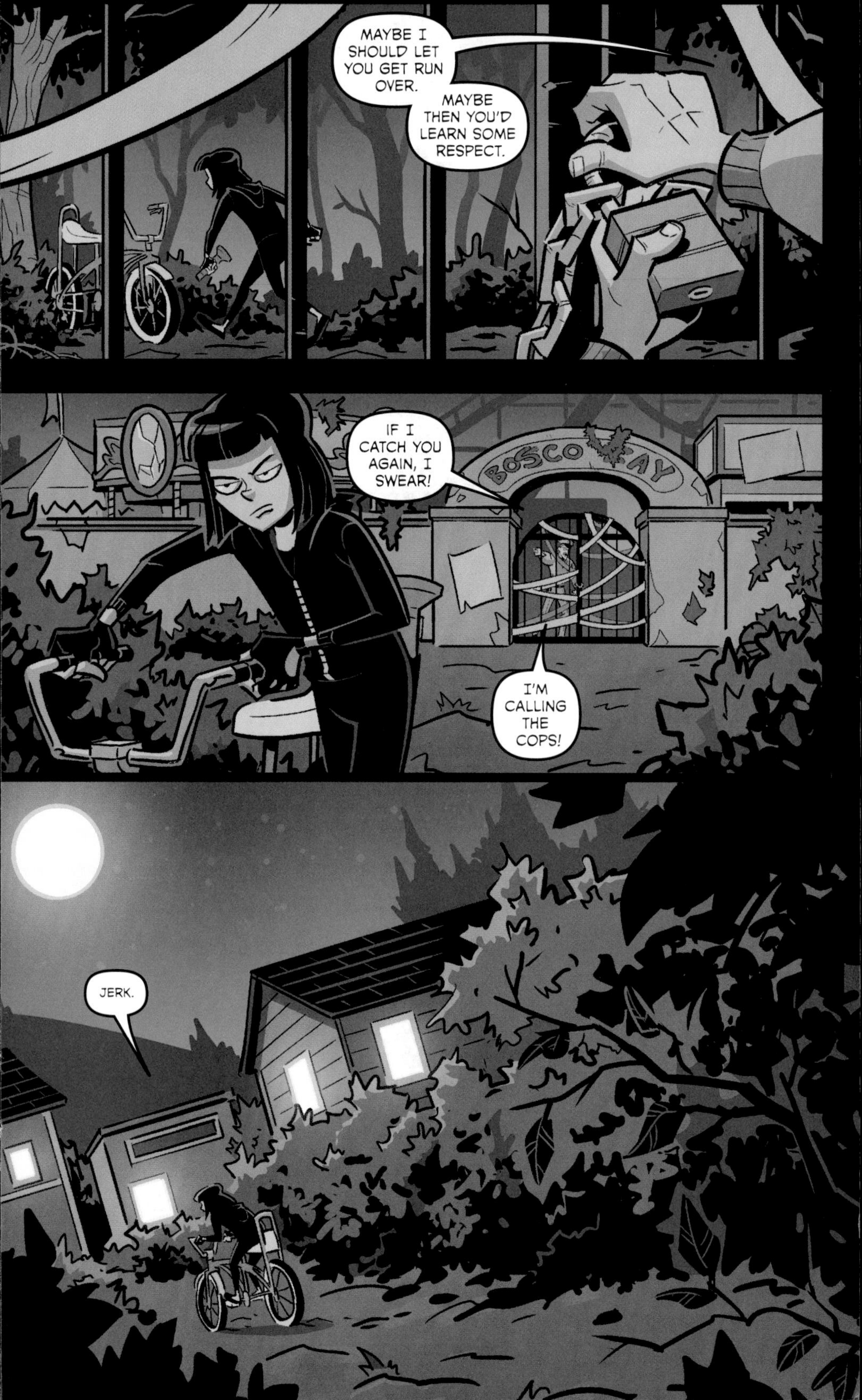
MAYBE I SHOULD LET YOU GET RUN OVER.
MAYBE THEN YOU'D LEARN SOME RESPECT.
IF I CATCH YOU AGAIN, I SWEAR!
I'M CALLING THE COPS!
JERK.

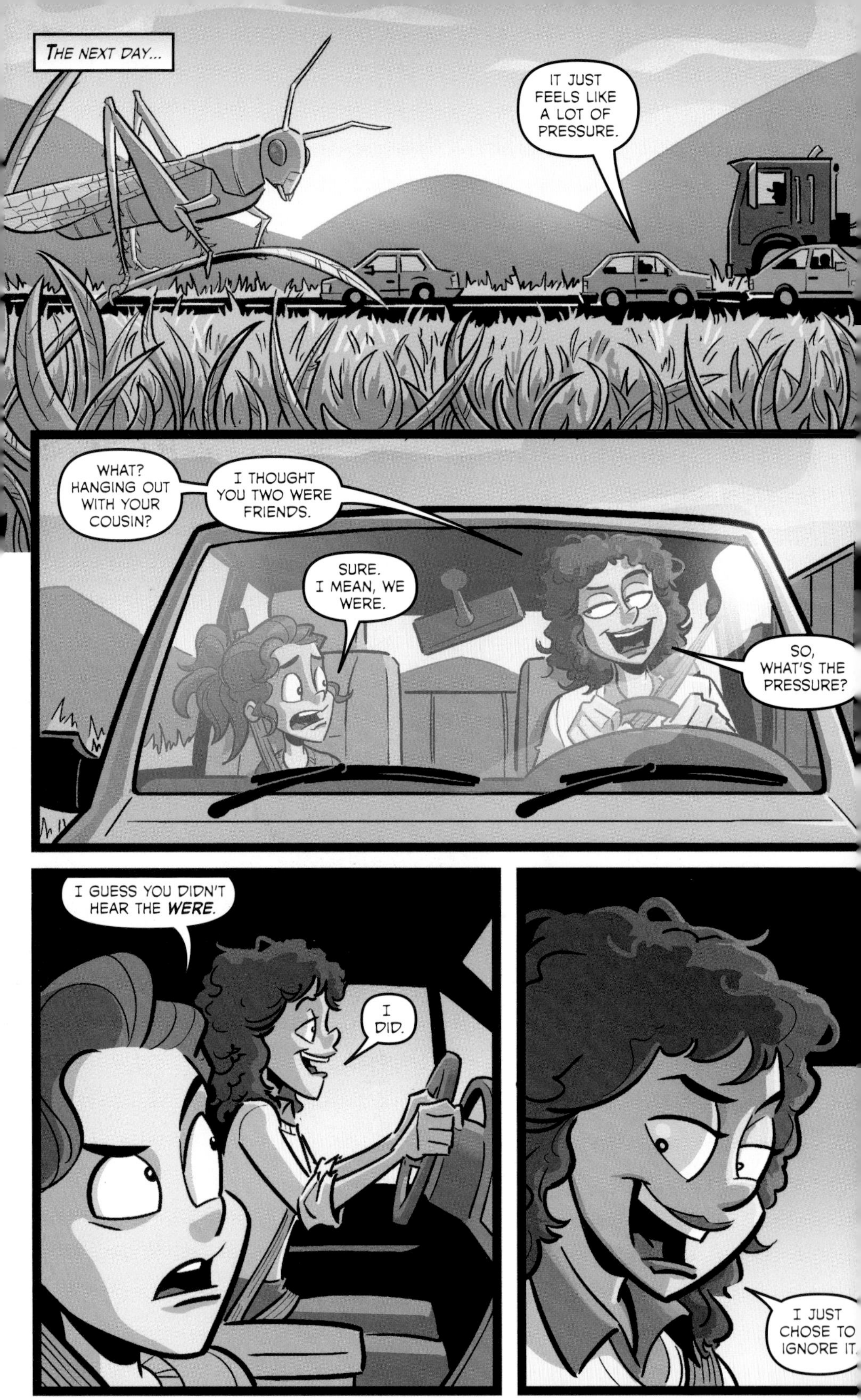
THE NEXT DAY...
IT JUST FEELS LIKE A LOT OF PRESSURE.
WHAT? HANGING OUT WITH YOUR COUSIN?
I THOUGHT YOU TWO WERE FRIENDS.
SURE. I MEAN, WE WERE.
SO, WHAT'S THE PRESSURE?
I GUESS YOU DIDN'T HEAR THE ***WERE***.
I DID.
I JUST CHOSE TO IGNORE IT.

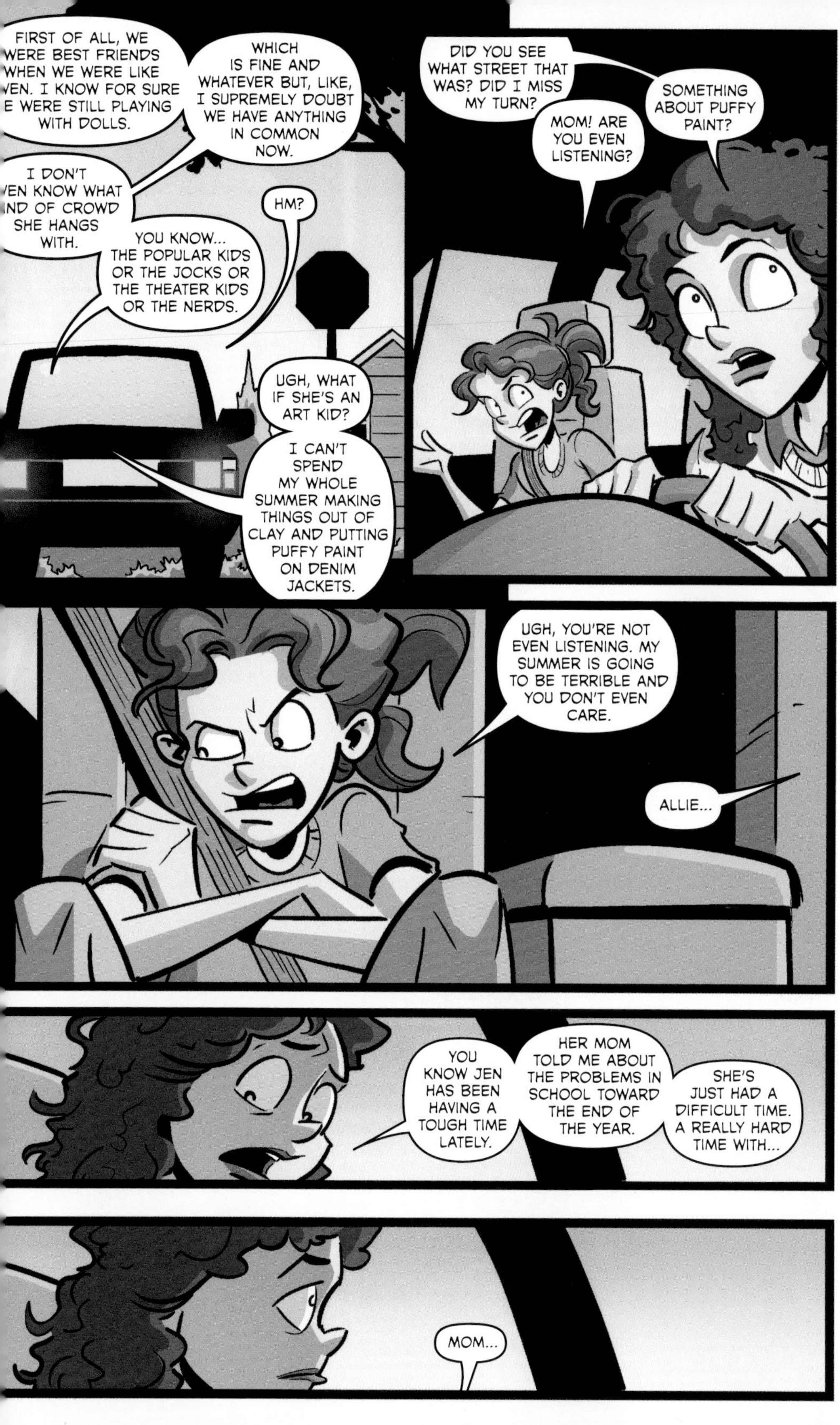
FIRST OF ALL, WE WERE BEST FRIENDS WHEN WE WERE LIKE VEN. I KNOW FOR SURE E WERE STILL PLAYING WITH DOLLS.
WHICH IS FINE AND WHATEVER BUT, LIKE, I SUPREMELY DOUBT WE HAVE ANYTHING IN COMMON NOW.
I DON'T VEN KNOW WHAT ND OF CROWD SHE HANGS WITH.
YOU KNOW... THE POPULAR KIDS OR THE JOCKS OR THE THEATER KIDS OR THE NERDS.
HM?
UGH, WHAT IF SHE'S AN ART KID?
I CAN'T SPEND MY WHOLE SUMMER MAKING THINGS OUT OF CLAY AND PUTTING PUFFY PAINT ON DENIM JACKETS.
DID YOU SEE WHAT STREET THAT WAS? DID I MISS MY TURN?
SOMETHING ABOUT PUFFY PAINT?
MOM! ARE YOU EVEN LISTENING?
UGH, YOU'RE NOT EVEN LISTENING. MY SUMMER IS GOING TO BE TERRIBLE AND YOU DON'T EVEN CARE.
ALLIE...
YOU KNOW JEN HAS BEEN HAVING A TOUGH TIME LATELY.
HER MOM TOLD ME ABOUT THE PROBLEMS IN SCHOOL TOWARD THE END OF THE YEAR.
SHE'S JUST HAD A DIFFICULT TIME. A REALLY HARD TIME WITH...
MOM...

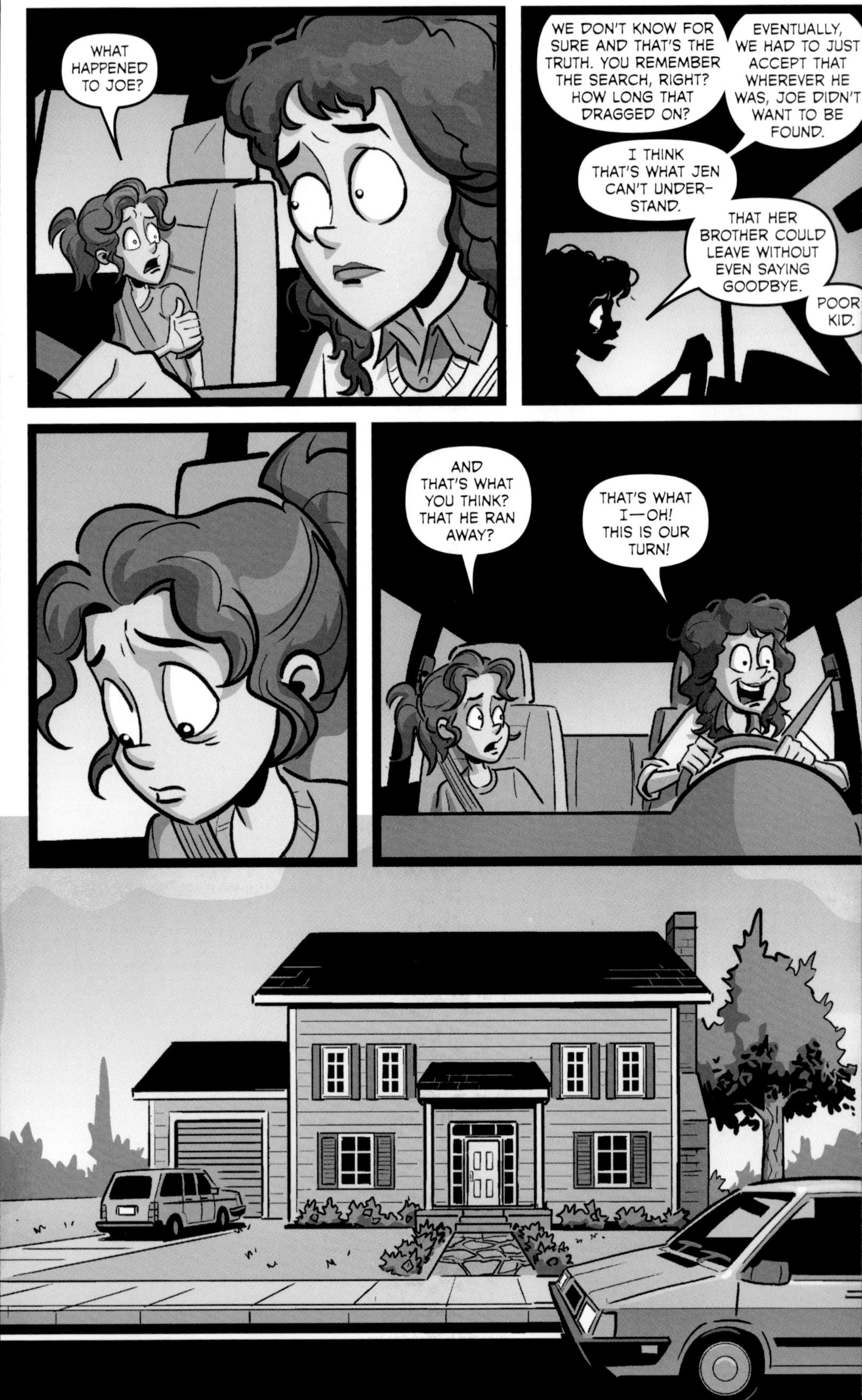
WHAT HAPPENED TO JOE?
WE DON'T KNOW FOR SURE AND THAT'S THE TRUTH. YOU REMEMBER THE SEARCH, RIGHT? HOW LONG THAT DRAGGED ON?
EVENTUALLY, WE HAD TO JUST ACCEPT THAT WHEREVER HE WAS, JOE DIDN'T WANT TO BE FOUND.
I THINK THAT'S WHAT JEN CAN'T UNDER-STAND.
THAT HER BROTHER COULD LEAVE WITHOUT EVEN SAYING GOODBYE.
POOR KID.
AND THAT'S WHAT YOU THINK? THAT HE RAN AWAY?
THAT'S WHAT I—OH! THIS IS OUR TURN!

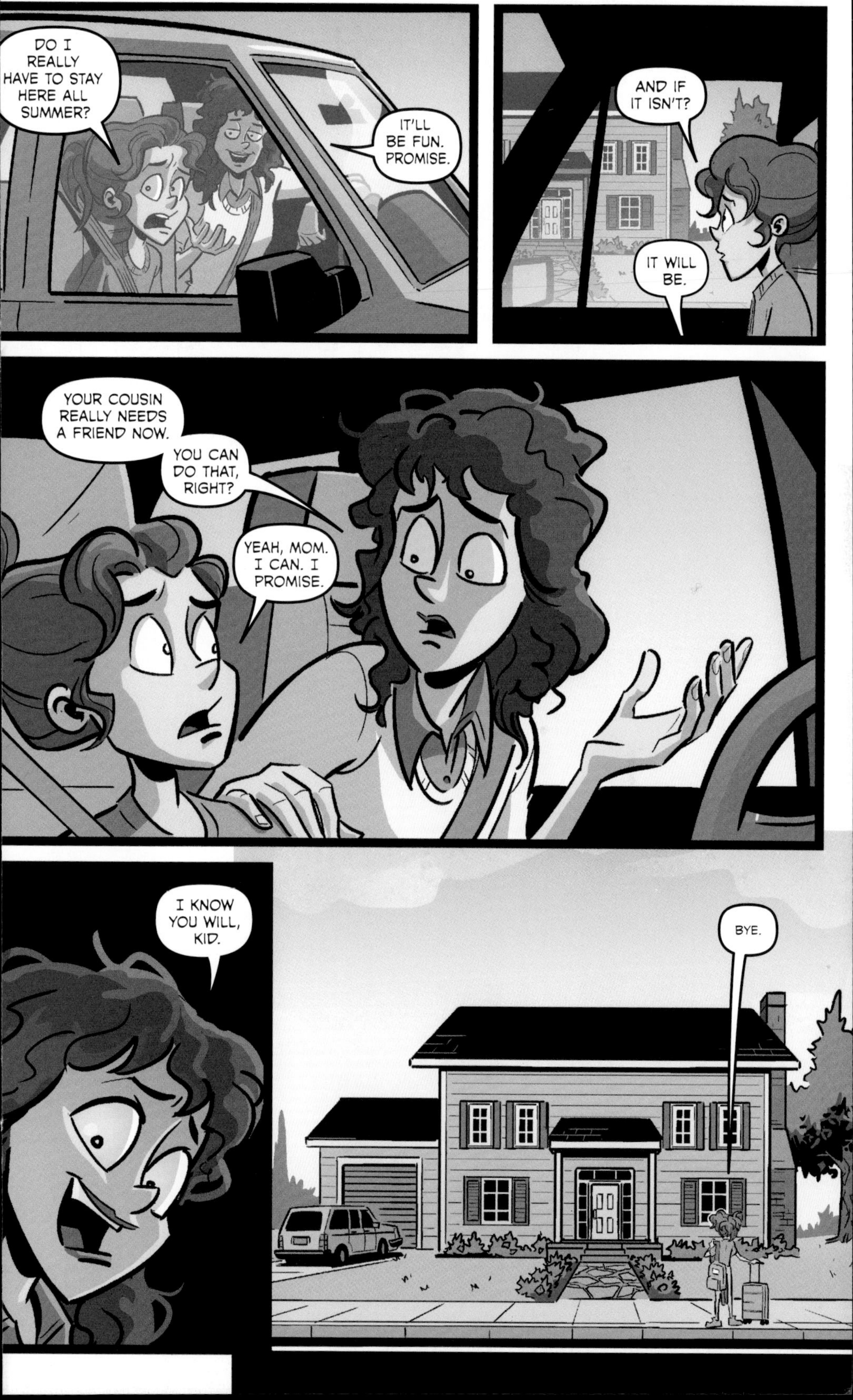
DO I REALLY HAVE TO STAY HERE ALL SUMMER?
IT'LL BE FUN. PROMISE.
AND IF IT ISN'T?
IT WILL BE.
YOUR COUSIN REALLY NEEDS A FRIEND NOW.
YOU CAN DO THAT, RIGHT?
YEAH, MOM. I CAN. I PROMISE.
I KNOW YOU WILL, KID.
BYE.

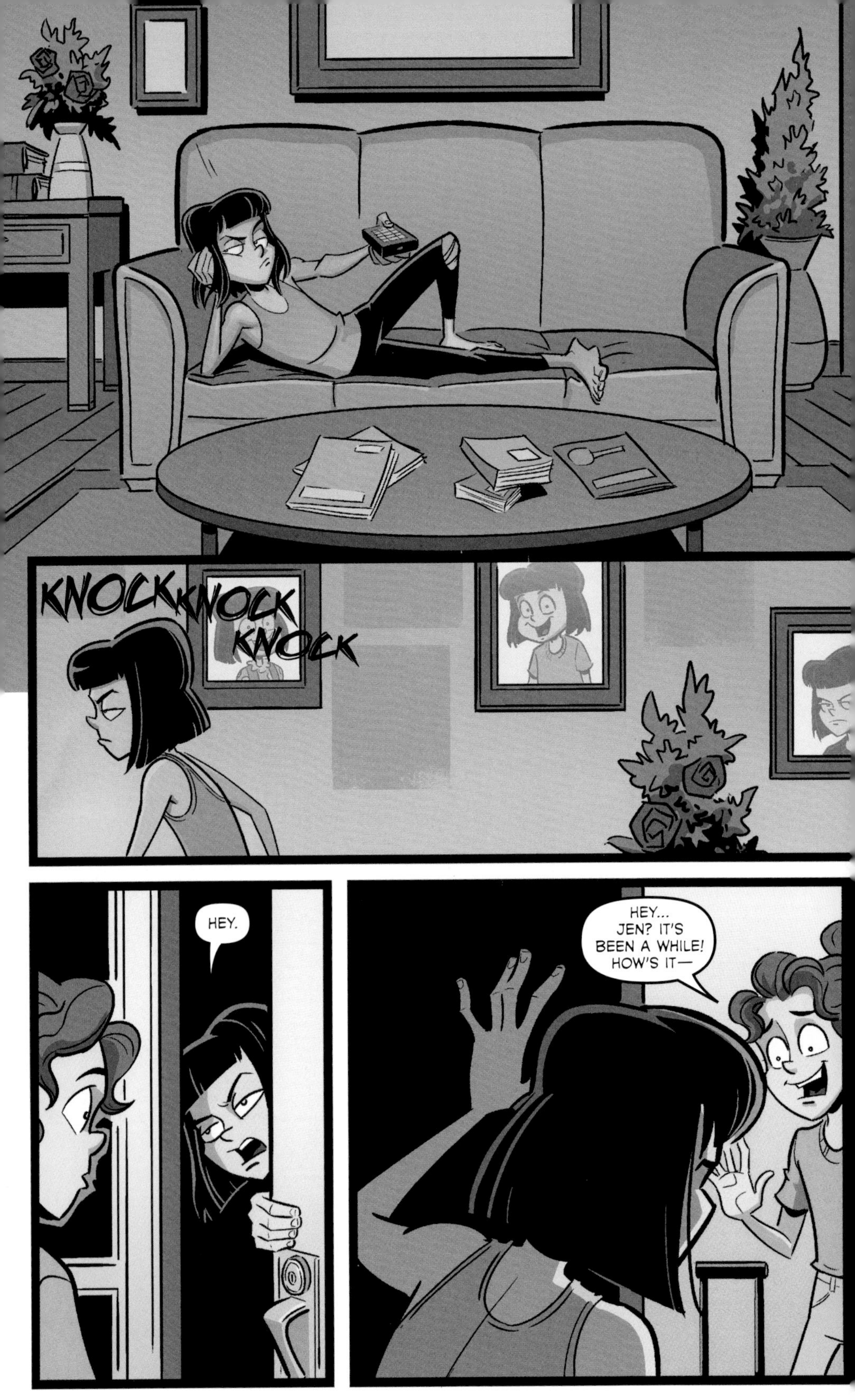
KNOCK KNOCK KNOCK
HEY.
HEY... JEN? IT'S BEEN A WHILE! HOW'S IT—

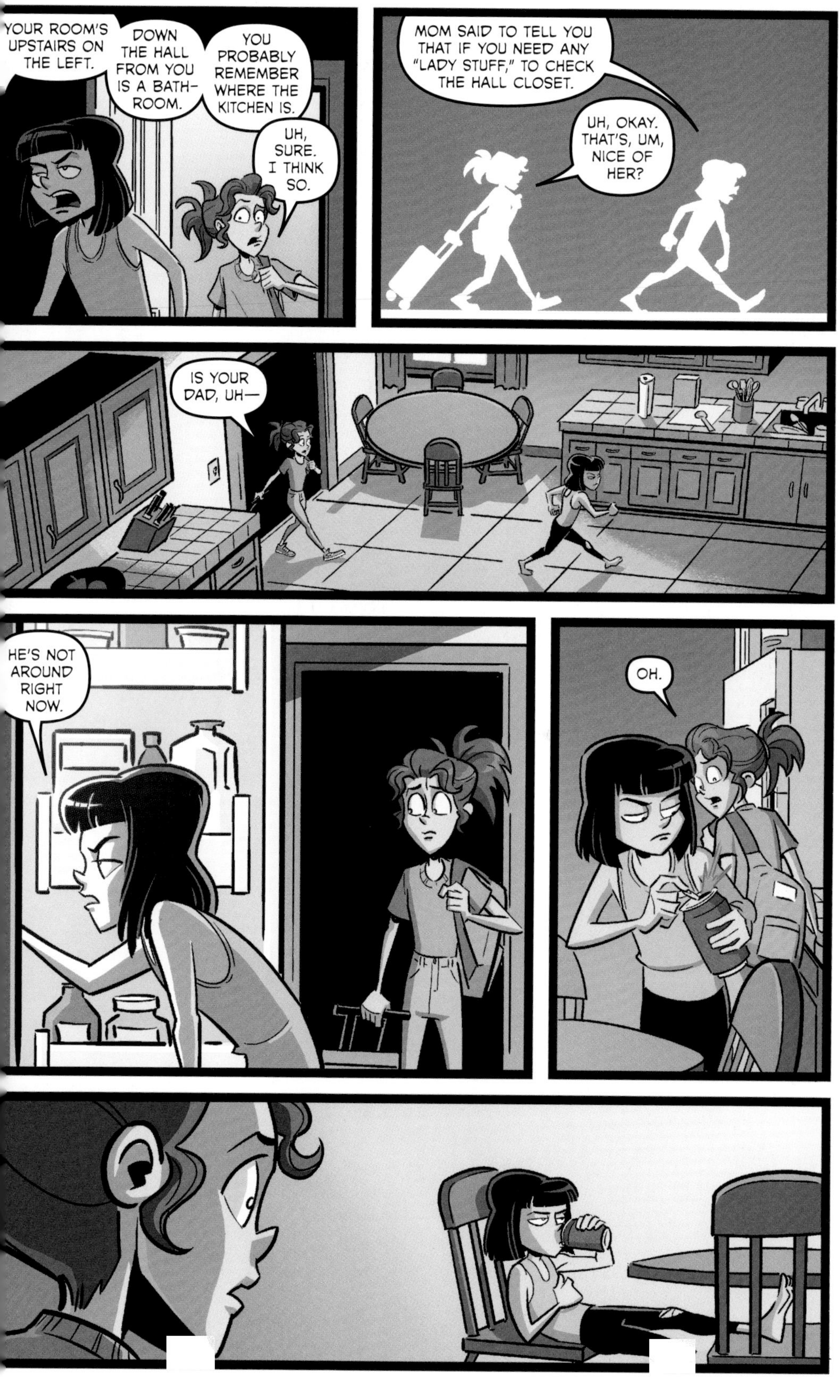

YOUR ROOM'S UPSTAIRS ON THE LEFT.
DOWN THE HALL FROM YOU IS A BATH-ROOM.
YOU PROBABLY REMEMBER WHERE THE KITCHEN IS.
UH, SURE. I THINK SO.
MOM SAID TO TELL YOU THAT IF YOU NEED ANY "LADY STUFF," TO CHECK THE HALL CLOSET.
UH, OKAY. THAT'S, UM, NICE OF HER?
IS YOUR DAD, UH—
HE'S NOT AROUND RIGHT NOW.
OH.

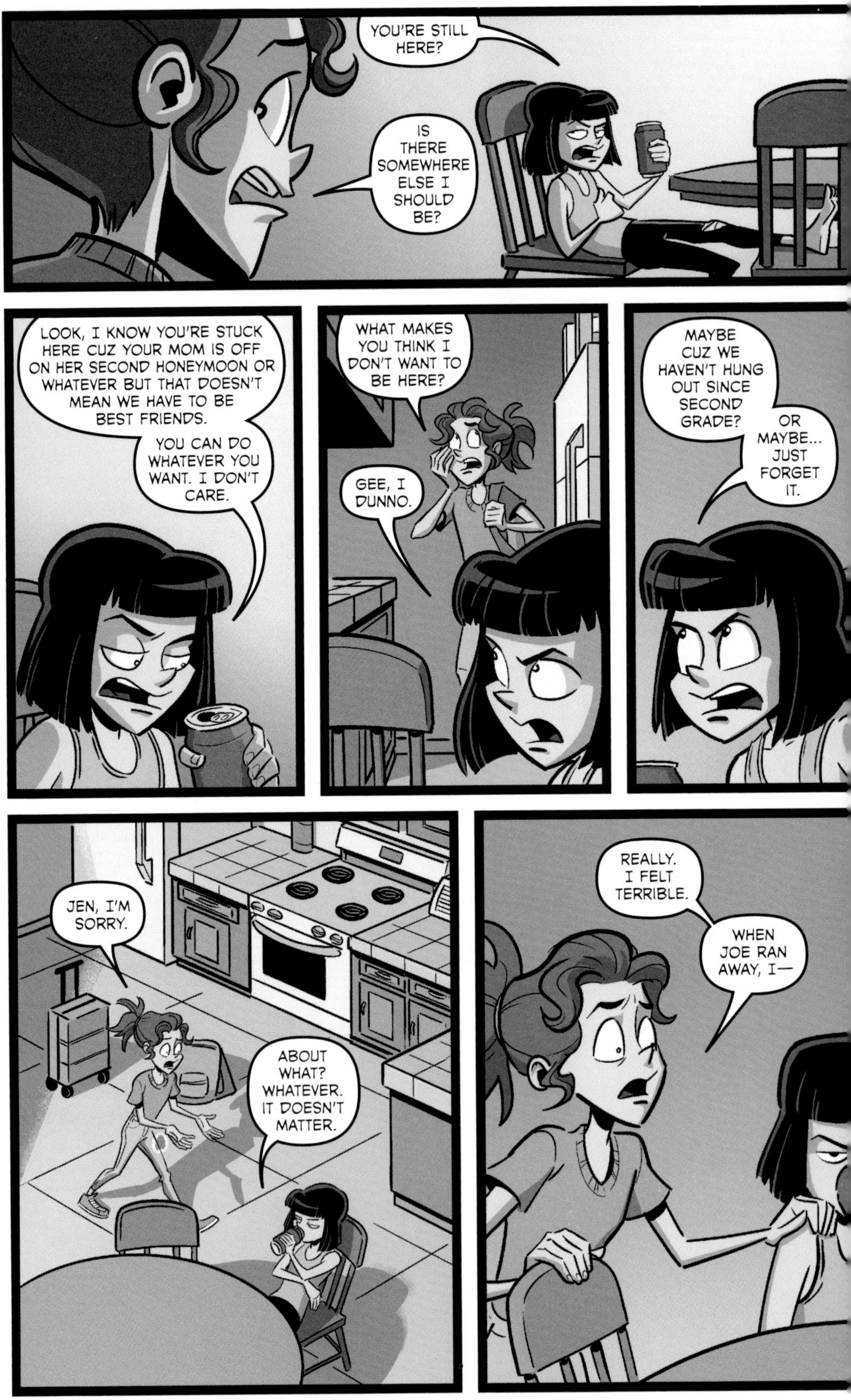

YOU'RE STILL HERE?
IS THERE SOMEWHERE ELSE I SHOULD BE?
LOOK, I KNOW YOU'RE STUCK HERE CUZ YOUR MOM IS OFF ON HER SECOND HONEYMOON OR WHATEVER BUT THAT DOESN'T MEAN WE HAVE TO BE BEST FRIENDS.
YOU CAN DO WHATEVER YOU WANT. I DON'T CARE.
WHAT MAKES YOU THINK I DON'T WANT TO BE HERE?
GEE, I DUNNO.
MAYBE CUZ WE HAVEN'T HUNG OUT SINCE SECOND GRADE?
OR MAYBE... JUST FORGET IT.
JEN, I'M SORRY.
ABOUT WHAT? WHATEVER. IT DOESN'T MATTER.
REALLY. I FELT TERRIBLE.
WHEN JOE RAN AWAY, I—

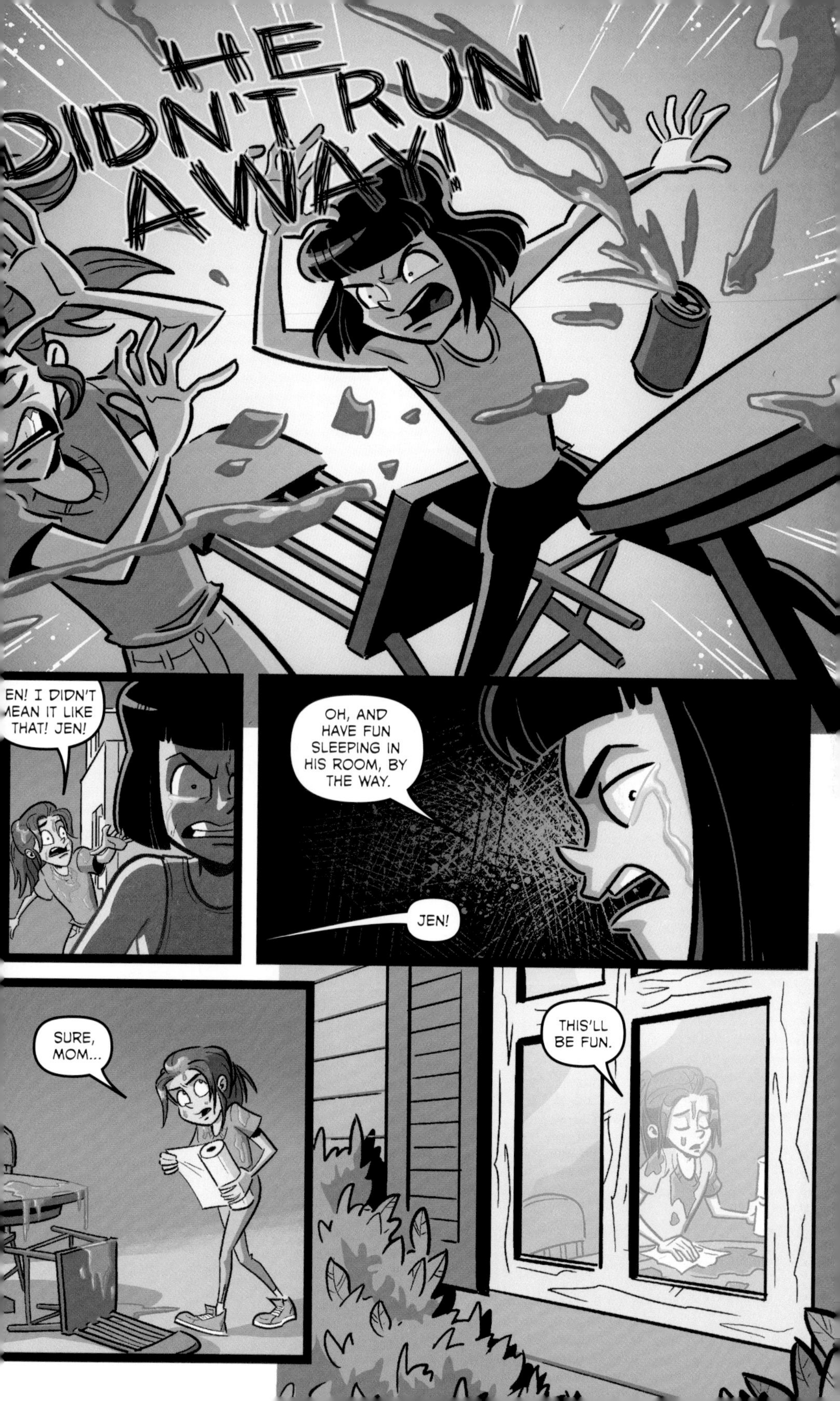
HE DIDN'T RUN AWAY!
EN! I DIDN'T MEAN IT LIKE THAT! JEN!
OH, AND HAVE FUN SLEEPING IN HIS ROOM, BY THE WAY.
JEN!
SURE, MOM...
THIS'LL BE FUN.

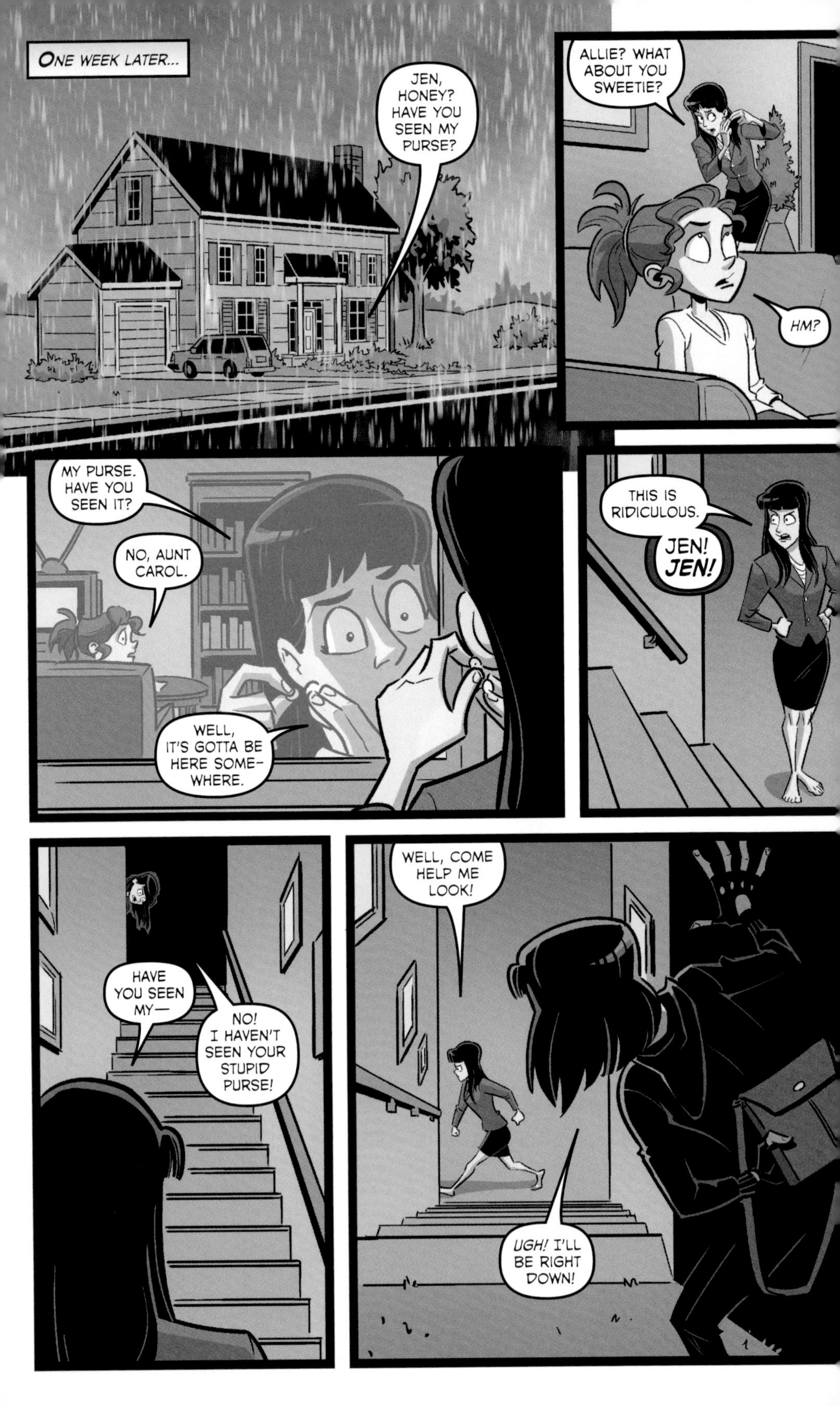

ONE WEEK LATER...
JEN, HONEY? HAVE YOU SEEN MY PURSE?
ALLIE? WHAT ABOUT YOU SWEETIE?
HM?
MY PURSE. HAVE YOU SEEN IT?
NO, AUNT CAROL.
WELL, IT'S GOTTA BE HERE SOME-WHERE.
THIS IS RIDICULOUS.
JEN! JEN!
HAVE YOU SEEN MY—
NO! I HAVEN'T SEEN YOUR STUPID PURSE!
WELL, COME HELP ME LOOK!
UGH! I'LL BE RIGHT DOWN!

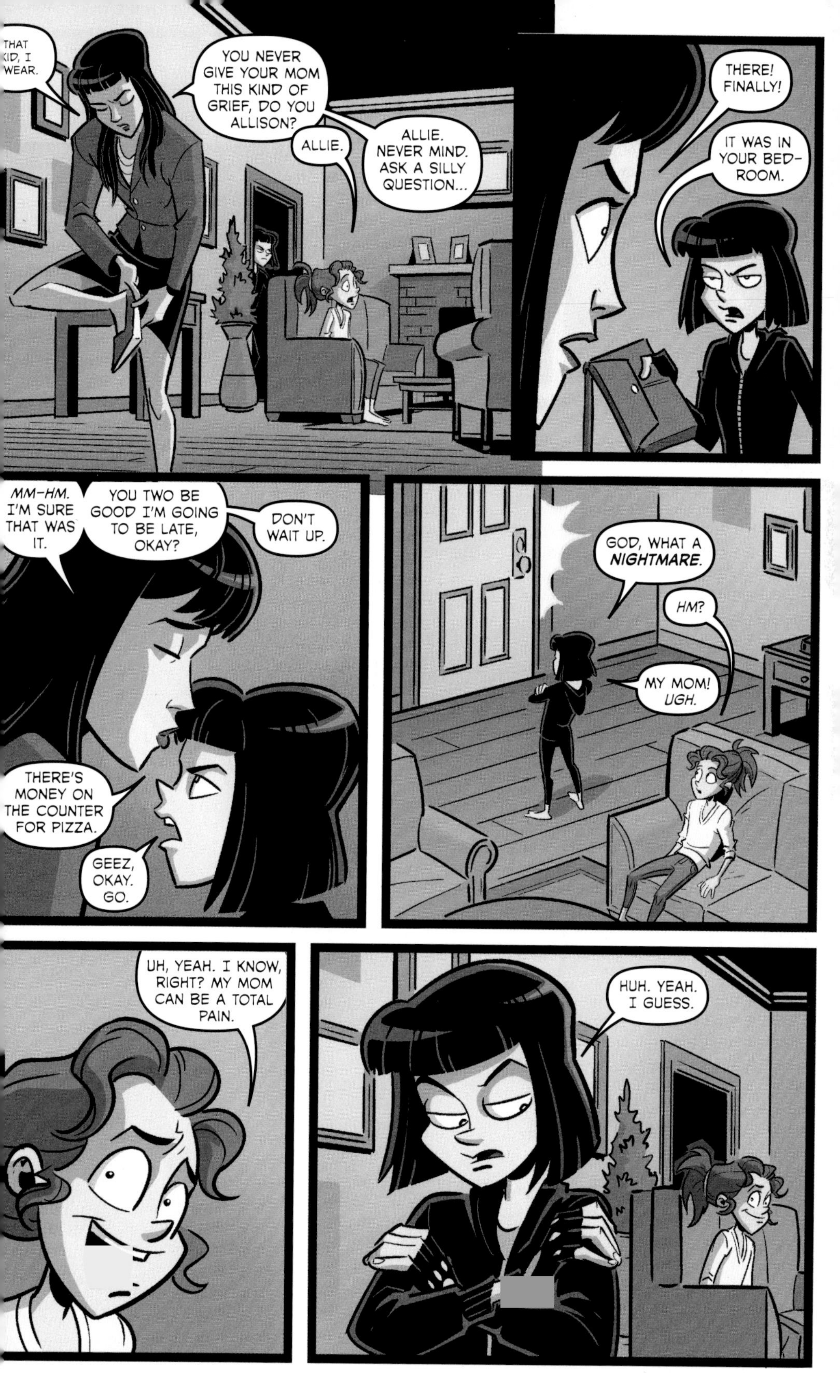

THAT
ID, I
WEAR.
YOU NEVER GIVE YOUR MOM THIS KIND OF GRIEF, DO YOU ALLISON?
ALLIE.
ALLIE. NEVER MIND. ASK A SILLY QUESTION...
THERE! FINALLY!
IT WAS IN YOUR BED-ROOM.
MM-HM. I'M SURE THAT WAS IT.
YOU TWO BE GOOD I'M GOING TO BE LATE, OKAY?
DON'T WAIT UP.
THERE'S MONEY ON THE COUNTER FOR PIZZA.
GEEZ, OKAY. GO.
GOD, WHAT A *NIGHTMARE*.
HM?
MY MOM! *UGH.*
UH, YEAH. I KNOW, RIGHT? MY MOM CAN BE A TOTAL PAIN.
HUH. YEAH. I GUESS.

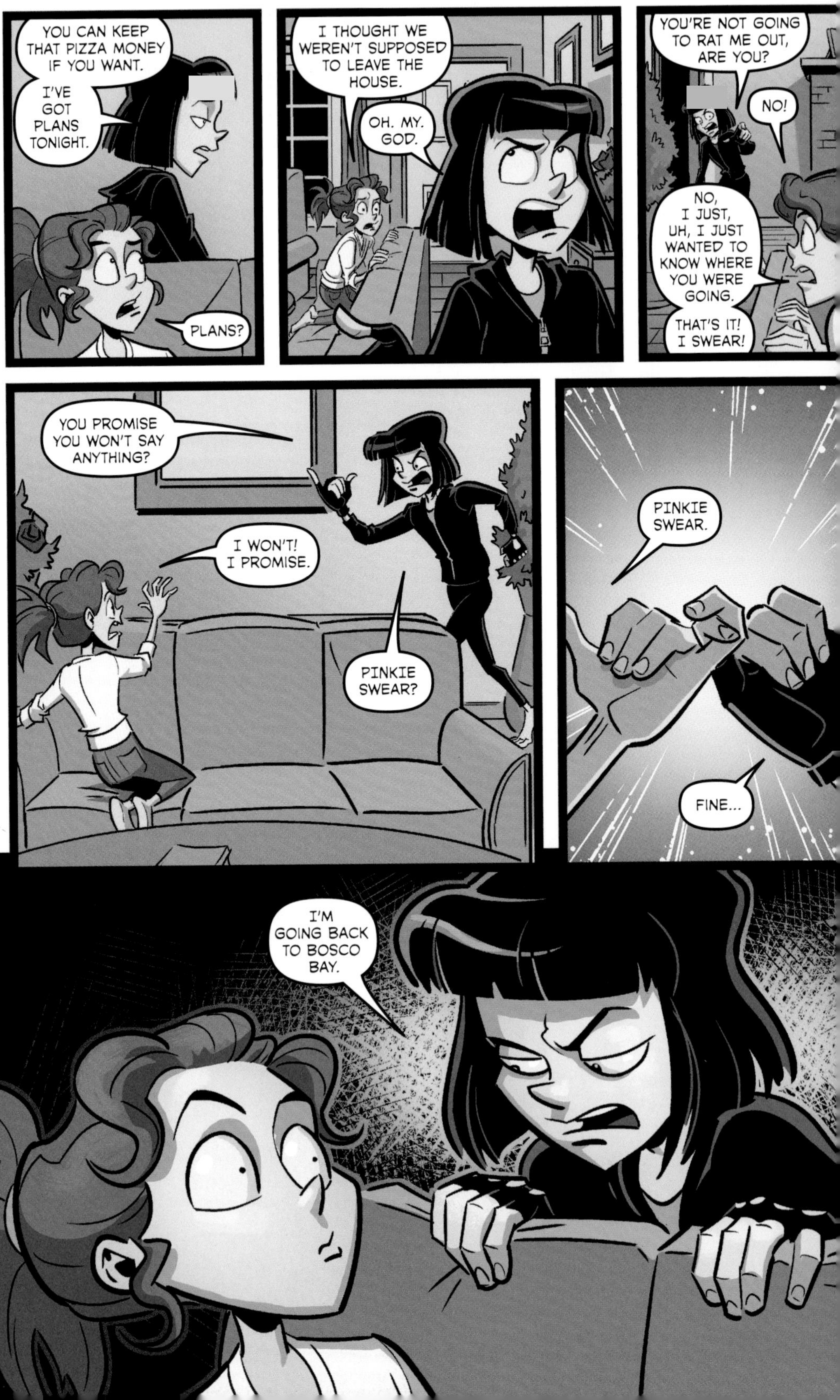
YOU CAN KEEP THAT PIZZA MONEY IF YOU WANT.
I'VE GOT PLANS TONIGHT.
PLANS?
I THOUGHT WE WEREN'T SUPPOSED TO LEAVE THE HOUSE.
OH. MY. GOD.
YOU'RE NOT GOING TO RAT ME OUT, ARE YOU?
NO!
NO, I JUST, UH, I JUST WANTED TO KNOW WHERE YOU WERE GOING.
THAT'S IT! I SWEAR!
YOU PROMISE YOU WON'T SAY ANYTHING?
I WON'T! I PROMISE.
PINKIE SWEAR?
PINKIE SWEAR.
FINE...
I'M GOING BACK TO BOSCO BAY.

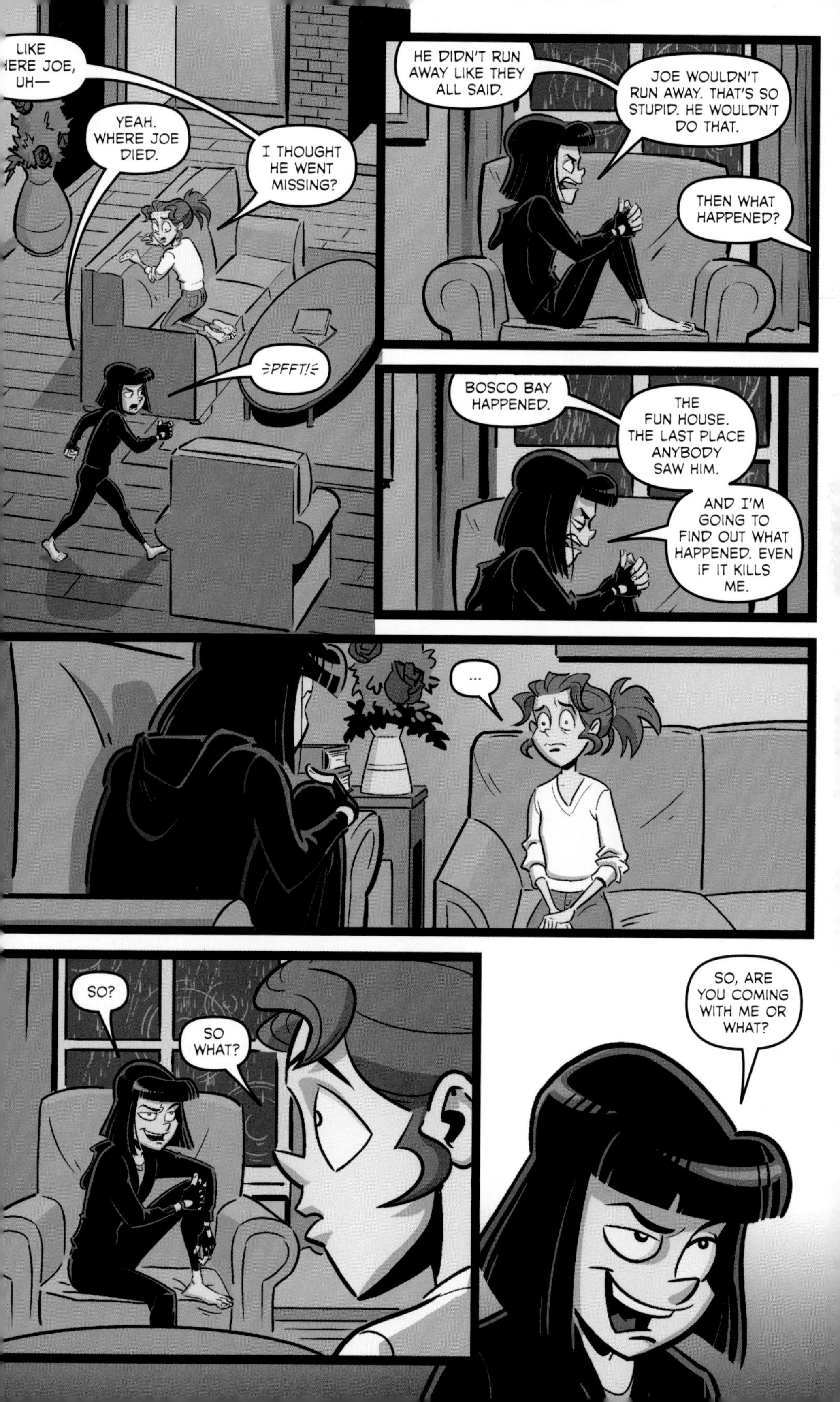
LIKE
ERE JOE,
UH—
YEAH.
WHERE JOE
DIED.
I THOUGHT
HE WENT
MISSING?
≥PFFT!≤
HE DIDN'T RUN
AWAY LIKE THEY
ALL SAID.
JOE WOULDN'T
RUN AWAY. THAT'S SO
STUPID. HE WOULDN'T
DO THAT.
THEN WHAT
HAPPENED?
BOSCO BAY
HAPPENED.
THE
FUN HOUSE.
THE LAST PLACE
ANYBODY
SAW HIM.
AND I'M
GOING TO
FIND OUT WHAT
HAPPENED. EVEN
IF IT KILLS
ME.
...
SO?
SO
WHAT?
SO, ARE
YOU COMING
WITH ME OR
WHAT?

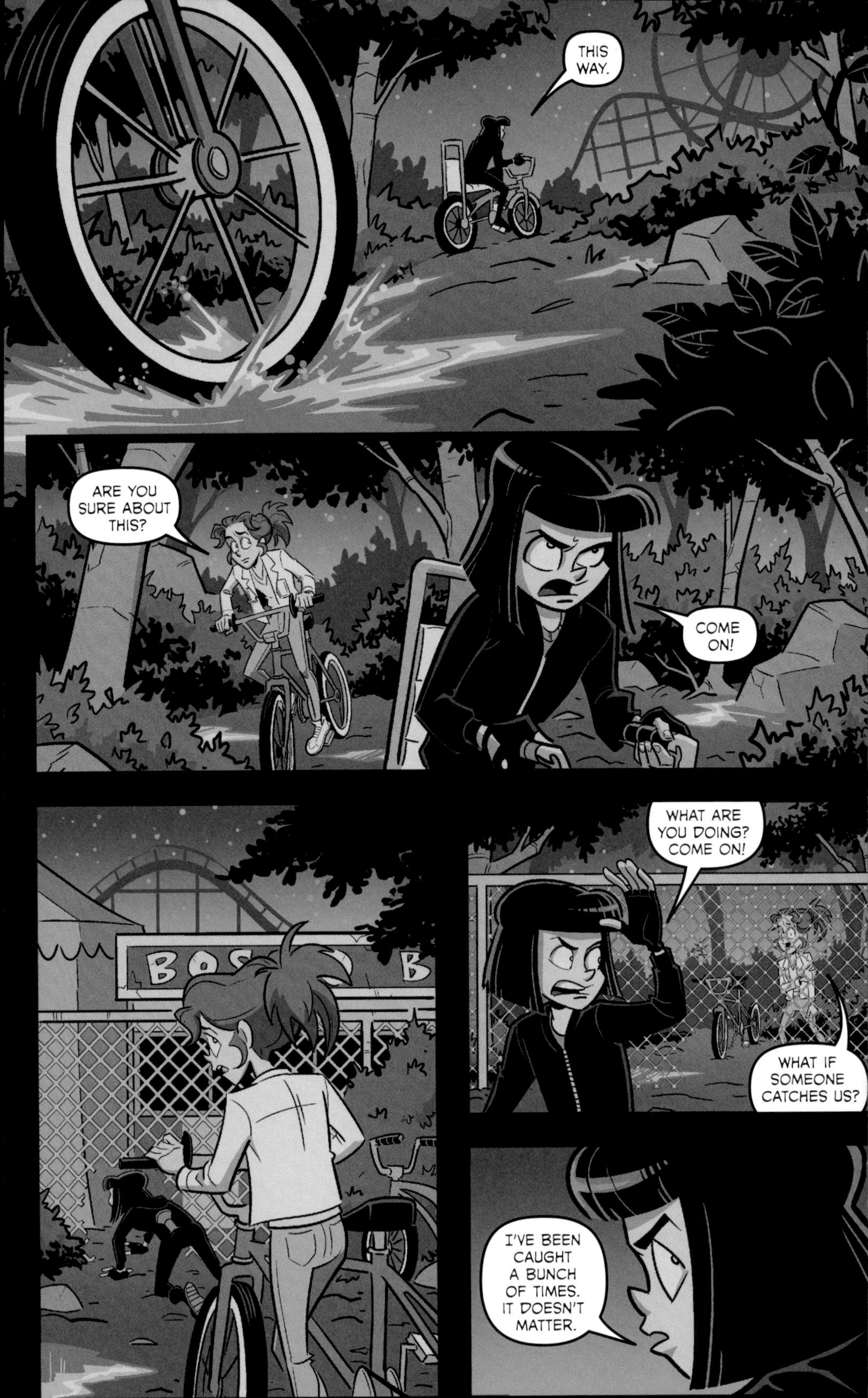
THIS WAY.
ARE YOU SURE ABOUT THIS?
COME ON!
BOS B
WHAT ARE YOU DOING? COME ON!
WHAT IF SOMEONE CATCHES US?
I'VE BEEN CAUGHT A BUNCH OF TIMES. IT DOESN'T MATTER.

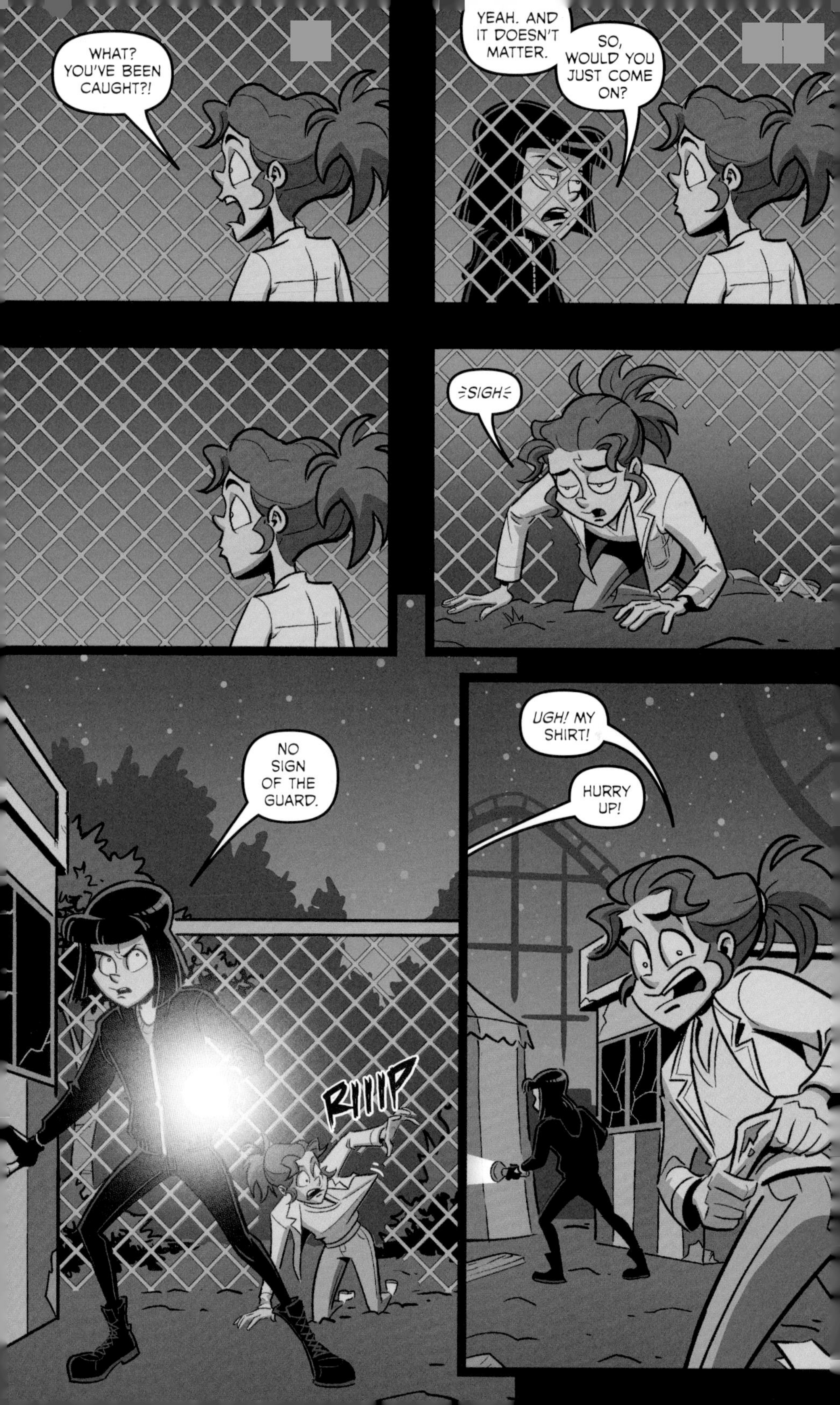
WHAT? YOU'VE BEEN CAUGHT?!
YEAH. AND IT DOESN'T MATTER.
SO, WOULD YOU JUST COME ON?
SIGH
NO SIGN OF THE GUARD.
RIIIP
UGH! MY SHIRT!
HURRY UP!

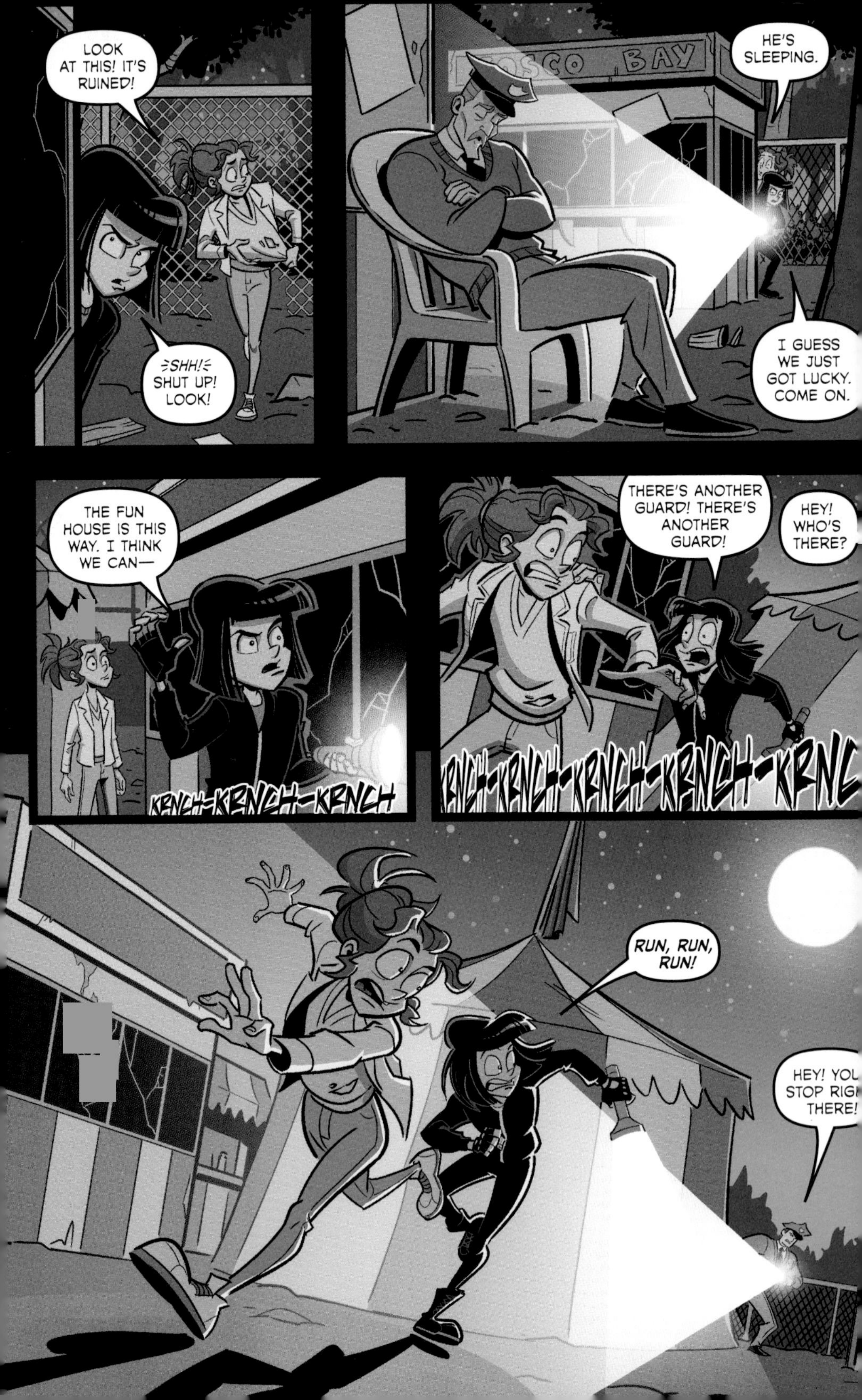
LOOK AT THIS! IT'S RUINED!
SHH! SHUT UP! LOOK!
HE'S SLEEPING.
I GUESS WE JUST GOT LUCKY. COME ON.
THE FUN HOUSE IS THIS WAY. I THINK WE CAN—
KRNCH-KRNCH-KRNCH
THERE'S ANOTHER GUARD! THERE'S ANOTHER GUARD!
HEY! WHO'S THERE?
KRNCH-KRNCH-KRNCH-KRNCH-KRNC
RUN, RUN, RUN!
HEY! YO STOP RIG THERE!

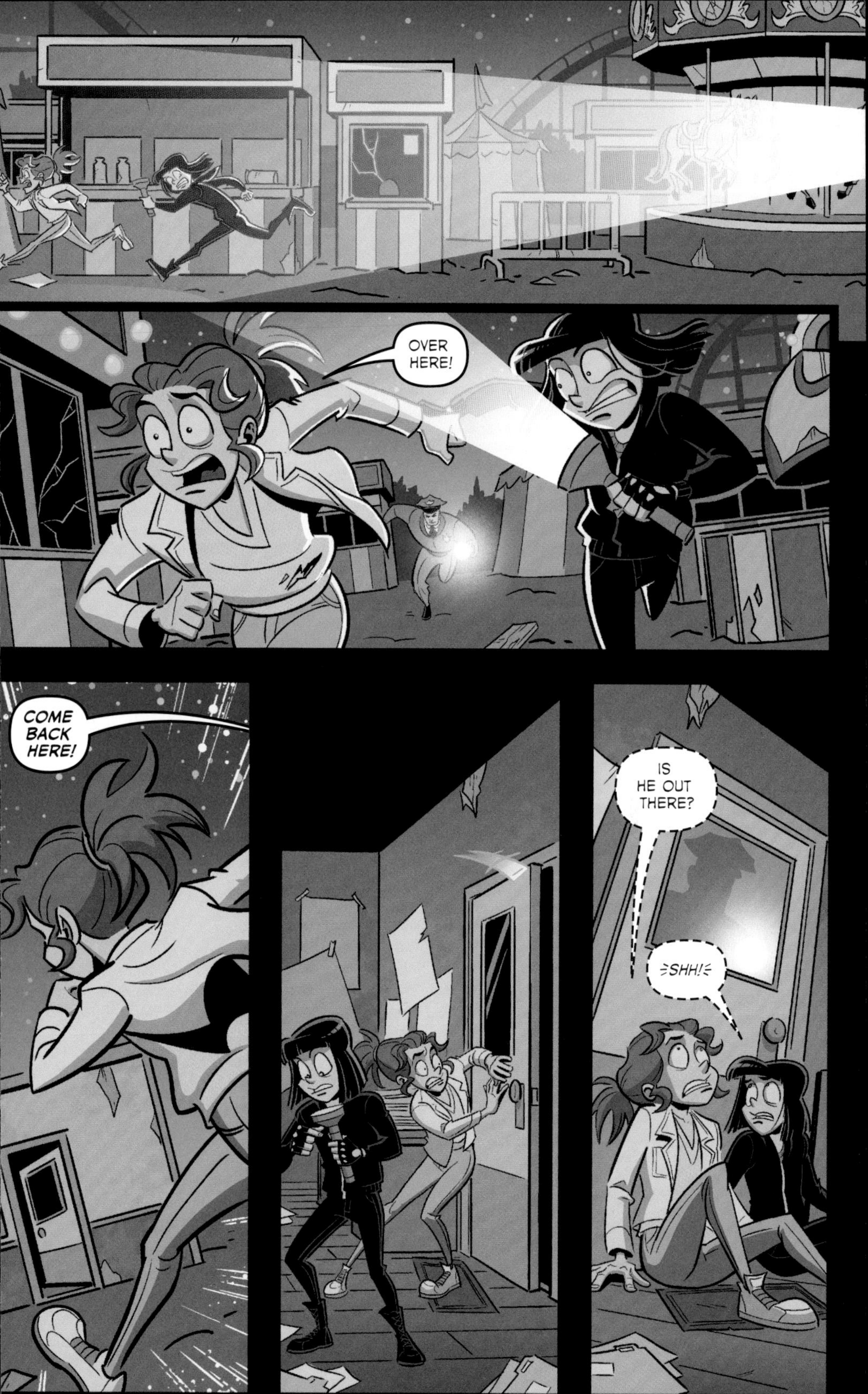
OVER HERE!
COME BACK HERE!
IS HE OUT THERE?
SHH!

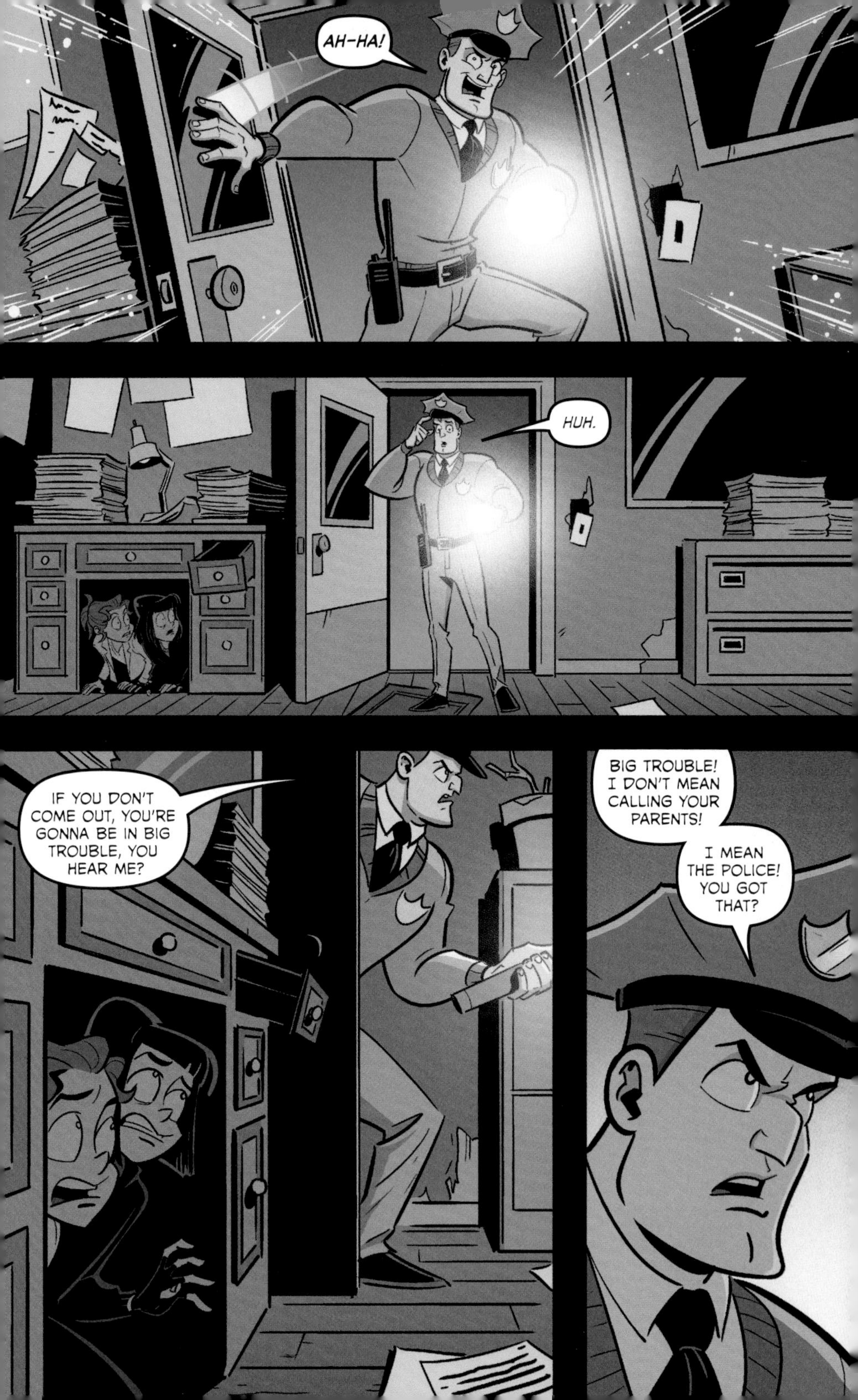
AH-HA!
HUH.
IF YOU DON'T COME OUT, YOU'RE GONNA BE IN BIG TROUBLE, YOU HEAR ME?
BIG TROUBLE! I DON'T MEAN CALLING YOUR PARENTS!
I MEAN THE POLICE! YOU GOT THAT?

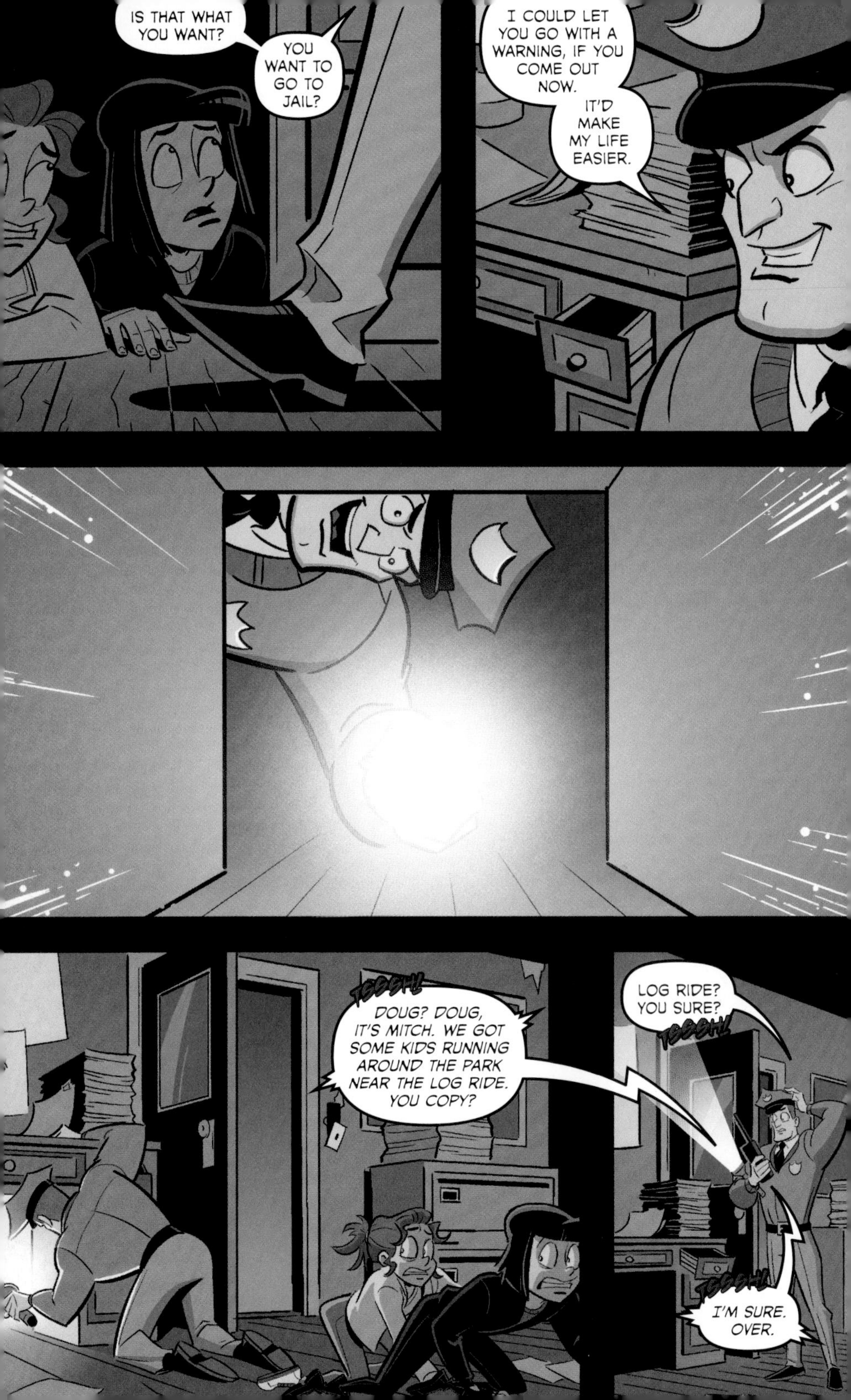
IS THAT WHAT YOU WANT?
YOU WANT TO GO TO JAIL?
I COULD LET YOU GO WITH A WARNING, IF YOU COME OUT NOW.
IT'D MAKE MY LIFE EASIER.
TSSSH!
DOUG? DOUG, IT'S MITCH. WE GOT SOME KIDS RUNNING AROUND THE PARK NEAR THE LOG RIDE. YOU COPY?
LOG RIDE? YOU SURE?
TSSSH!
TSSSH!
I'M SURE. OVER.

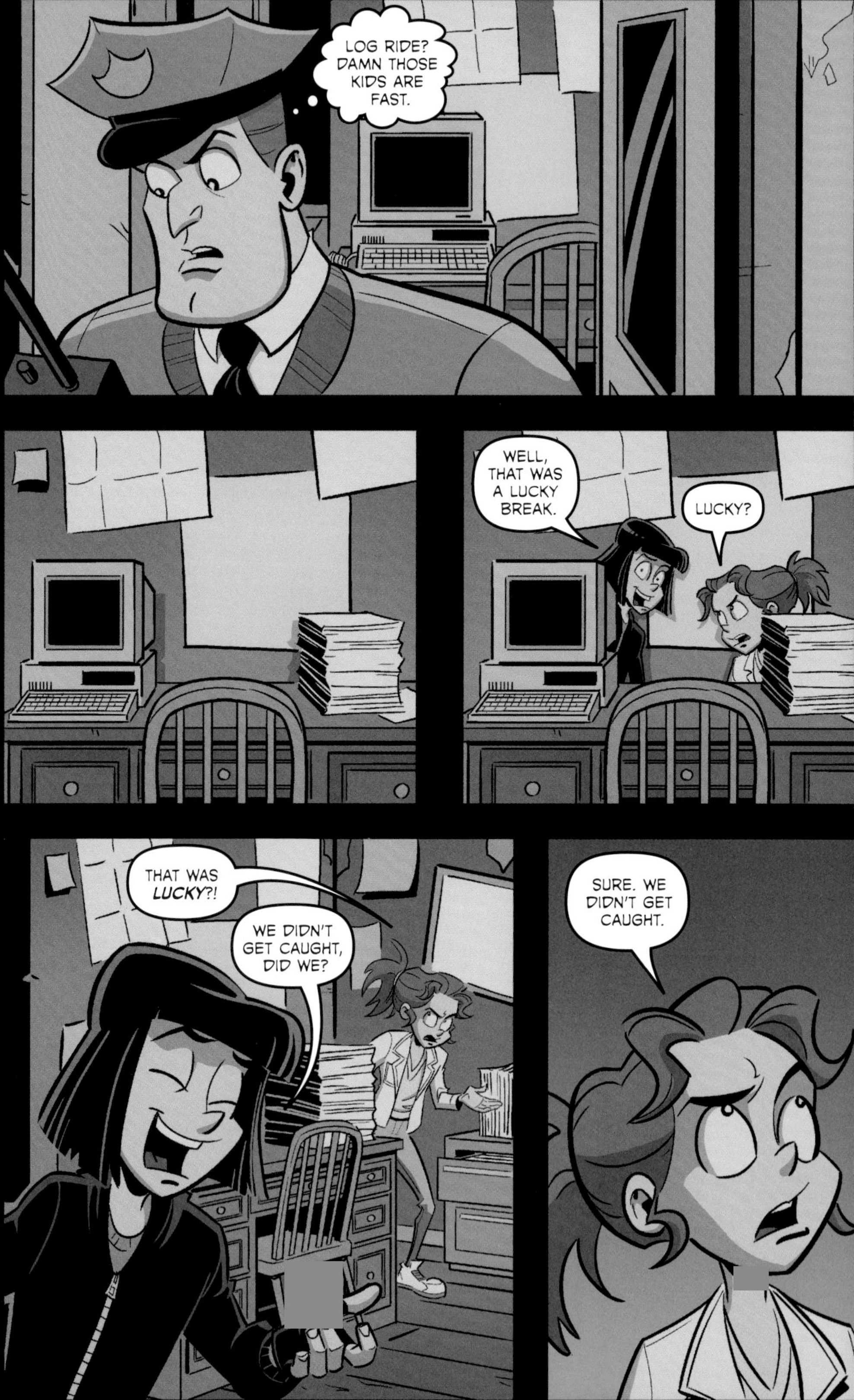
LOG RIDE? DAMN THOSE KIDS ARE FAST.
WELL, THAT WAS A LUCKY BREAK.
LUCKY?
THAT WAS *LUCKY*?!
WE DIDN'T GET CAUGHT, DID WE?
SURE. WE DIDN'T GET CAUGHT.

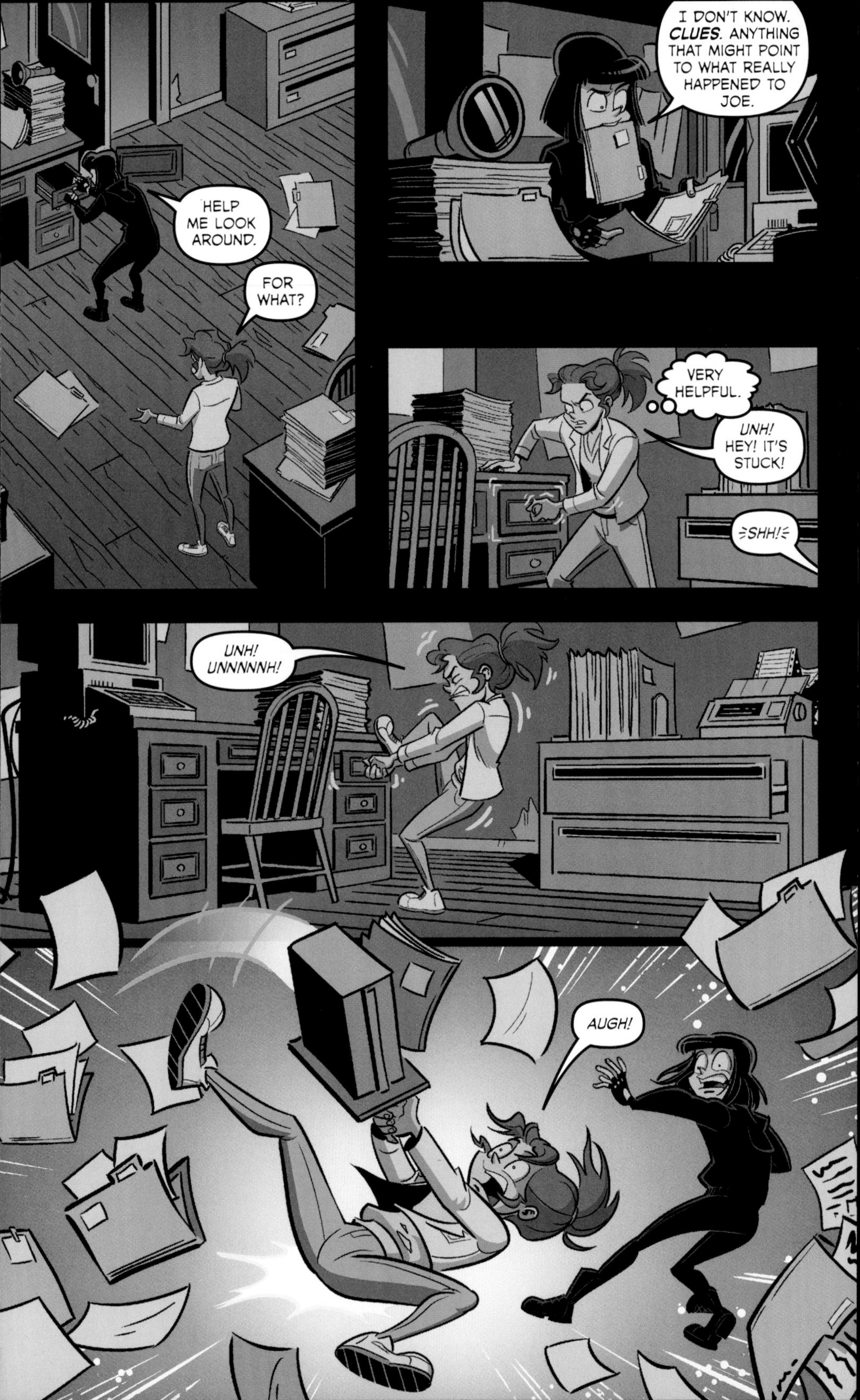
HELP ME LOOK AROUND.
FOR WHAT?
I DON'T KNOW. *CLUES*. ANYTHING THAT MIGHT POINT TO WHAT REALLY HAPPENED TO JOE.
VERY HELPFUL.
UNH! HEY! IT'S STUCK!
SHH!
UNH! UNNNNNH!
AUGH!

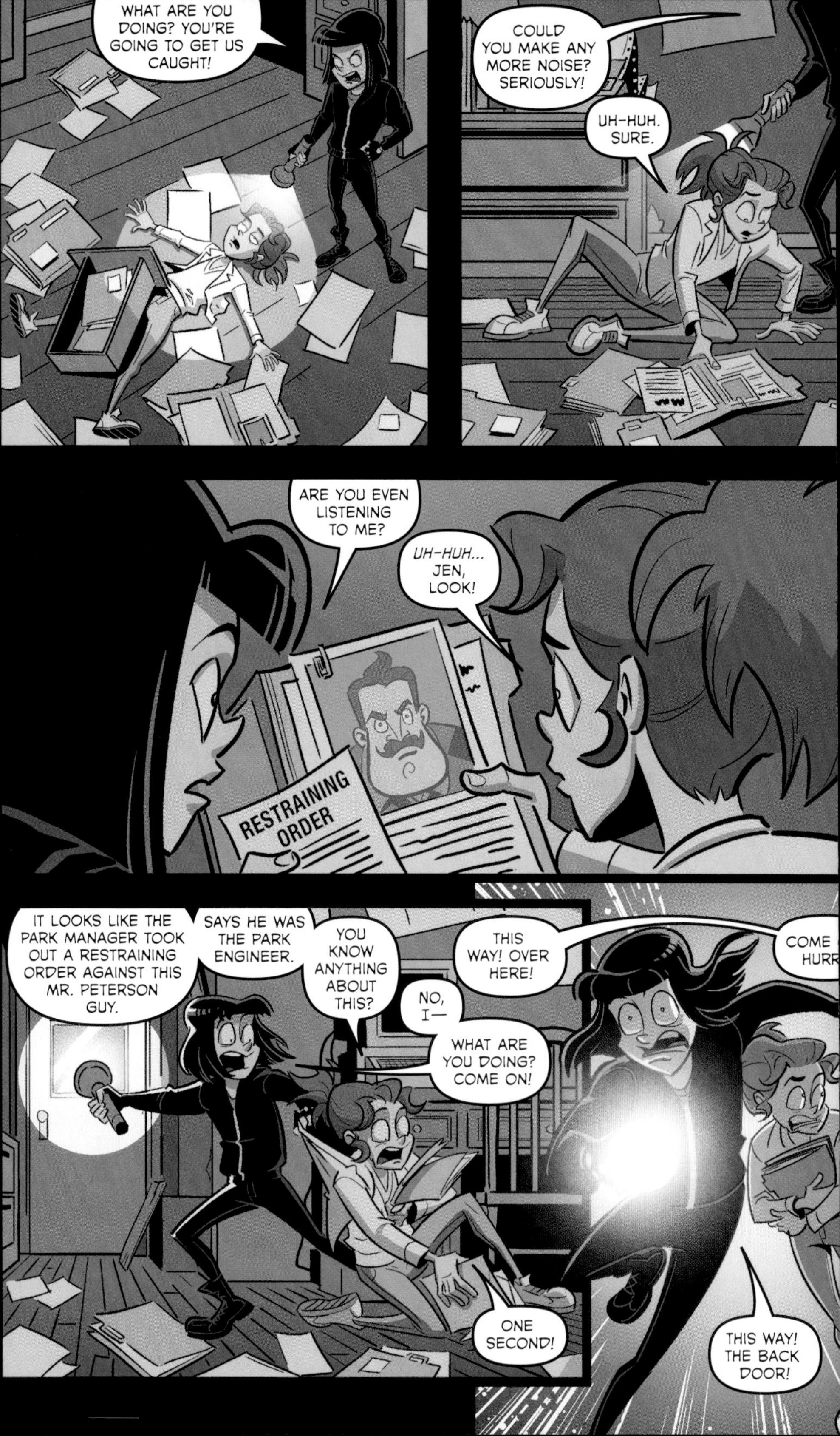
WHAT ARE YOU DOING? YOU'RE GOING TO GET US CAUGHT!
COULD YOU MAKE ANY MORE NOISE? SERIOUSLY!
UH-HUH. SURE.
ARE YOU EVEN LISTENING TO ME?
UH-HUH... JEN, LOOK!
RESTRAINING ORDER
IT LOOKS LIKE THE PARK MANAGER TOOK OUT A RESTRAINING ORDER AGAINST THIS MR. PETERSON GUY.
SAYS HE WAS THE PARK ENGINEER.
YOU KNOW ANYTHING ABOUT THIS?
NO, I—
THIS WAY! OVER HERE!
WHAT ARE YOU DOING? COME ON!
ONE SECOND!
THIS WAY! THE BACK DOOR!

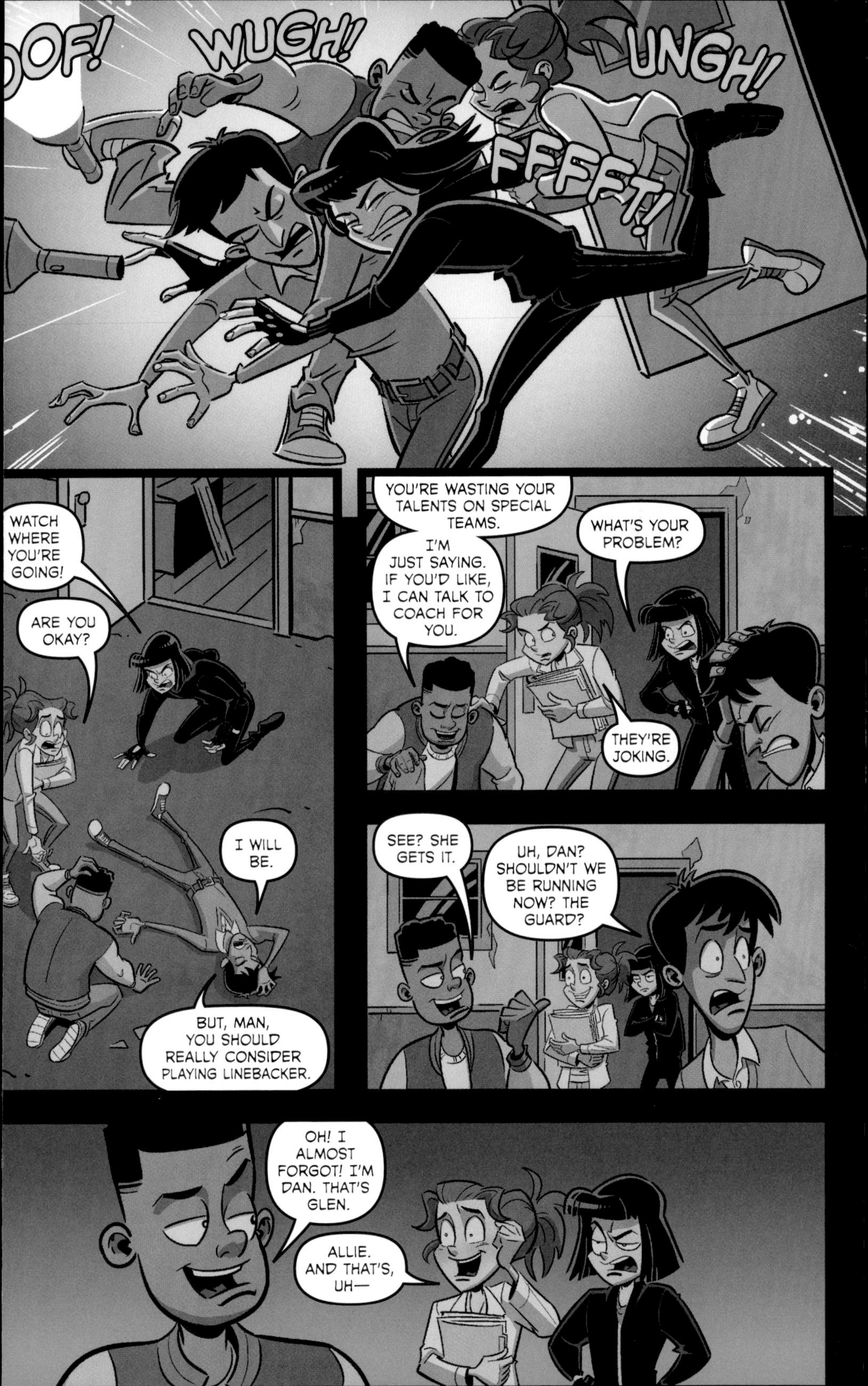
OOF!
WUGH!
UNGH!
FFFFT!
WATCH WHERE YOU'RE GOING!
ARE YOU OKAY?
I WILL BE.
BUT, MAN, YOU SHOULD REALLY CONSIDER PLAYING LINEBACKER.
YOU'RE WASTING YOUR TALENTS ON SPECIAL TEAMS.
I'M JUST SAYING. IF YOU'D LIKE, I CAN TALK TO COACH FOR YOU.
WHAT'S YOUR PROBLEM?
THEY'RE JOKING.
SEE? SHE GETS IT.
UH, DAN? SHOULDN'T WE BE RUNNING NOW? THE GUARD?
OH! I ALMOST FORGOT! I'M DAN. THAT'S GLEN.
ALLIE. AND THAT'S, UH—

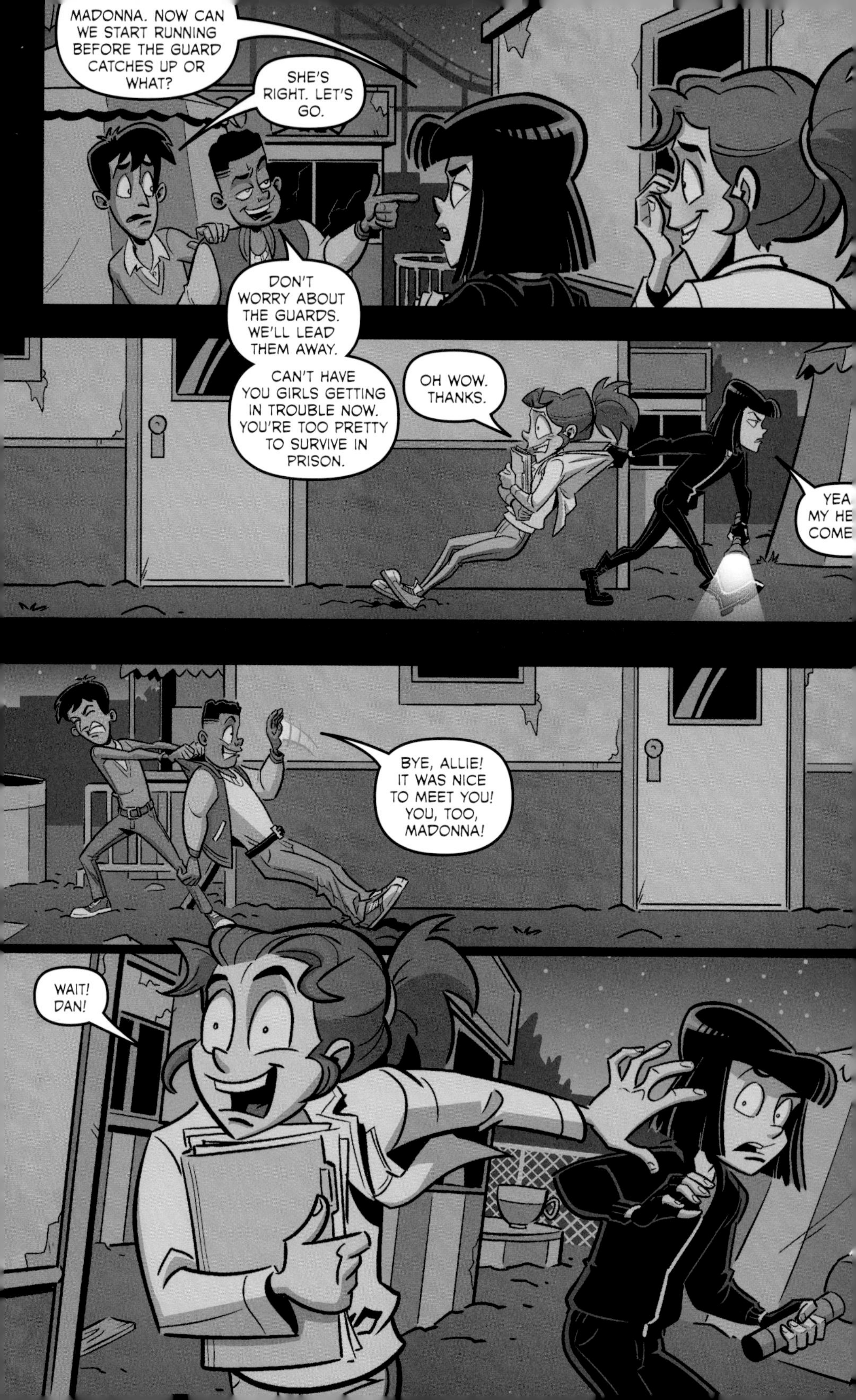
MADONNA. NOW CAN WE START RUNNING BEFORE THE GUARD CATCHES UP OR WHAT?
SHE'S RIGHT. LET'S GO.
DON'T WORRY ABOUT THE GUARDS. WE'LL LEAD THEM AWAY.
CAN'T HAVE YOU GIRLS GETTING IN TROUBLE NOW. YOU'RE TOO PRETTY TO SURVIVE IN PRISON.
OH WOW. THANKS.
YEA
MY HE
COME
BYE, ALLIE! IT WAS NICE TO MEET YOU! YOU, TOO, MADONNA!
WAIT! DAN!

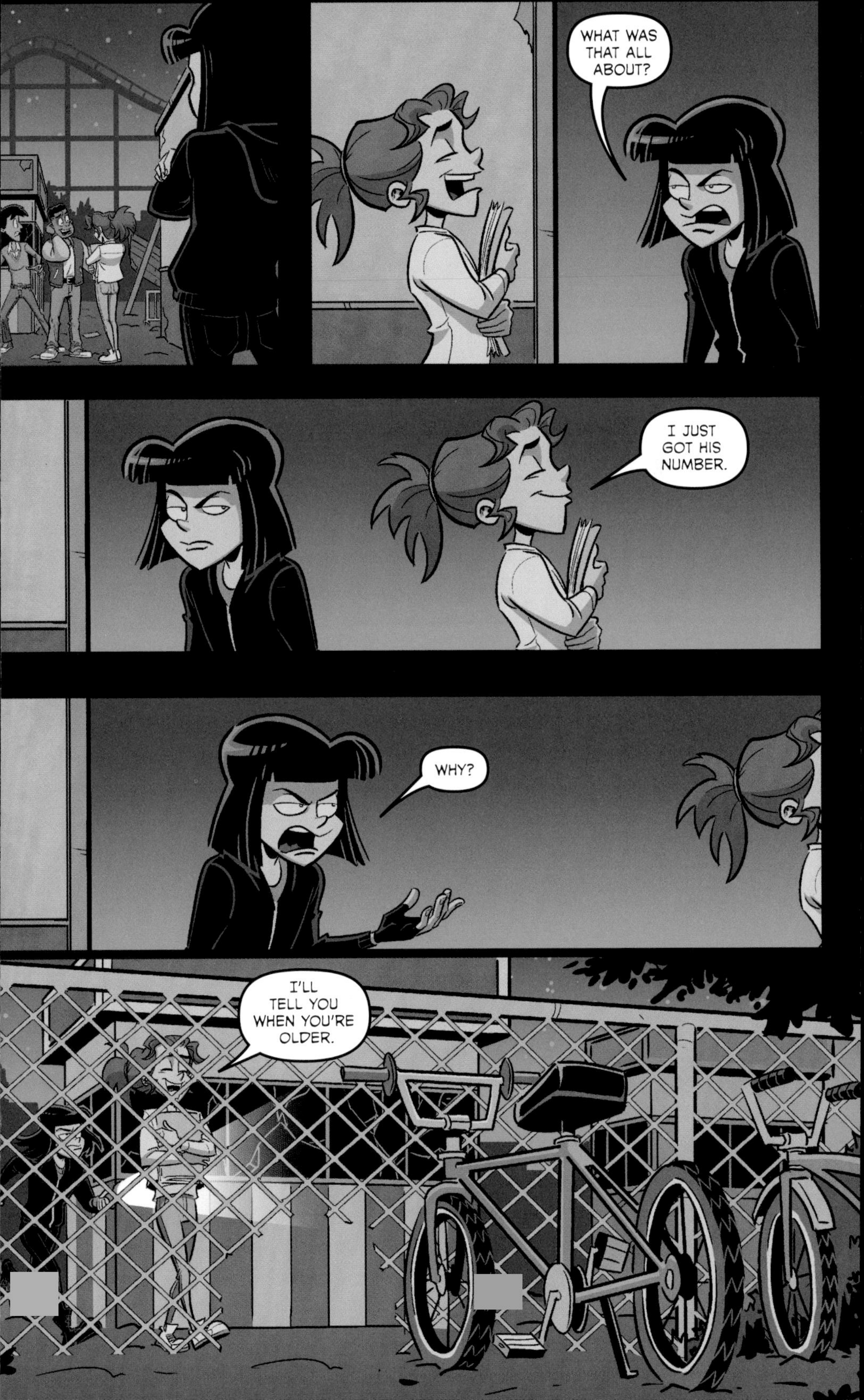
WHAT WAS THAT ALL ABOUT?
I JUST GOT HIS NUMBER.
WHY?
I'LL TELL YOU WHEN YOU'RE OLDER.

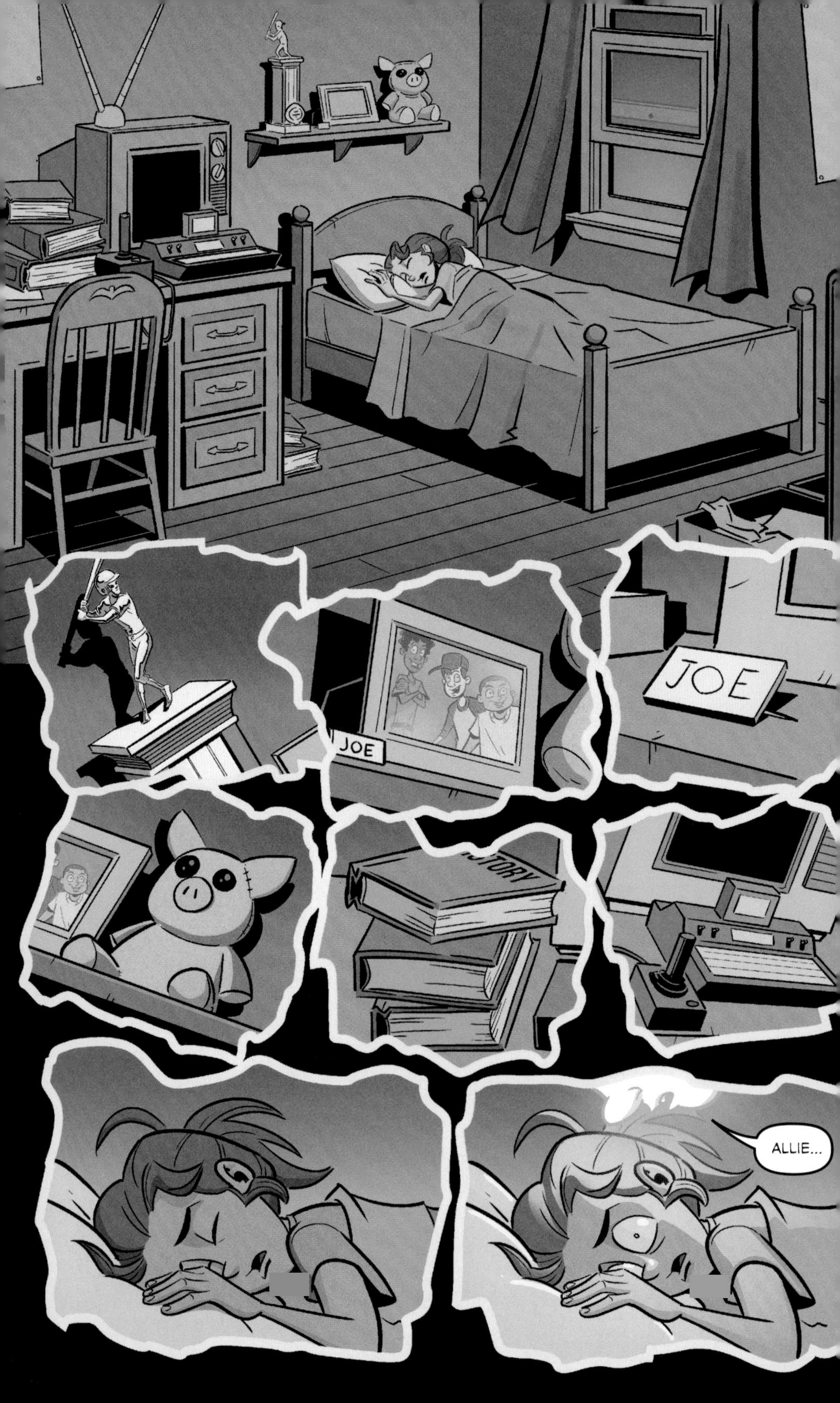
JOE
JOE
HISTORY
ALLIE...

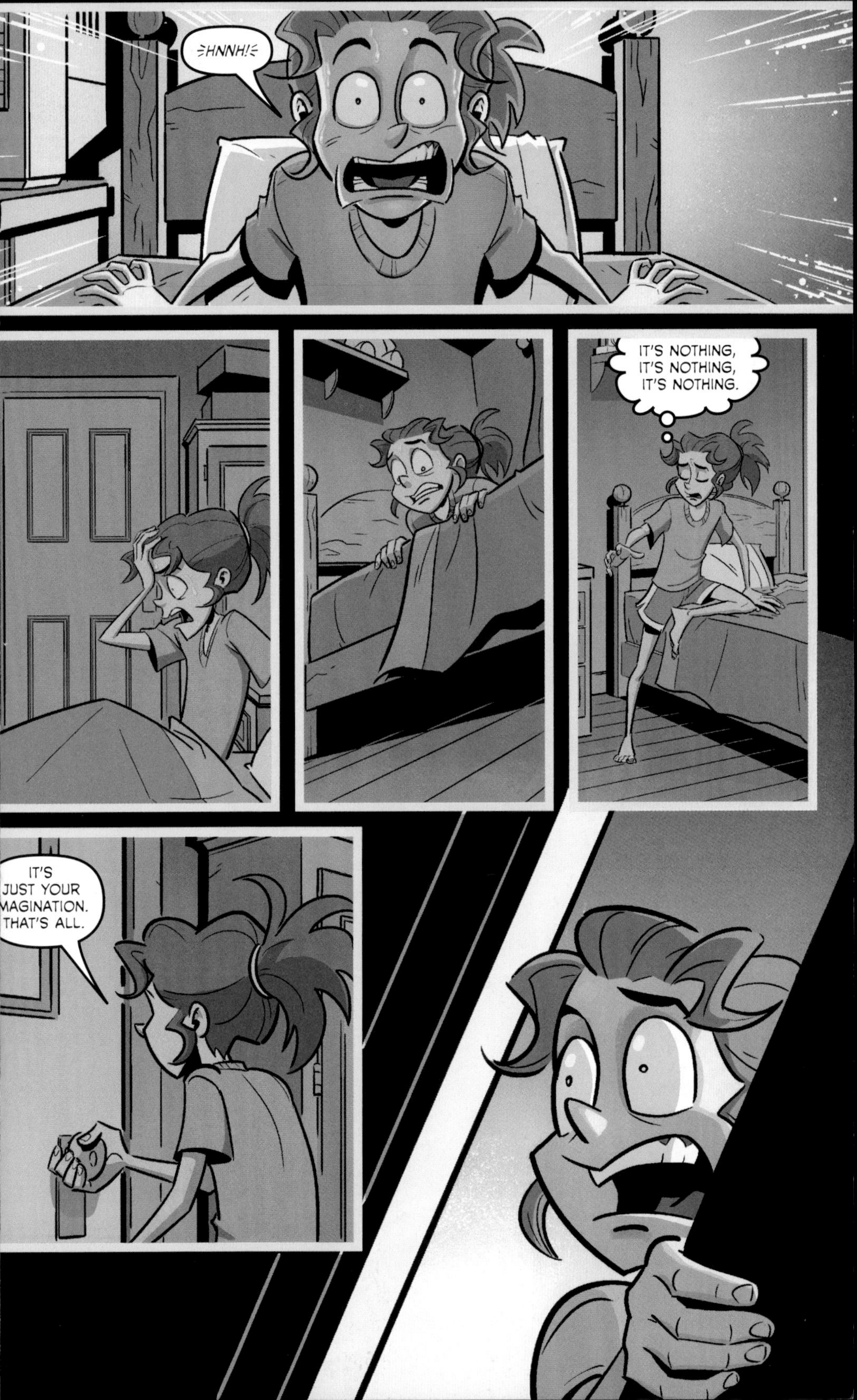

HNNH!
IT'S NOTHING, IT'S NOTHING, IT'S NOTHING.
IT'S JUST YOUR MAGINATION. THAT'S ALL.

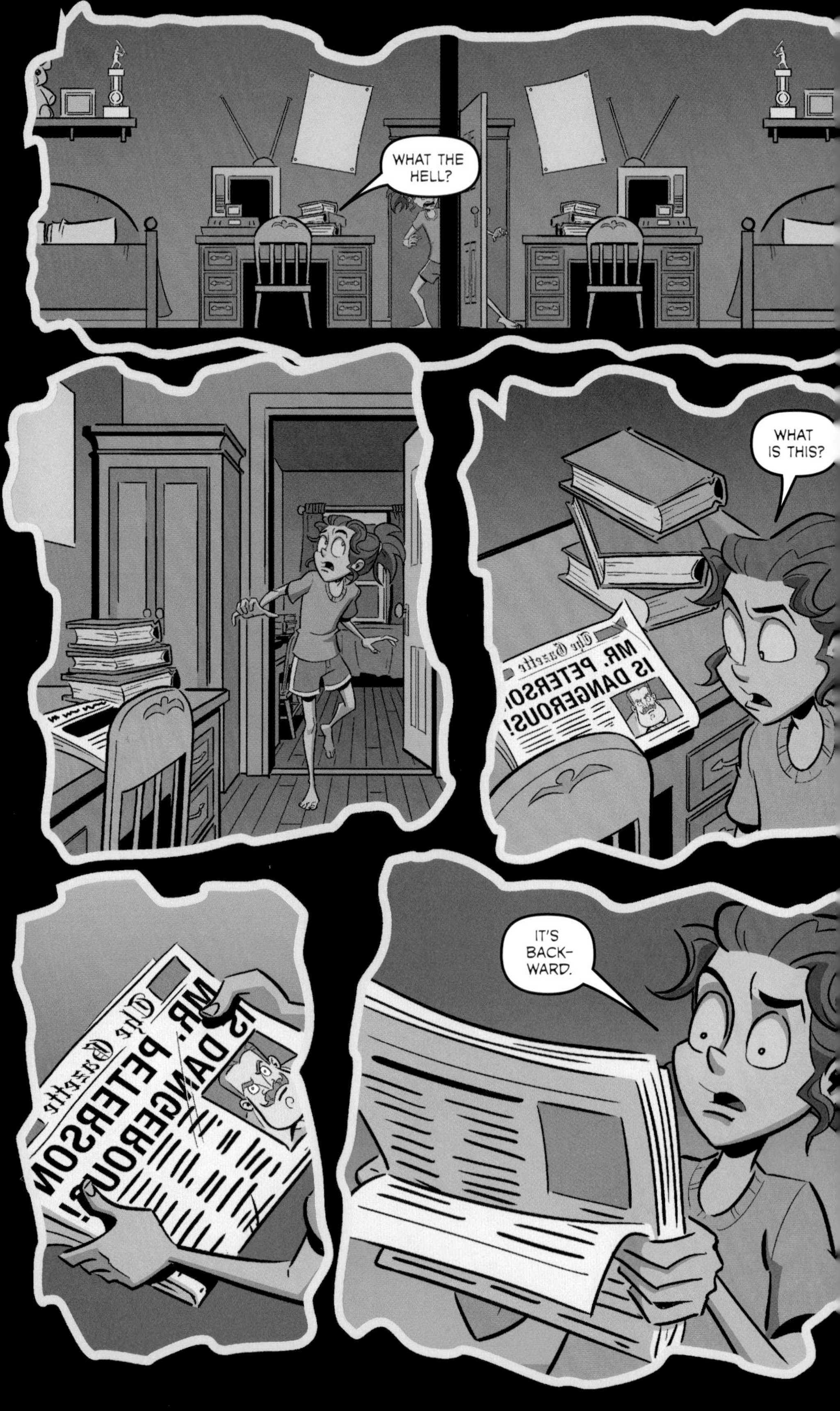
WHAT THE HELL?
WHAT IS THIS?
The Gazette
MR. PETERSON IS DANGEROUS!
IT'S BACKWARD.

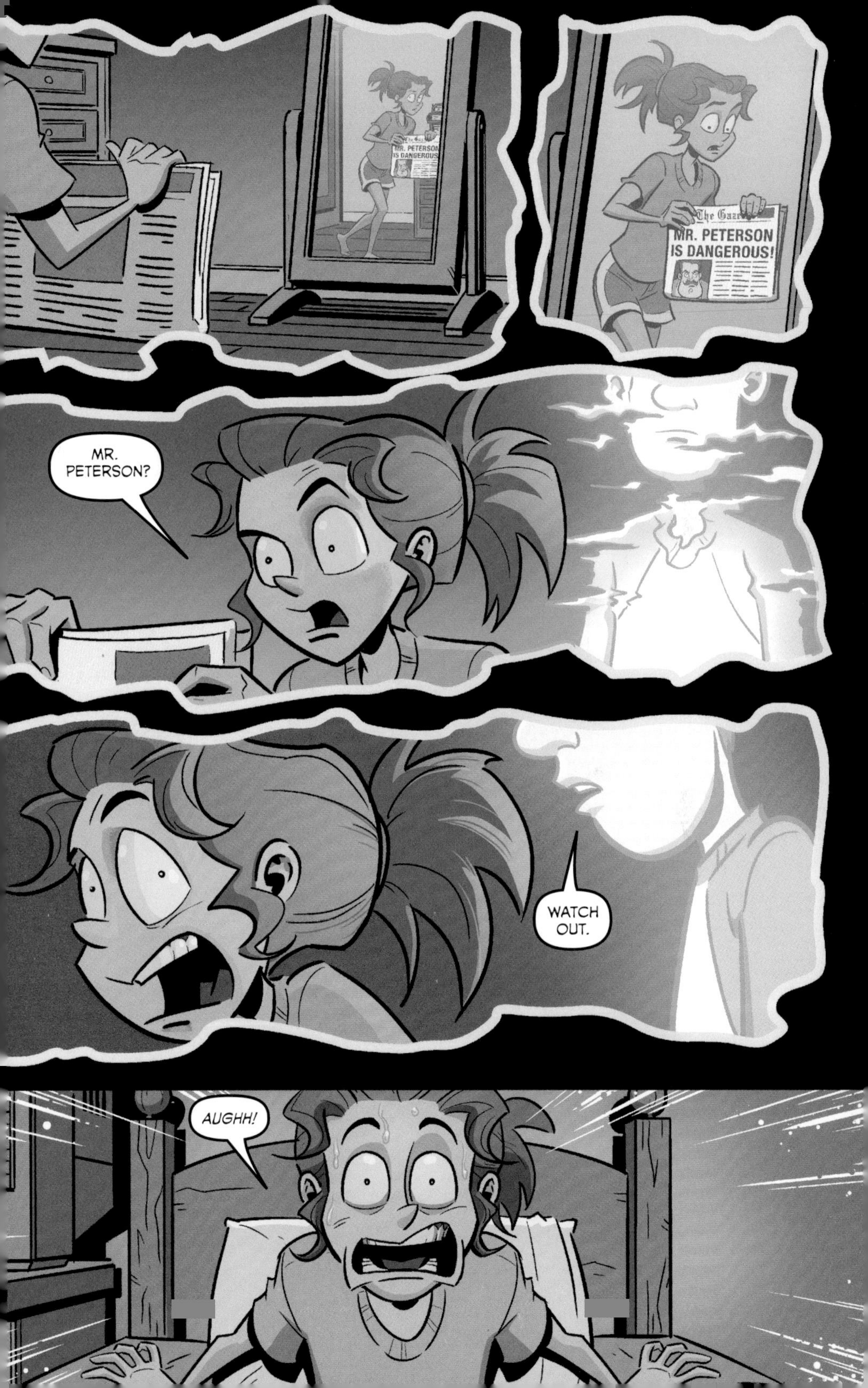
MR. PETERSON
IS DANGEROUS
The Gaz
MR. PETERSON
IS DANGEROUS!
MR. PETERSON?
WATCH OUT.
AUGHH!

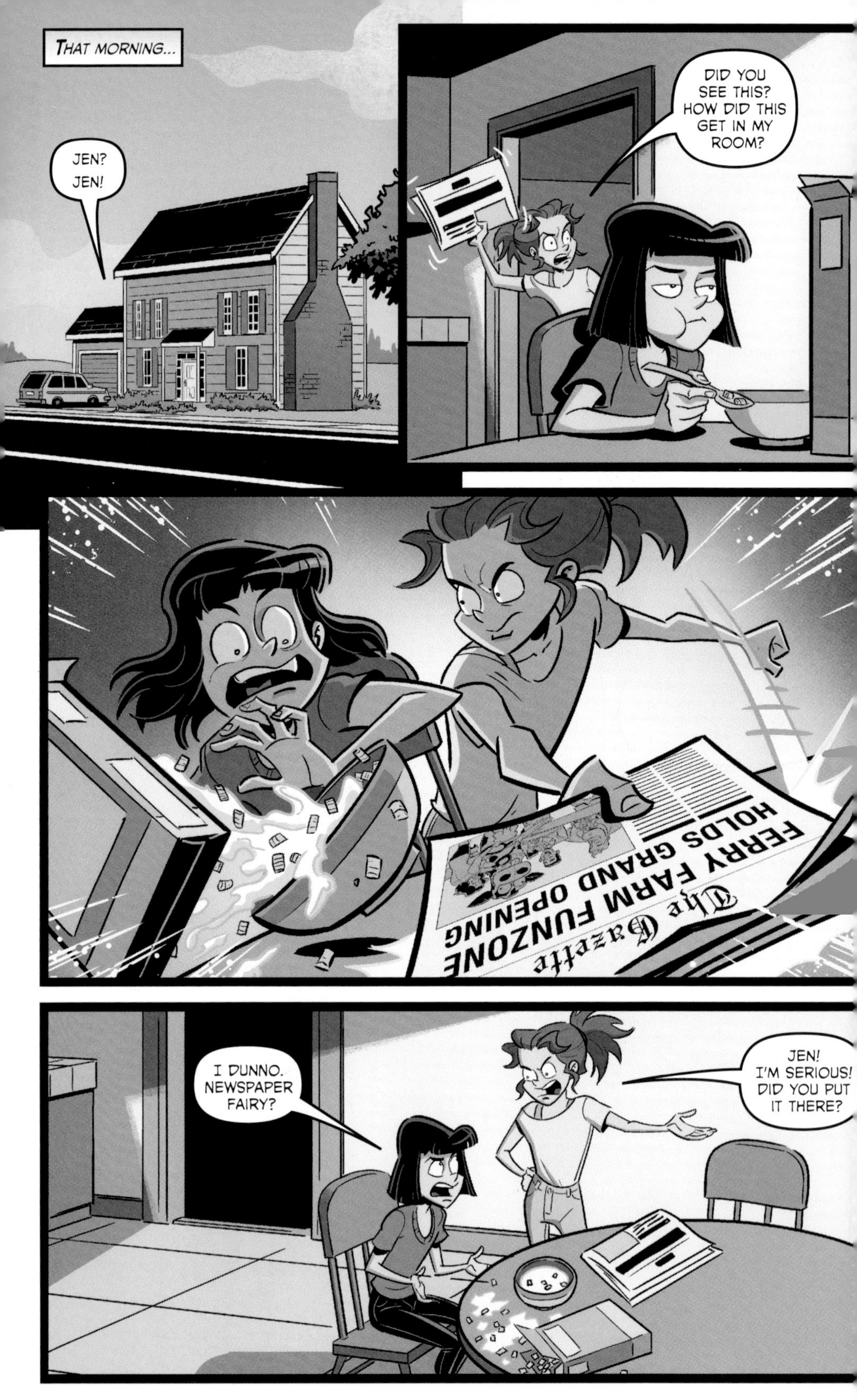
THAT MORNING...
JEN? JEN!
DID YOU SEE THIS? HOW DID THIS GET IN MY ROOM?
The Gazette
FERRY FARM FUNZONE HOLDS GRAND OPENING
I DUNNO. NEWSPAPER FAIRY?
JEN! I'M SERIOUS! DID YOU PUT IT THERE?

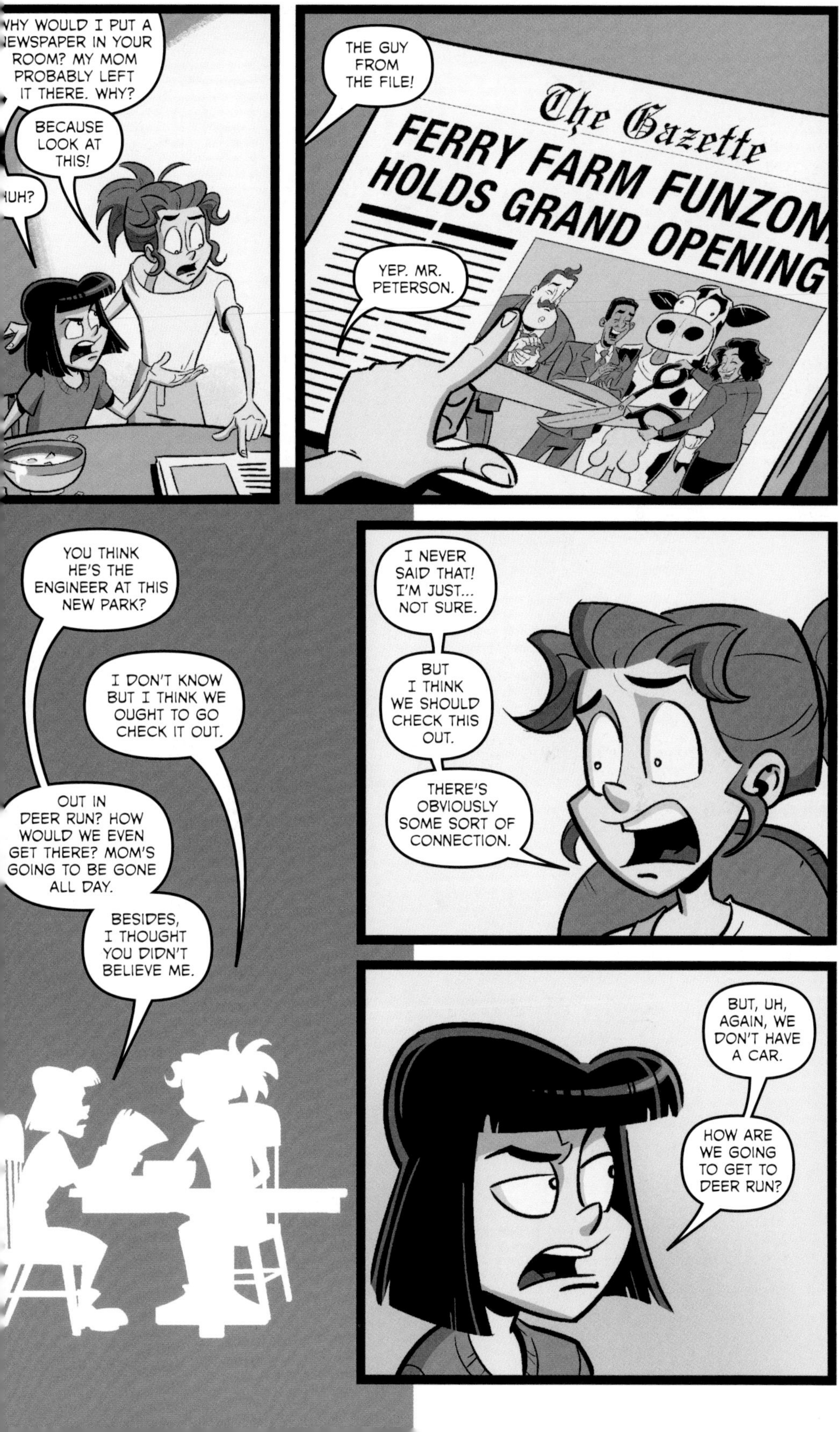

WHY WOULD I PUT A NEWSPAPER IN YOUR ROOM? MY MOM PROBABLY LEFT IT THERE. WHY?
BECAUSE LOOK AT THIS!
HUH?
THE GUY FROM THE FILE!
The Gazette
FERRY FARM FUNZON HOLDS GRAND OPENING
YEP. MR. PETERSON.
YOU THINK HE'S THE ENGINEER AT THIS NEW PARK?
I DON'T KNOW BUT I THINK WE OUGHT TO GO CHECK IT OUT.
OUT IN DEER RUN? HOW WOULD WE EVEN GET THERE? MOM'S GOING TO BE GONE ALL DAY.
BESIDES, I THOUGHT YOU DIDN'T BELIEVE ME.
I NEVER SAID THAT! I'M JUST... NOT SURE.
BUT I THINK WE SHOULD CHECK THIS OUT.
THERE'S OBVIOUSLY SOME SORT OF CONNECTION.
BUT, UH, AGAIN, WE DON'T HAVE A CAR.
HOW ARE WE GOING TO GET TO DEER RUN?

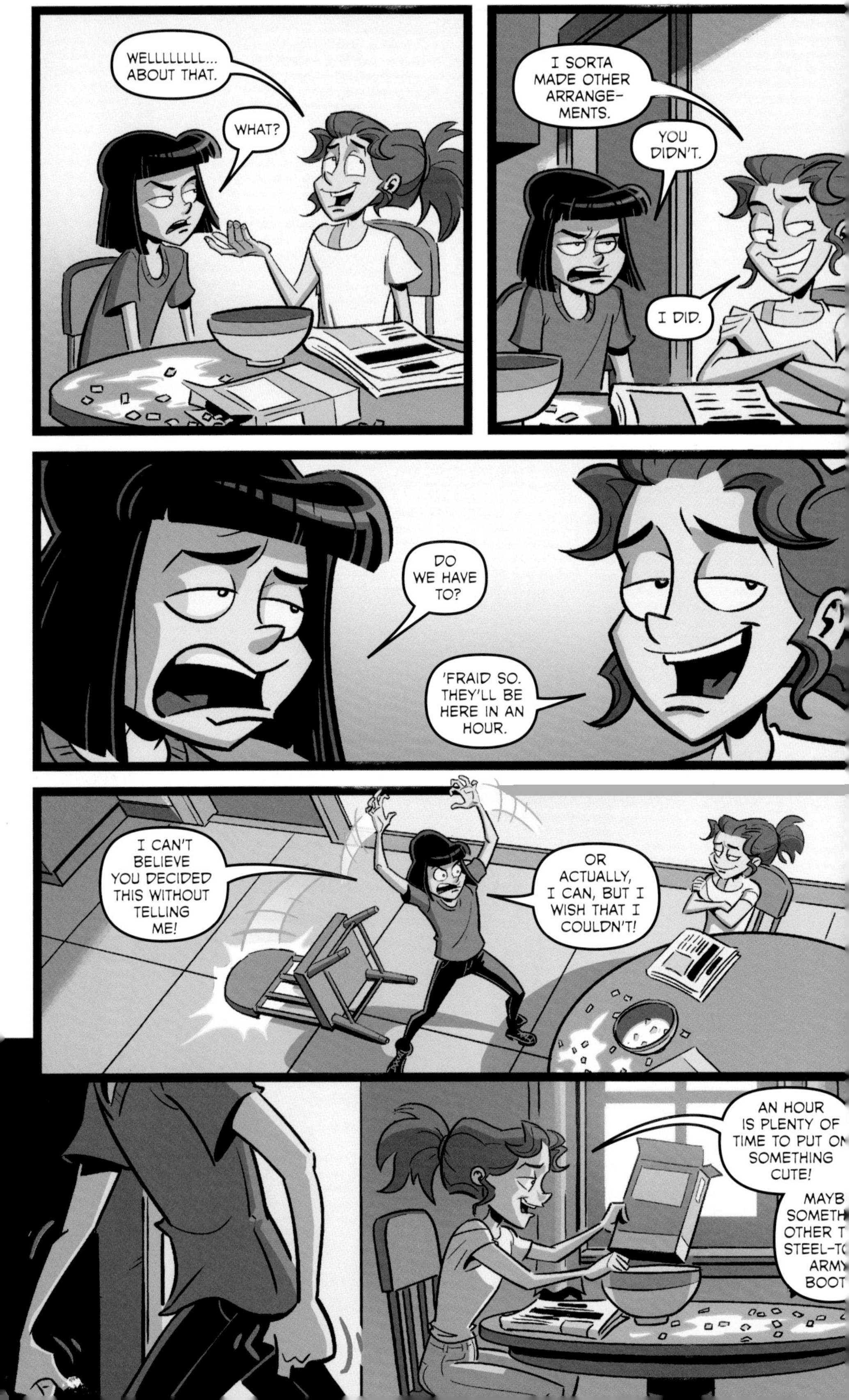
WELLLLLLLL... ABOUT THAT.
WHAT?
I SORTA MADE OTHER ARRANGE-MENTS.
YOU DIDN'T.
I DID.
DO WE HAVE TO?
'FRAID SO. THEY'LL BE HERE IN AN HOUR.
I CAN'T BELIEVE YOU DECIDED THIS WITHOUT TELLING ME!
OR ACTUALLY, I CAN, BUT I WISH THAT I COULDN'T!
AN HOUR IS PLENTY OF TIME TO PUT O
SOMETHING CUTE!
MAYB
SOMETH
OTHER T
STEEL-T
ARMY
BOOT

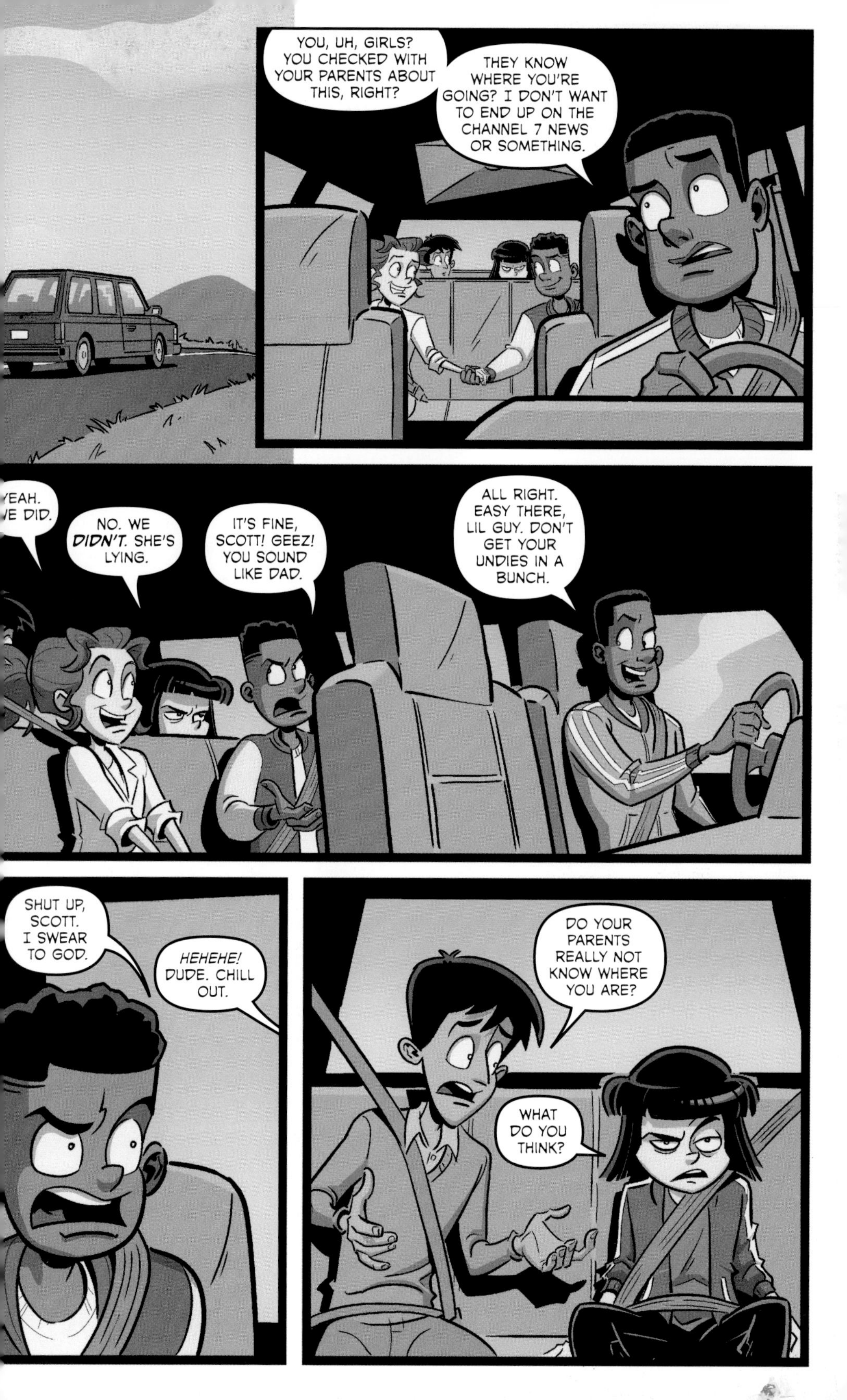

YOU, UH, GIRLS? YOU CHECKED WITH YOUR PARENTS ABOUT THIS, RIGHT?
THEY KNOW WHERE YOU'RE GOING? I DON'T WANT TO END UP ON THE CHANNEL 7 NEWS OR SOMETHING.
YEAH. WE DID.
NO. WE *DIDN'T*. SHE'S LYING.
IT'S FINE, SCOTT! GEEZ! YOU SOUND LIKE DAD.
ALL RIGHT. EASY THERE, LIL GUY. DON'T GET YOUR UNDIES IN A BUNCH.
SHUT UP, SCOTT. I SWEAR TO GOD.
HEHEHE! DUDE. CHILL OUT.
DO YOUR PARENTS REALLY NOT KNOW WHERE YOU ARE?
WHAT DO YOU THINK?

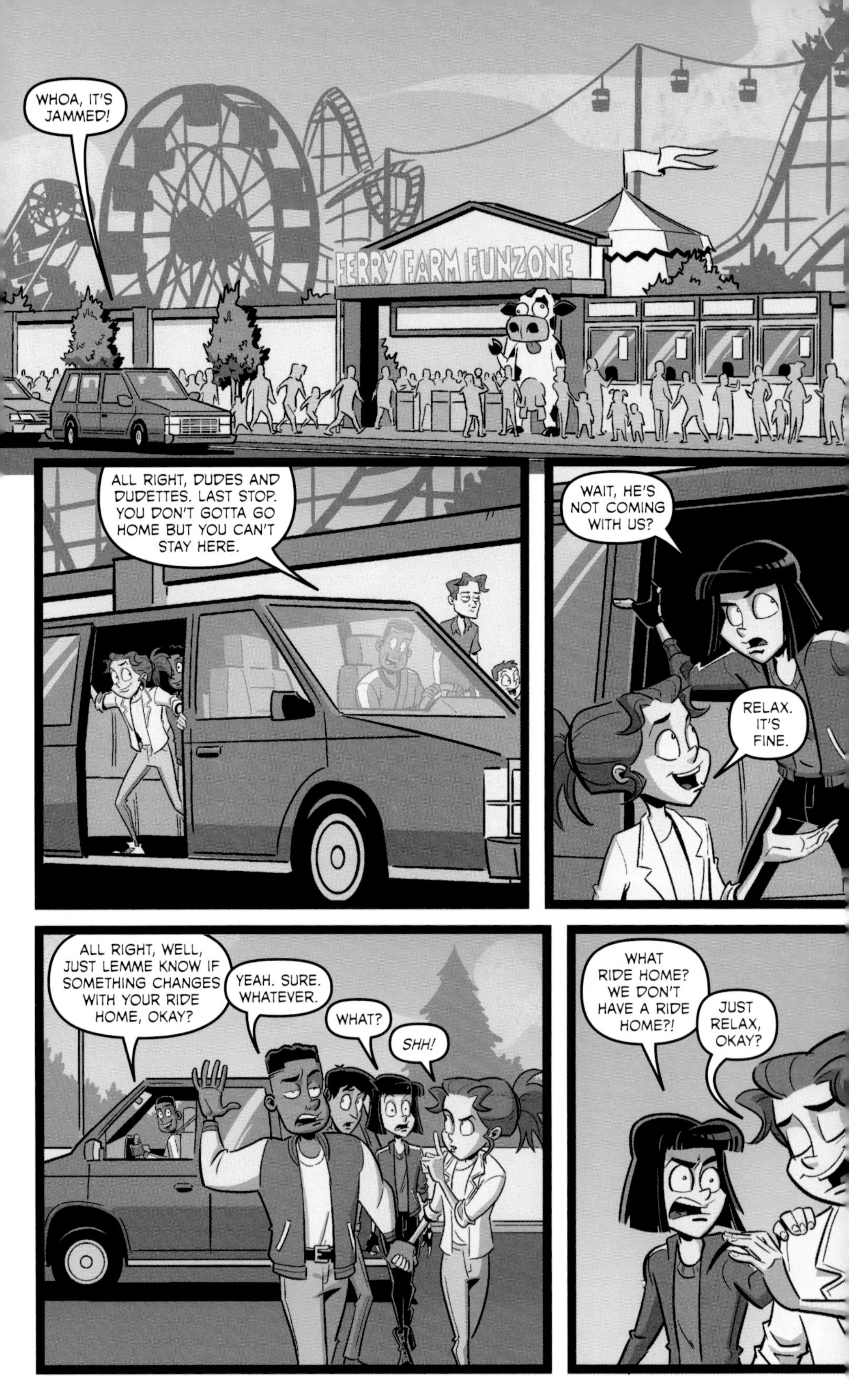
WHOA, IT'S JAMMED!
FERRY FARM FUNZONE
ALL RIGHT, DUDES AND DUDETTES. LAST STOP. YOU DON'T GOTTA GO HOME BUT YOU CAN'T STAY HERE.
WAIT, HE'S NOT COMING WITH US?
RELAX. IT'S FINE.
ALL RIGHT, WELL, JUST LEMME KNOW IF SOMETHING CHANGES WITH YOUR RIDE HOME, OKAY?
YEAH. SURE. WHATEVER.
WHAT?
SHH!
WHAT RIDE HOME? WE DON'T HAVE A RIDE HOME?!
JUST RELAX, OKAY?

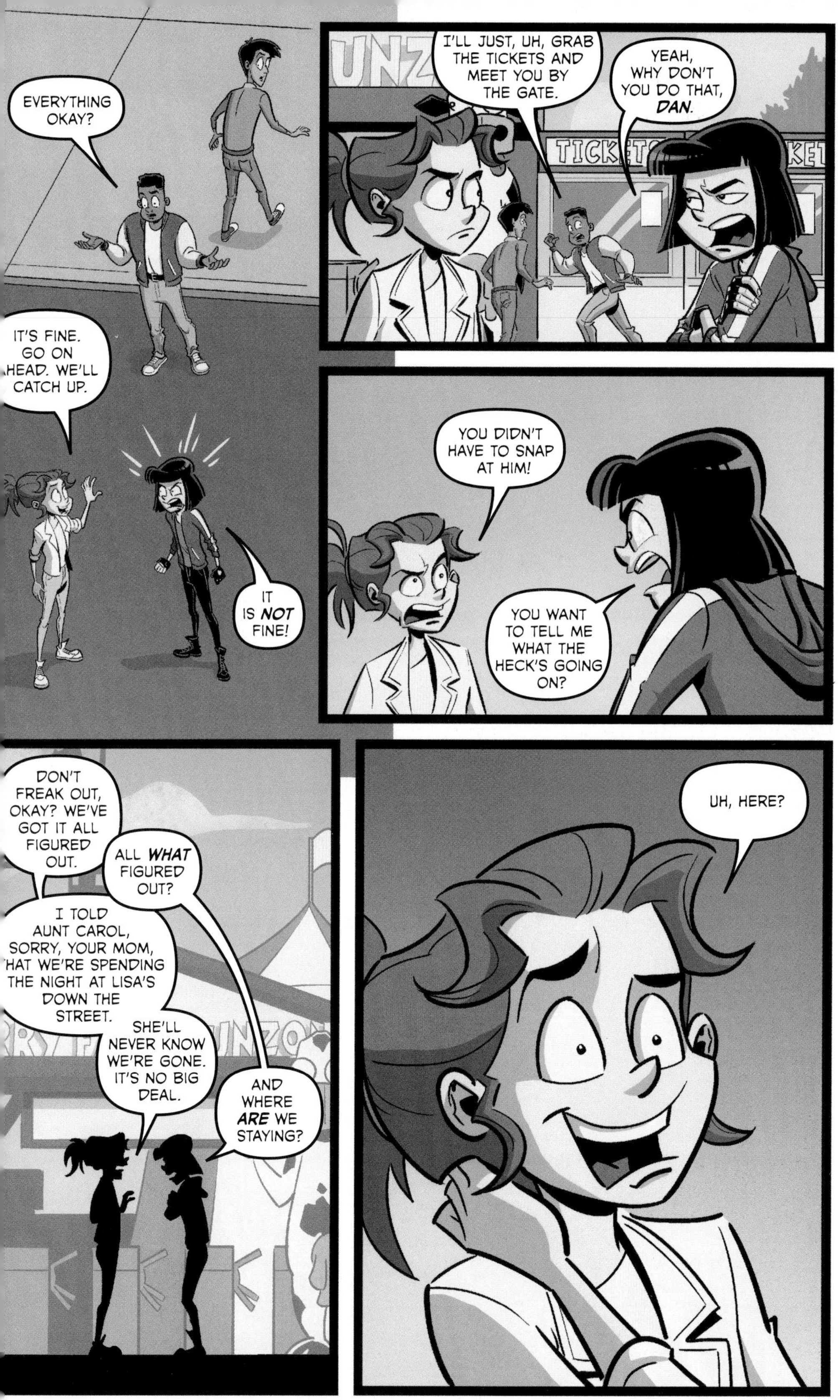

EVERYTHING OKAY?
I'LL JUST, UH, GRAB THE TICKETS AND MEET YOU BY THE GATE.
YEAH, WHY DON'T YOU DO THAT, DAN.
TICKETS
IT'S FINE. GO ON AHEAD. WE'LL CATCH UP.
IT IS NOT FINE!
YOU DIDN'T HAVE TO SNAP AT HIM!
YOU WANT TO TELL ME WHAT THE HECK'S GOING ON?
DON'T FREAK OUT, OKAY? WE'VE GOT IT ALL FIGURED OUT.
ALL WHAT FIGURED OUT?
I TOLD AUNT CAROL, SORRY, YOUR MOM, THAT WE'RE SPENDING THE NIGHT AT LISA'S DOWN THE STREET.
SHE'LL NEVER KNOW WE'RE GONE. IT'S NO BIG DEAL.
AND WHERE ARE WE STAYING?
UH, HERE?

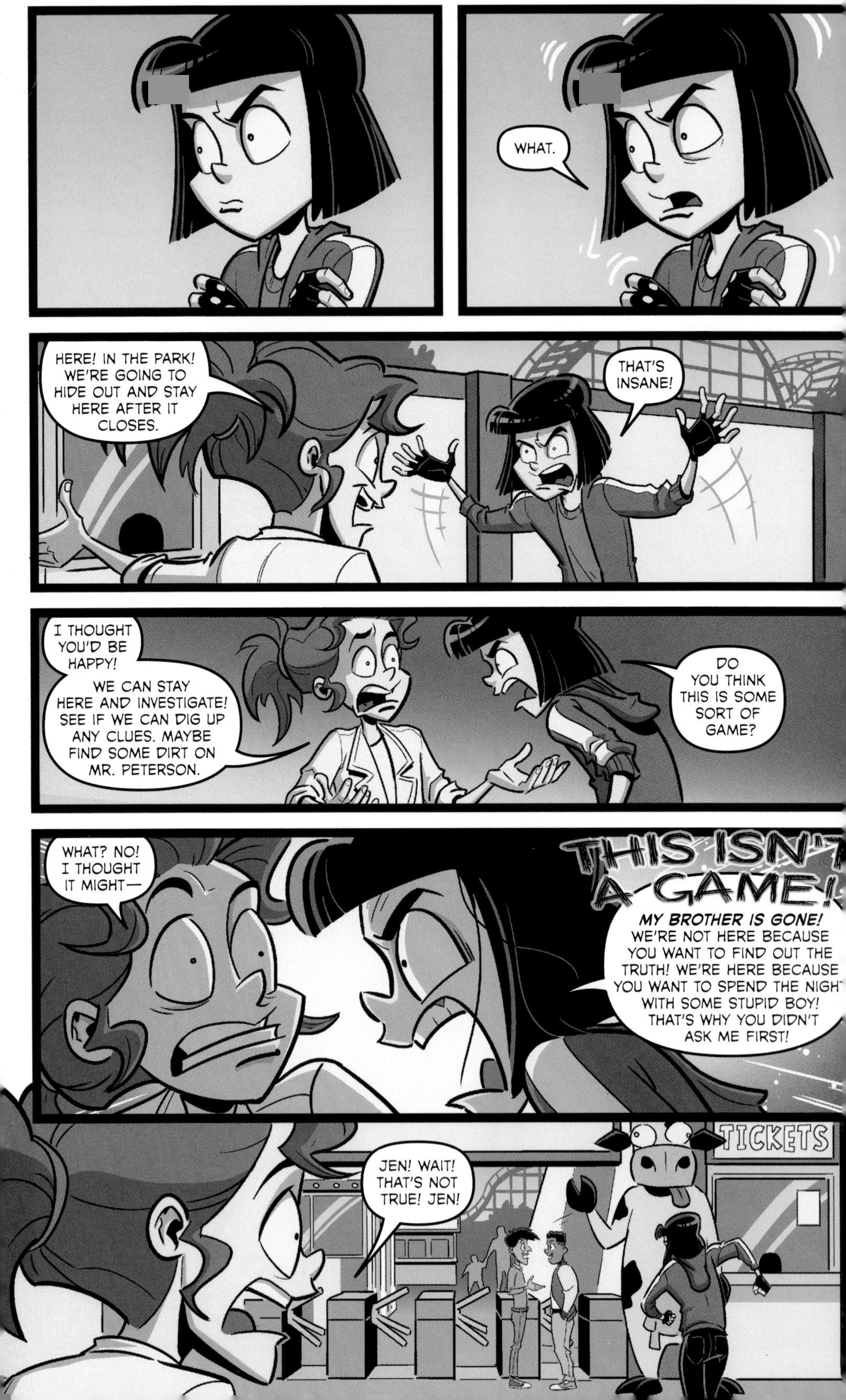
WHAT.
HERE! IN THE PARK! WE'RE GOING TO HIDE OUT AND STAY HERE AFTER IT CLOSES.
THAT'S INSANE!
I THOUGHT YOU'D BE HAPPY!
WE CAN STAY HERE AND INVESTIGATE! SEE IF WE CAN DIG UP ANY CLUES. MAYBE FIND SOME DIRT ON MR. PETERSON.
DO YOU THINK THIS IS SOME SORT OF GAME?
WHAT? NO! I THOUGHT IT MIGHT—
THIS ISN'T A GAME!
MY BROTHER IS GONE! WE'RE NOT HERE BECAUSE YOU WANT TO FIND OUT THE TRUTH! WE'RE HERE BECAUSE YOU WANT TO SPEND THE NIGHT WITH SOME STUPID BOY! THAT'S WHY YOU DIDN'T ASK ME FIRST!
TICKETS
JEN! WAIT! THAT'S NOT TRUE! JEN!

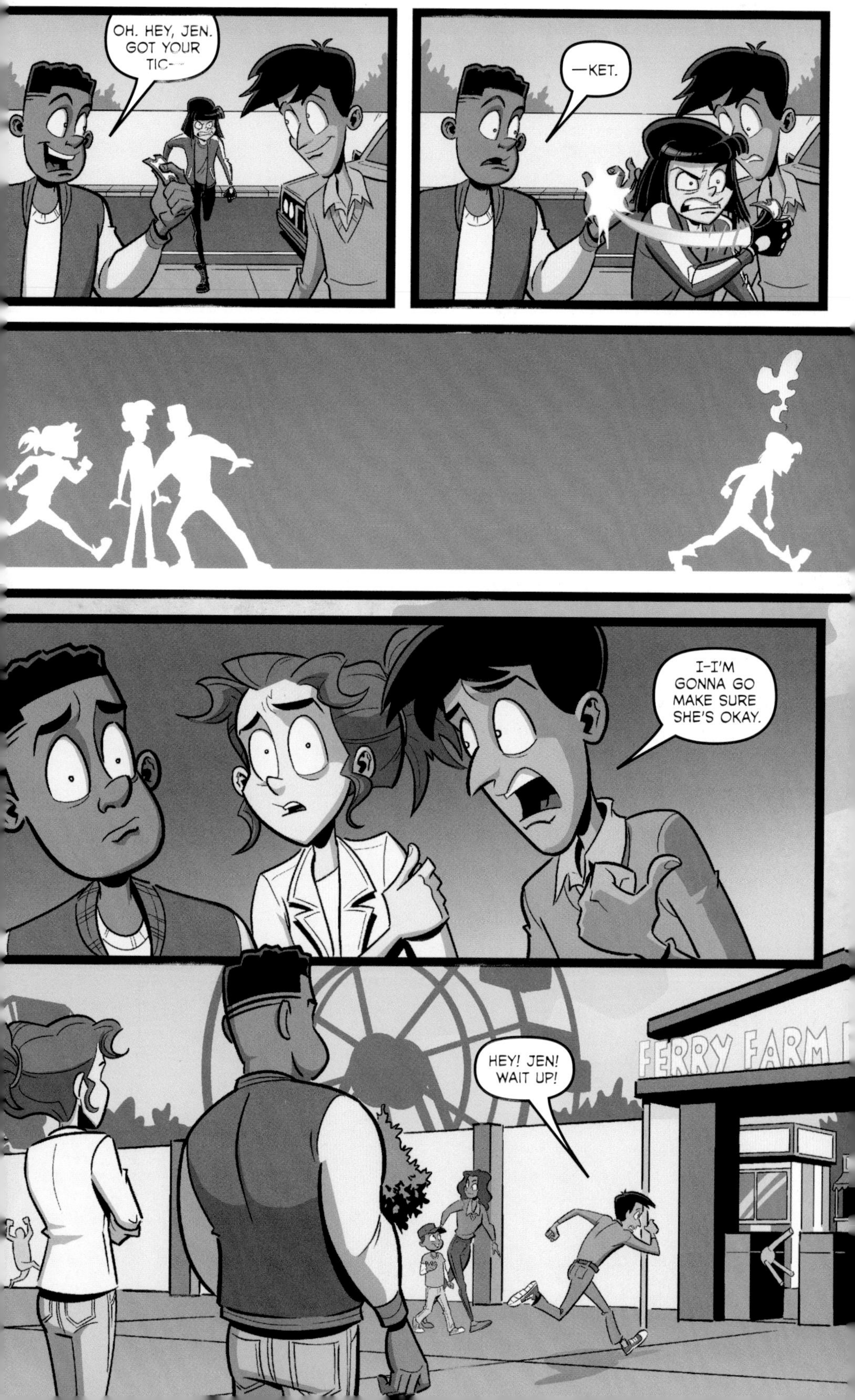
OH. HEY, JEN. GOT YOUR TIC—
—KET.
I-I'M GONNA GO MAKE SURE SHE'S OKAY.
FERRY FARM
HEY! JEN! WAIT UP!

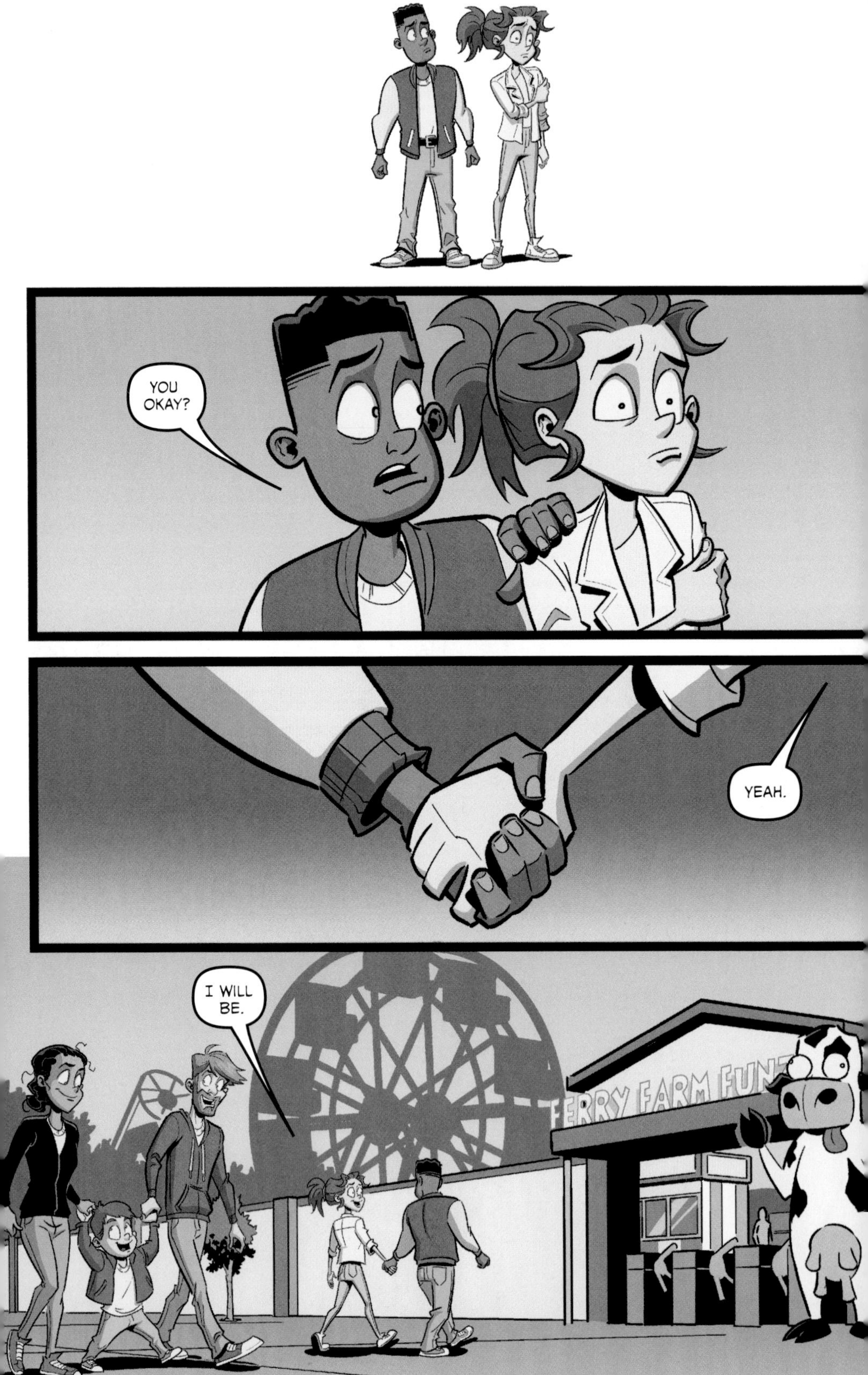
YOU OKAY?
YEAH.
I WILL BE.
FERRY FARM FUN

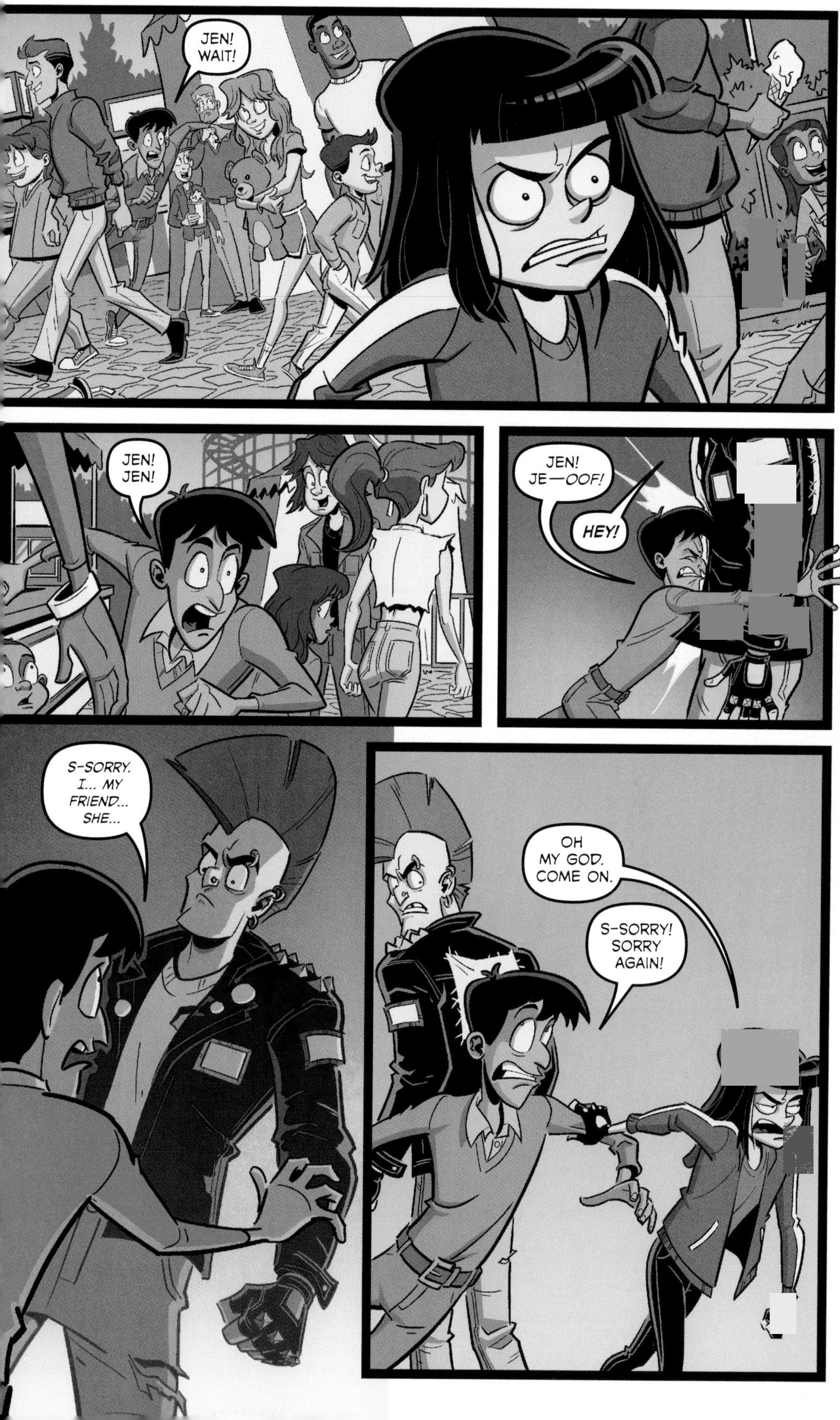
JEN! WAIT!
JEN! JEN!
JEN! JE—OOF!
HEY!
S-SORRY. I... MY FRIEND... SHE...
OH MY GOD. COME ON.
S-SORRY! SORRY AGAIN!

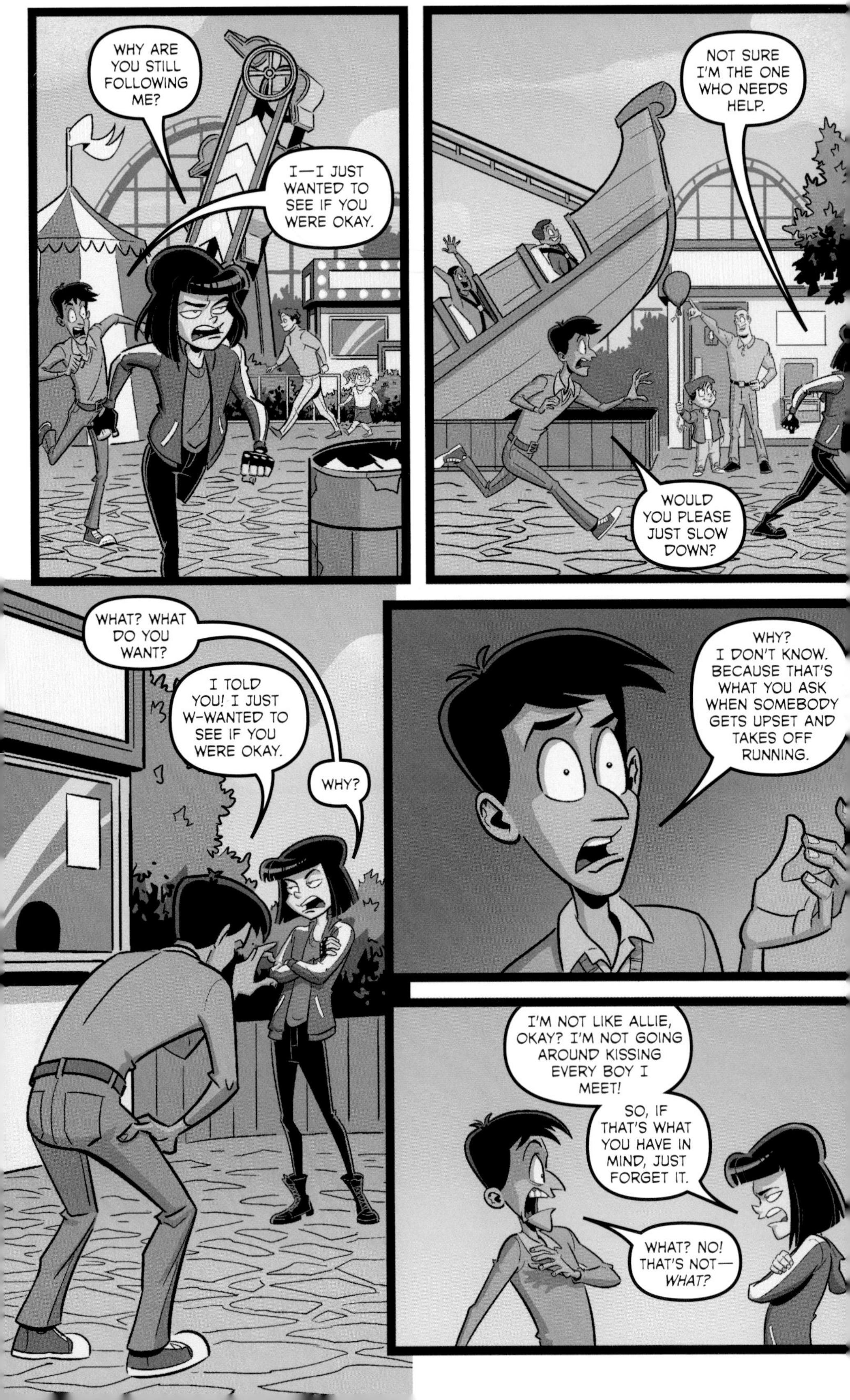
WHY ARE YOU STILL FOLLOWING ME?
I—I JUST WANTED TO SEE IF YOU WERE OKAY.
NOT SURE I'M THE ONE WHO NEEDS HELP.
WOULD YOU PLEASE JUST SLOW DOWN?
WHAT? WHAT DO YOU WANT?
I TOLD YOU! I JUST W-WANTED TO SEE IF YOU WERE OKAY.
WHY?
WHY? I DON'T KNOW. BECAUSE THAT'S WHAT YOU ASK WHEN SOMEBODY GETS UPSET AND TAKES OFF RUNNING.
I'M NOT LIKE ALLIE, OKAY? I'M NOT GOING AROUND KISSING EVERY BOY I MEET!
SO, IF THAT'S WHAT YOU HAVE IN MIND, JUST FORGET IT.
WHAT? NO! THAT'S NOT—*WHAT?*

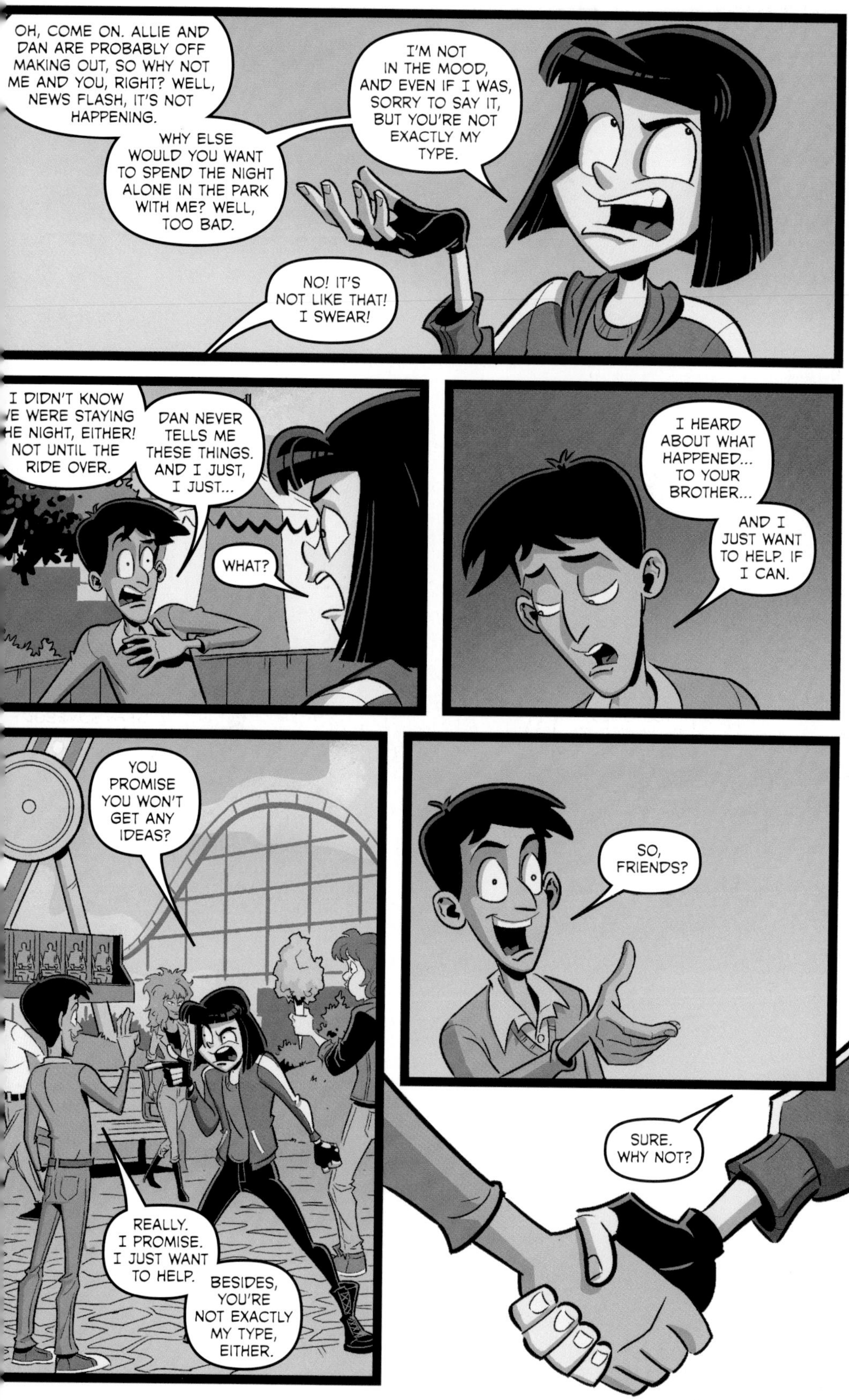

OH, COME ON. ALLIE AND DAN ARE PROBABLY OFF MAKING OUT, SO WHY NOT ME AND YOU, RIGHT? WELL, NEWS FLASH, IT'S NOT HAPPENING.
WHY ELSE WOULD YOU WANT TO SPEND THE NIGHT ALONE IN THE PARK WITH ME? WELL, TOO BAD.
I'M NOT IN THE MOOD, AND EVEN IF I WAS, SORRY TO SAY IT, BUT YOU'RE NOT EXACTLY MY TYPE.
NO! IT'S NOT LIKE THAT! I SWEAR!
I DIDN'T KNOW /E WERE STAYING HE NIGHT, EITHER! NOT UNTIL THE RIDE OVER.
DAN NEVER TELLS ME THESE THINGS. AND I JUST, I JUST...
WHAT?
I HEARD ABOUT WHAT HAPPENED... TO YOUR BROTHER...
AND I JUST WANT TO HELP. IF I CAN.
YOU PROMISE YOU WON'T GET ANY IDEAS?
REALLY. I PROMISE. I JUST WANT TO HELP.
BESIDES, YOU'RE NOT EXACTLY MY TYPE, EITHER.
SO, FRIENDS?
SURE. WHY NOT?

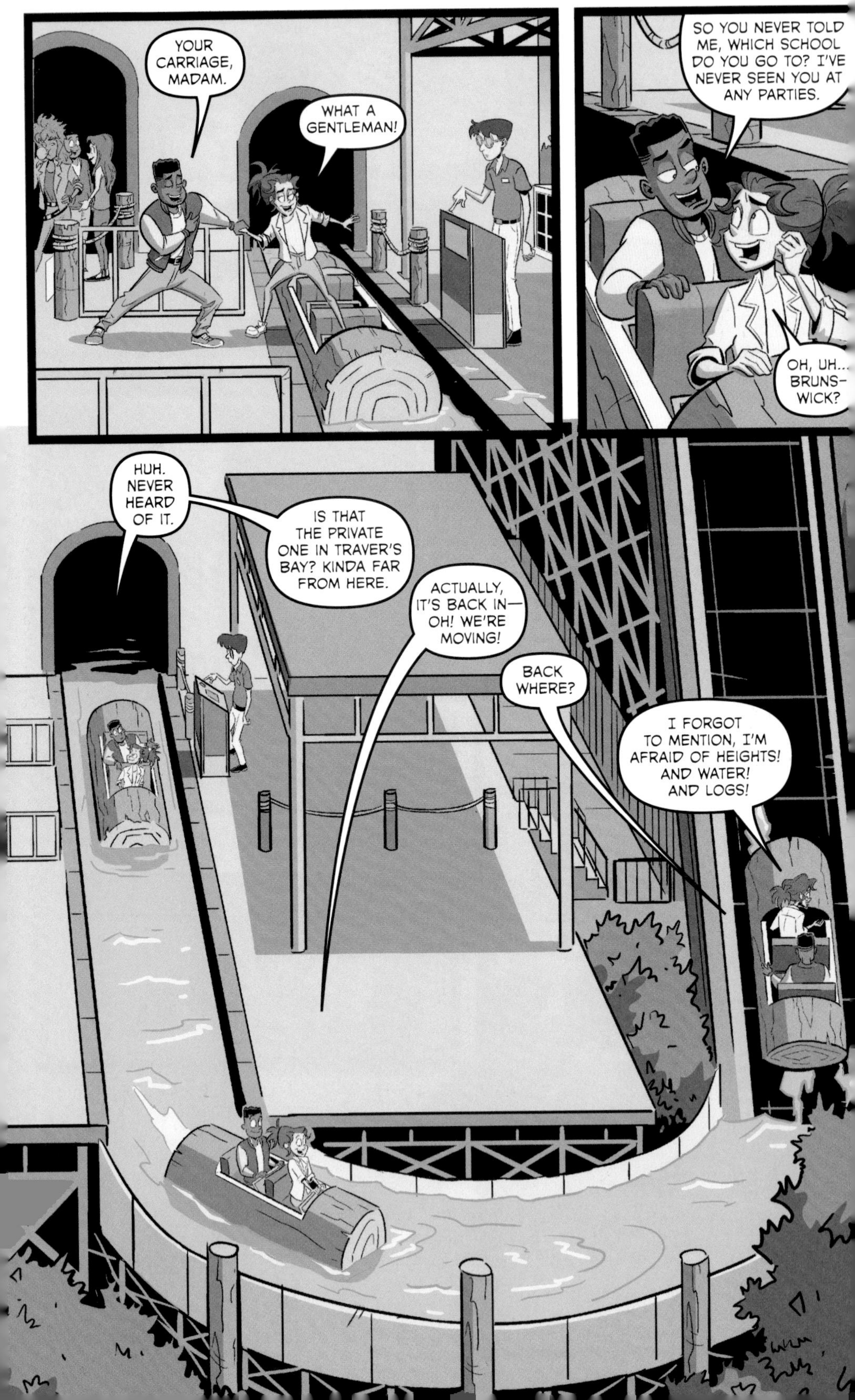
YOUR CARRIAGE, MADAM.
WHAT A GENTLEMAN!
SO YOU NEVER TOLD ME, WHICH SCHOOL DO YOU GO TO? I'VE NEVER SEEN YOU AT ANY PARTIES.
OH, UH... BRUNS-WICK?
HUH. NEVER HEARD OF IT.
IS THAT THE PRIVATE ONE IN TRAVER'S BAY? KINDA FAR FROM HERE.
ACTUALLY, IT'S BACK IN— OH! WE'RE MOVING!
BACK WHERE?
I FORGOT TO MENTION, I'M AFRAID OF HEIGHTS! AND WATER! AND LOGS!

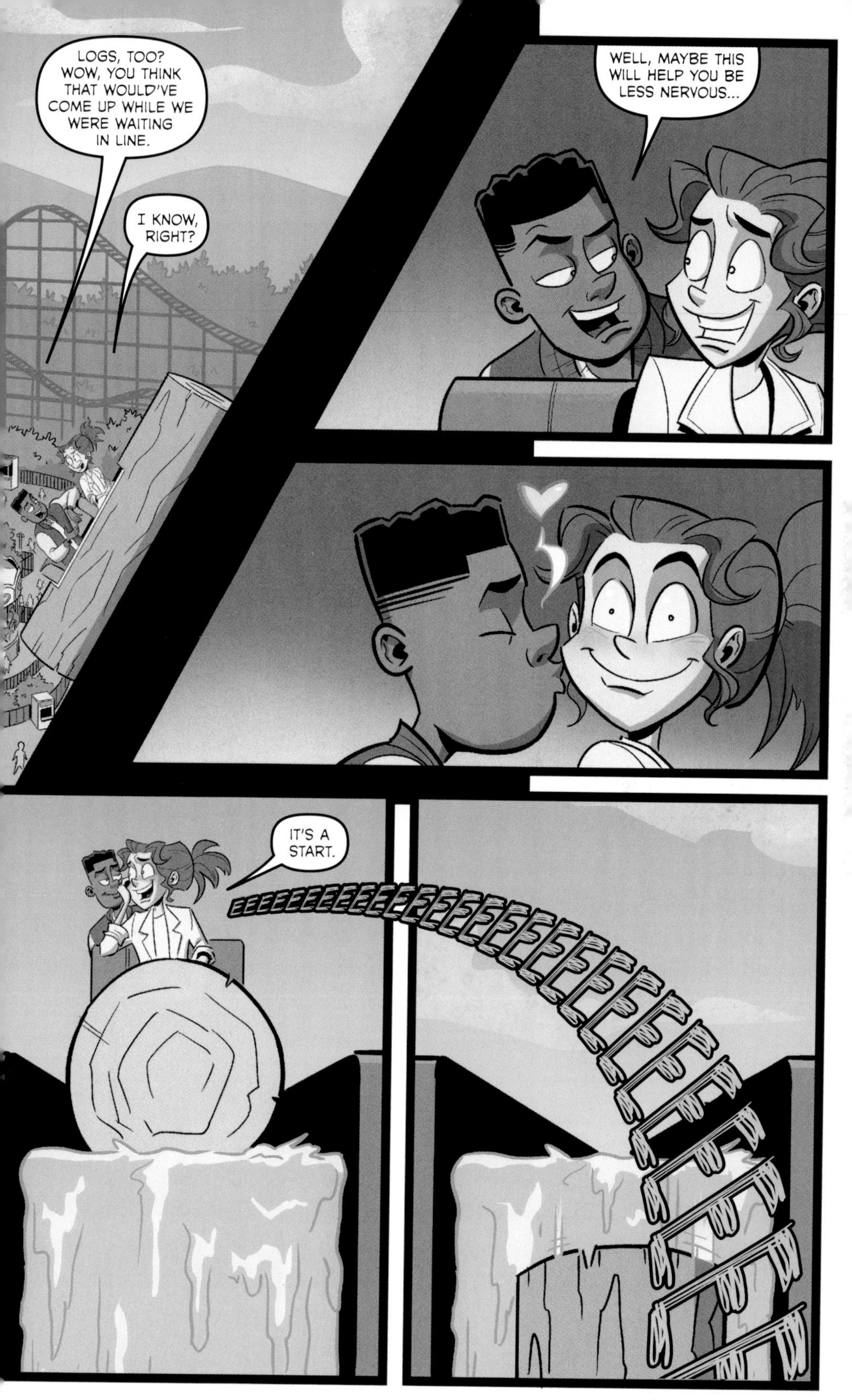

LOGS, TOO? WOW, YOU THINK THAT WOULD'VE COME UP WHILE WE WERE WAITING IN LINE.
I KNOW, RIGHT?
WELL, MAYBE THIS WILL HELP YOU BE LESS NERVOUS...
IT'S A START.
EEEEEEEEEEEEEEEEEEEEEEEEEEEEEEEEEEEEEE

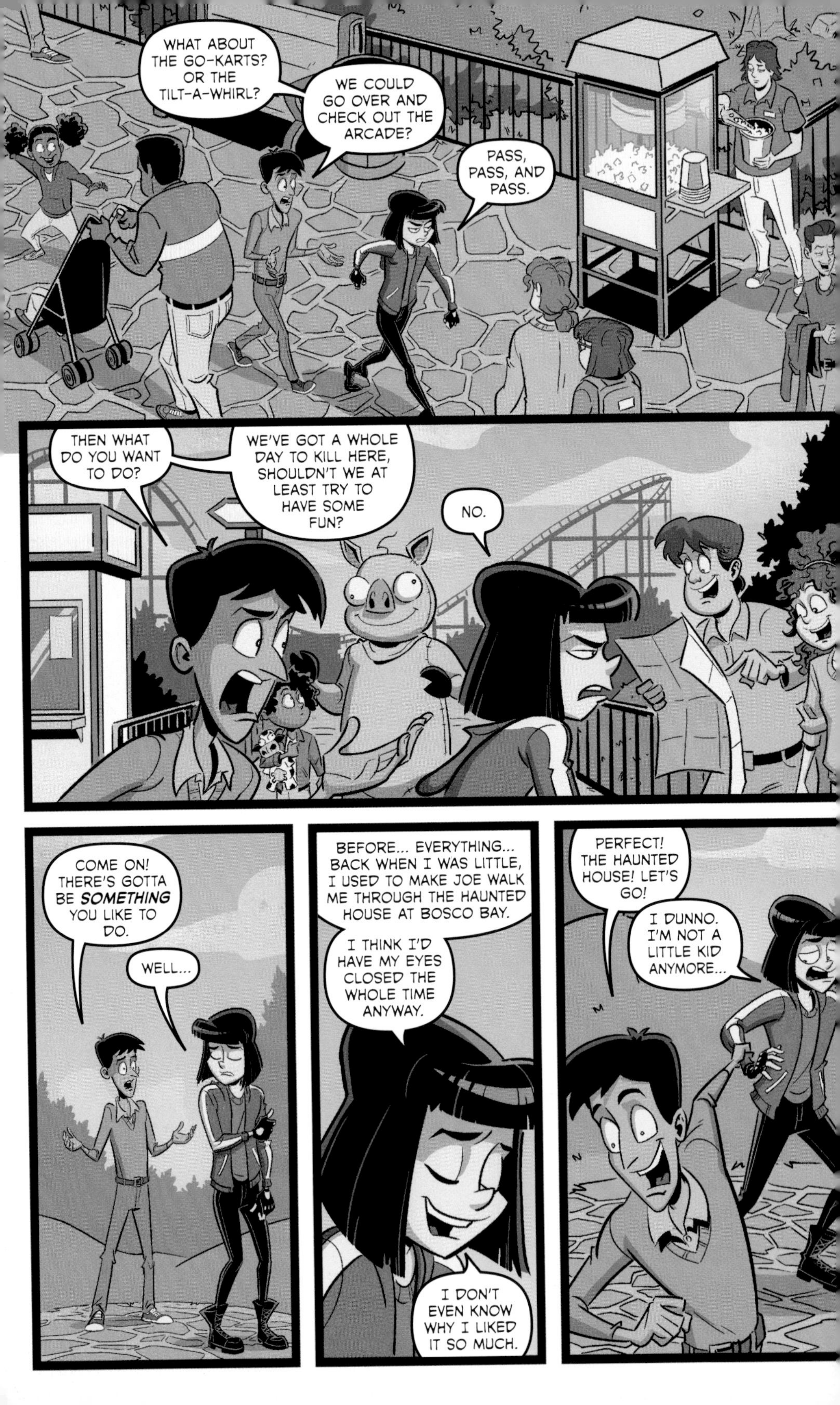

WHAT ABOUT THE GO-KARTS? OR THE TILT-A-WHIRL?
WE COULD GO OVER AND CHECK OUT THE ARCADE?
PASS, PASS, AND PASS.
THEN WHAT DO YOU WANT TO DO?
WE'VE GOT A WHOLE DAY TO KILL HERE, SHOULDN'T WE AT LEAST TRY TO HAVE SOME FUN?
NO.
COME ON! THERE'S GOTTA BE *SOMETHING* YOU LIKE TO DO.
WELL...
BEFORE... EVERYTHING... BACK WHEN I WAS LITTLE, I USED TO MAKE JOE WALK ME THROUGH THE HAUNTED HOUSE AT BOSCO BAY.
I THINK I'D HAVE MY EYES CLOSED THE WHOLE TIME ANYWAY.
I DON'T EVEN KNOW WHY I LIKED IT SO MUCH.
PERFECT! THE HAUNTED HOUSE! LET'S GO!
I DUNNO. I'M NOT A LITTLE KID ANYMORE...

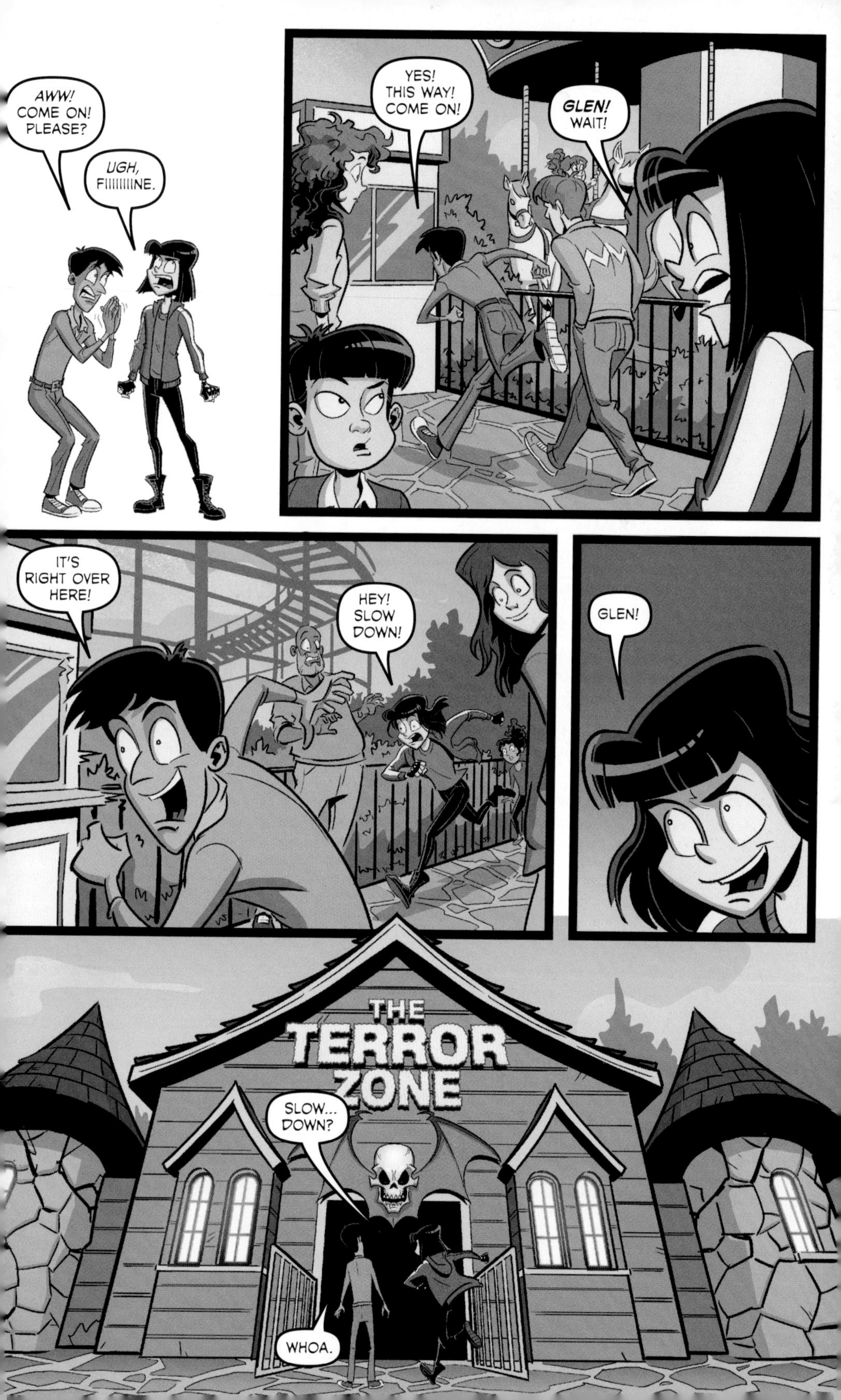
AWW! COME ON! PLEASE?
UGH, FIIIIIIINE.
YES! THIS WAY! COME ON!
GLEN! WAIT!
IT'S RIGHT OVER HERE!
HEY! SLOW DOWN!
GLEN!
THE TERROR ZONE
SLOW... DOWN?
WHOA.

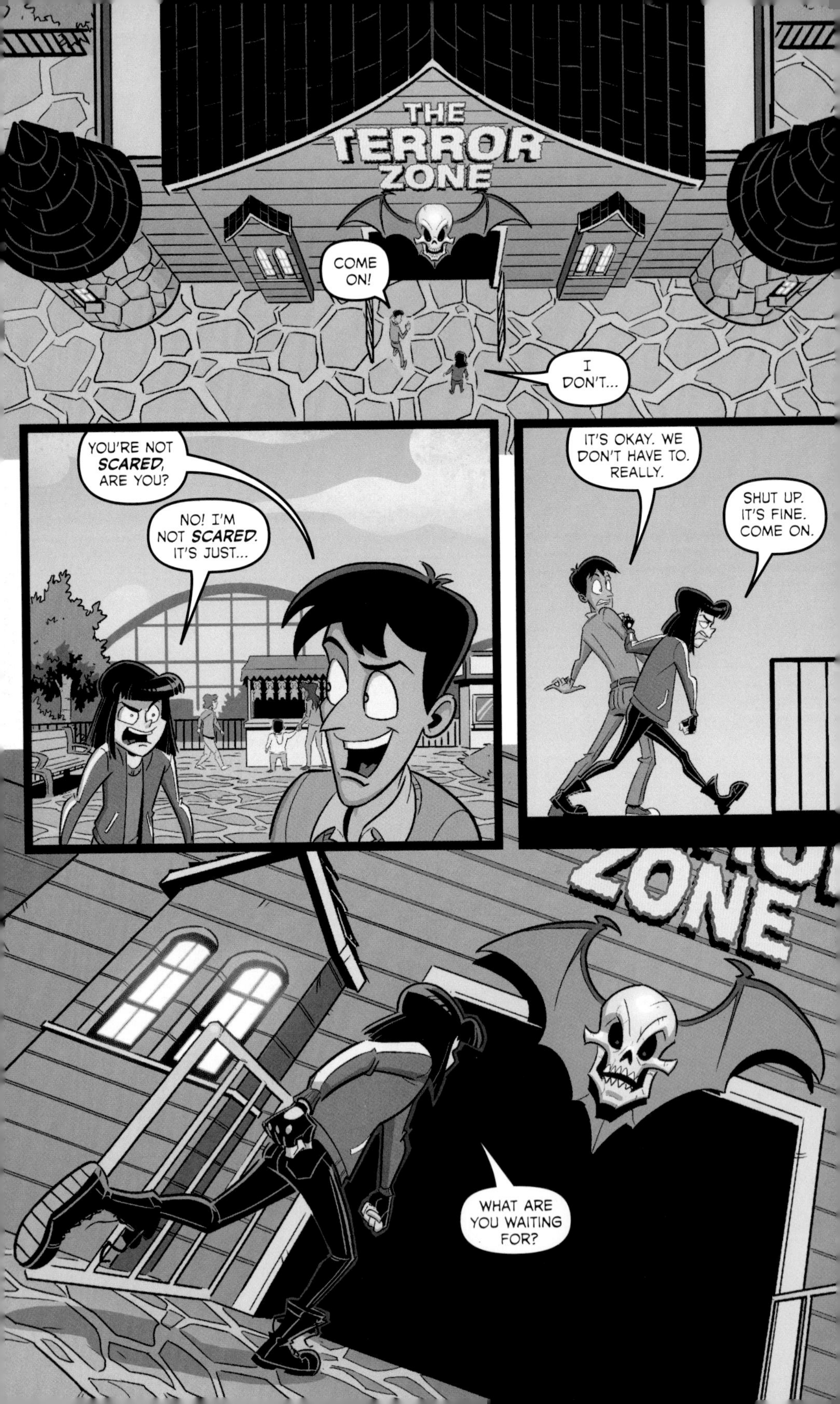
THE TERROR ZONE
COME ON!
I DON'T...
YOU'RE NOT *SCARED*, ARE YOU?
NO! I'M NOT *SCARED*. IT'S JUST...
IT'S OKAY. WE DON'T HAVE TO. REALLY.
SHUT UP. IT'S FINE. COME ON.
ZONE
WHAT ARE YOU WAITING FOR?

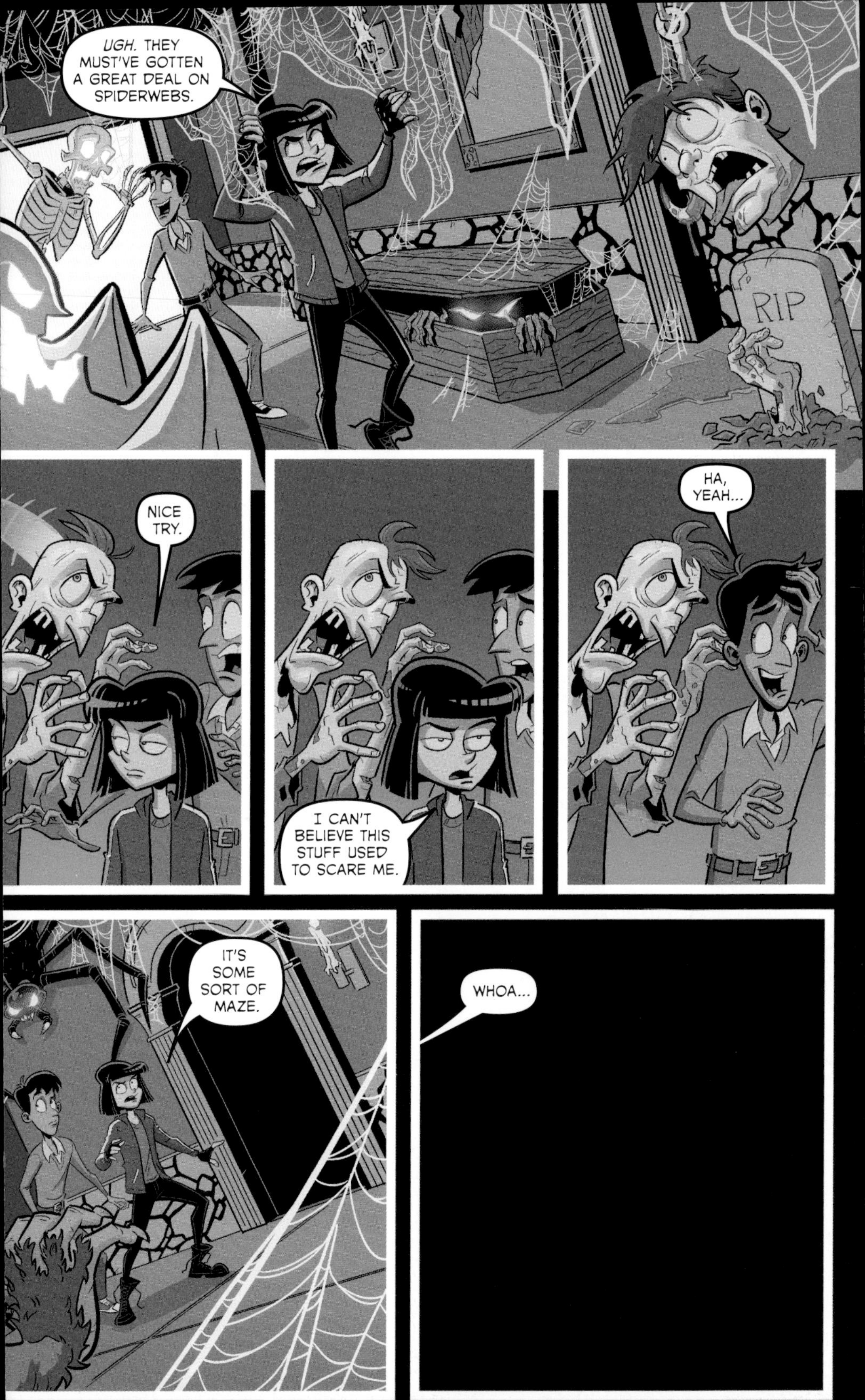
UGH. THEY MUST'VE GOTTEN A GREAT DEAL ON SPIDERWEBS.
RIP
NICE TRY.
I CAN'T BELIEVE THIS STUFF USED TO SCARE ME.
HA, YEAH...
IT'S SOME SORT OF MAZE.
WHOA...

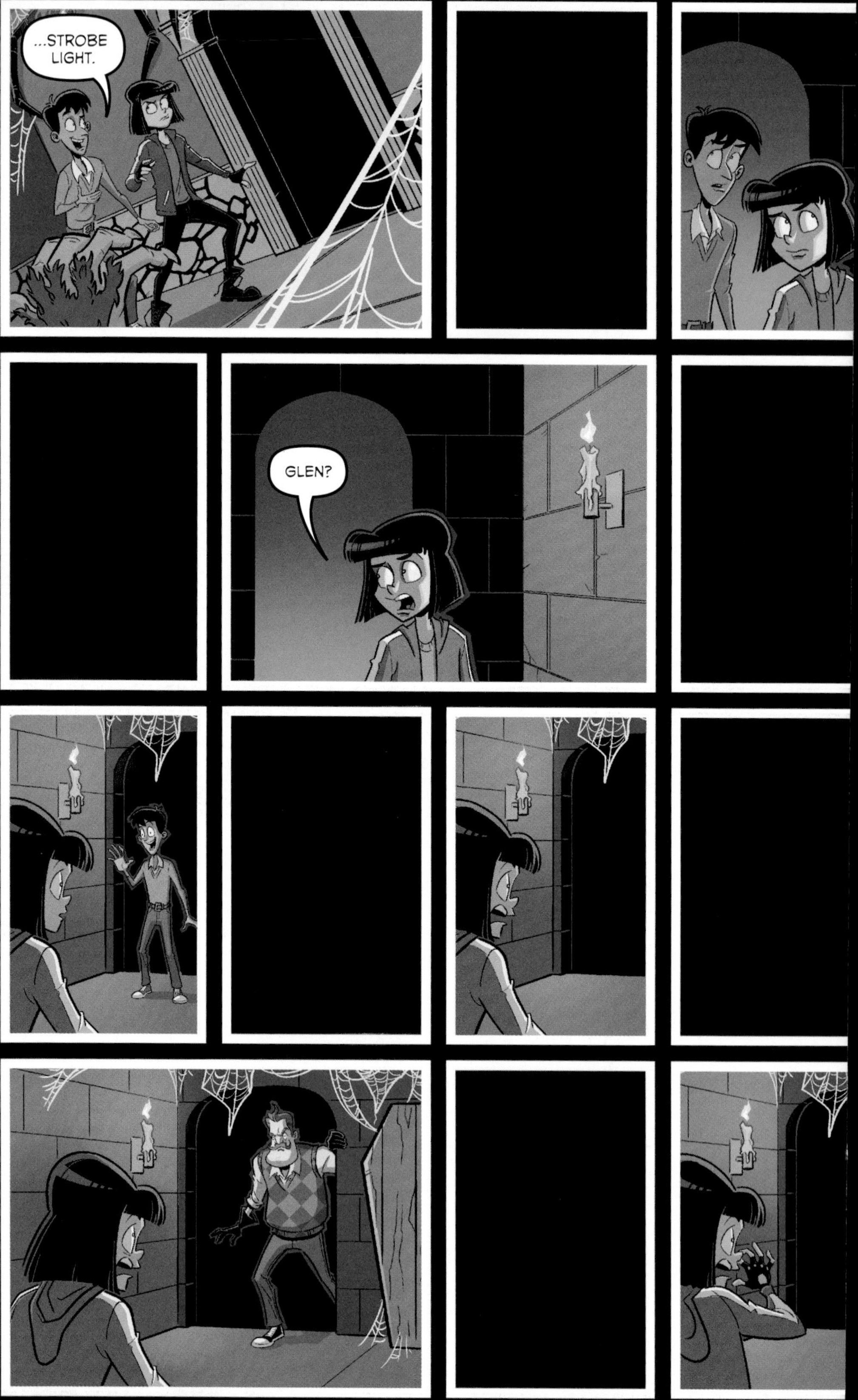
...STROBE LIGHT.
GLEN?

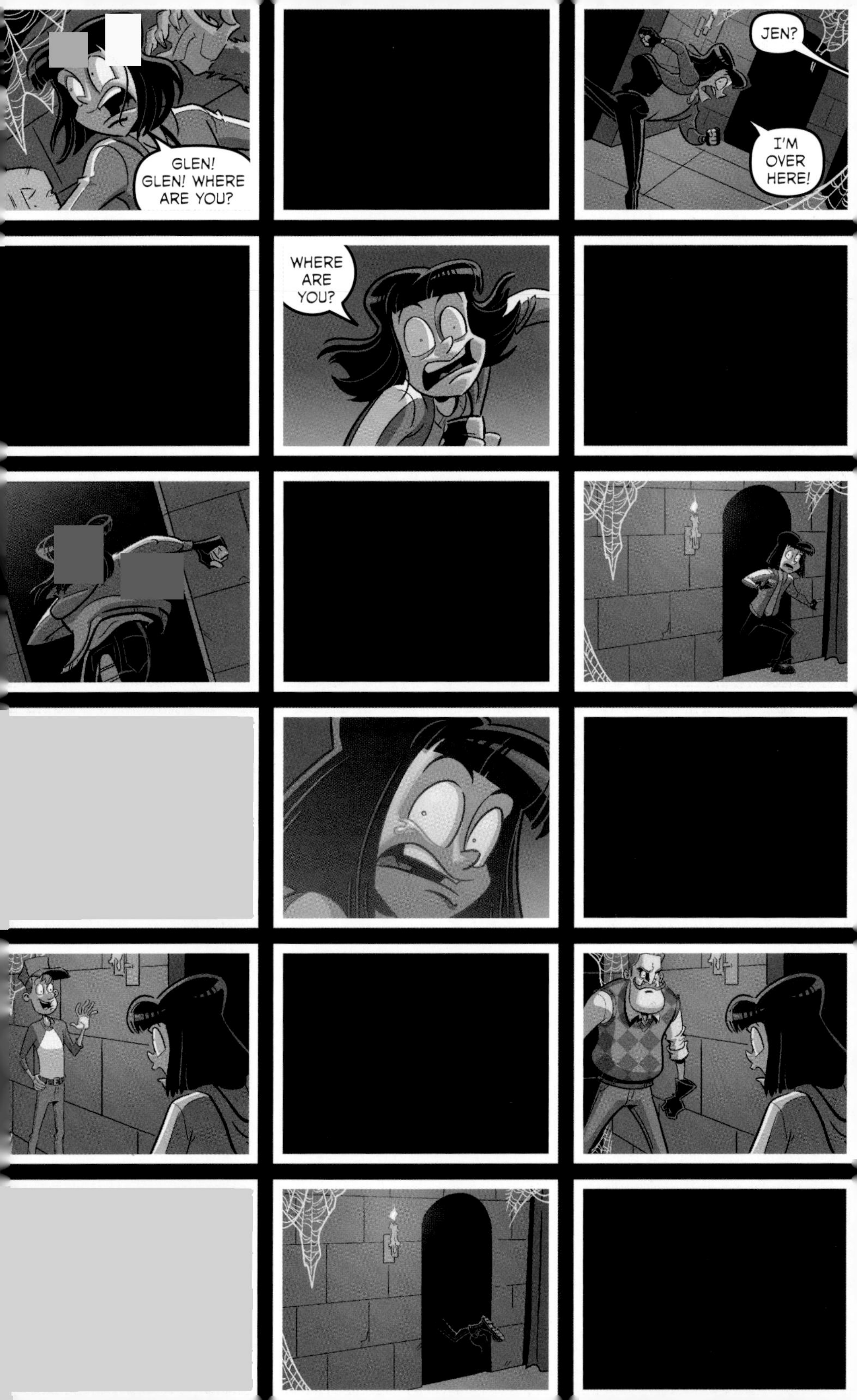
GLEN! GLEN! WHERE ARE YOU?
JEN?
I'M OVER HERE!
WHERE ARE YOU?

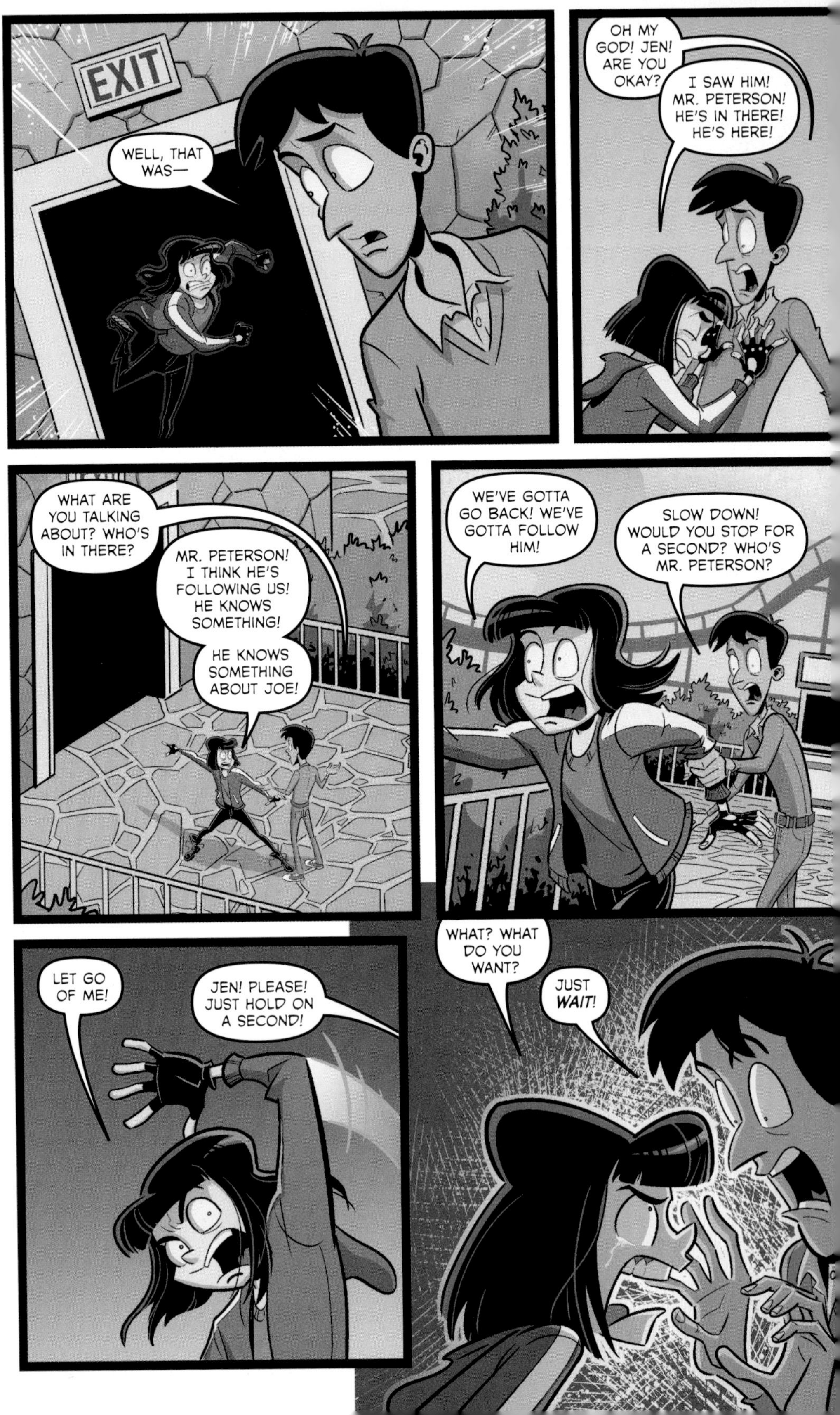
EXIT
WELL, THAT WAS—
OH MY GOD! JEN! ARE YOU OKAY?
I SAW HIM! MR. PETERSON! HE'S IN THERE! HE'S HERE!
WHAT ARE YOU TALKING ABOUT? WHO'S IN THERE?
MR. PETERSON! I THINK HE'S FOLLOWING US! HE KNOWS SOMETHING!
HE KNOWS SOMETHING ABOUT JOE!
WE'VE GOTTA GO BACK! WE'VE GOTTA FOLLOW HIM!
SLOW DOWN! WOULD YOU STOP FOR A SECOND? WHO'S MR. PETERSON?
LET GO OF ME!
JEN! PLEASE! JUST HOLD ON A SECOND!
WHAT? WHAT DO YOU WANT?
JUST *WAIT*!

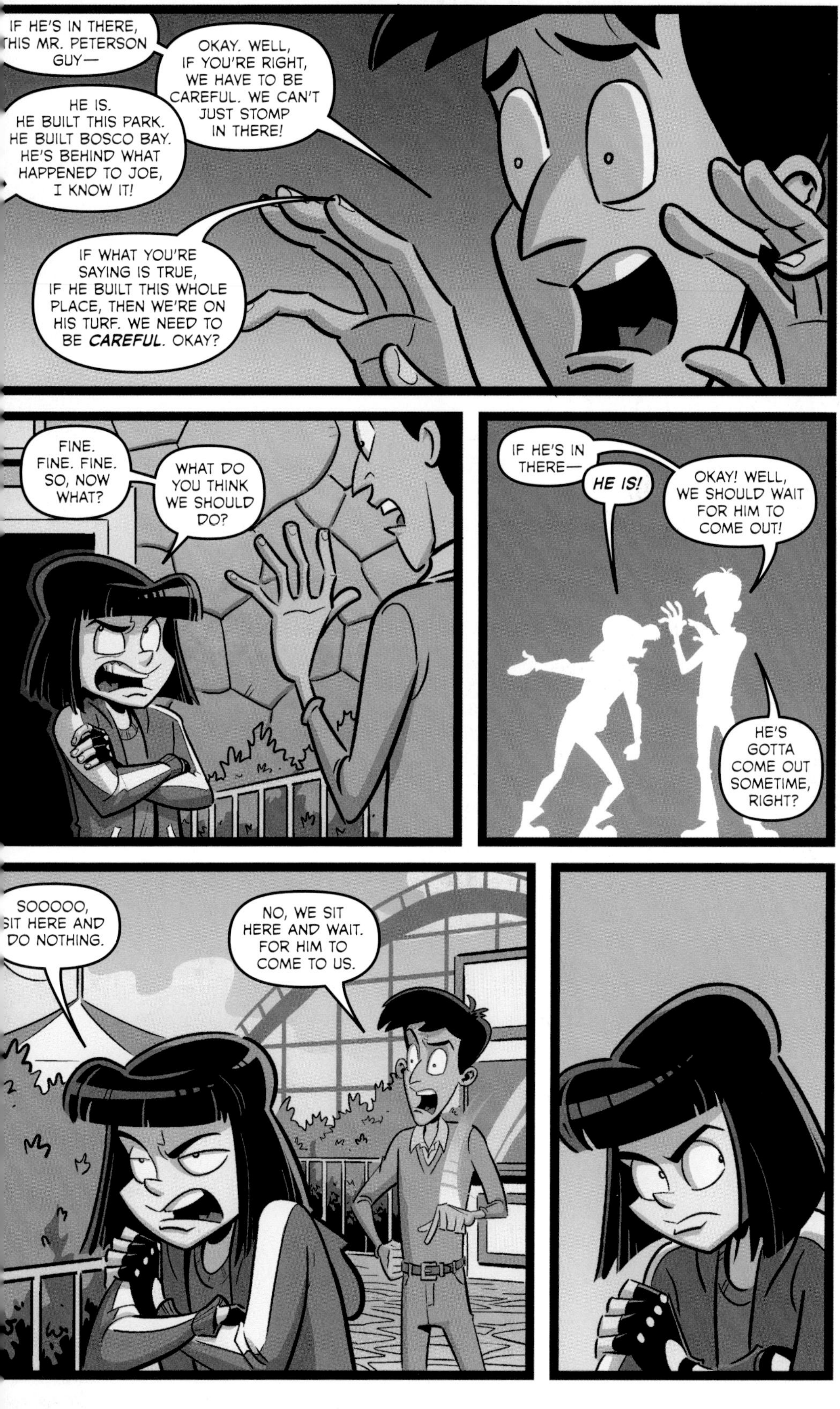
IF HE'S IN THERE, THIS MR. PETERSON GUY—
OKAY. WELL, IF YOU'RE RIGHT, WE HAVE TO BE CAREFUL. WE CAN'T JUST STOMP IN THERE!
HE IS. HE BUILT THIS PARK. HE BUILT BOSCO BAY. HE'S BEHIND WHAT HAPPENED TO JOE, I KNOW IT!
IF WHAT YOU'RE SAYING IS TRUE, IF HE BUILT THIS WHOLE PLACE, THEN WE'RE ON HIS TURF. WE NEED TO BE CAREFUL. OKAY?
FINE. FINE. FINE. SO, NOW WHAT?
WHAT DO YOU THINK WE SHOULD DO?
IF HE'S IN THERE—
HE IS!
OKAY! WELL, WE SHOULD WAIT FOR HIM TO COME OUT!
HE'S GOTTA COME OUT SOMETIME, RIGHT?
SOOOOO, SIT HERE AND DO NOTHING.
NO, WE SIT HERE AND WAIT. FOR HIM TO COME TO US.

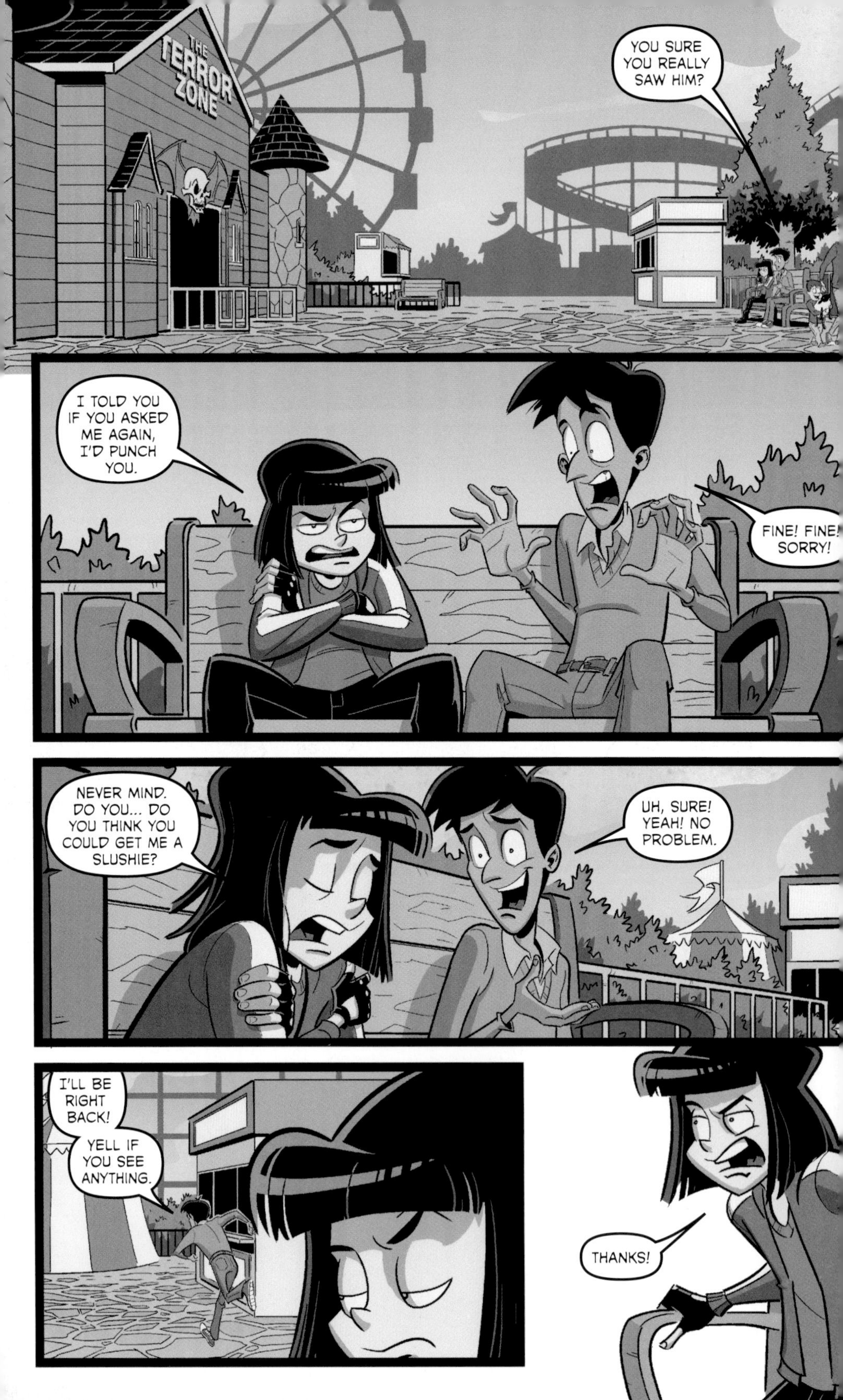
THE TERROR ZONE
YOU SURE YOU REALLY SAW HIM?
I TOLD YOU IF YOU ASKED ME AGAIN, I'D PUNCH YOU.
FINE! FINE! SORRY!
NEVER MIND. DO YOU... DO YOU THINK YOU COULD GET ME A SLUSHIE?
UH, SURE! YEAH! NO PROBLEM.
I'LL BE RIGHT BACK!
YELL IF YOU SEE ANYTHING.
THANKS!

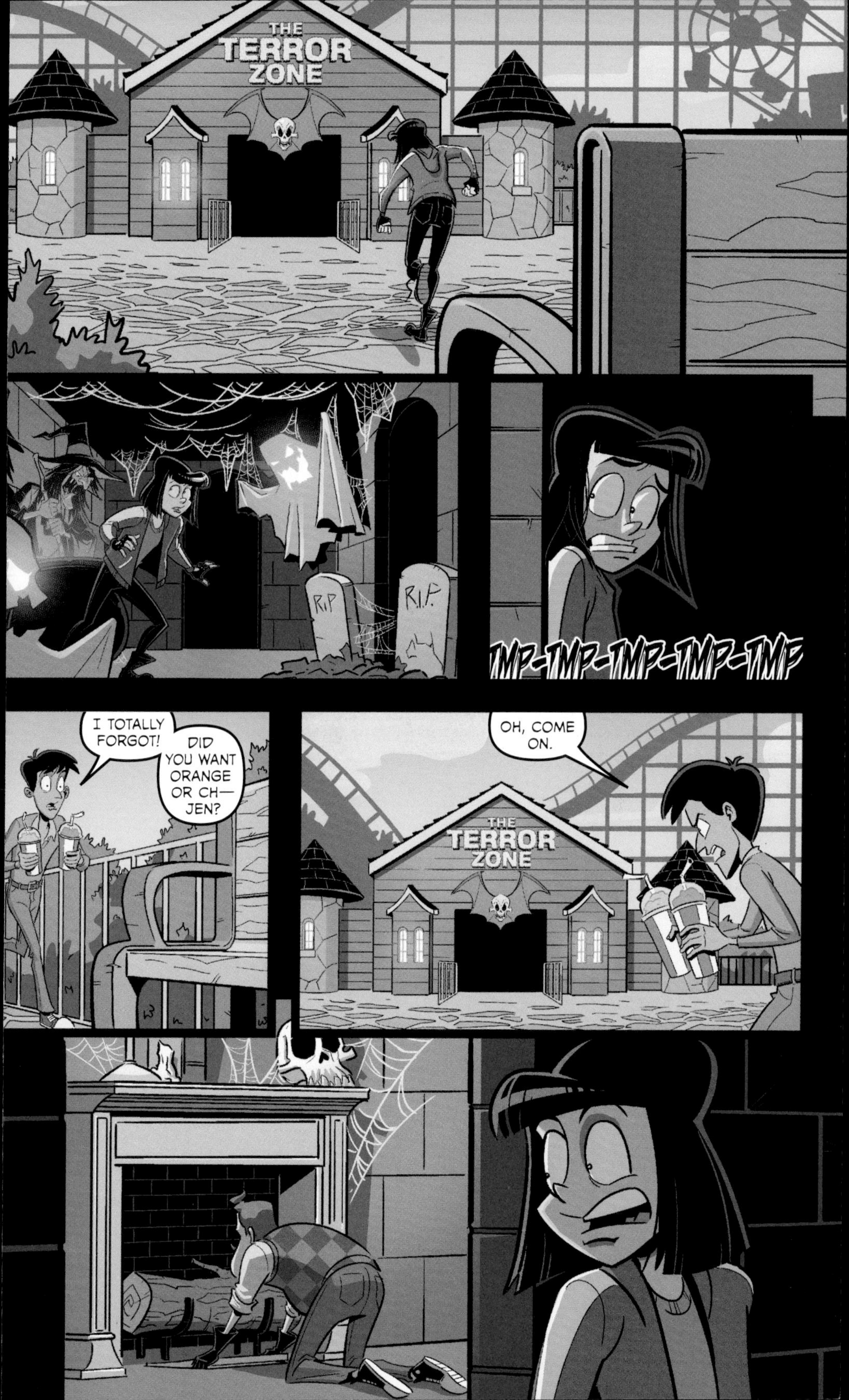
THE TERROR ZONE
R.I.P
R.I.P.
TMP-TMP-TMP-TMP-TMP
I TOTALLY FORGOT!
DID YOU WANT ORANGE OR CH— JEN?
OH, COME ON.
THE TERROR ZONE

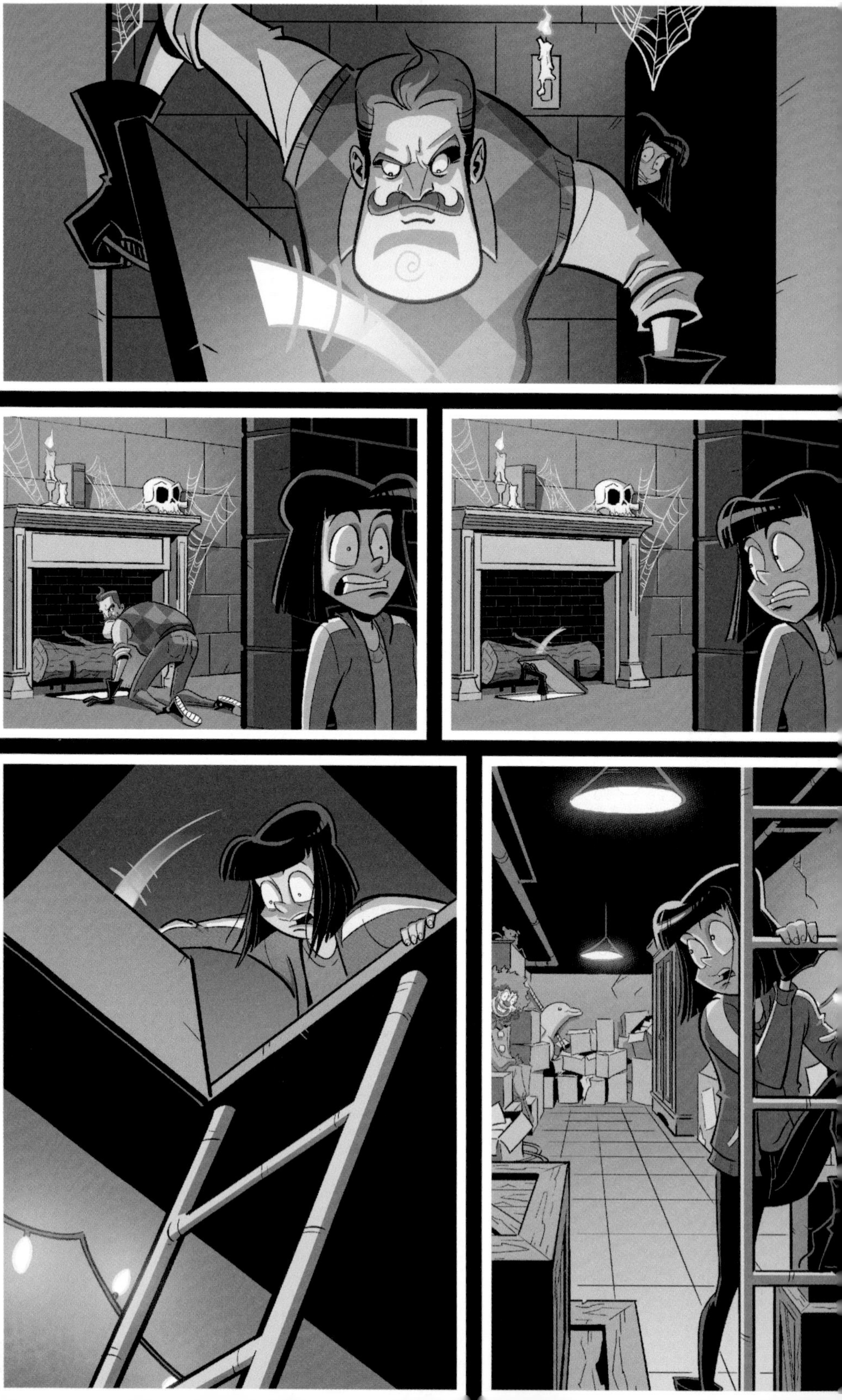

TMP-TMP-TMP-TMP-TMP

TMP-TMP-TMP

WHUM-PANG

TMP-TMP-TMP-TMP

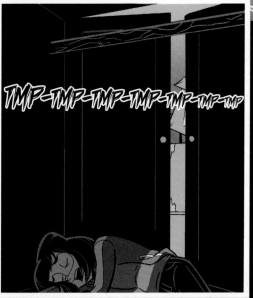

TMP-TMP-TMP-TMP-TMP-TMP-TMP

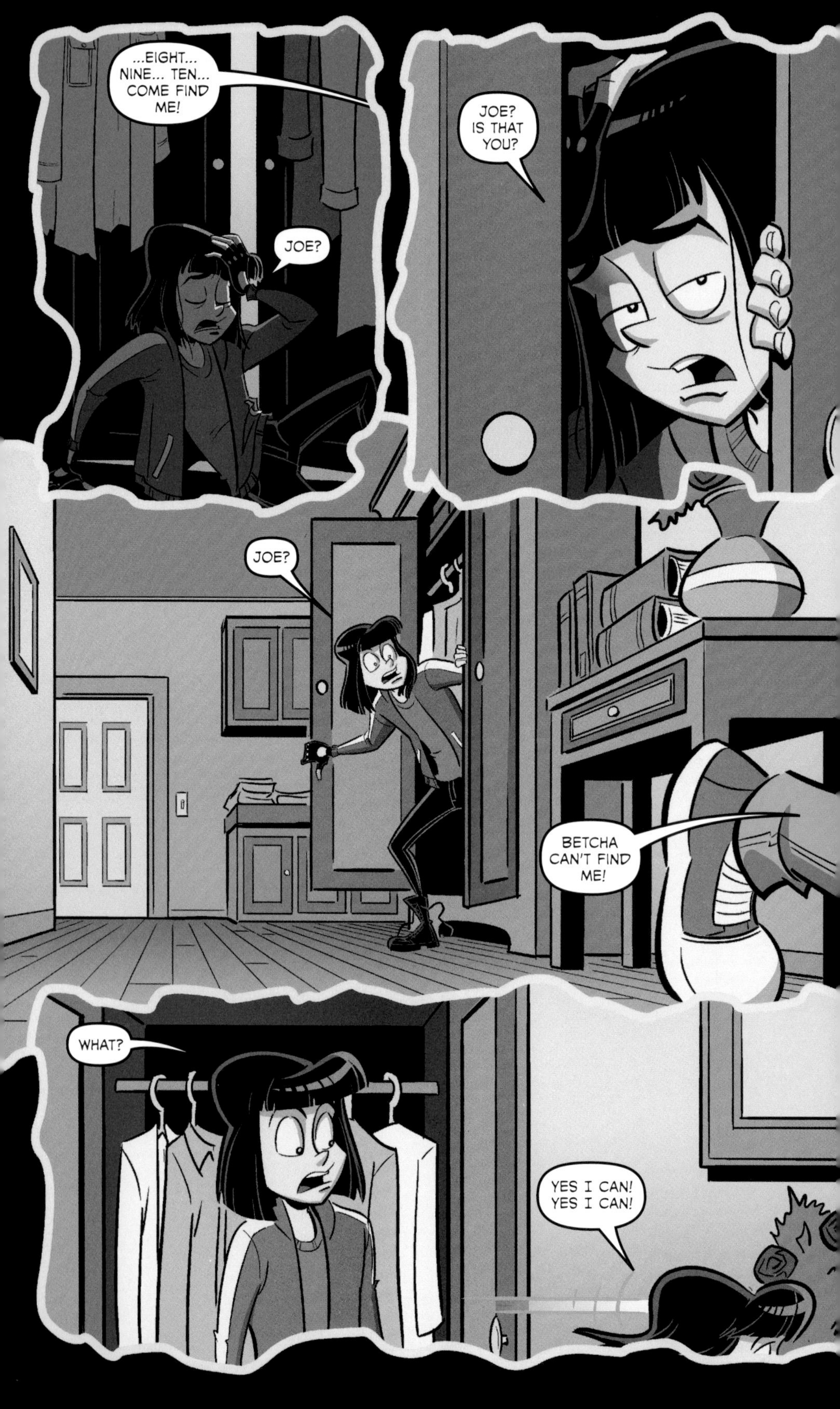
...EIGHT... NINE... TEN... COME FIND ME!
JOE?
JOE? IS THAT YOU?
JOE?
BETCHA CAN'T FIND ME!
WHAT?
YES I CAN! YES I CAN!

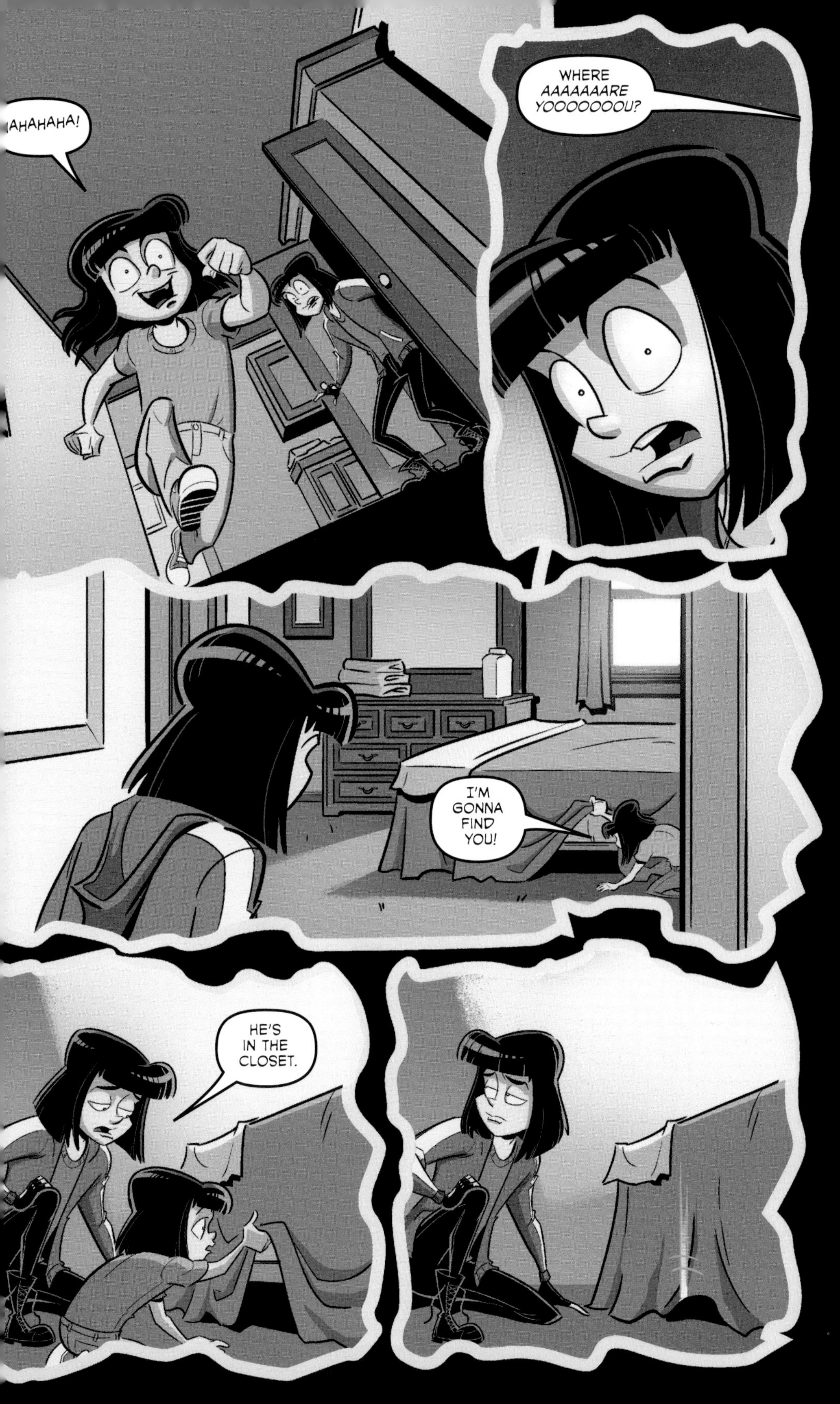
AHAHAHA!
WHERE AAAAAAARE YOOOOOOOU?
I'M GONNA FIND YOU!
HE'S IN THE CLOSET.

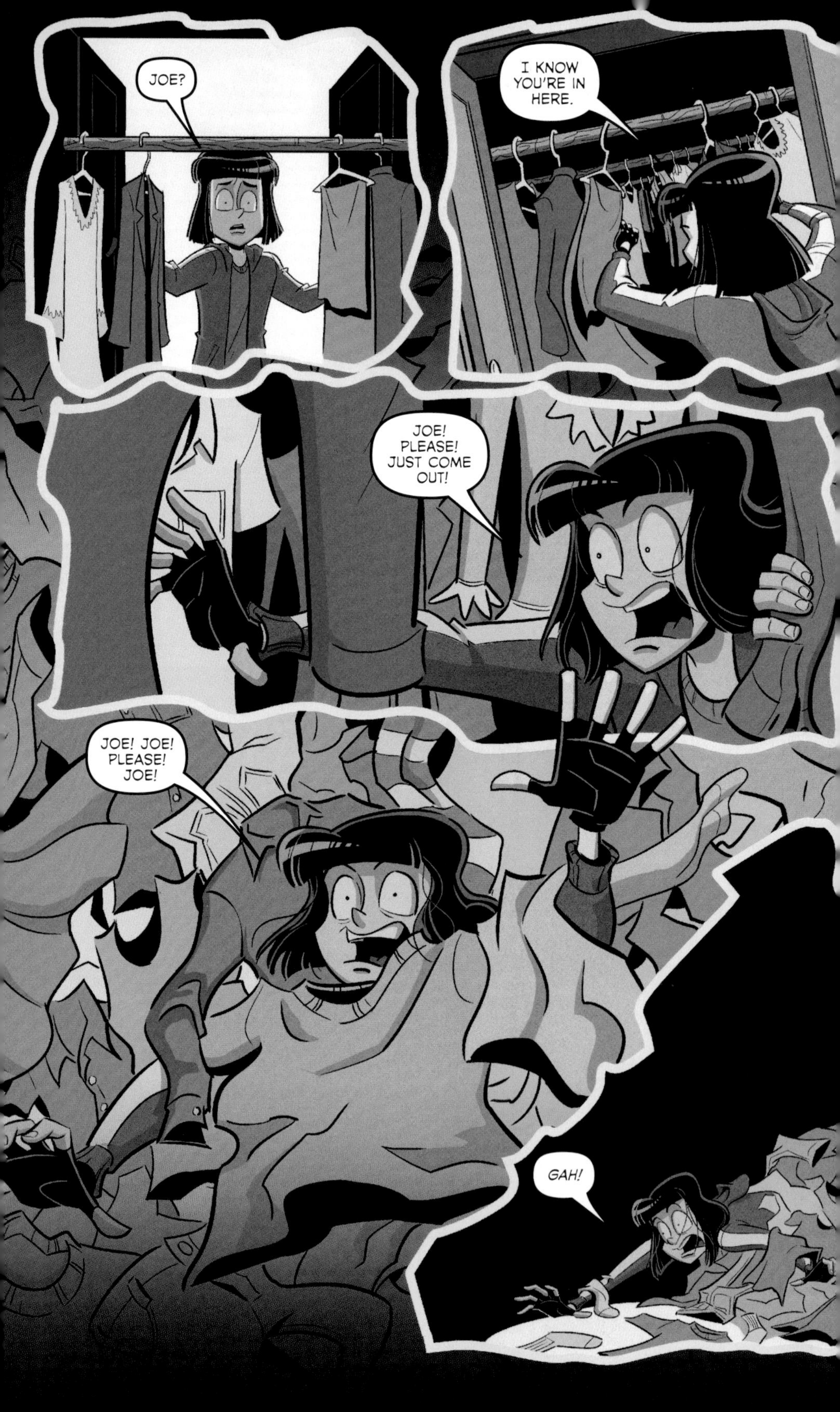
JOE?
I KNOW YOU'RE IN HERE.
JOE! PLEASE! JUST COME OUT!
JOE! JOE! PLEASE! JOE!
GAH!

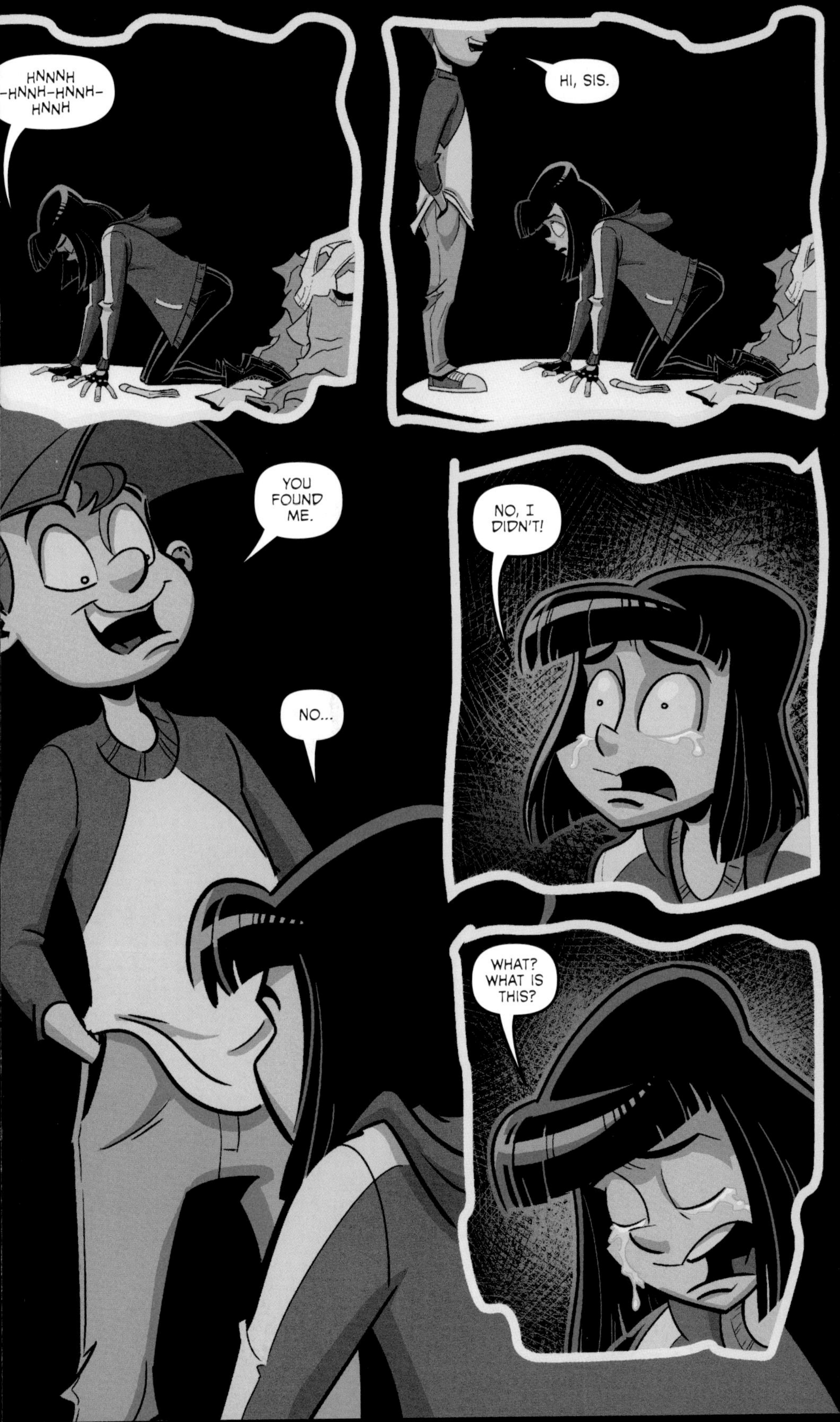
HNNNH -HNNH-HNNH-HNNH
HI, SIS.
YOU FOUND ME.
NO, I DIDN'T!
NO...
WHAT? WHAT IS THIS?

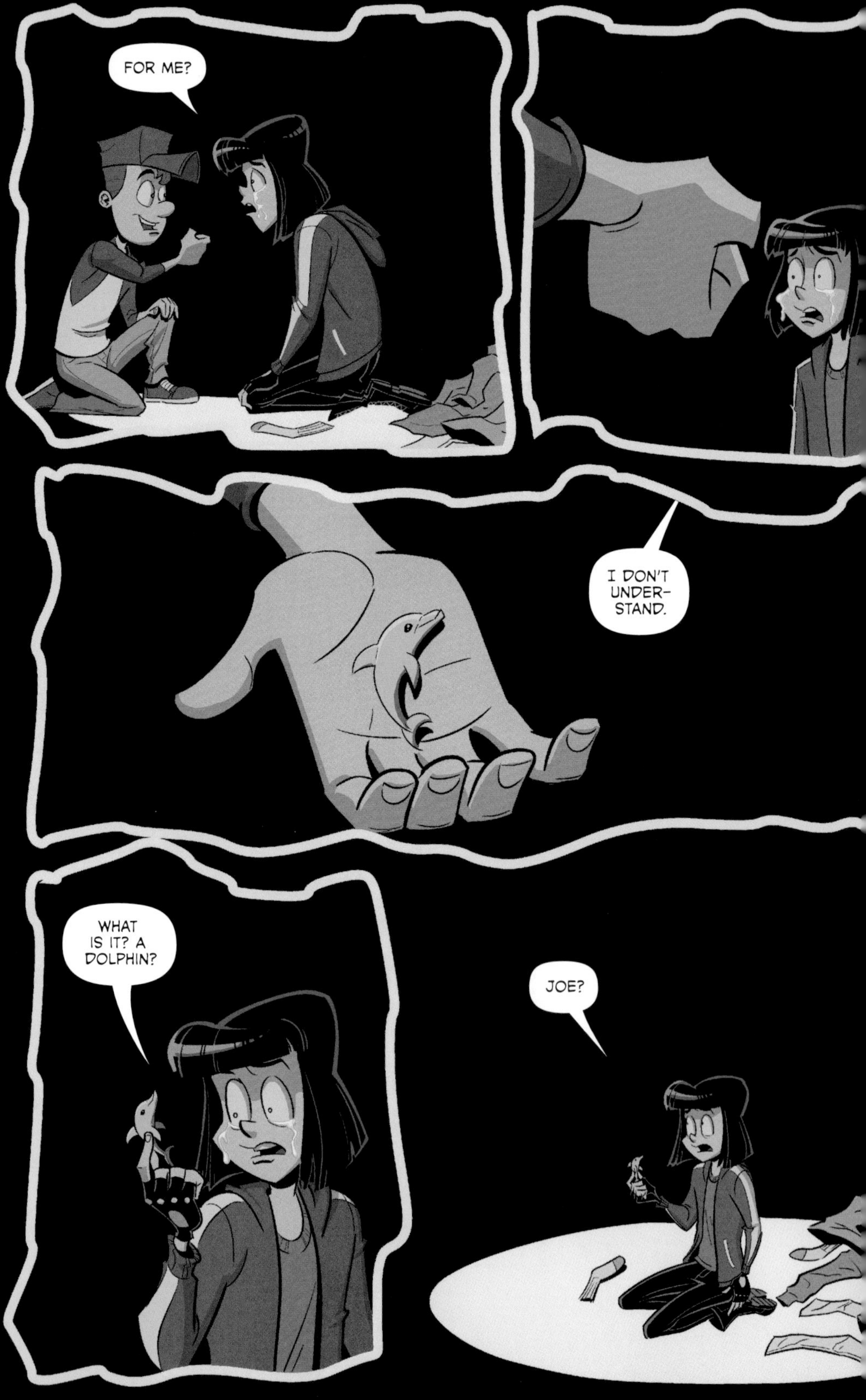
FOR ME?
I DON'T UNDER-STAND.
WHAT IS IT? A DOLPHIN?
JOE?

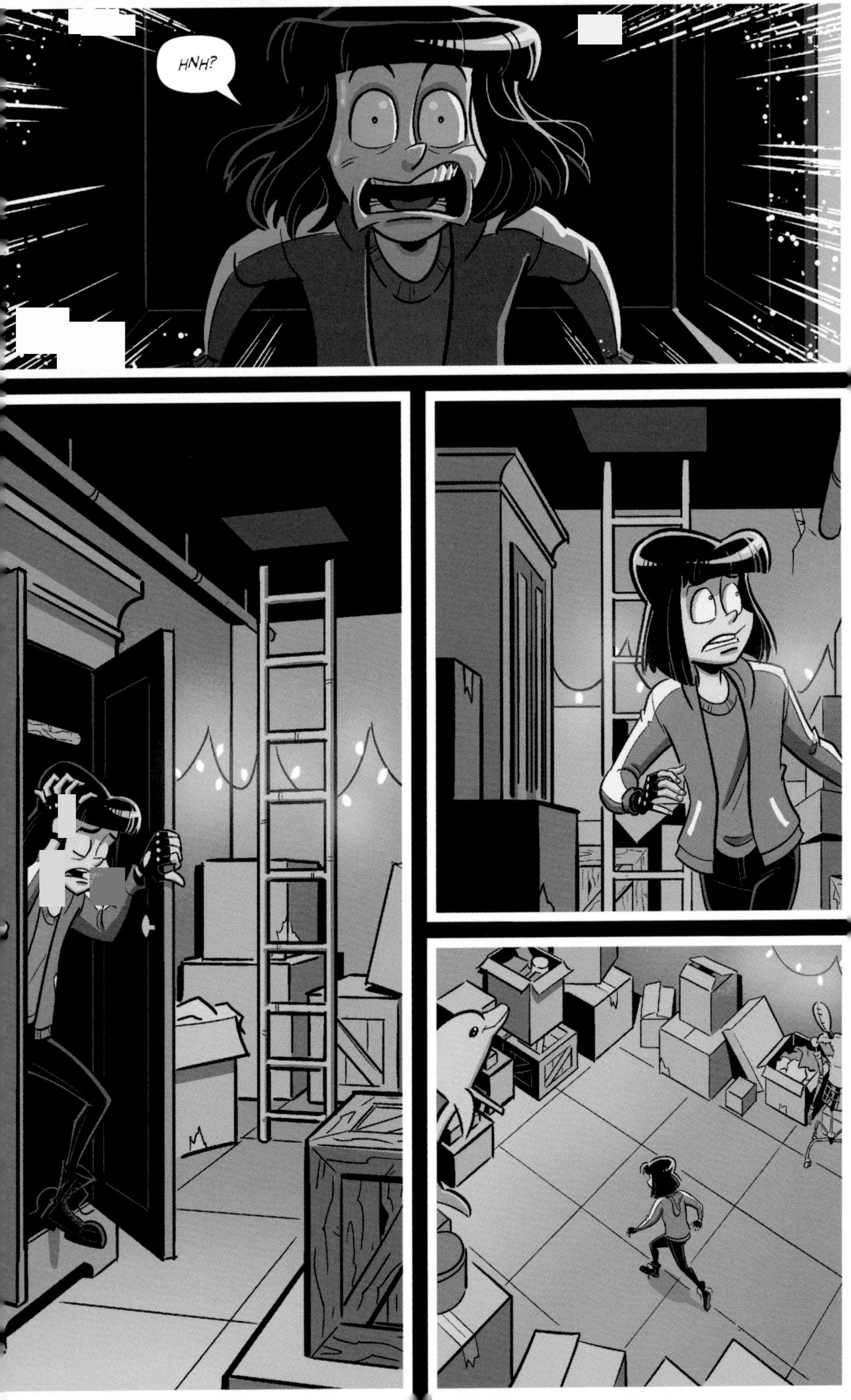
HNH?

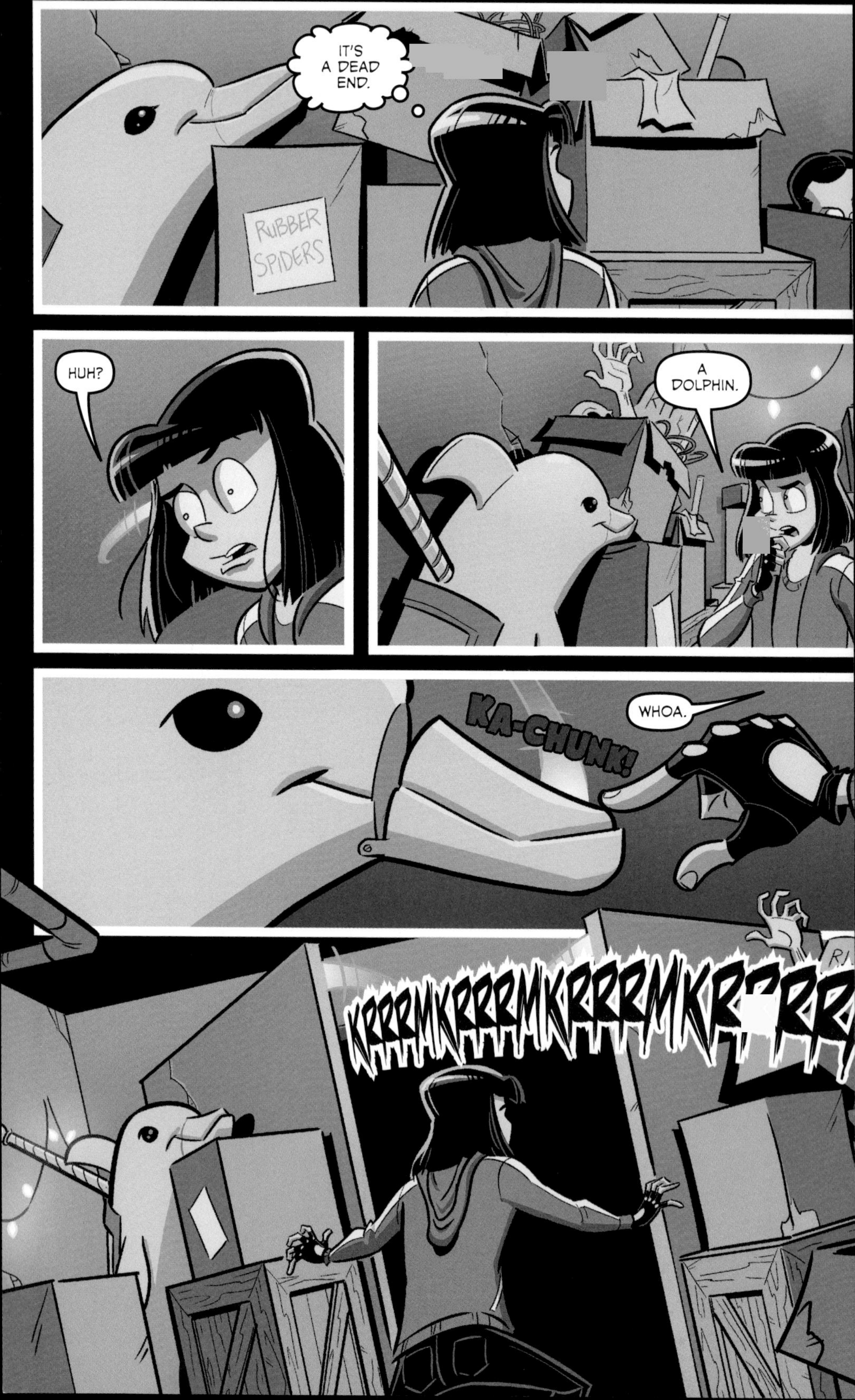
IT'S A DEAD END.
RUBBER SPIDERS
HUH?
A DOLPHIN.
KA-CHUNK!
WHOA.
KRRRMKRRRMKRRRMKR

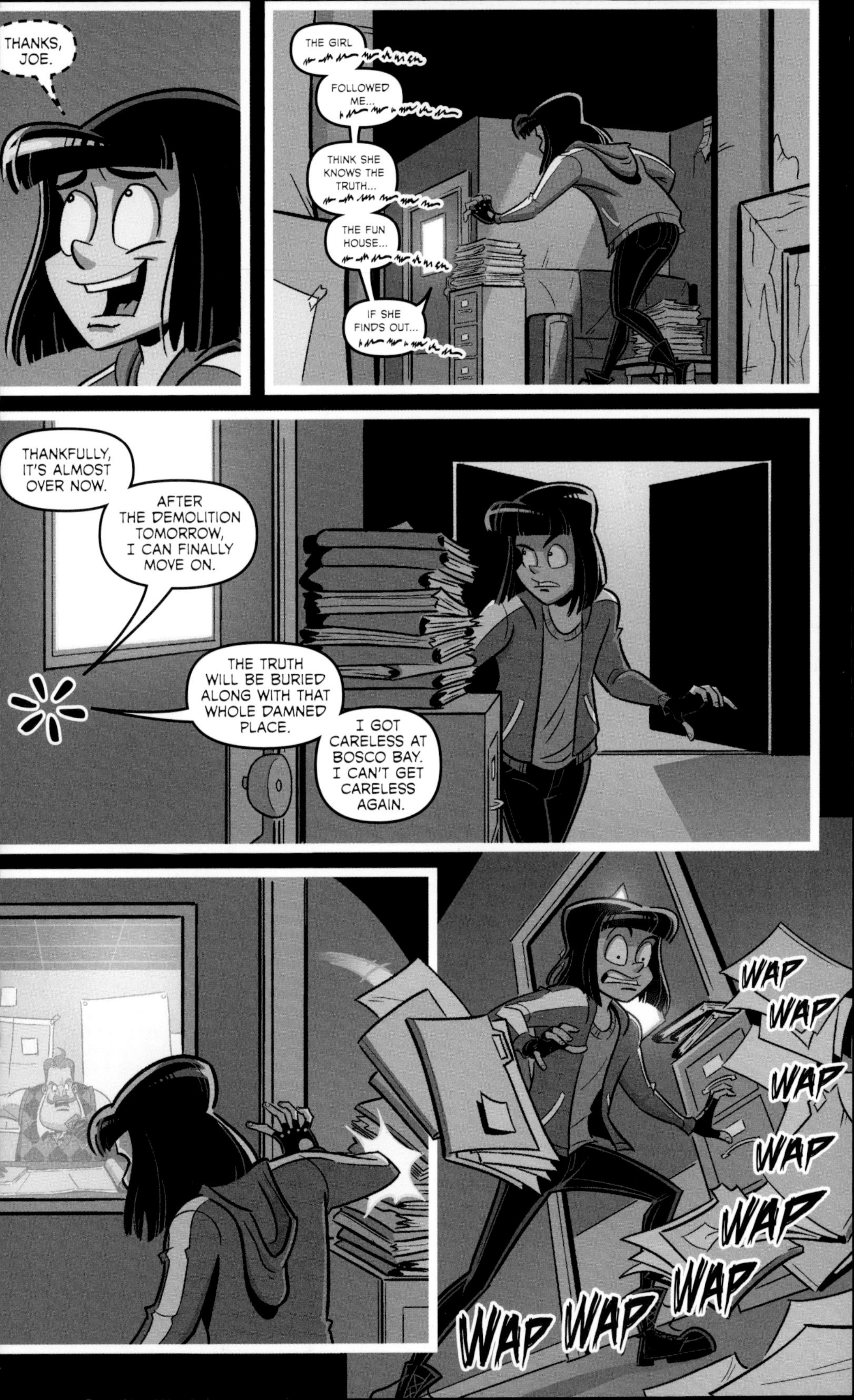
THANKS, JOE.
THE GIRL
FOLLOWED ME...
THINK SHE KNOWS THE TRUTH...
THE FUN HOUSE...
IF SHE FINDS OUT...
THANKFULLY, IT'S ALMOST OVER NOW.
AFTER THE DEMOLITION TOMORROW, I CAN FINALLY MOVE ON.
THE TRUTH WILL BE BURIED ALONG WITH THAT WHOLE DAMNED PLACE.
I GOT CARELESS AT BOSCO BAY. I CAN'T GET CARELESS AGAIN.
WAP
WAP
WAP
WAP
WAP
WAP
WAP WAP

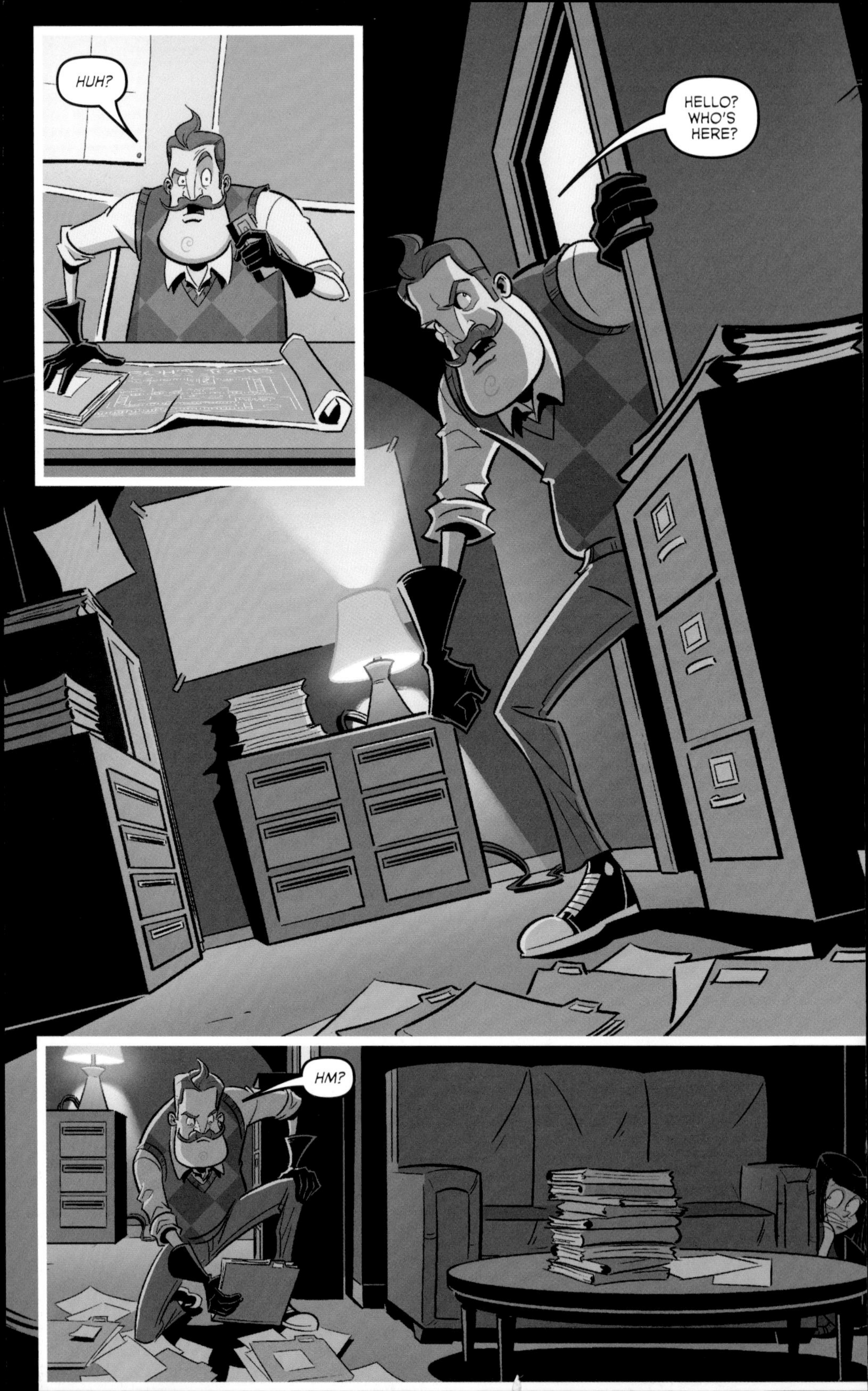
HUH?
HELLO? WHO'S HERE?
HM?

IS ANYBODY HERE?

GET A GRIP, TEDDY. YOU'RE LOSING IT.

IT'LL ALL BE OVER SOON. IT'LL ALL BE OVER SOON.

KA-CHUNK!

KRRRMKOORMKOOOMKOORK

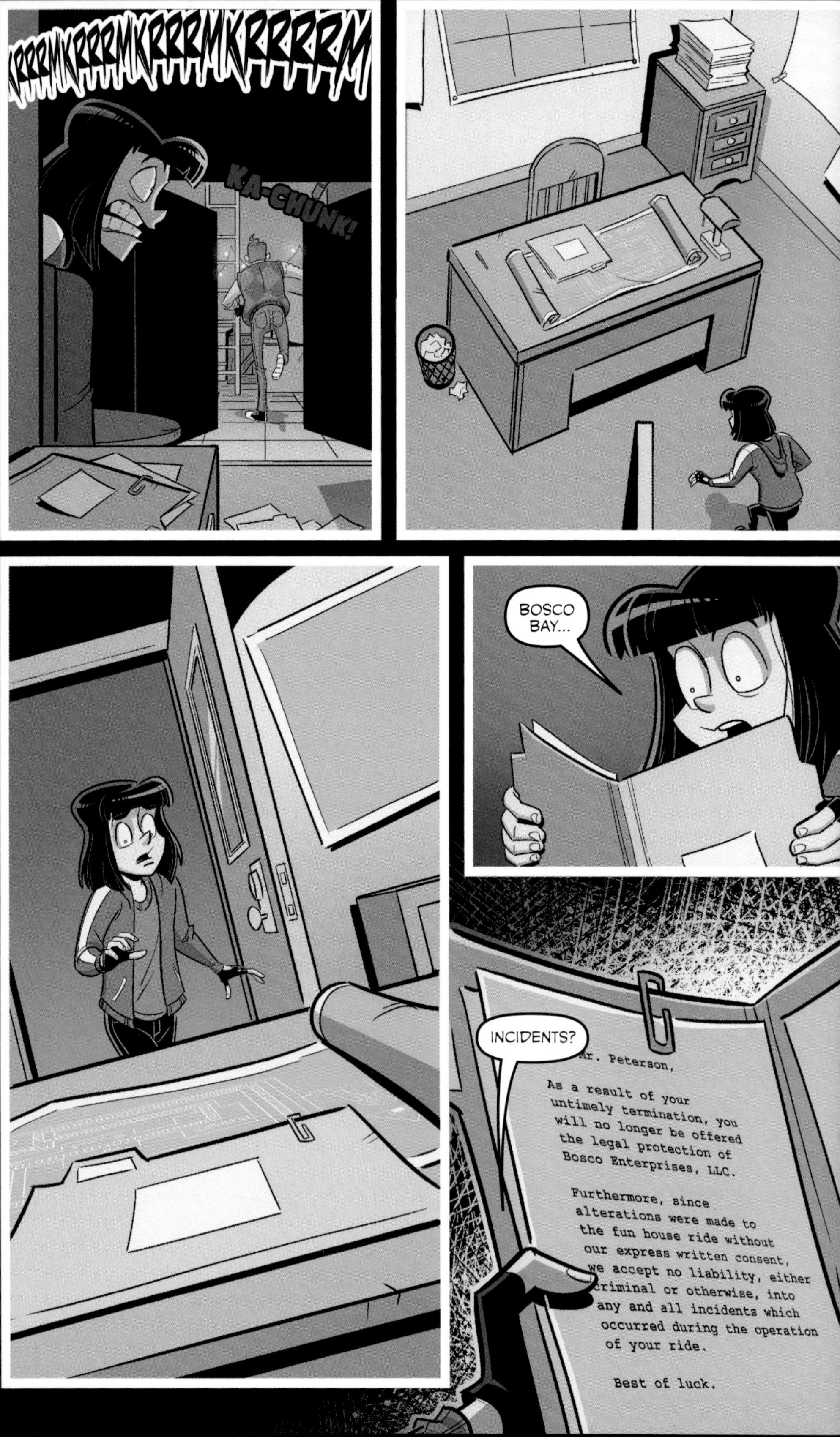
KRRRMKRRRMKRRRMKRRRRM
KA-CHUNK!
BOSCO BAY...
INCIDENTS?
Mr. Peterson,
As a result of your untimely termination, you will no longer be offered the legal protection of Bosco Enterprises, LLC.
Furthermore, since alterations were made to the fun house ride without our express written consent, we accept no liability, either criminal or otherwise, into any and all incidents which occurred during the operation of your ride.
Best of luck.

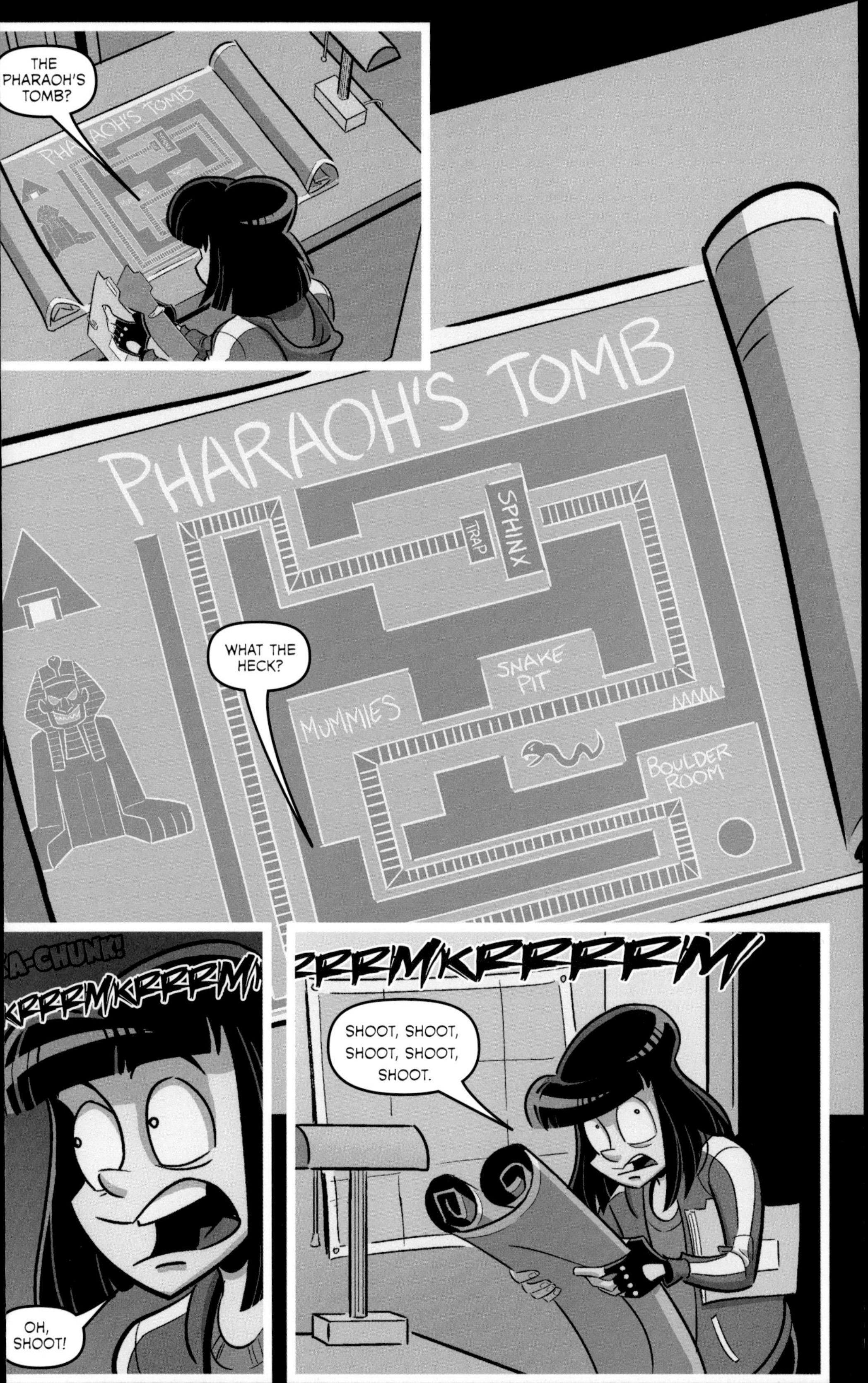
THE PHARAOH'S TOMB?
PHARAOH'S TOMB
SPHINX
TRAP
SNAKE PIT
MUMMIES
BOULDER ROOM
WHAT THE HECK?
KA-CHUNK!
KRRRMKRRRRM
KRRRMKRRRRRM
SHOOT, SHOOT, SHOOT, SHOOT, SHOOT.
OH, SHOOT!

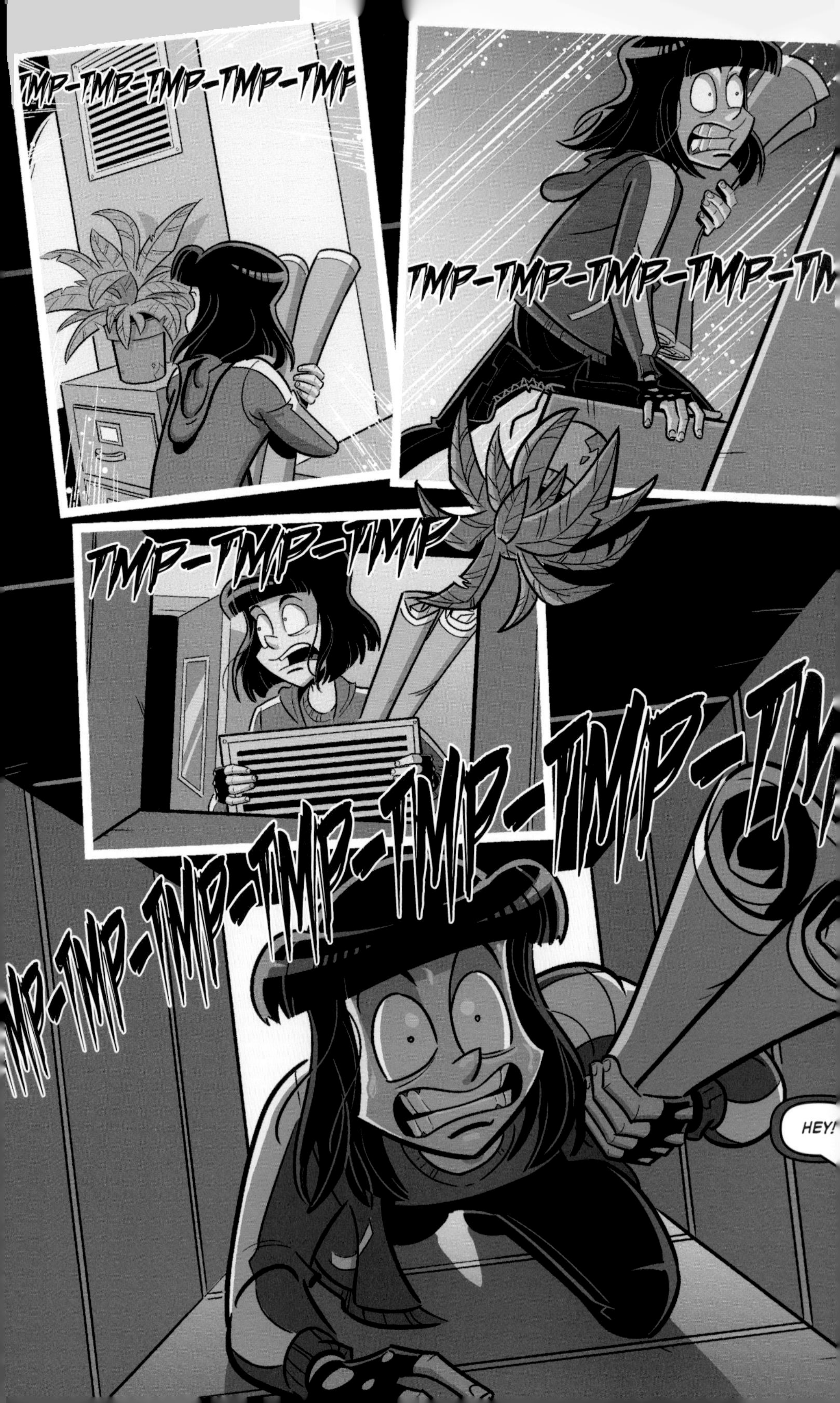
TMP-TMP-TMP-TMP-TMP
TMP-TMP-TMP-TMP-TM
TMP-TMP-TMP
MP-TMP-TMP-TMP-TMP-TMP-TM
HEY!

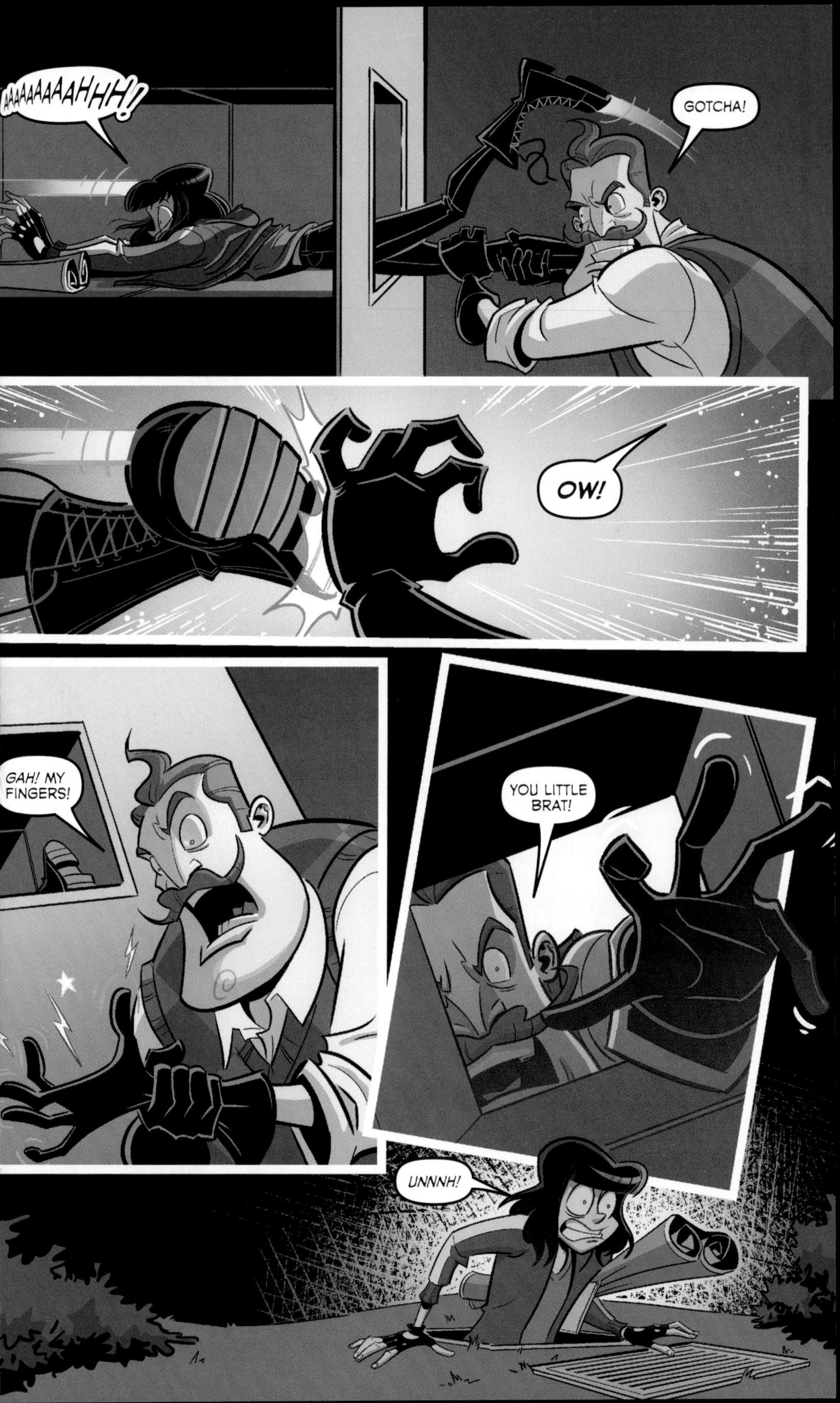

AAAAAAAAAHHH!
GOTCHA!
OW!
GAH! MY FINGERS!
YOU LITTLE BRAT!
UNNNH!

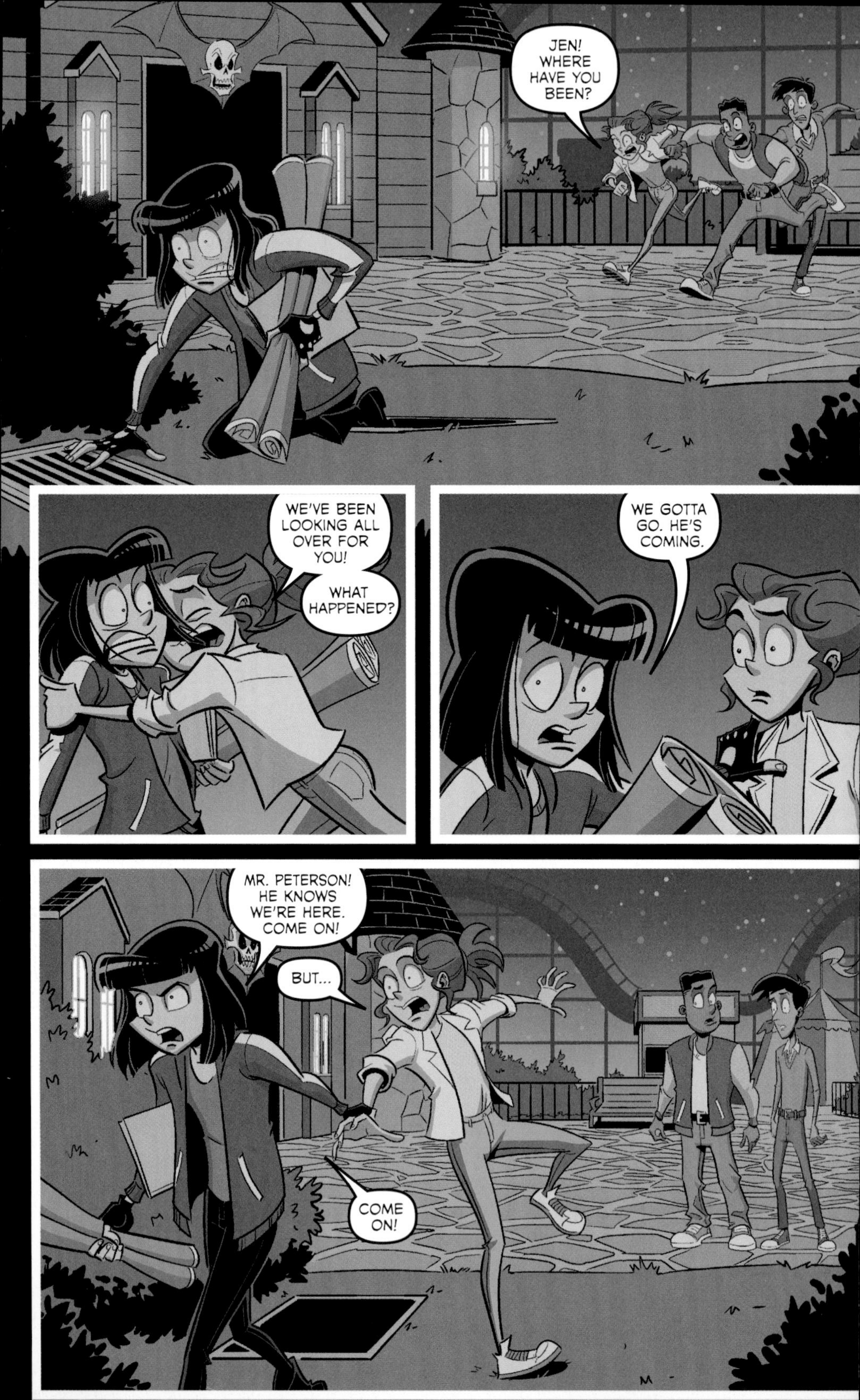

JEN! WHERE HAVE YOU BEEN?
WE'VE BEEN LOOKING ALL OVER FOR YOU!
WHAT HAPPENED?
WE GOTTA GO. HE'S COMING.
MR. PETERSON! HE KNOWS WE'RE HERE. COME ON!
BUT...
COME ON!

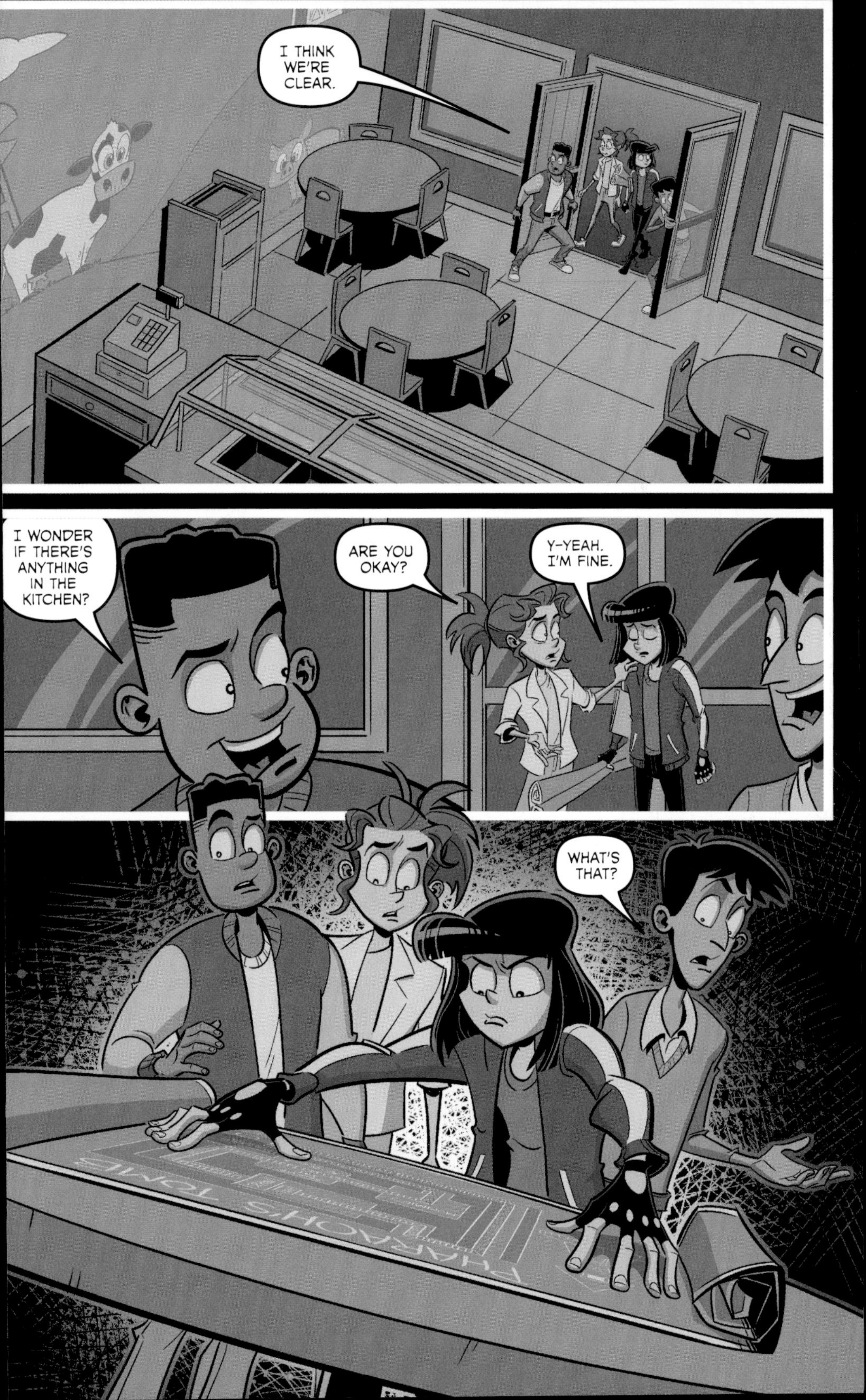
I THINK WE'RE CLEAR.
I WONDER IF THERE'S ANYTHING IN THE KITCHEN?
ARE YOU OKAY?
Y-YEAH. I'M FINE.
WHAT'S THAT?
PHARAOH'S TOMB

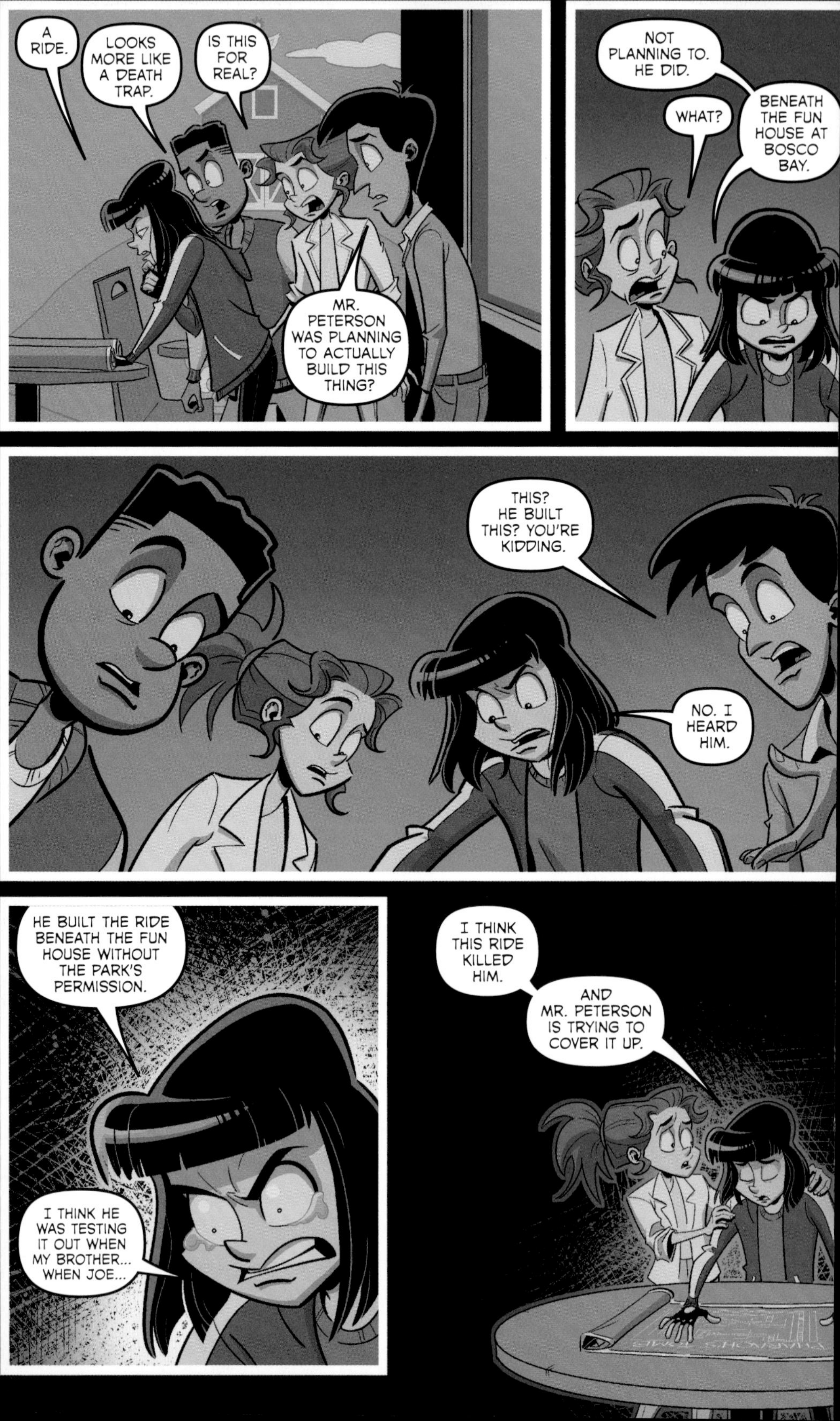
A RIDE.
LOOKS MORE LIKE A DEATH TRAP.
IS THIS FOR REAL?
MR. PETERSON WAS PLANNING TO ACTUALLY BUILD THIS THING?
NOT PLANNING TO. HE DID.
WHAT?
BENEATH THE FUN HOUSE AT BOSCO BAY.
THIS? HE BUILT THIS? YOU'RE KIDDING.
NO. I HEARD HIM.
HE BUILT THE RIDE BENEATH THE FUN HOUSE WITHOUT THE PARK'S PERMISSION.
I THINK HE WAS TESTING IT OUT WHEN MY BROTHER... WHEN JOE...
I THINK THIS RIDE KILLED HIM.
AND MR. PETERSON IS TRYING TO COVER IT UP.

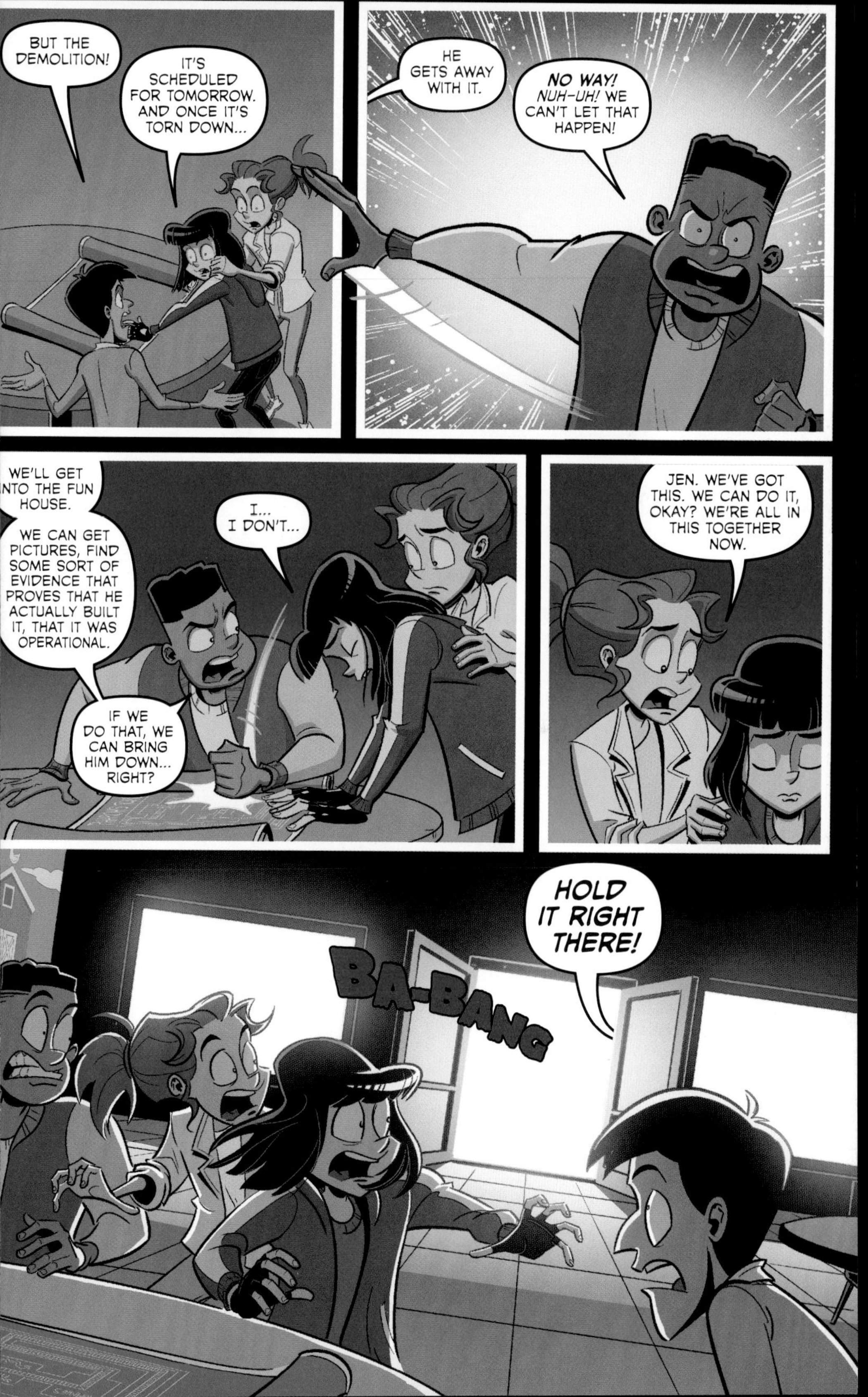

BUT THE DEMOLITION!
IT'S SCHEDULED FOR TOMORROW. AND ONCE IT'S TORN DOWN...
HE GETS AWAY WITH IT.
NO WAY! NUH-UH! WE CAN'T LET THAT HAPPEN!
WE'LL GET INTO THE FUN HOUSE.
WE CAN GET PICTURES, FIND SOME SORT OF EVIDENCE THAT PROVES THAT HE ACTUALLY BUILT IT, THAT IT WAS OPERATIONAL.
I... I DON'T...
IF WE DO THAT, WE CAN BRING HIM DOWN... RIGHT?
JEN. WE'VE GOT THIS. WE CAN DO IT, OKAY? WE'RE ALL IN THIS TOGETHER NOW.
BA-BANG
HOLD IT RIGHT THERE!

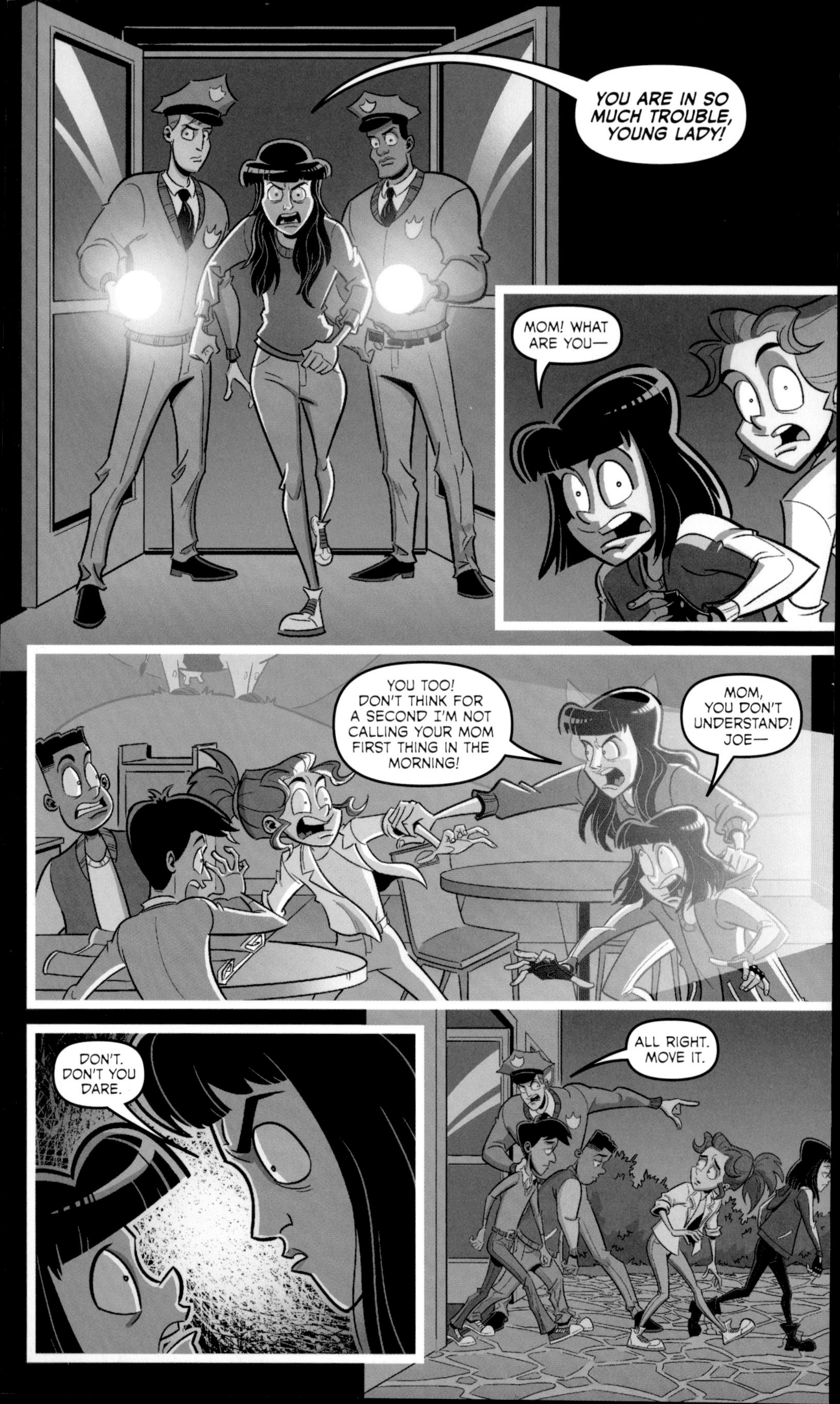
YOU ARE IN SO MUCH TROUBLE, YOUNG LADY!
MOM! WHAT ARE YOU—
YOU TOO! DON'T THINK FOR A SECOND I'M NOT CALLING YOUR MOM FIRST THING IN THE MORNING!
MOM, YOU DON'T UNDERSTAND! JOE—
DON'T. DON'T YOU DARE.
ALL RIGHT. MOVE IT.

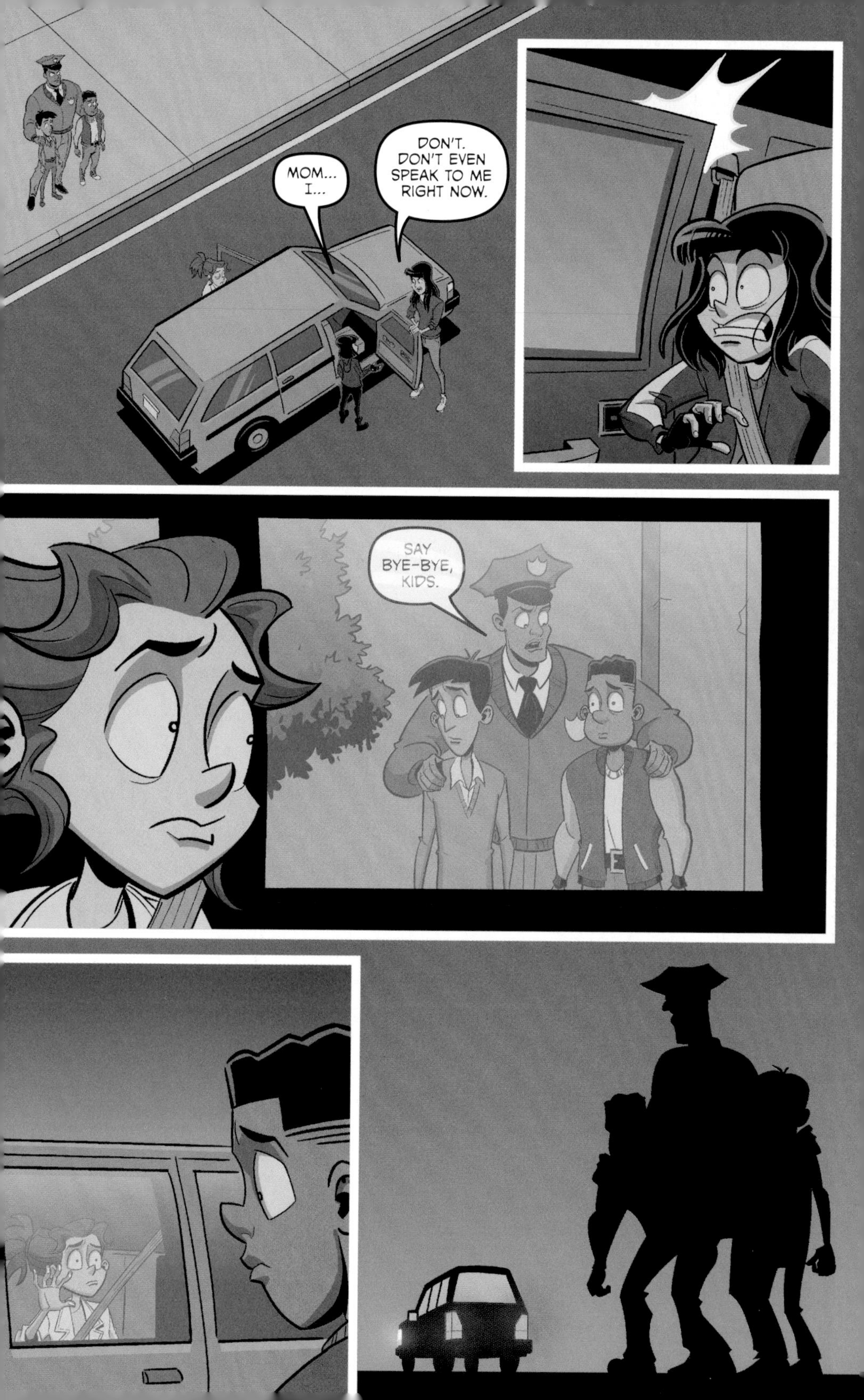
MOM... I...
DON'T. DON'T EVEN SPEAK TO ME RIGHT NOW.
SAY BYE-BYE, KIDS.

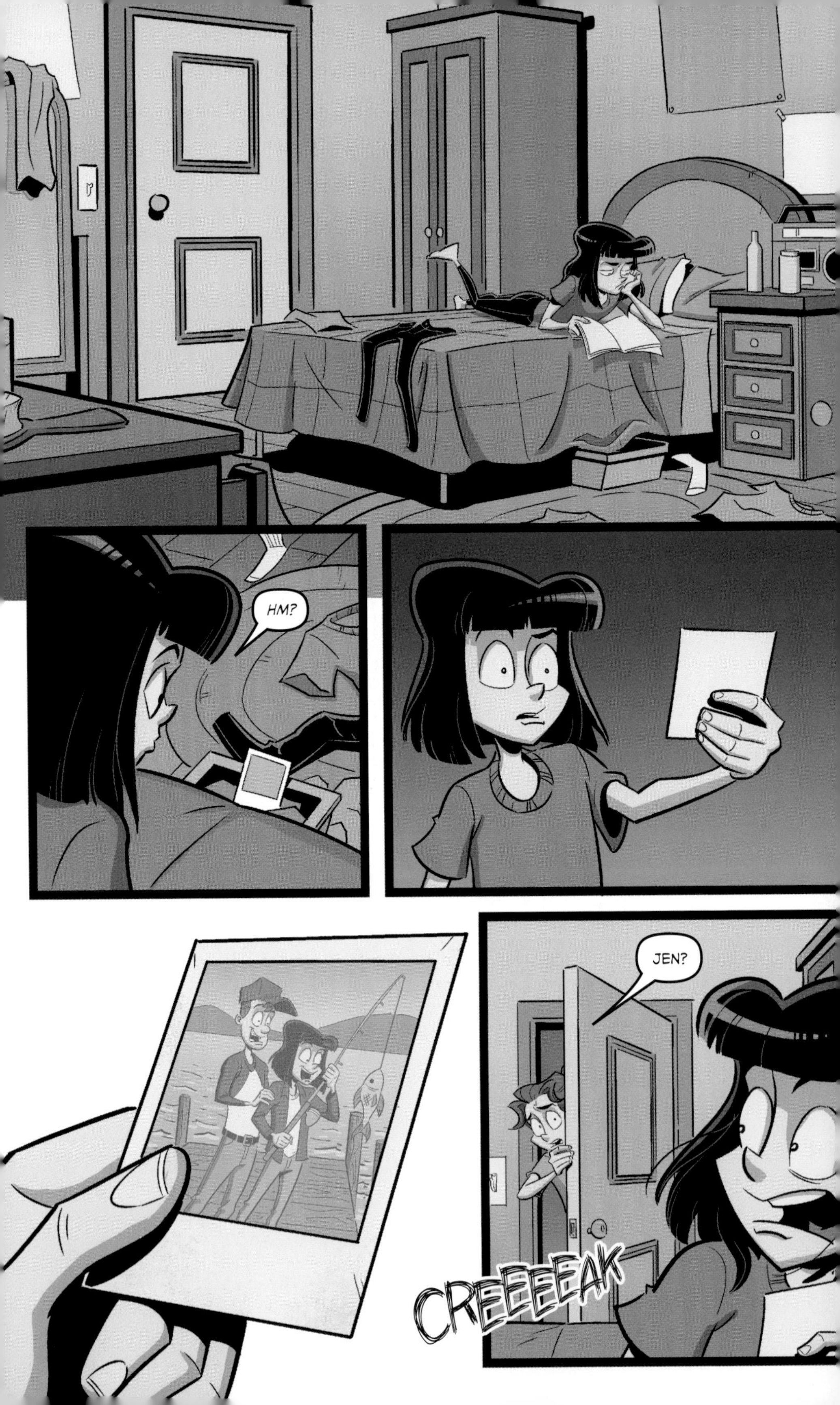
HM?
JEN?
CREEEEAK

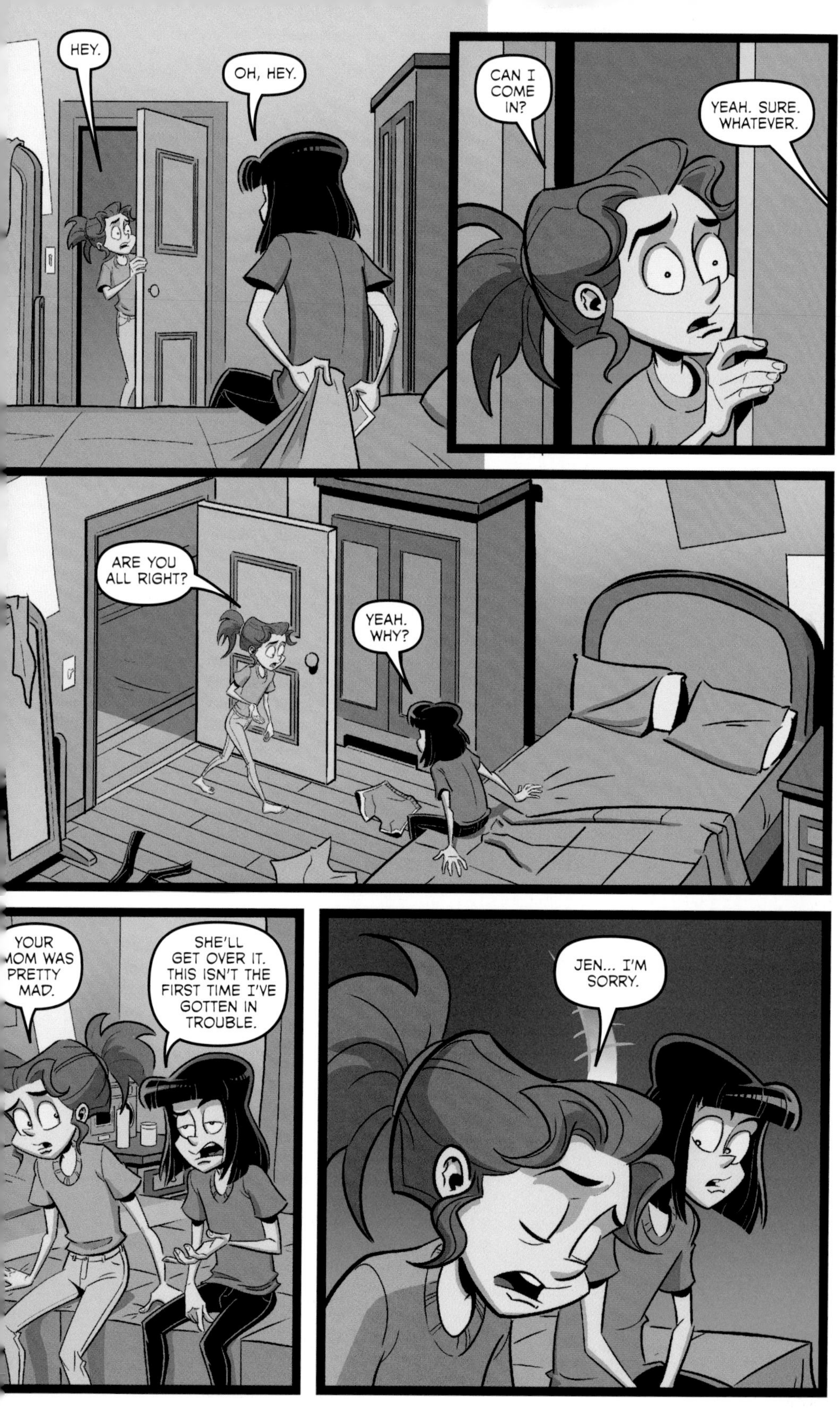
HEY.
OH, HEY.
CAN I COME IN?
YEAH. SURE. WHATEVER.
ARE YOU ALL RIGHT?
YEAH. WHY?
YOUR MOM WAS PRETTY MAD.
SHE'LL GET OVER IT. THIS ISN'T THE FIRST TIME I'VE GOTTEN IN TROUBLE.
JEN... I'M SORRY.

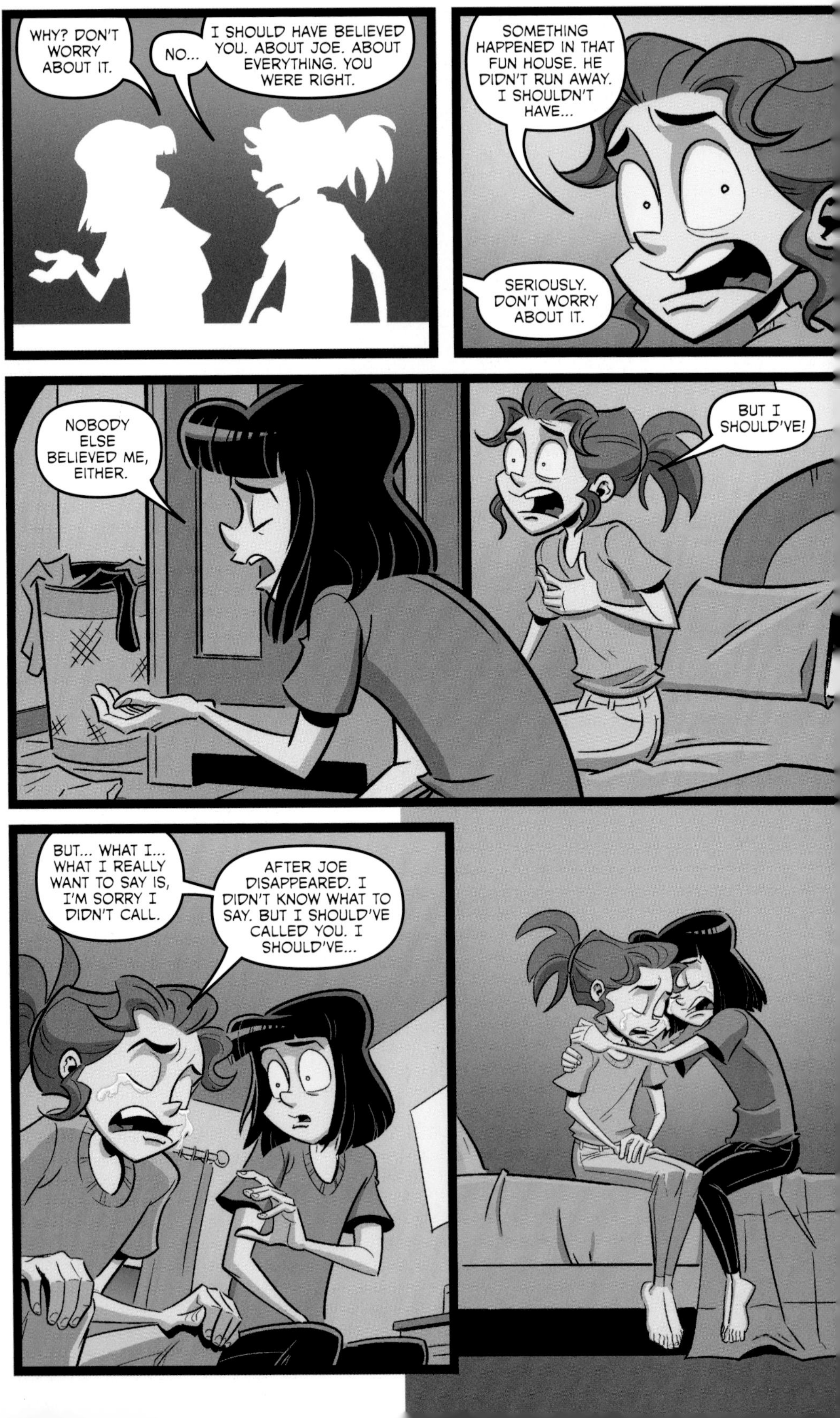
WHY? DON'T WORRY ABOUT IT.
NO...
I SHOULD HAVE BELIEVED YOU. ABOUT JOE. ABOUT EVERYTHING. YOU WERE RIGHT.
SOMETHING HAPPENED IN THAT FUN HOUSE. HE DIDN'T RUN AWAY. I SHOULDN'T HAVE...
SERIOUSLY. DON'T WORRY ABOUT IT.
NOBODY ELSE BELIEVED ME, EITHER.
BUT I SHOULD'VE!
BUT... WHAT I... WHAT I REALLY WANT TO SAY IS, I'M SORRY I DIDN'T CALL.
AFTER JOE DISAPPEARED. I DIDN'T KNOW WHAT TO SAY. BUT I SHOULD'VE CALLED YOU. I SHOULD'VE...

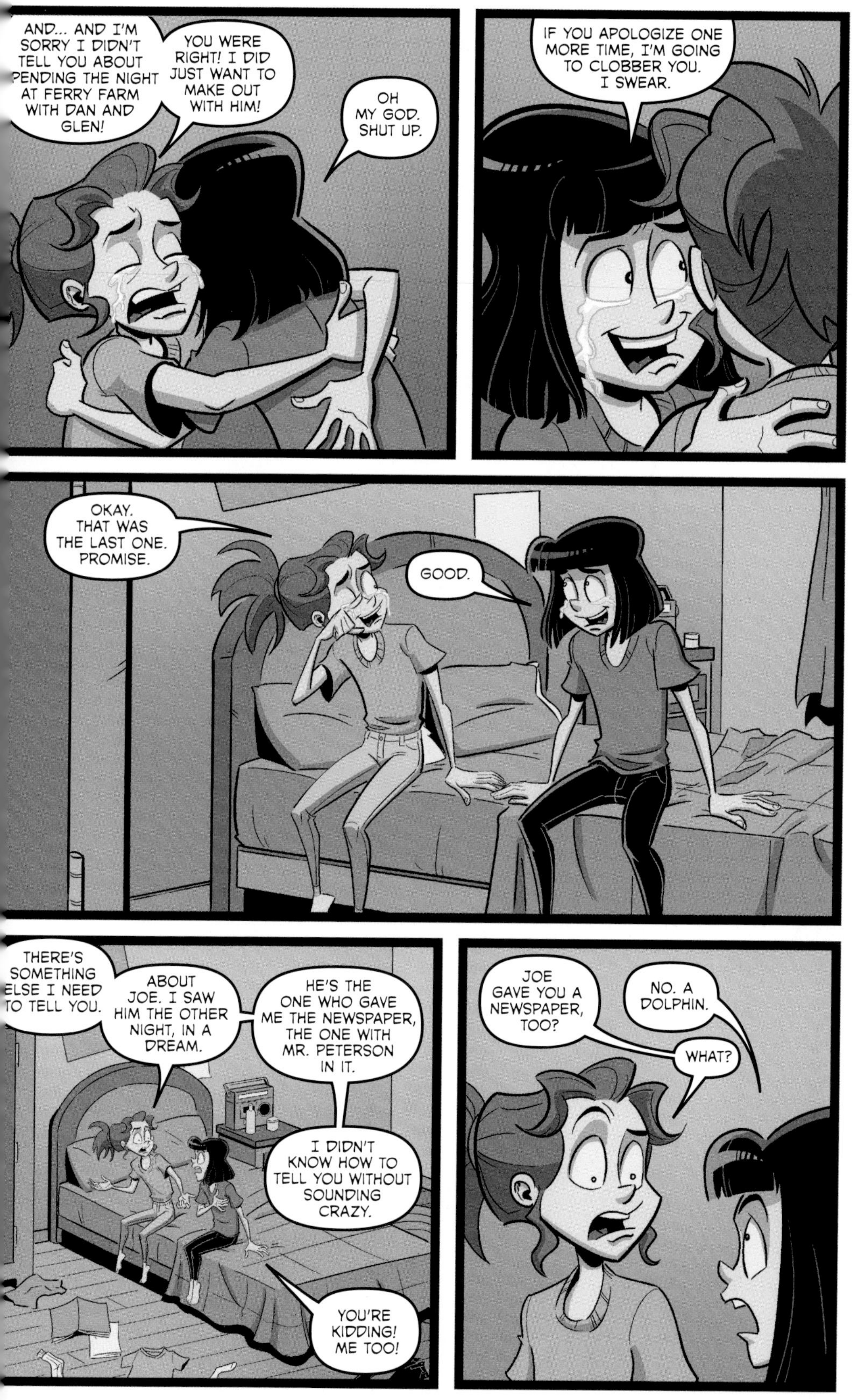

AND... AND I'M SORRY I DIDN'T TELL YOU ABOUT PENDING THE NIGHT AT FERRY FARM WITH DAN AND GLEN!
YOU WERE RIGHT! I DID JUST WANT TO MAKE OUT WITH HIM!
OH MY GOD. SHUT UP.
IF YOU APOLOGIZE ONE MORE TIME, I'M GOING TO CLOBBER YOU. I SWEAR.
OKAY. THAT WAS THE LAST ONE. PROMISE.
GOOD.
THERE'S SOMETHING ELSE I NEED TO TELL YOU.
ABOUT JOE. I SAW HIM THE OTHER NIGHT, IN A DREAM.
HE'S THE ONE WHO GAVE ME THE NEWSPAPER, THE ONE WITH MR. PETERSON IN IT.
I DIDN'T KNOW HOW TO TELL YOU WITHOUT SOUNDING CRAZY.
YOU'RE KIDDING! ME TOO!
JOE GAVE YOU A NEWSPAPER, TOO?
NO. A DOLPHIN.
WHAT?

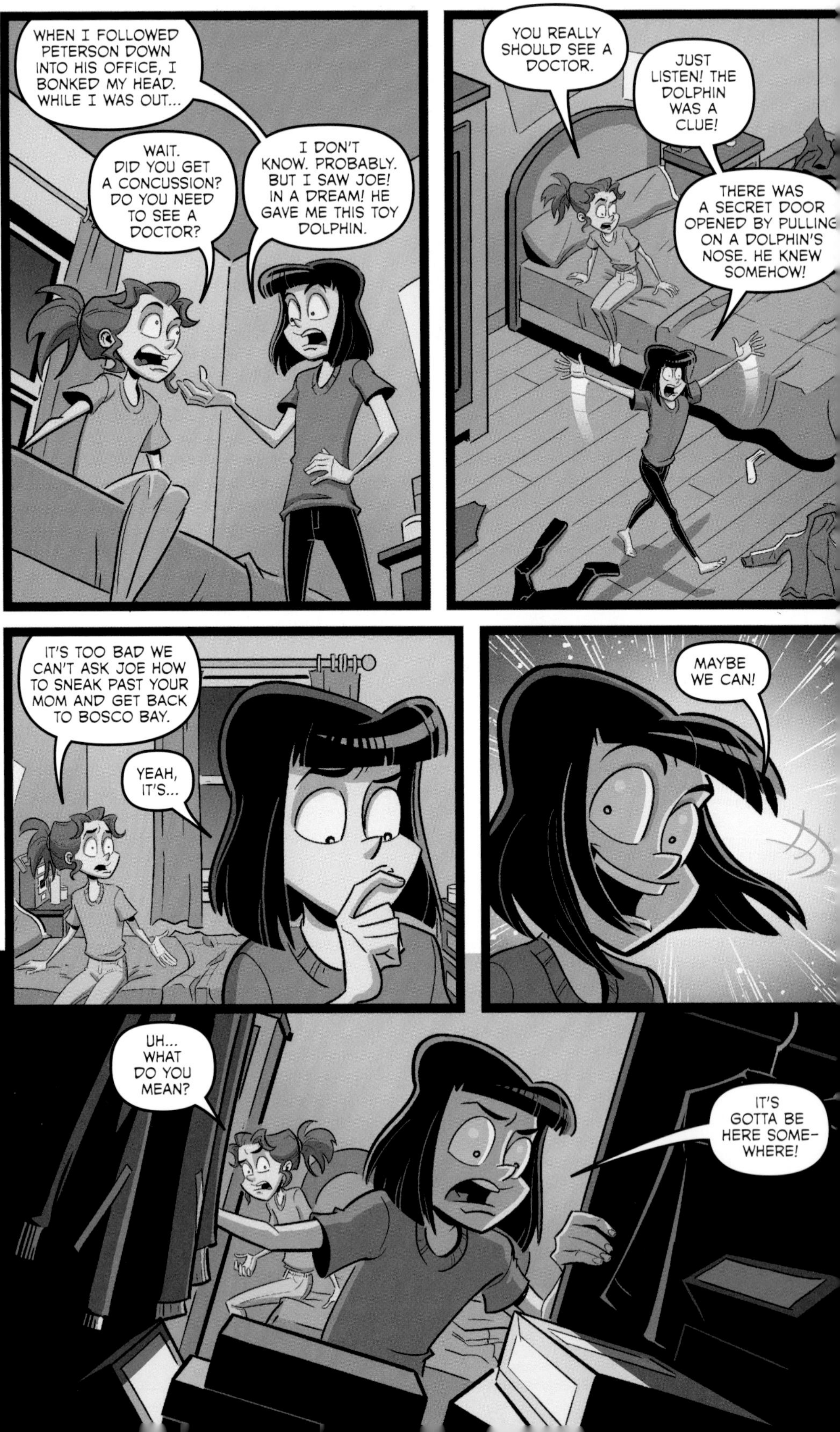
WHEN I FOLLOWED PETERSON DOWN INTO HIS OFFICE, I BONKED MY HEAD. WHILE I WAS OUT...
WAIT. DID YOU GET A CONCUSSION? DO YOU NEED TO SEE A DOCTOR?
I DON'T KNOW. PROBABLY. BUT I SAW JOE! IN A DREAM! HE GAVE ME THIS TOY DOLPHIN.
YOU REALLY SHOULD SEE A DOCTOR.
JUST LISTEN! THE DOLPHIN WAS A CLUE!
THERE WAS A SECRET DOOR OPENED BY PULLING ON A DOLPHIN'S NOSE. HE KNEW SOMEHOW!
IT'S TOO BAD WE CAN'T ASK JOE HOW TO SNEAK PAST YOUR MOM AND GET BACK TO BOSCO BAY.
YEAH, IT'S...
MAYBE WE CAN!
UH... WHAT DO YOU MEAN?
IT'S GOTTA BE HERE SOME-WHERE!

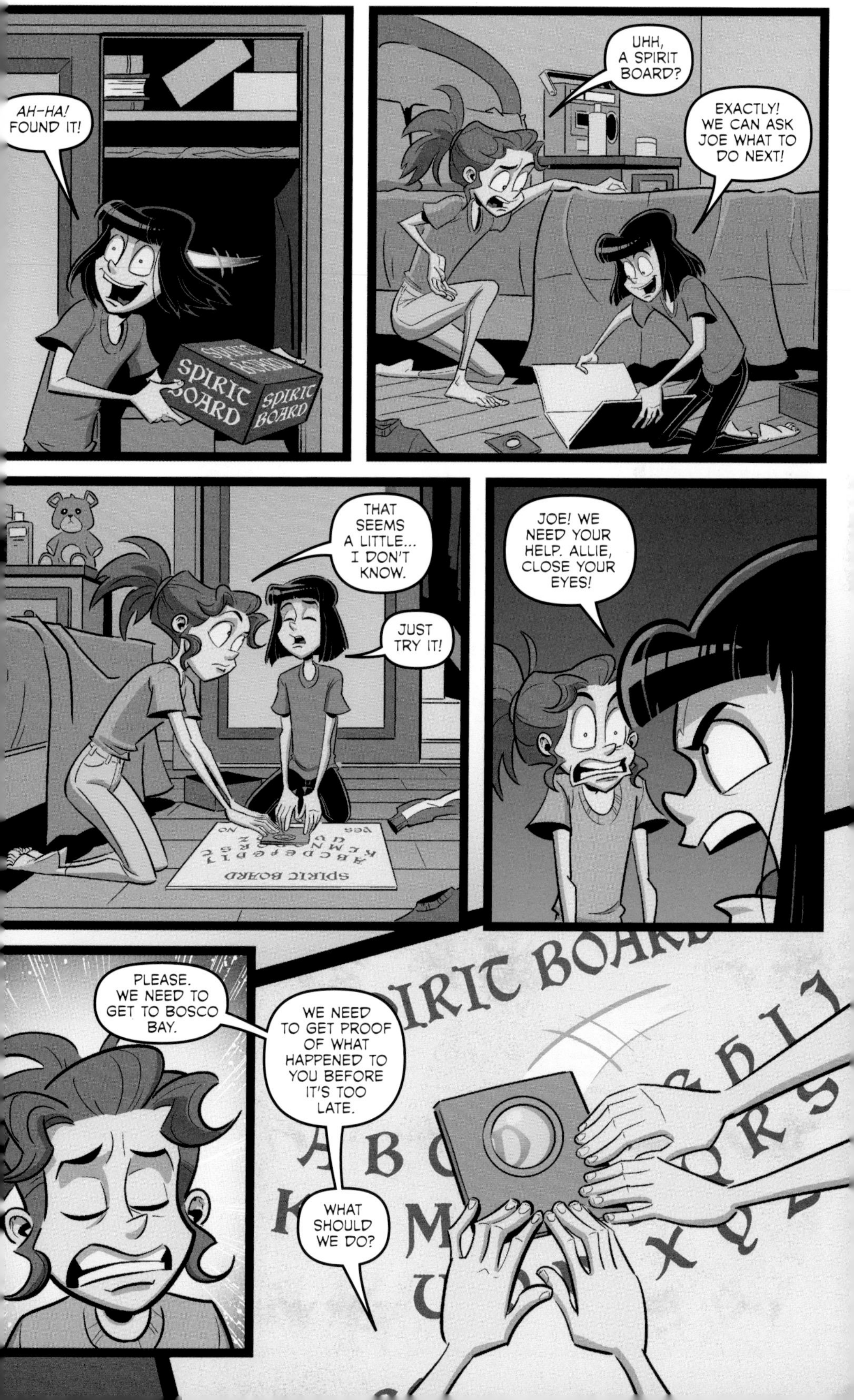
AH-HA! FOUND IT!
SPIRIT BOARD
UHH, A SPIRIT BOARD?
EXACTLY! WE CAN ASK JOE WHAT TO DO NEXT!
THAT SEEMS A LITTLE... I DON'T KNOW.
JUST TRY IT!
SPIRIT BOARD
JOE! WE NEED YOUR HELP. ALLIE, CLOSE YOUR EYES!
PLEASE. WE NEED TO GET TO BOSCO BAY.
WE NEED TO GET PROOF OF WHAT HAPPENED TO YOU BEFORE IT'S TOO LATE.
WHAT SHOULD WE DO?

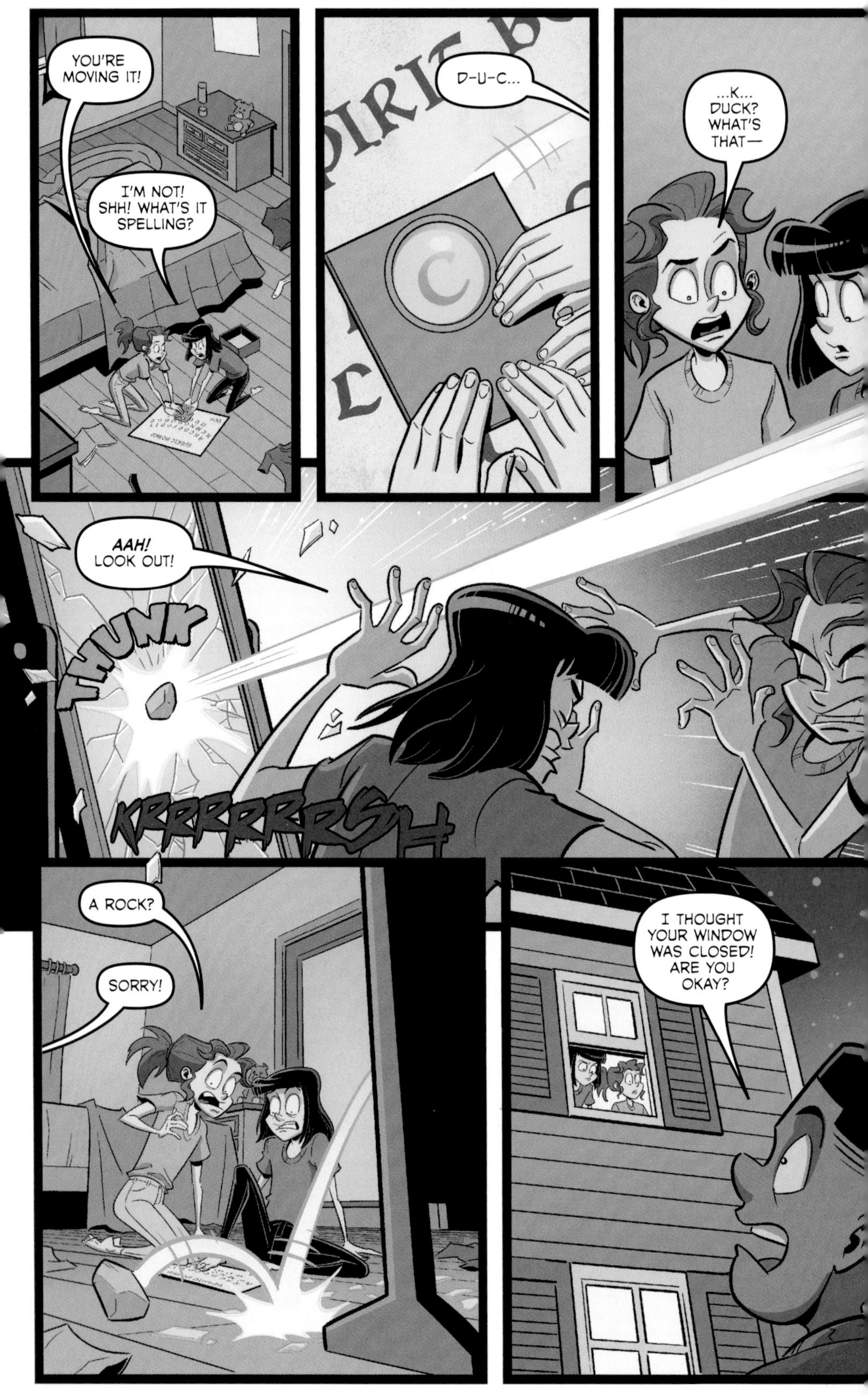

YOU'RE MOVING IT!
I'M NOT! SHH! WHAT'S IT SPELLING?
D-U-C...
...K... DUCK? WHAT'S THAT—
AAH! LOOK OUT!
THUNK
KRRRRRRSH
A ROCK?
SORRY!
I THOUGHT YOUR WINDOW WAS CLOSED! ARE YOU OKAY?

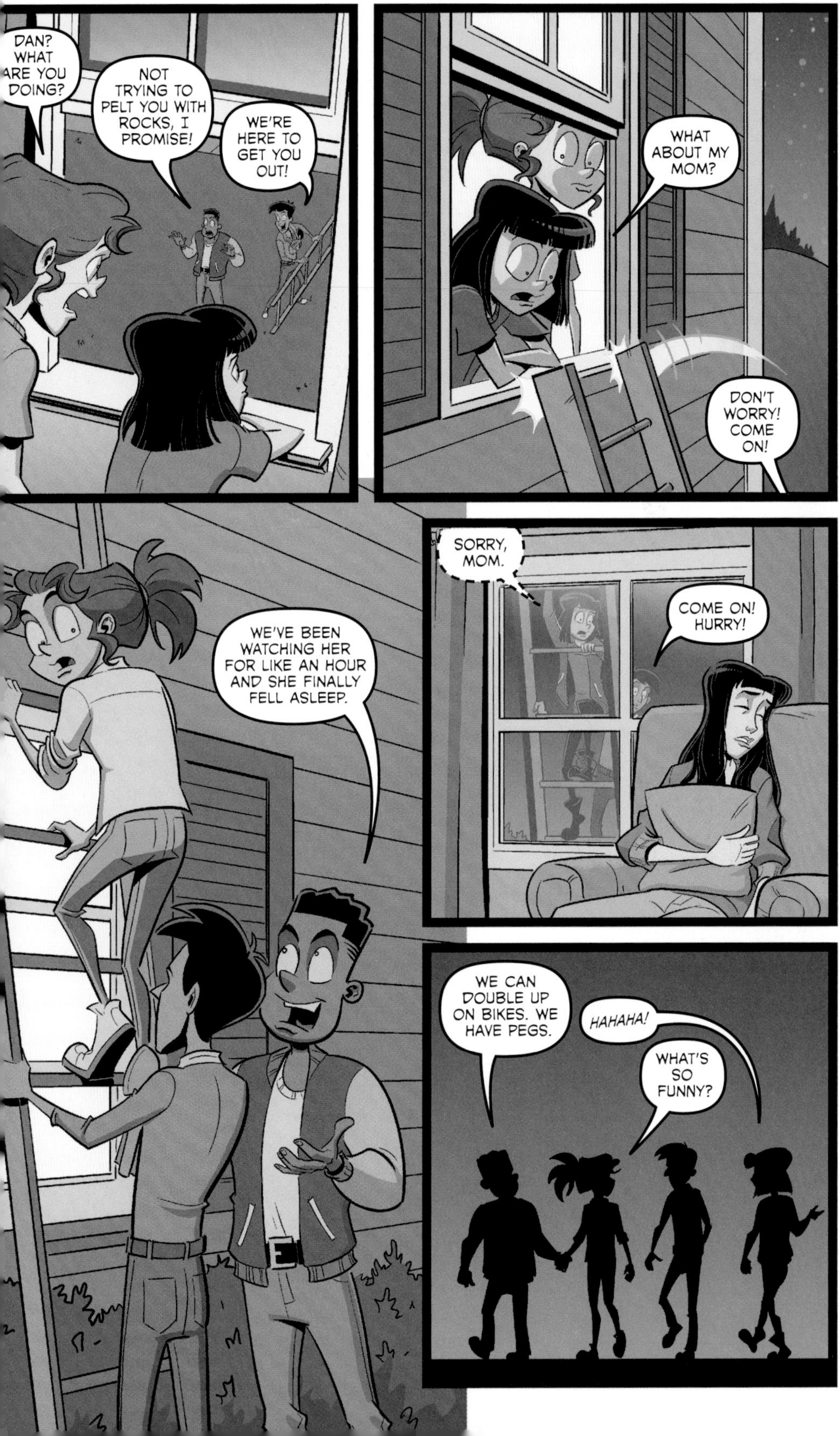
DAN? WHAT ARE YOU DOING?
NOT TRYING TO PELT YOU WITH ROCKS, I PROMISE!
WE'RE HERE TO GET YOU OUT!
WHAT ABOUT MY MOM?
DON'T WORRY! COME ON!
WE'VE BEEN WATCHING HER FOR LIKE AN HOUR AND SHE FINALLY FELL ASLEEP.
SORRY, MOM.
COME ON! HURRY!
WE CAN DOUBLE UP ON BIKES. WE HAVE PEGS.
HAHAHA!
WHAT'S SO FUNNY?

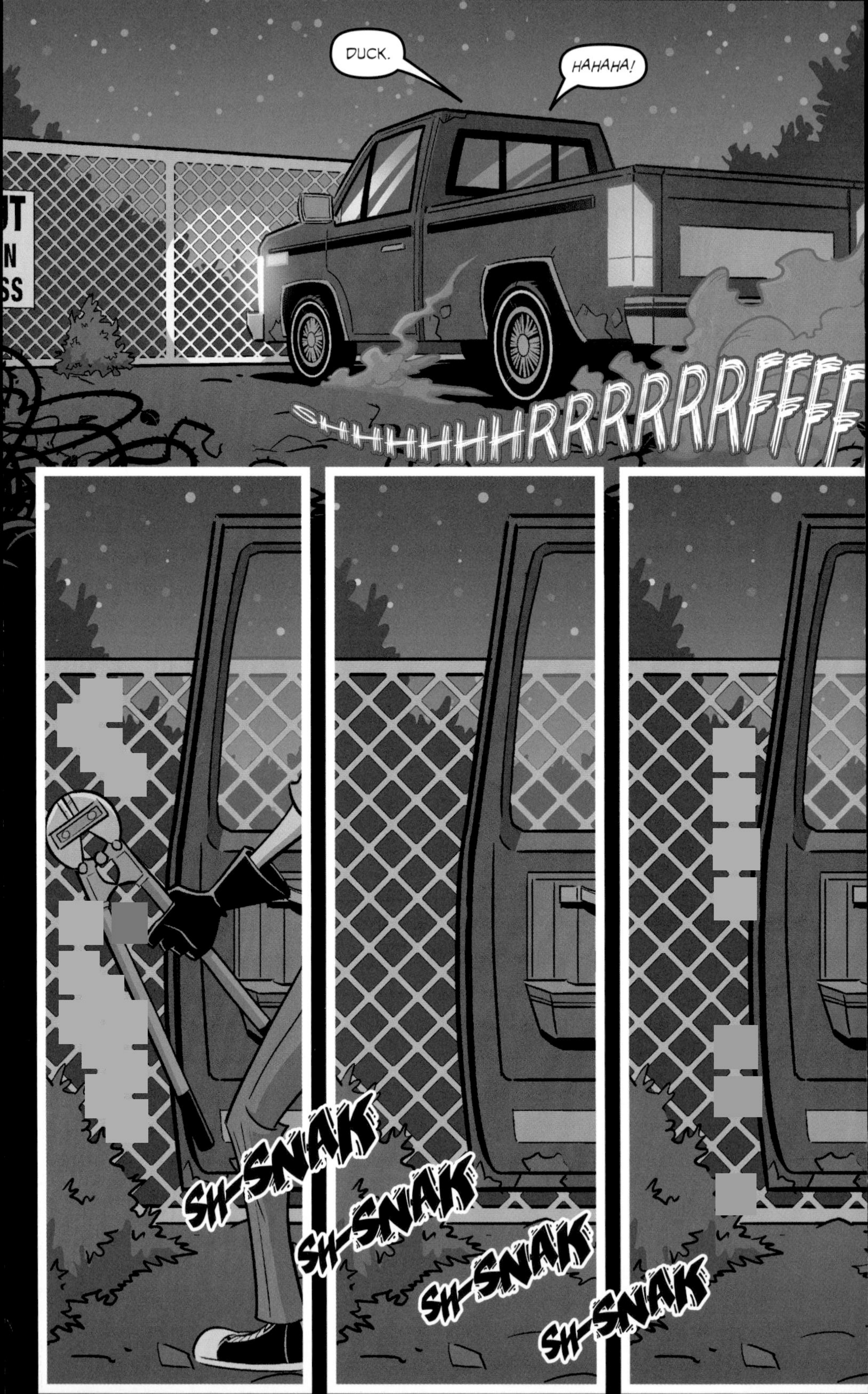
DUCK.
HAHAHA!
SHHHHHHHHHRRRRRRRFFFFF
SH-SNAK
SH-SNAK
SH-SNAK
SH-SNAK

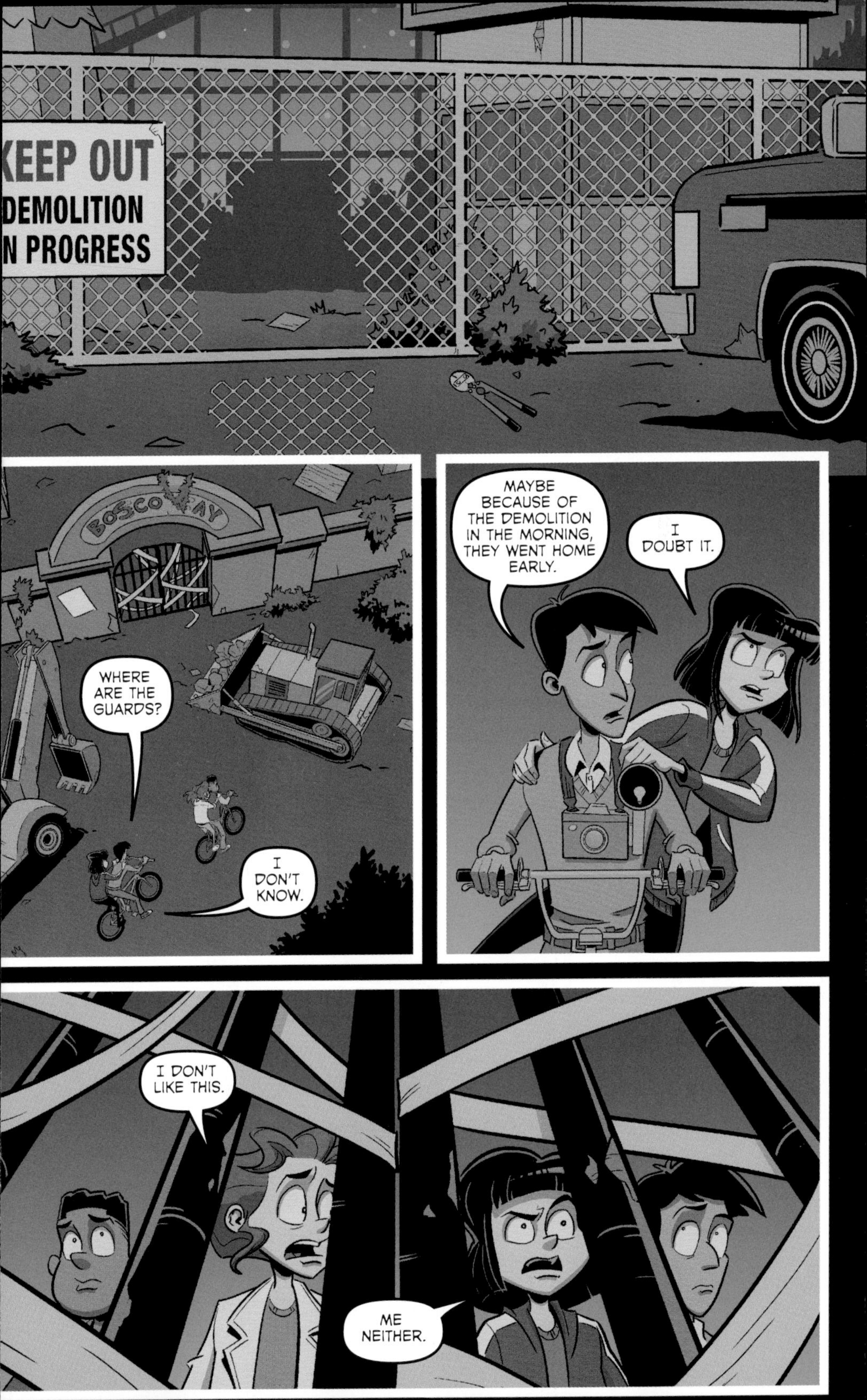
KEEP OUT
DEMOLITION
N PROGRESS
BOSCO
WHERE ARE THE GUARDS?
I DON'T KNOW.
MAYBE BECAUSE OF THE DEMOLITION IN THE MORNING, THEY WENT HOME EARLY.
I DOUBT IT.
I DON'T LIKE THIS.
ME NEITHER.

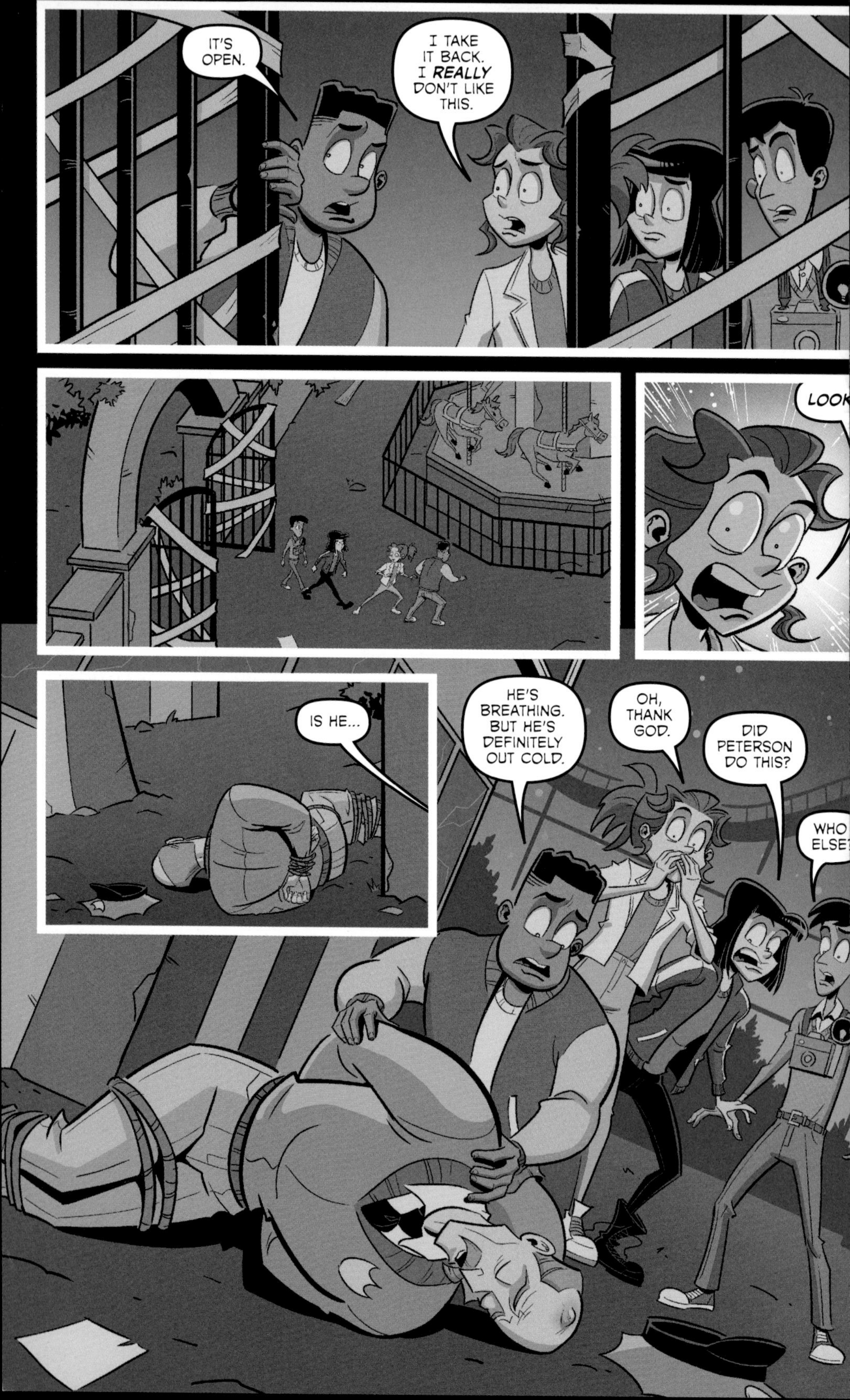
IT'S OPEN.
I TAKE IT BACK. I *REALLY* DON'T LIKE THIS.
LOOK
IS HE...
HE'S BREATHING. BUT HE'S DEFINITELY OUT COLD.
OH, THANK GOD.
DID PETERSON DO THIS?
WHO ELSE

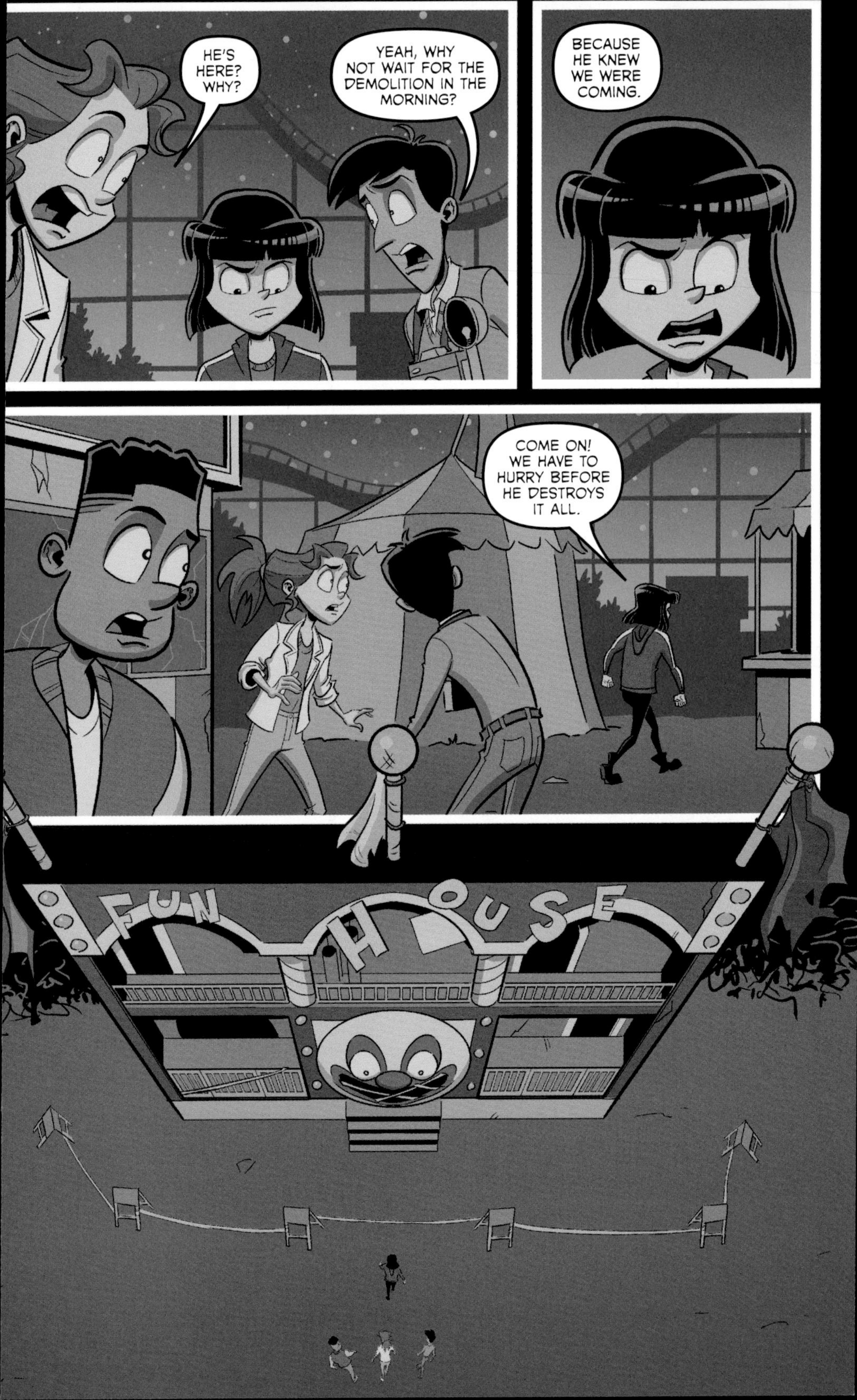
HE'S HERE? WHY?
YEAH, WHY NOT WAIT FOR THE DEMOLITION IN THE MORNING?
BECAUSE HE KNEW WE WERE COMING.
COME ON! WE HAVE TO HURRY BEFORE HE DESTROYS IT ALL.
FUN HOUSE

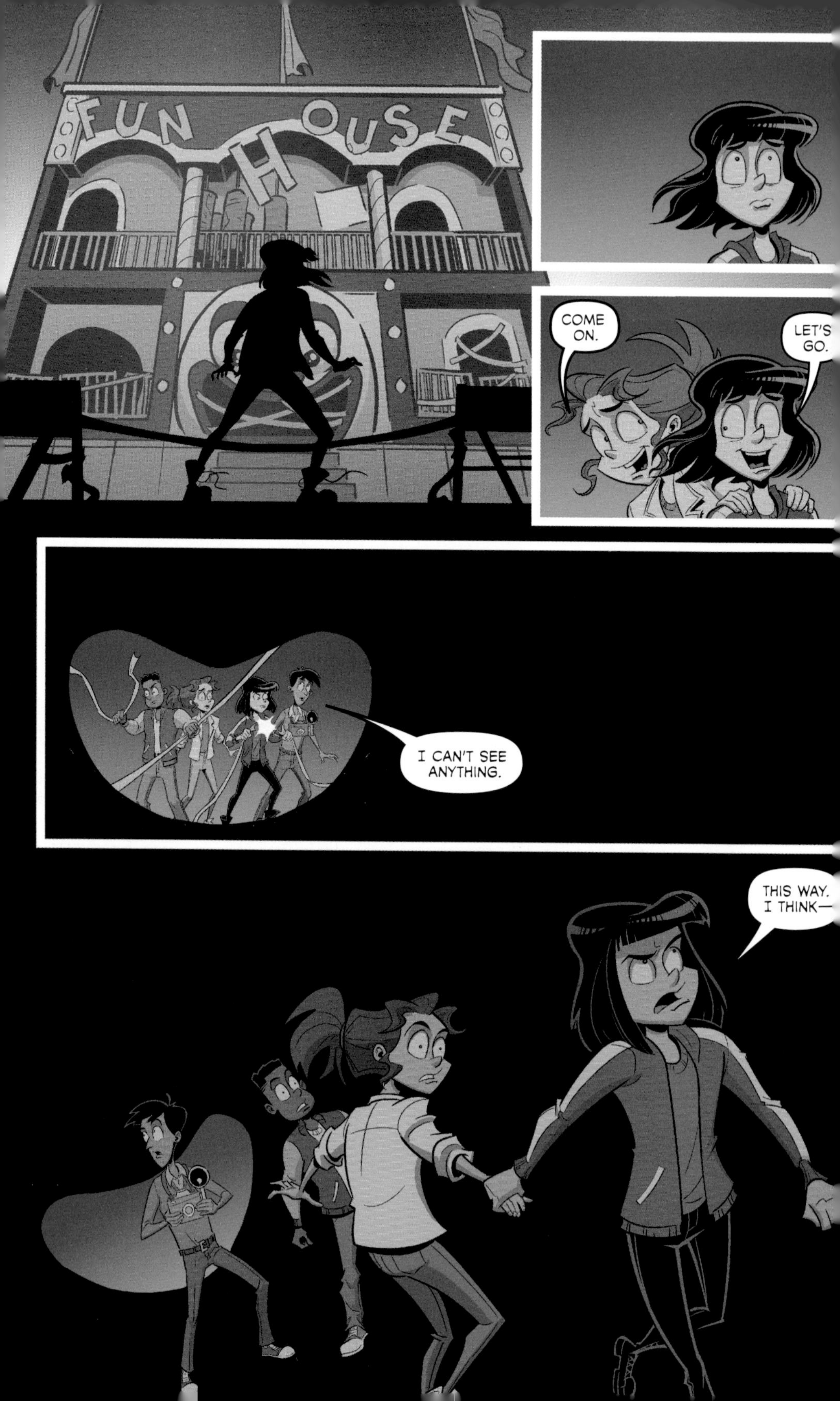
FUN HOUSE
COME ON.
LET'S GO.
I CAN'T SEE ANYTHING.
THIS WAY. I THINK—

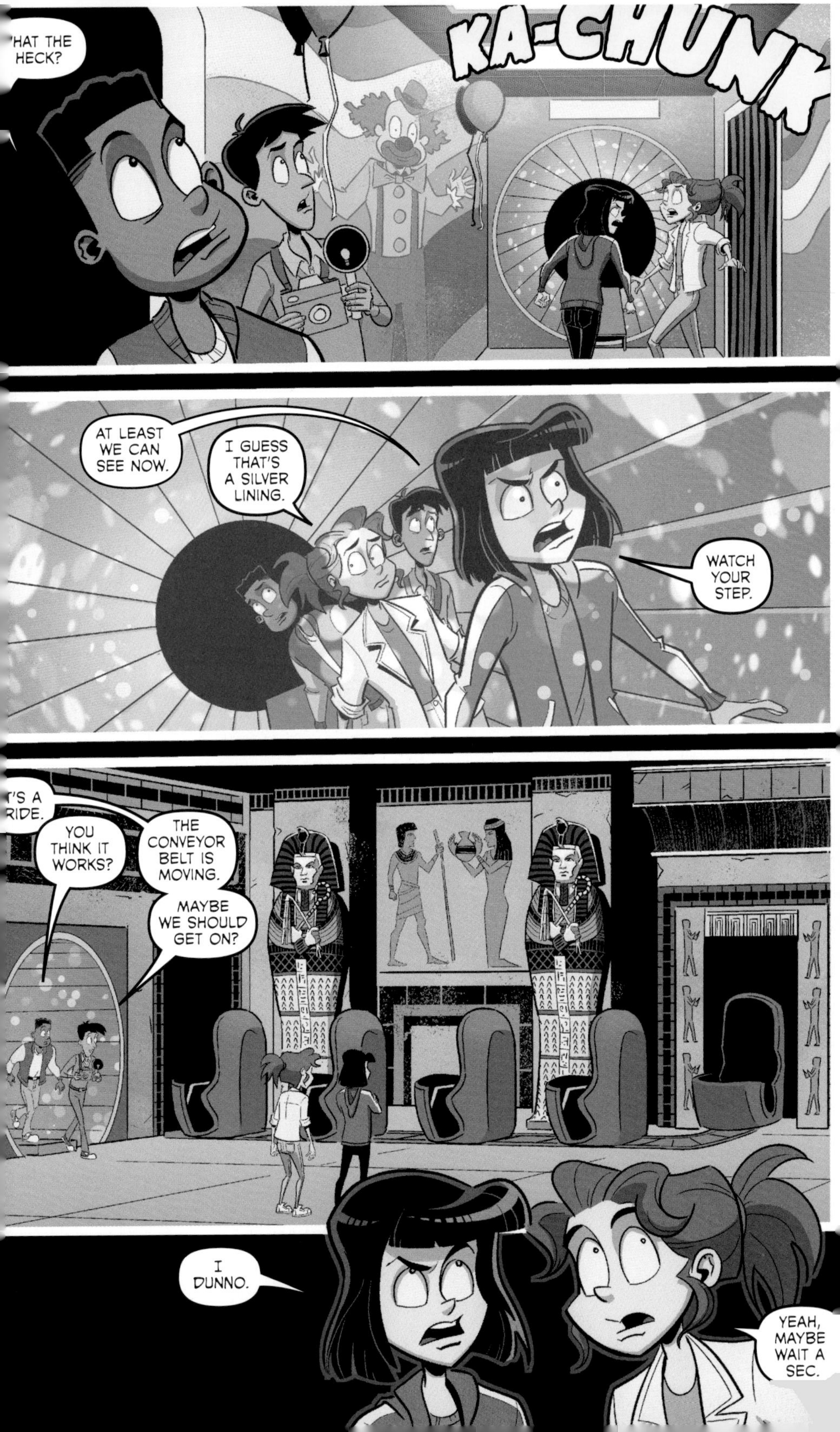
HAT THE HECK?
KA-CHUNK
AT LEAST WE CAN SEE NOW.
I GUESS THAT'S A SILVER LINING.
WATCH YOUR STEP.
T'S A RIDE.
YOU THINK IT WORKS?
THE CONVEYOR BELT IS MOVING.
MAYBE WE SHOULD GET ON?
I DUNNO.
YEAH, MAYBE WAIT A SEC.

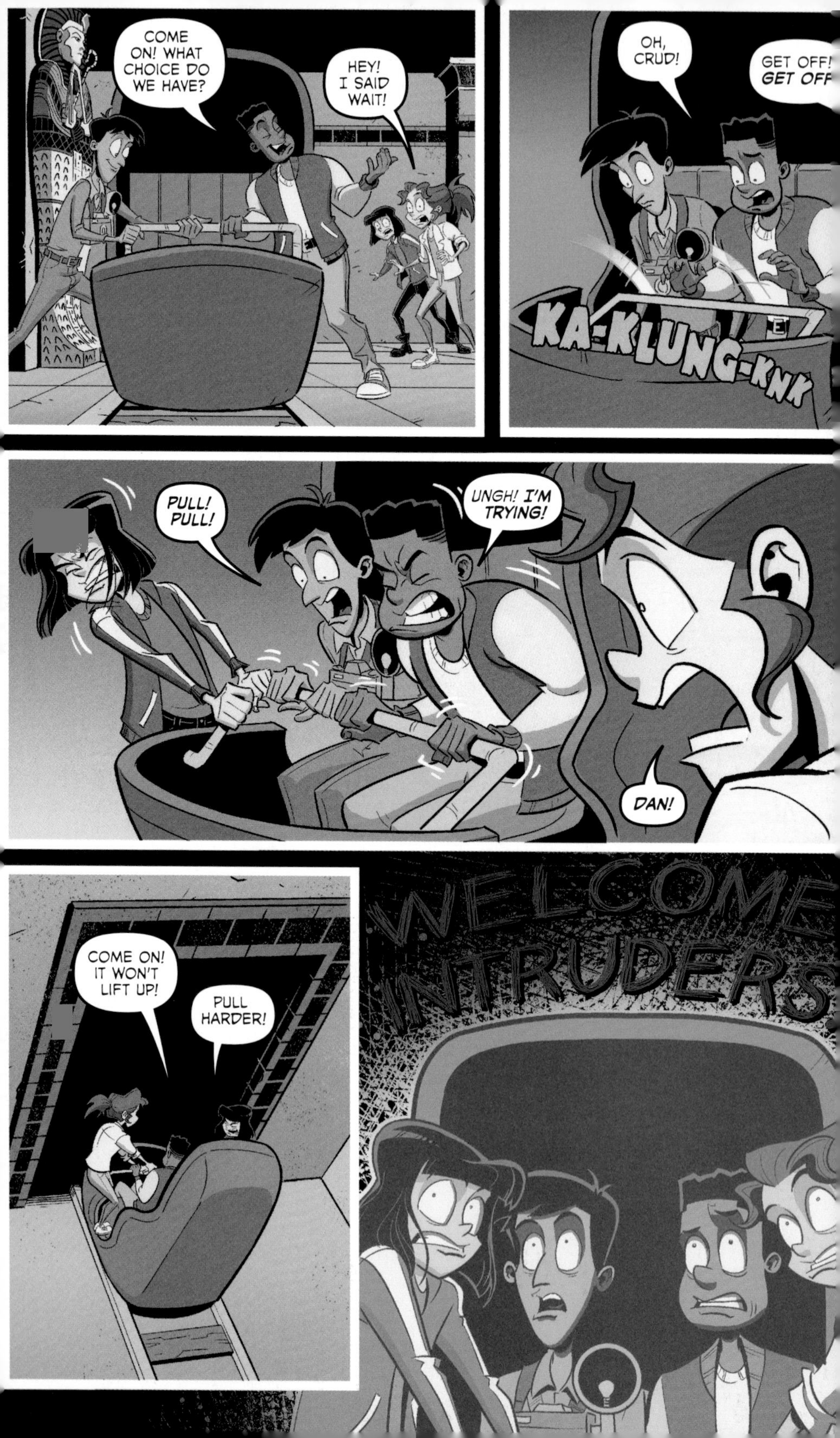
COME ON! WHAT CHOICE DO WE HAVE?
HEY! I SAID WAIT!
OH, CRUD!
GET OFF! GET OFF
KA-KLUNG-KNK
PULL! PULL!
UNGH! I'M TRYING!
DAN!
COME ON! IT WON'T LIFT UP!
PULL HARDER!
WELCOME INTRUDERS

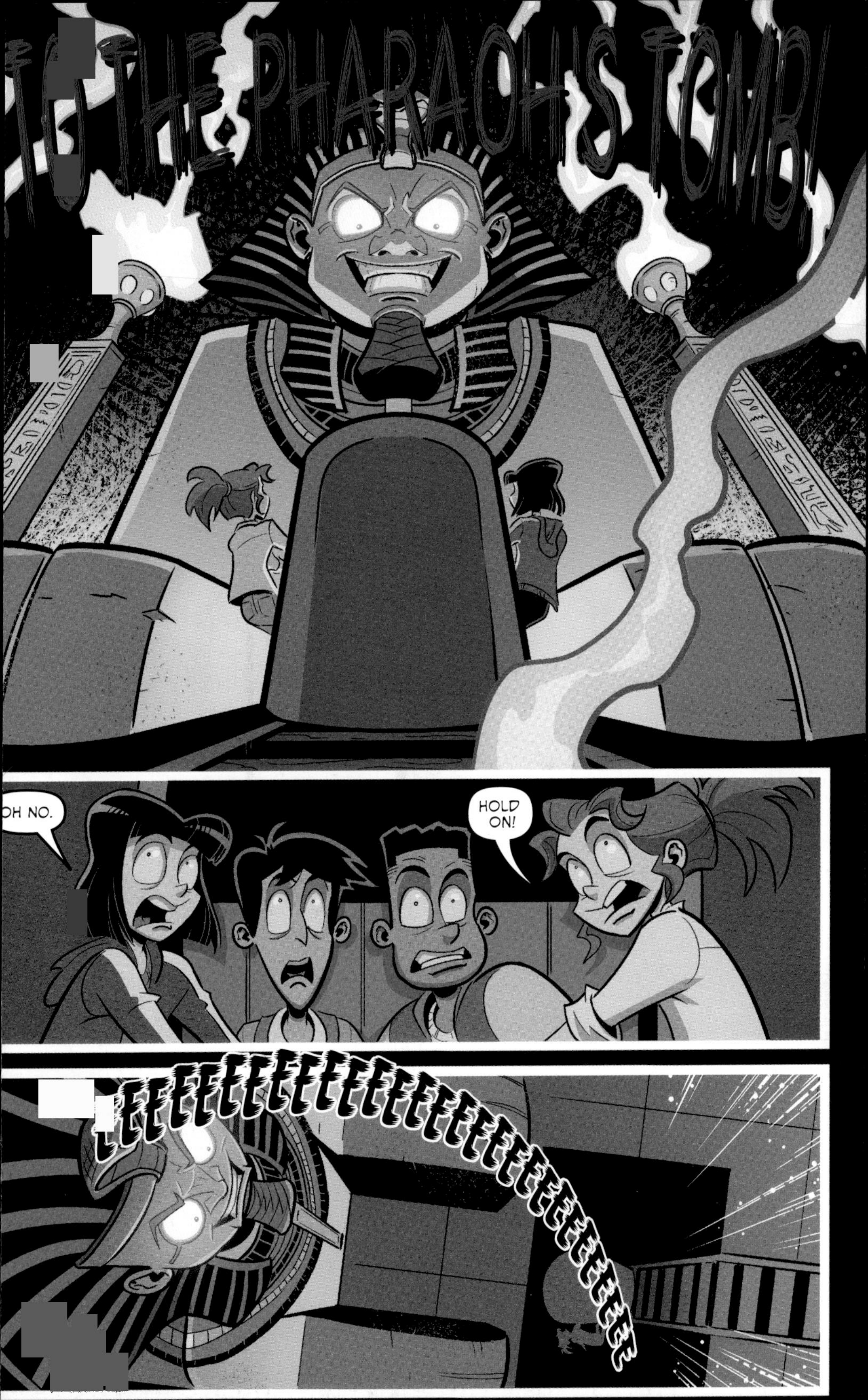

TO THE PHARAOH'S TOMB!
OH NO.
HOLD ON!
EEEEEEEEEEEEEEEEEEEEEEEEEEEEEEEEEEEEEEEE

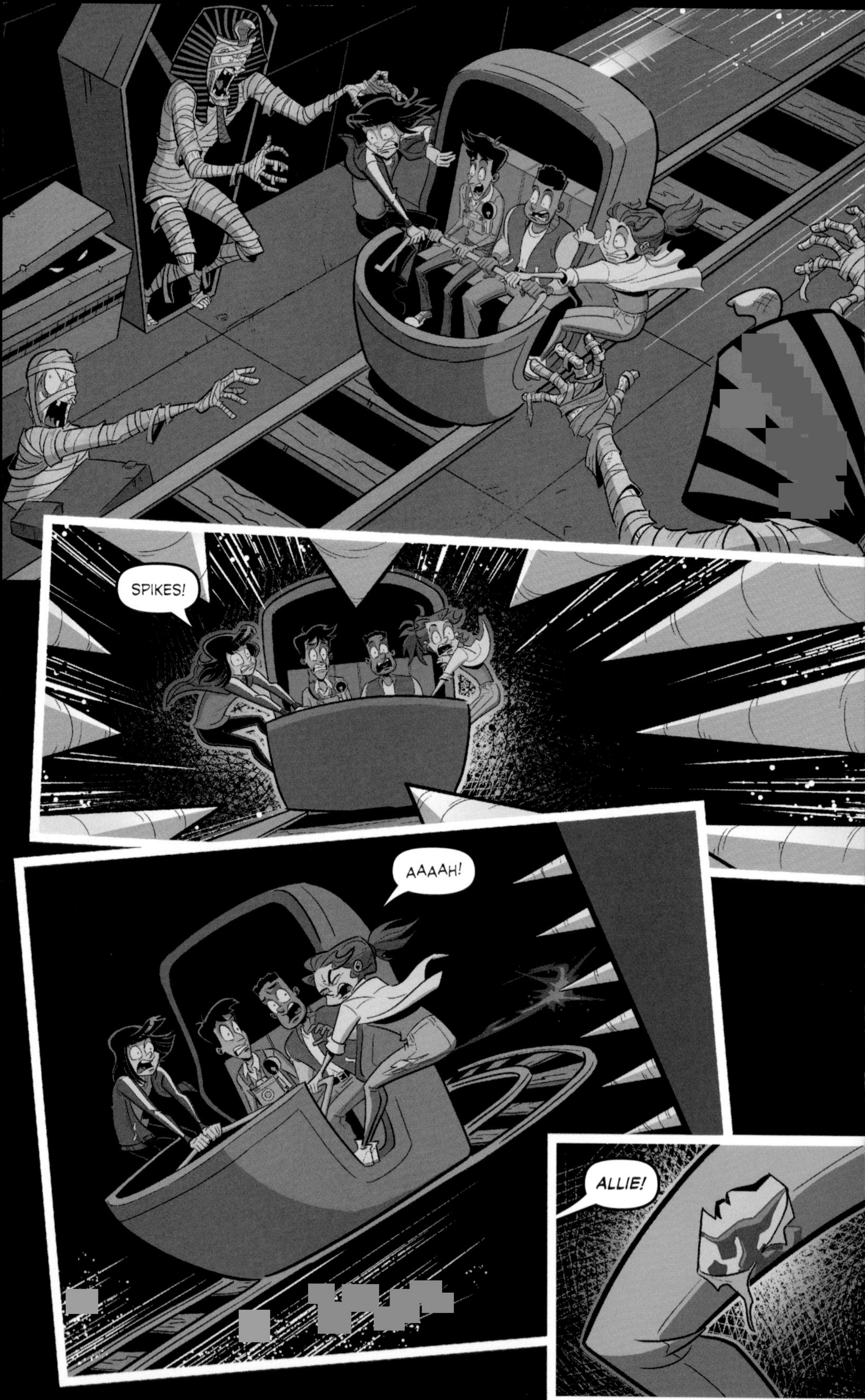
SPIKES!
AAAAH!
ALLIE!

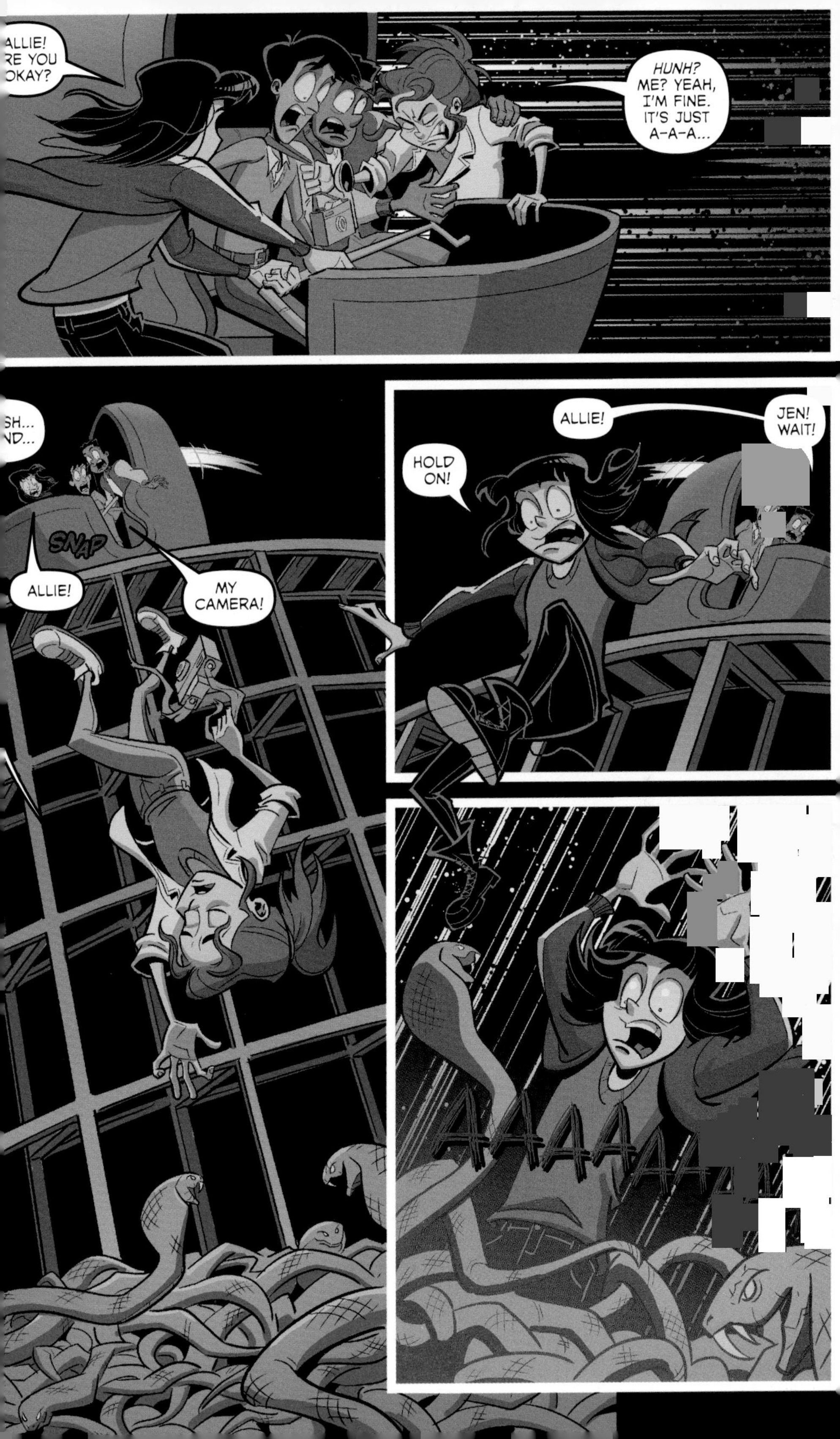

ALLIE!
RE YOU
OKAY?
HUNH? ME? YEAH, I'M FINE. IT'S JUST A-A-A...
SH...
ND...
SNAP
ALLIE!
MY CAMERA!
ALLIE!
JEN! WAIT!
HOLD ON!
AAAAA

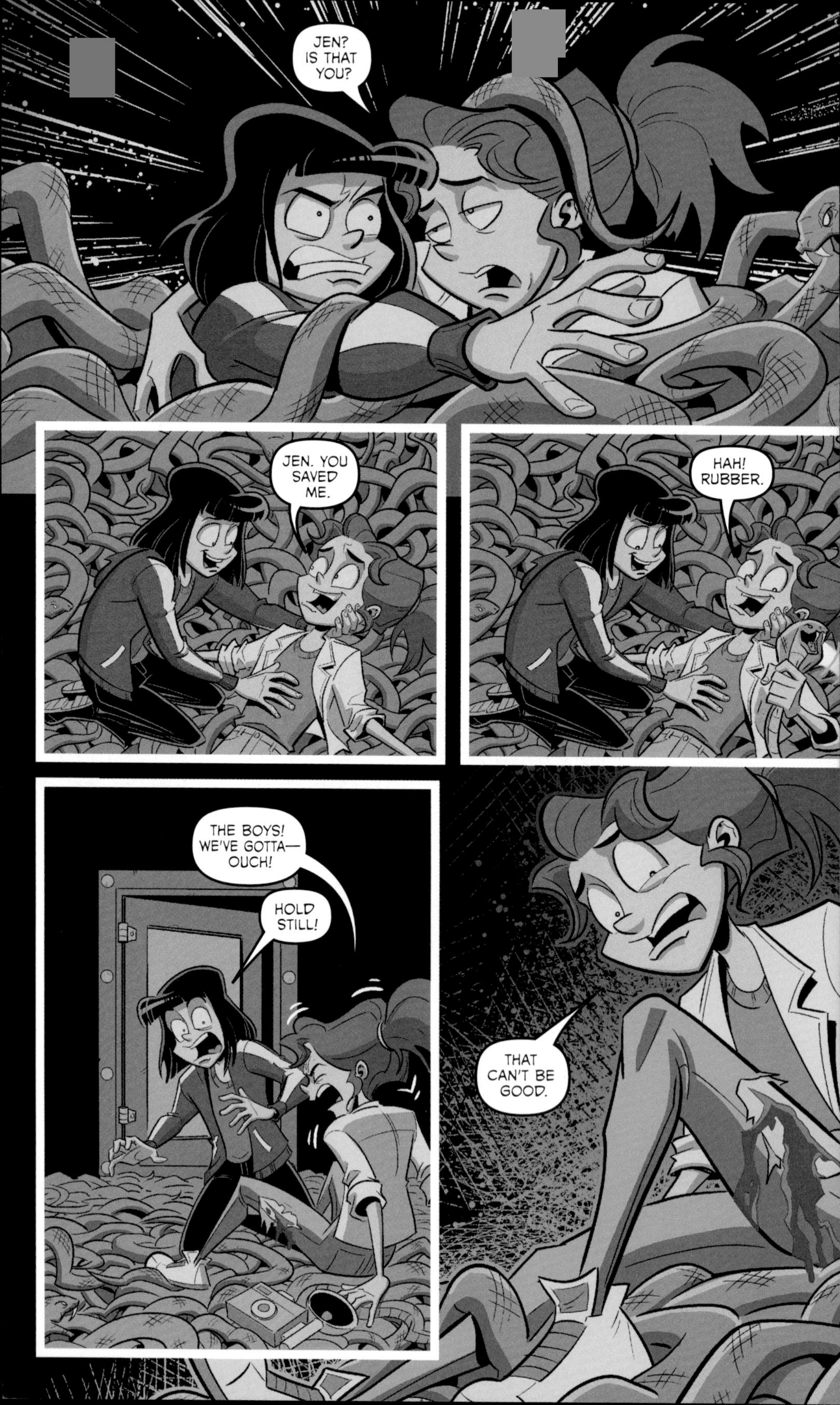
JEN? IS THAT YOU?
JEN. YOU SAVED ME.
HAH! RUBBER.
THE BOYS! WE'VE GOTTA— OUCH!
HOLD STILL!
THAT CAN'T BE GOOD.

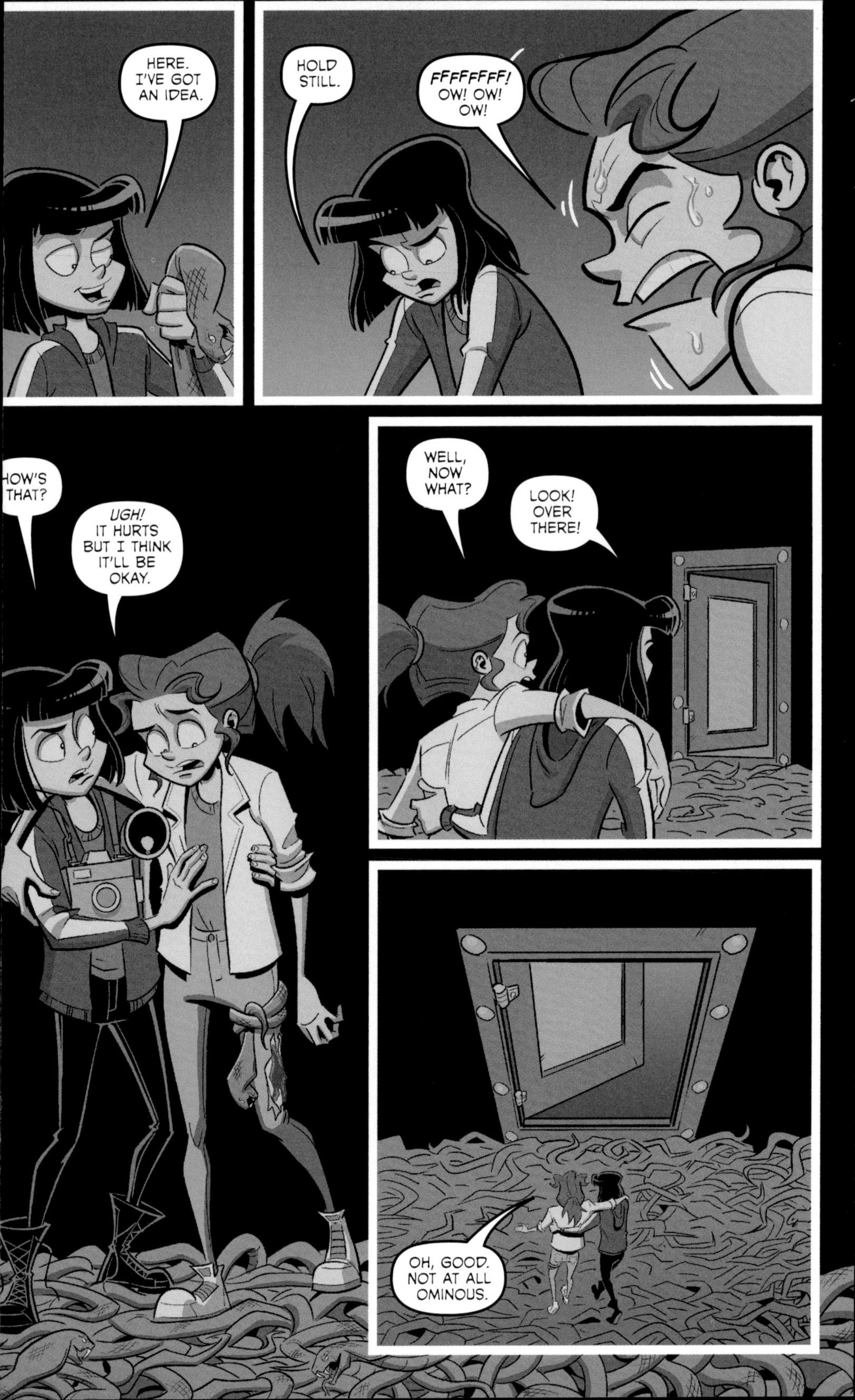
HERE. I'VE GOT AN IDEA.
HOLD STILL.
FFFFFFFF! OW! OW! OW!
HOW'S THAT?
UGH! IT HURTS BUT I THINK IT'LL BE OKAY.
WELL, NOW WHAT?
LOOK! OVER THERE!
OH, GOOD. NOT AT ALL OMINOUS.

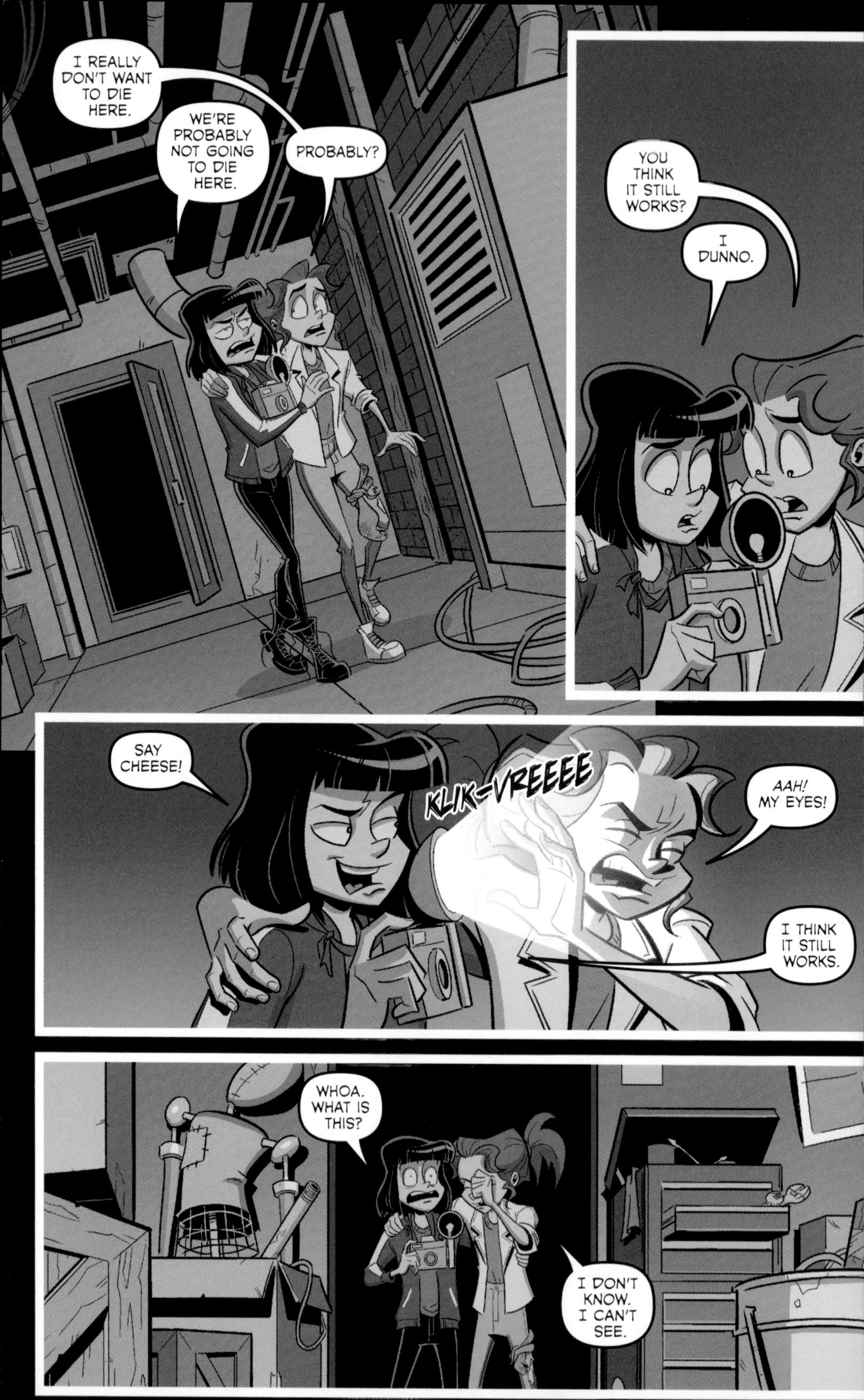
I REALLY DON'T WANT TO DIE HERE.
WE'RE PROBABLY NOT GOING TO DIE HERE.
PROBABLY?
YOU THINK IT STILL WORKS?
I DUNNO.
SAY CHEESE!
KLIK-VREEEE
AAH! MY EYES!
I THINK IT STILL WORKS.
WHOA. WHAT IS THIS?
I DON'T KNOW. I CAN'T SEE.

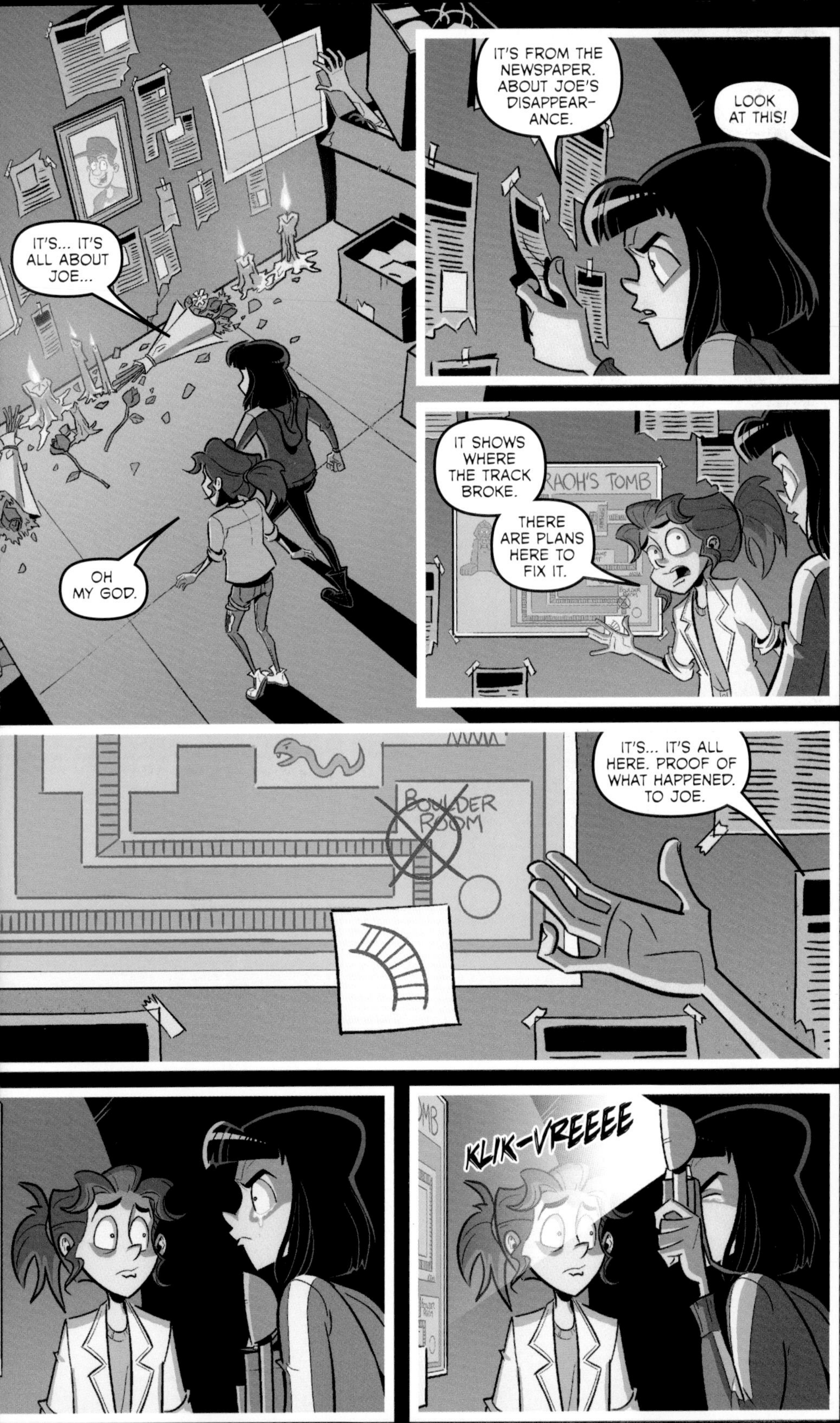
IT'S... IT'S ALL ABOUT JOE...
OH MY GOD.
LOOK AT THIS!
IT'S FROM THE NEWSPAPER. ABOUT JOE'S DISAPPEAR-ANCE.
IT SHOWS WHERE THE TRACK BROKE.
THERE ARE PLANS HERE TO FIX IT.
BOULDER ROOM
IT'S... IT'S ALL HERE. PROOF OF WHAT HAPPENED. TO JOE.
KLIK-VREEEE

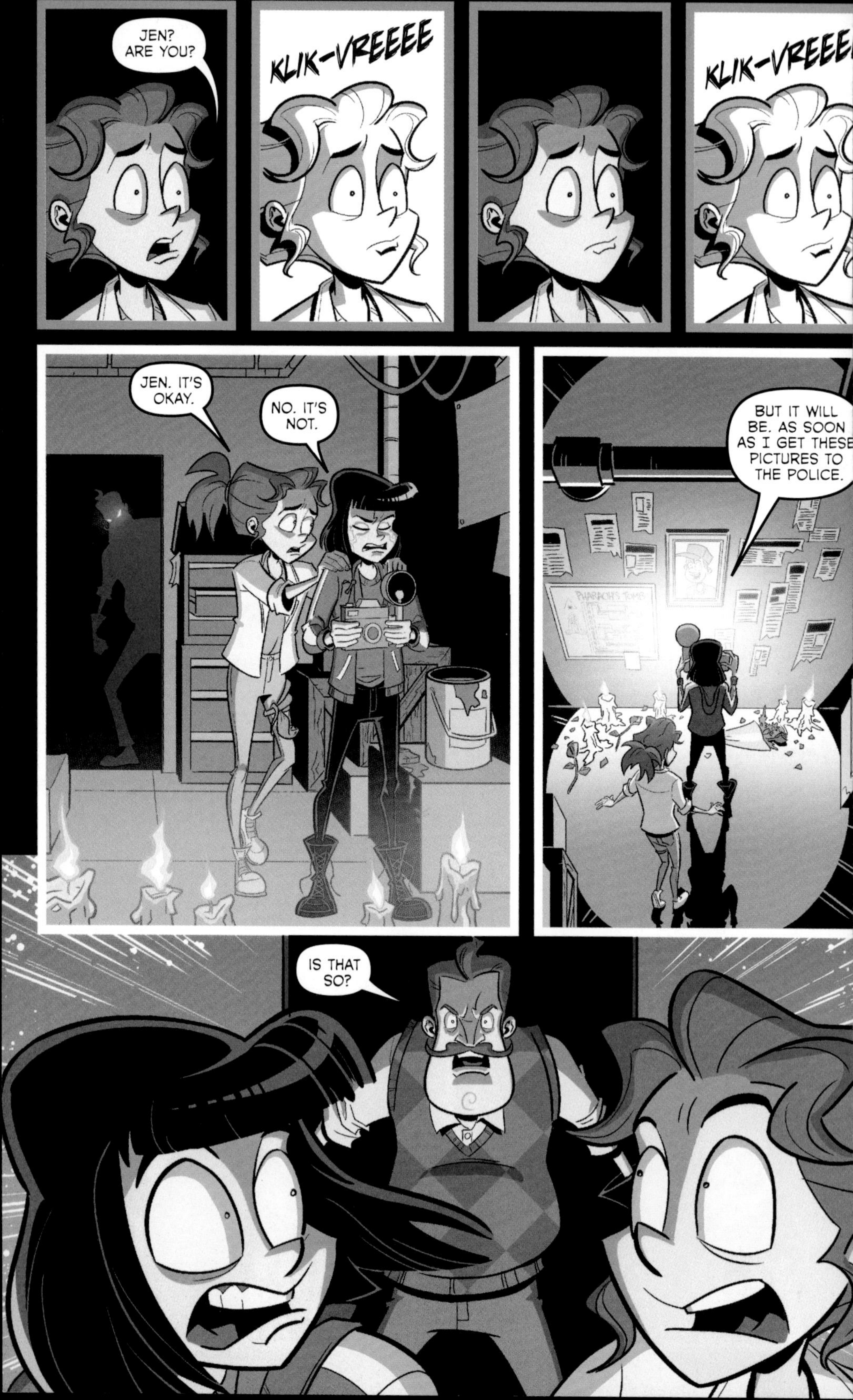
JEN? ARE YOU?
KLIK-VREEEE
KLIK-VREEEE
JEN. IT'S OKAY.
NO. IT'S NOT.
BUT IT WILL BE. AS SOON AS I GET THESE PICTURES TO THE POLICE.
PHARAOH'S TOMB
IS THAT SO?

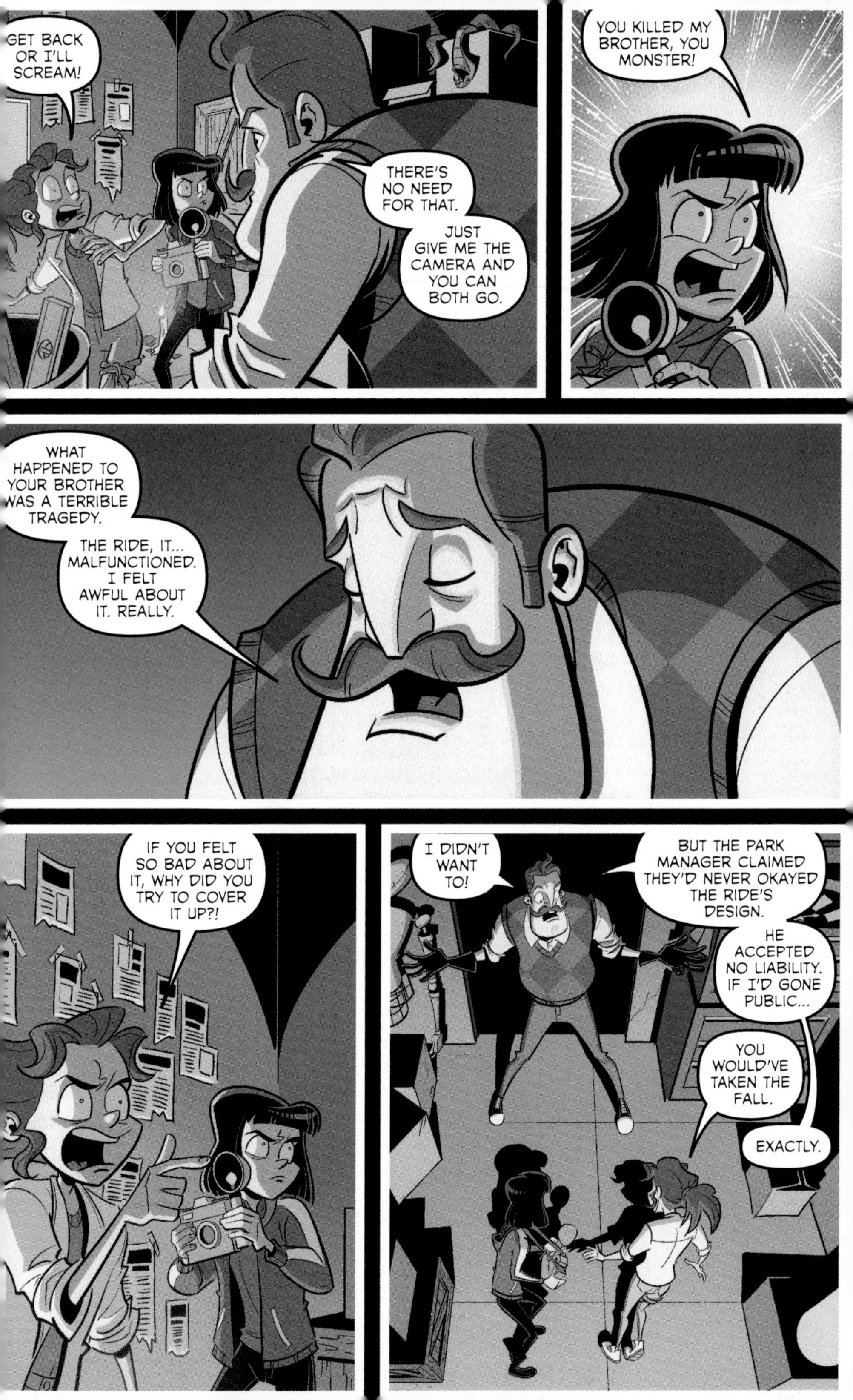
GET BACK OR I'LL SCREAM!
THERE'S NO NEED FOR THAT.
JUST GIVE ME THE CAMERA AND YOU CAN BOTH GO.
YOU KILLED MY BROTHER, YOU MONSTER!
WHAT HAPPENED TO YOUR BROTHER WAS A TERRIBLE TRAGEDY.
THE RIDE, IT... MALFUNCTIONED. I FELT AWFUL ABOUT IT. REALLY.
IF YOU FELT SO BAD ABOUT IT, WHY DID YOU TRY TO COVER IT UP?!
I DIDN'T WANT TO!
BUT THE PARK MANAGER CLAIMED THEY'D NEVER OKAYED THE RIDE'S DESIGN.
HE ACCEPTED NO LIABILITY. IF I'D GONE PUBLIC...
YOU WOULD'VE TAKEN THE FALL.
EXACTLY.

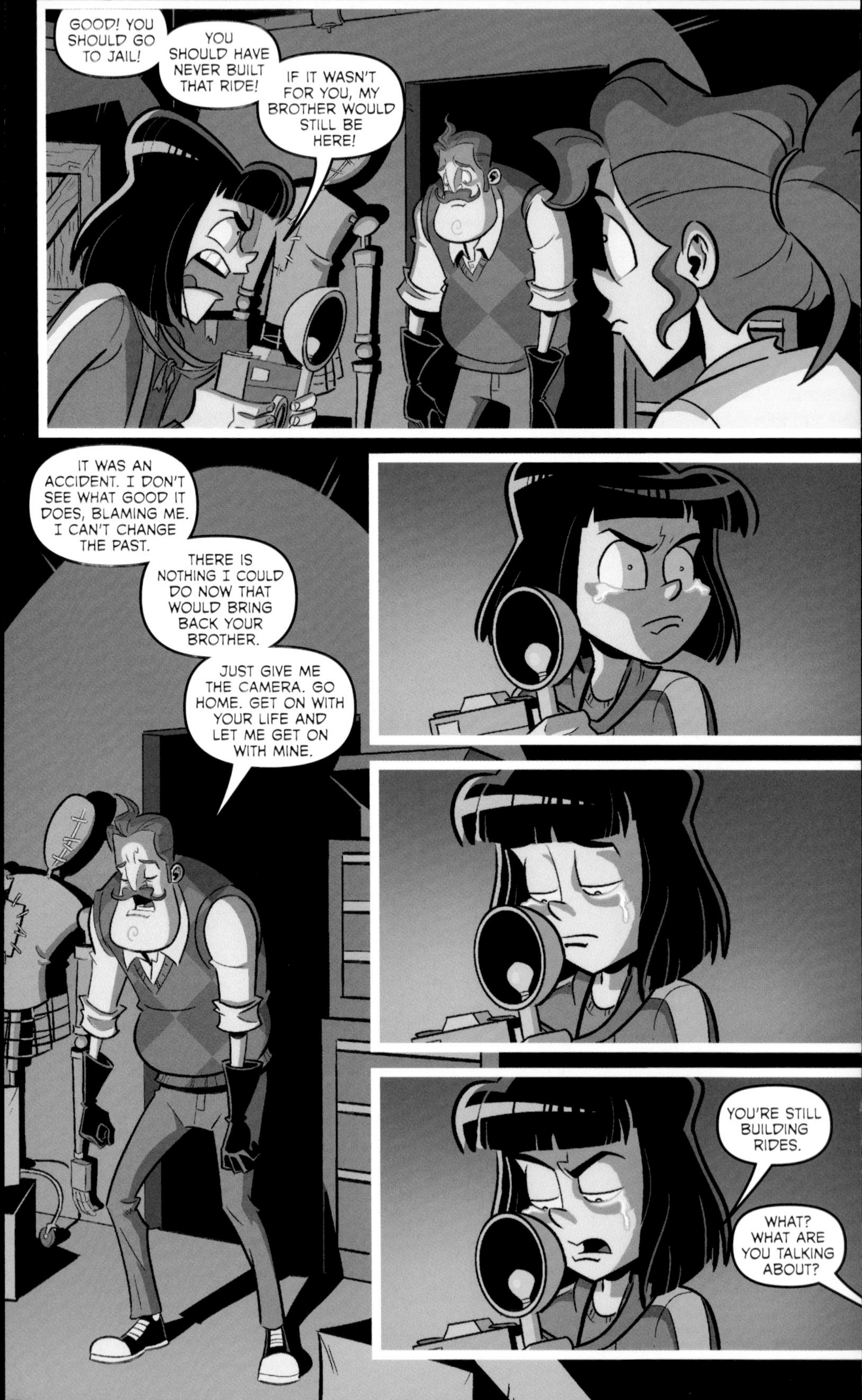
GOOD! YOU SHOULD GO TO JAIL!
YOU SHOULD HAVE NEVER BUILT THAT RIDE!
IF IT WASN'T FOR YOU, MY BROTHER WOULD STILL BE HERE!
IT WAS AN ACCIDENT. I DON'T SEE WHAT GOOD IT DOES, BLAMING ME. I CAN'T CHANGE THE PAST.
THERE IS NOTHING I COULD DO NOW THAT WOULD BRING BACK YOUR BROTHER.
JUST GIVE ME THE CAMERA. GO HOME. GET ON WITH YOUR LIFE AND LET ME GET ON WITH MINE.
YOU'RE STILL BUILDING RIDES.
WHAT? WHAT ARE YOU TALKING ABOUT?

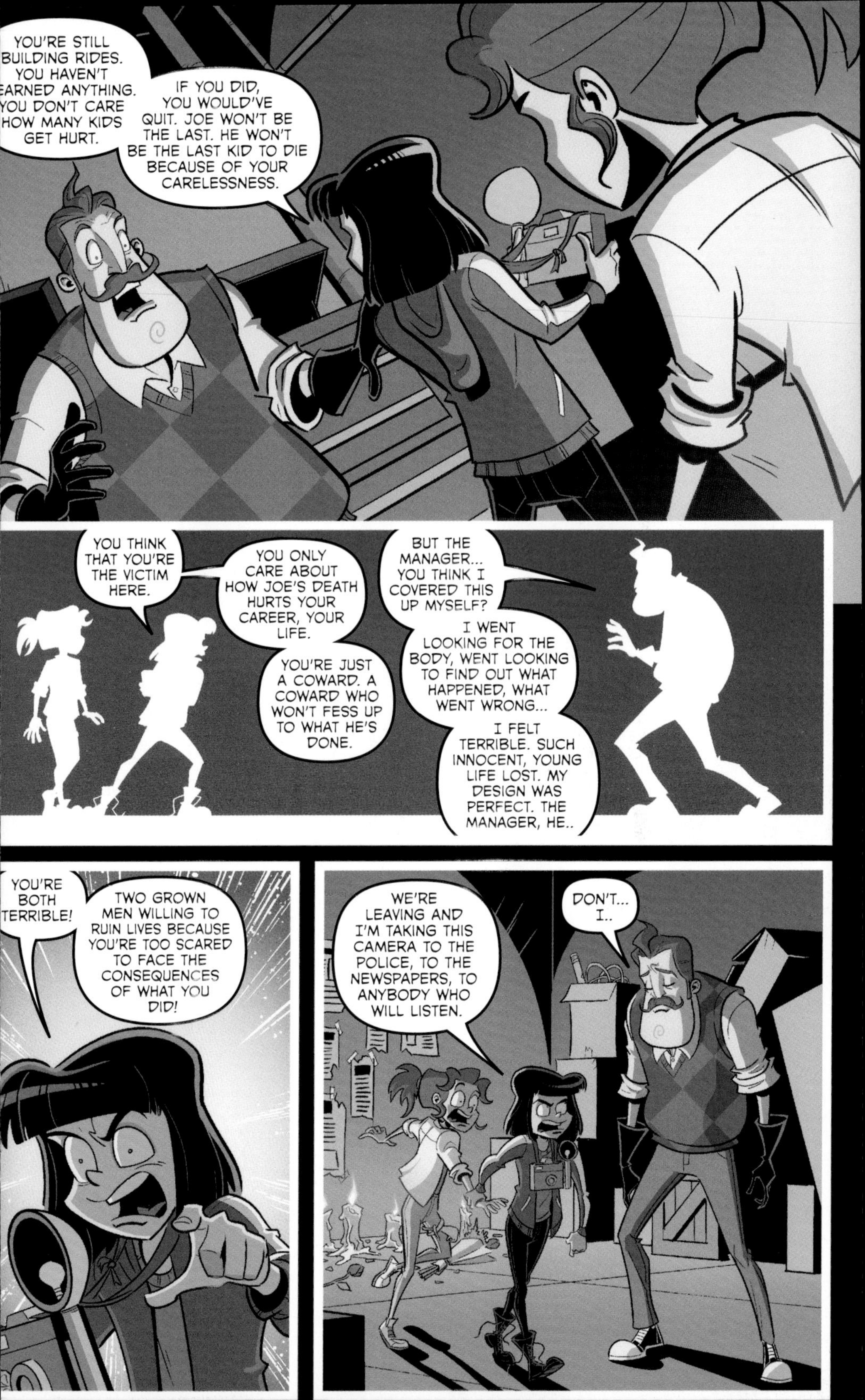
YOU'RE STILL BUILDING RIDES. YOU HAVEN'T EARNED ANYTHING. YOU DON'T CARE HOW MANY KIDS GET HURT.
IF YOU DID, YOU WOULD'VE QUIT. JOE WON'T BE THE LAST. HE WON'T BE THE LAST KID TO DIE BECAUSE OF YOUR CARELESSNESS.
YOU THINK THAT YOU'RE THE VICTIM HERE.
YOU ONLY CARE ABOUT HOW JOE'S DEATH HURTS YOUR CAREER, YOUR LIFE.
YOU'RE JUST A COWARD. A COWARD WHO WON'T FESS UP TO WHAT HE'S DONE.
BUT THE MANAGER... YOU THINK I COVERED THIS UP MYSELF?
I WENT LOOKING FOR THE BODY, WENT LOOKING TO FIND OUT WHAT HAPPENED, WHAT WENT WRONG...
I FELT TERRIBLE. SUCH INNOCENT, YOUNG LIFE LOST. MY DESIGN WAS PERFECT. THE MANAGER, HE..
YOU'RE BOTH TERRIBLE!
TWO GROWN MEN WILLING TO RUIN LIVES BECAUSE YOU'RE TOO SCARED TO FACE THE CONSEQUENCES OF WHAT YOU DID!
WE'RE LEAVING AND I'M TAKING THIS CAMERA TO THE POLICE, TO THE NEWSPAPERS, TO ANYBODY WHO WILL LISTEN.
DON'T... I..

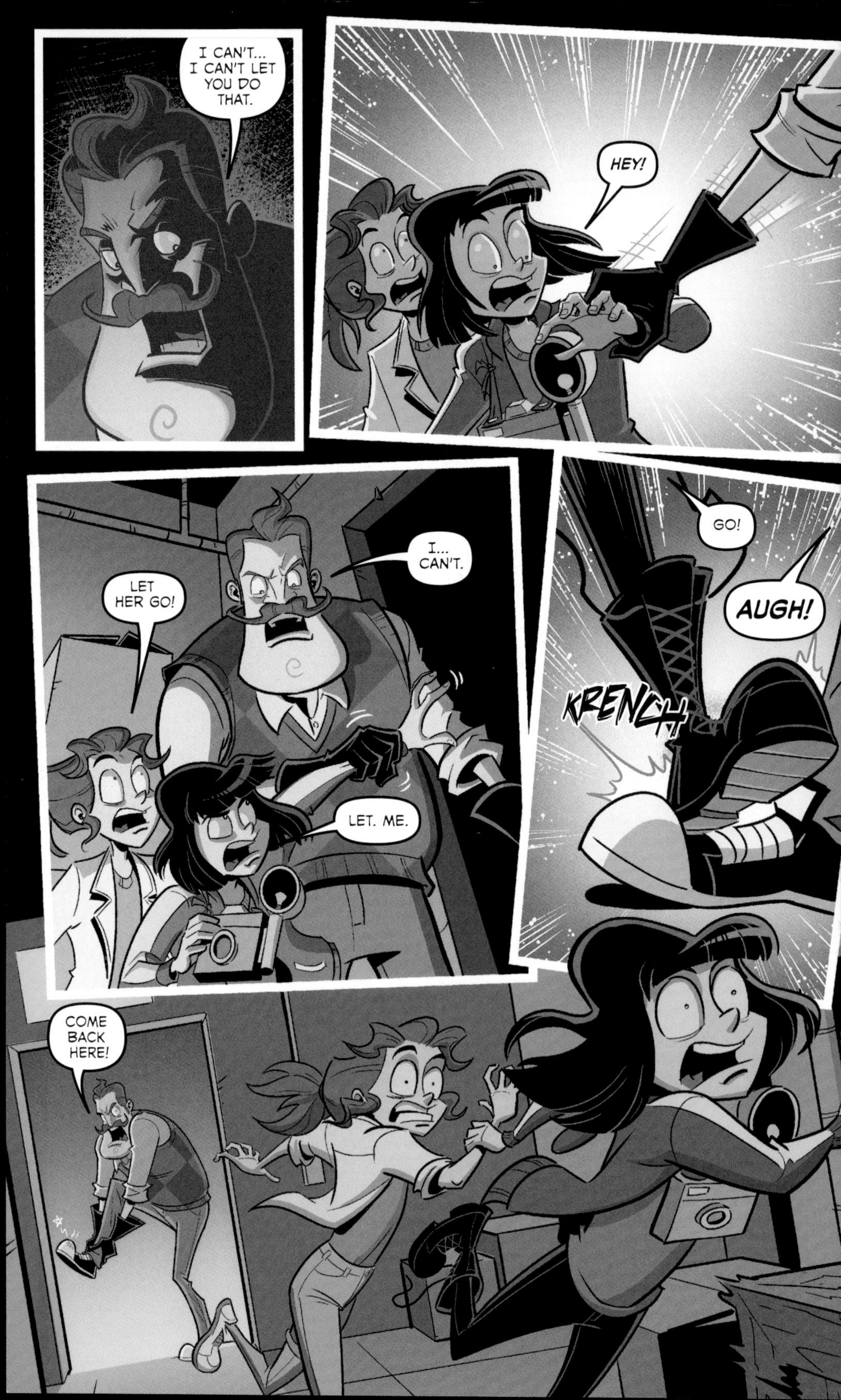
I CAN'T... I CAN'T LET YOU DO THAT.
HEY!
I... CAN'T.
LET HER GO!
LET. ME.
GO!
AUGH!
KRENCH
COME BACK HERE!

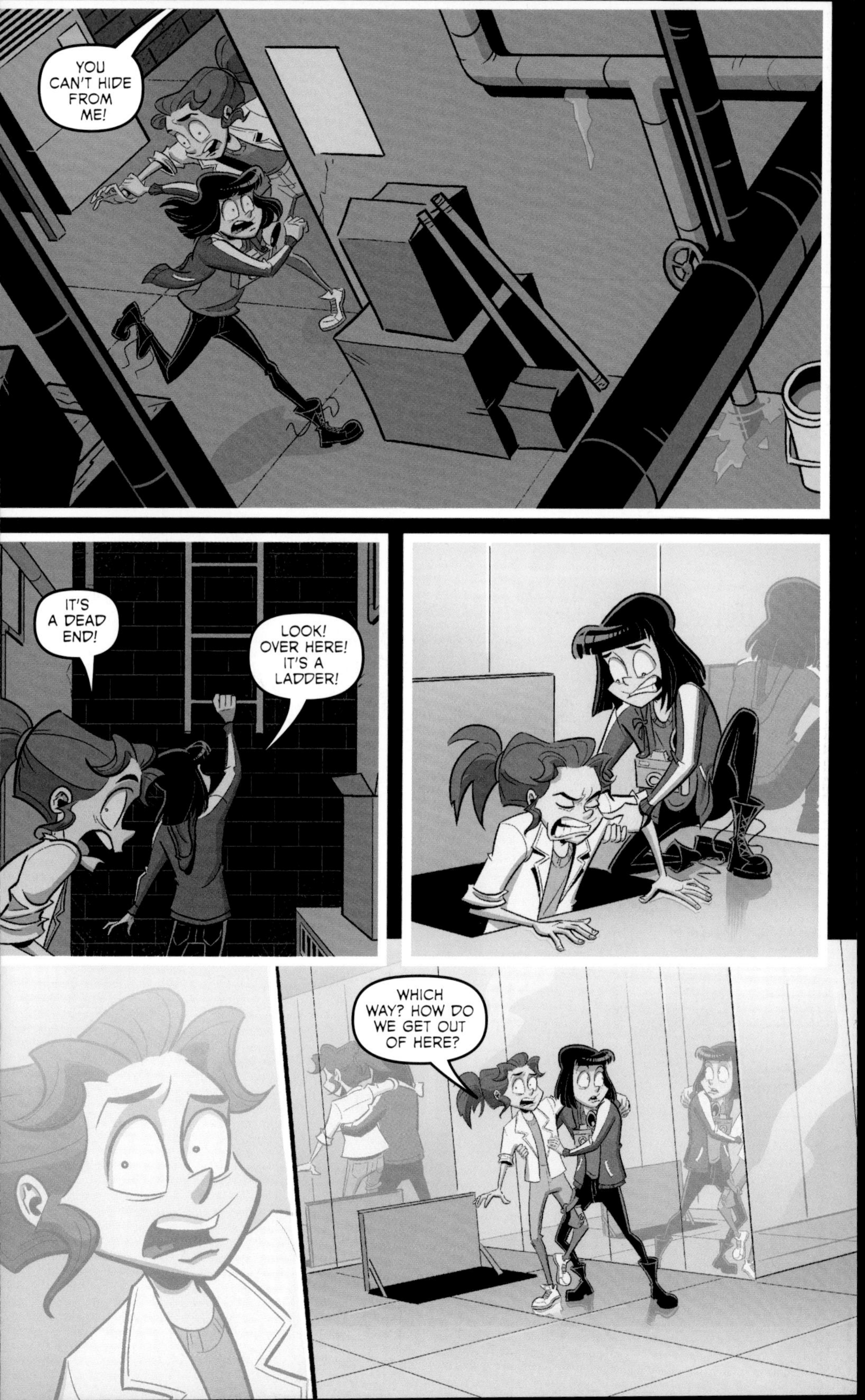
YOU CAN'T HIDE FROM ME!
IT'S A DEAD END!
LOOK! OVER HERE! IT'S A LADDER!
WHICH WAY? HOW DO WE GET OUT OF HERE?

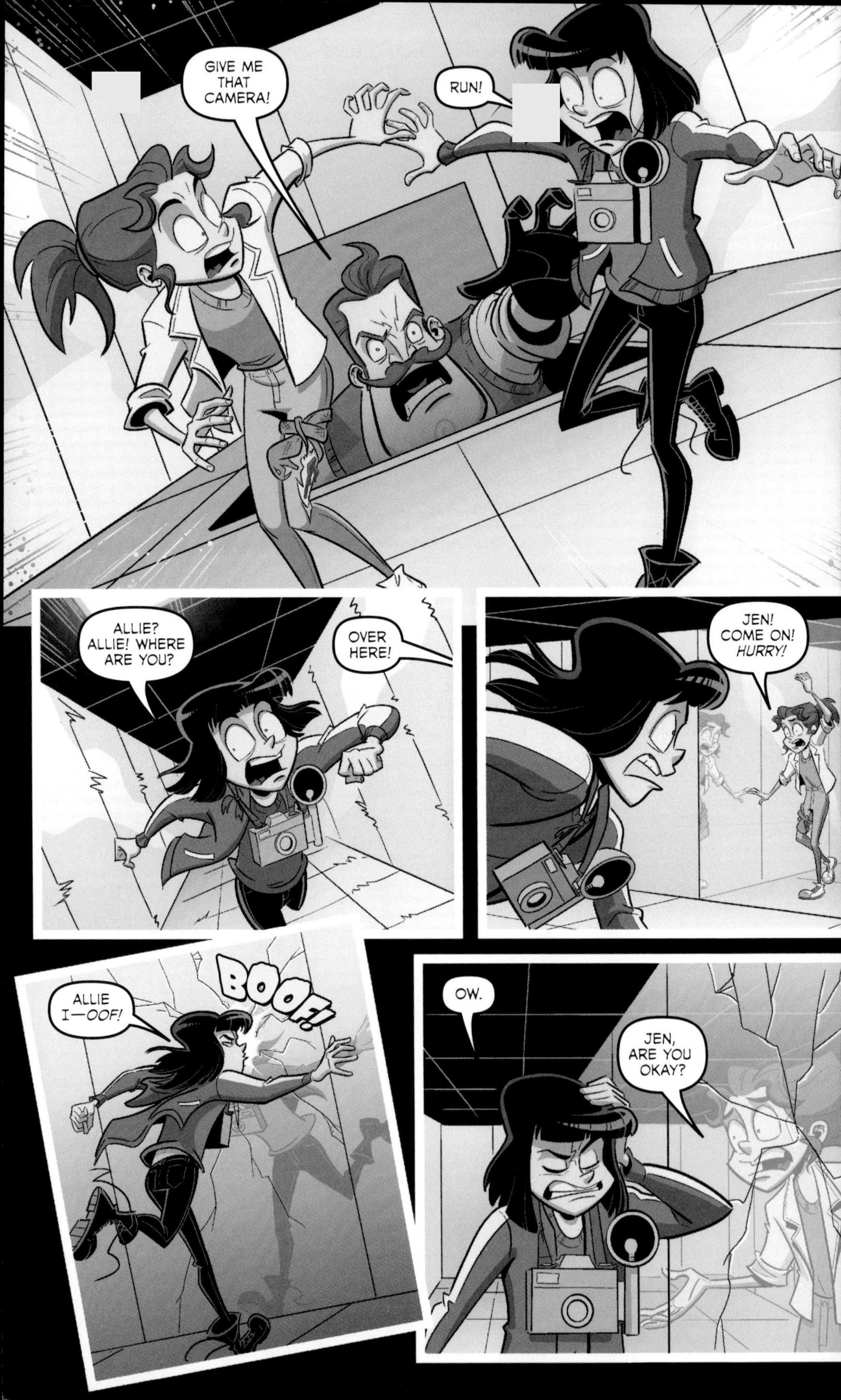
GIVE ME THAT CAMERA!
RUN!
ALLIE? ALLIE! WHERE ARE YOU?
OVER HERE!
JEN! COME ON! *HURRY!*
ALLIE I—*OOF!*
BOOF!
OW.
JEN, ARE YOU OKAY?

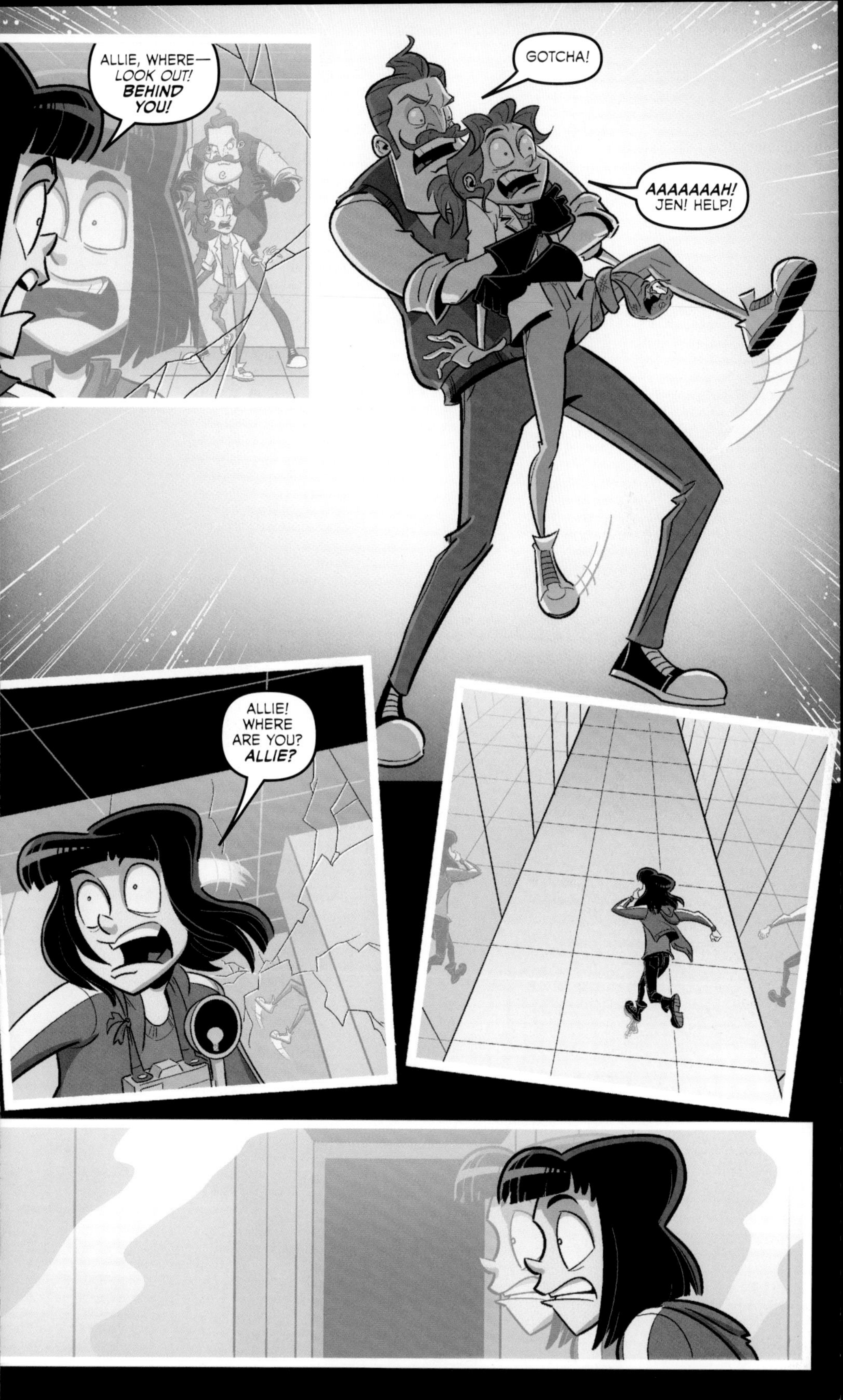
ALLIE, WHERE— LOOK OUT! BEHIND YOU!
GOTCHA!
AAAAAAAH! JEN! HELP!
ALLIE! WHERE ARE YOU? ALLIE?

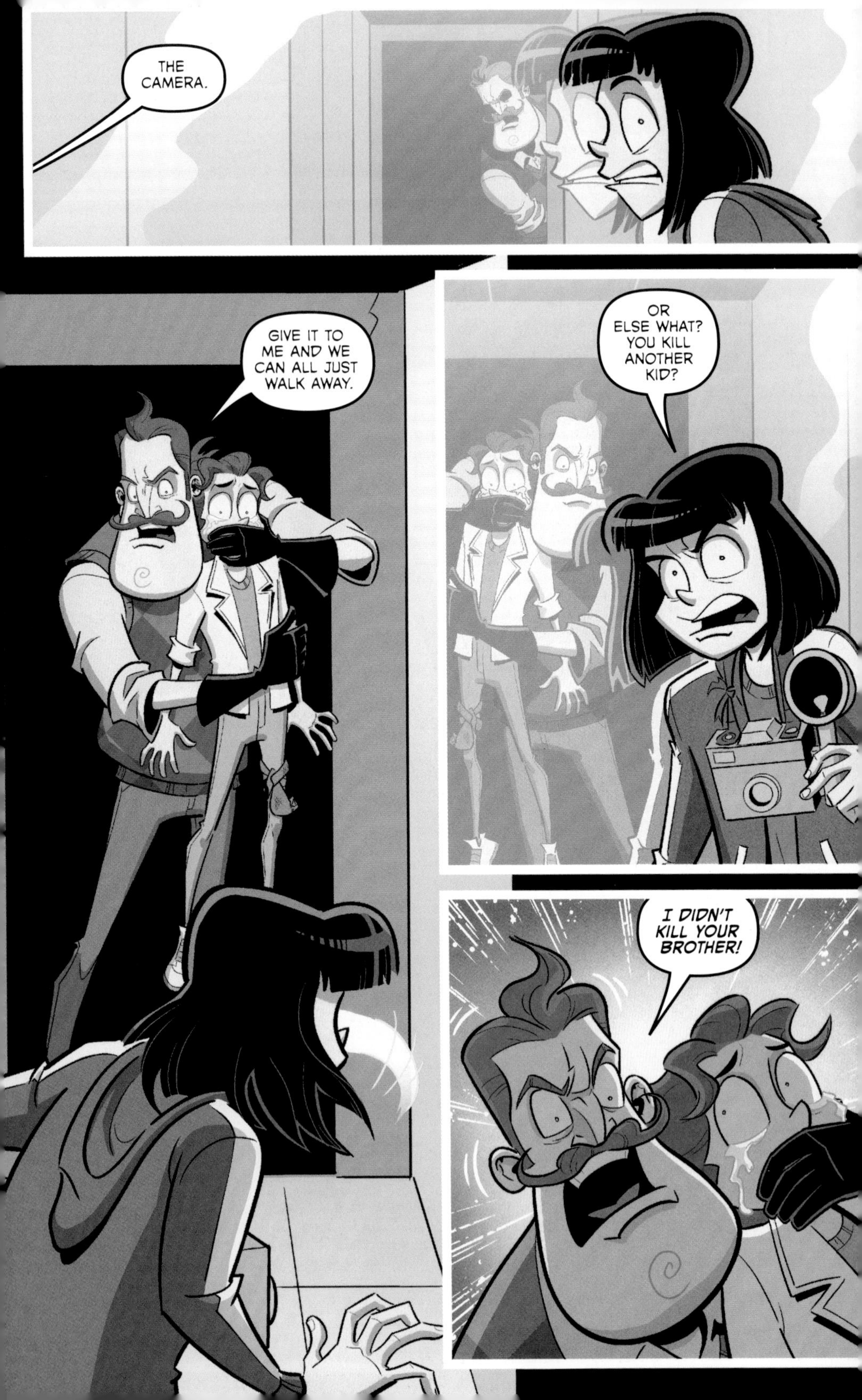
THE CAMERA.
GIVE IT TO ME AND WE CAN ALL JUST WALK AWAY.
OR ELSE WHAT? YOU KILL ANOTHER KID?
I DIDN'T KILL YOUR BROTHER!

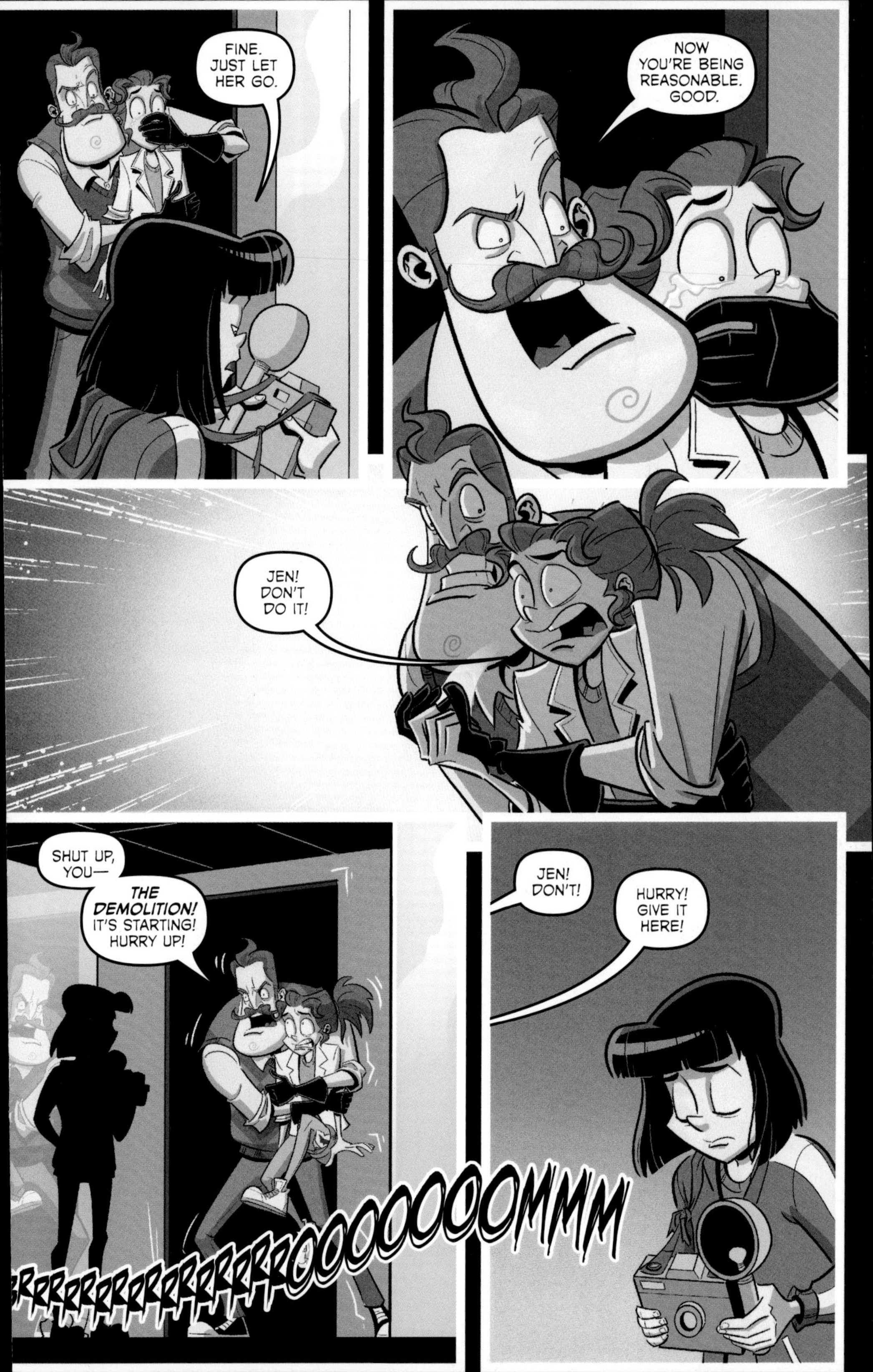
FINE. JUST LET HER GO.
NOW YOU'RE BEING REASONABLE. GOOD.
JEN! DON'T DO IT!
SHUT UP, YOU—
THE DEMOLITION! IT'S STARTING! HURRY UP!
JEN! DON'T!
HURRY! GIVE IT HERE!
BRRRRRRRRRRRRRRRRRRROOOOOOOOOMMMM

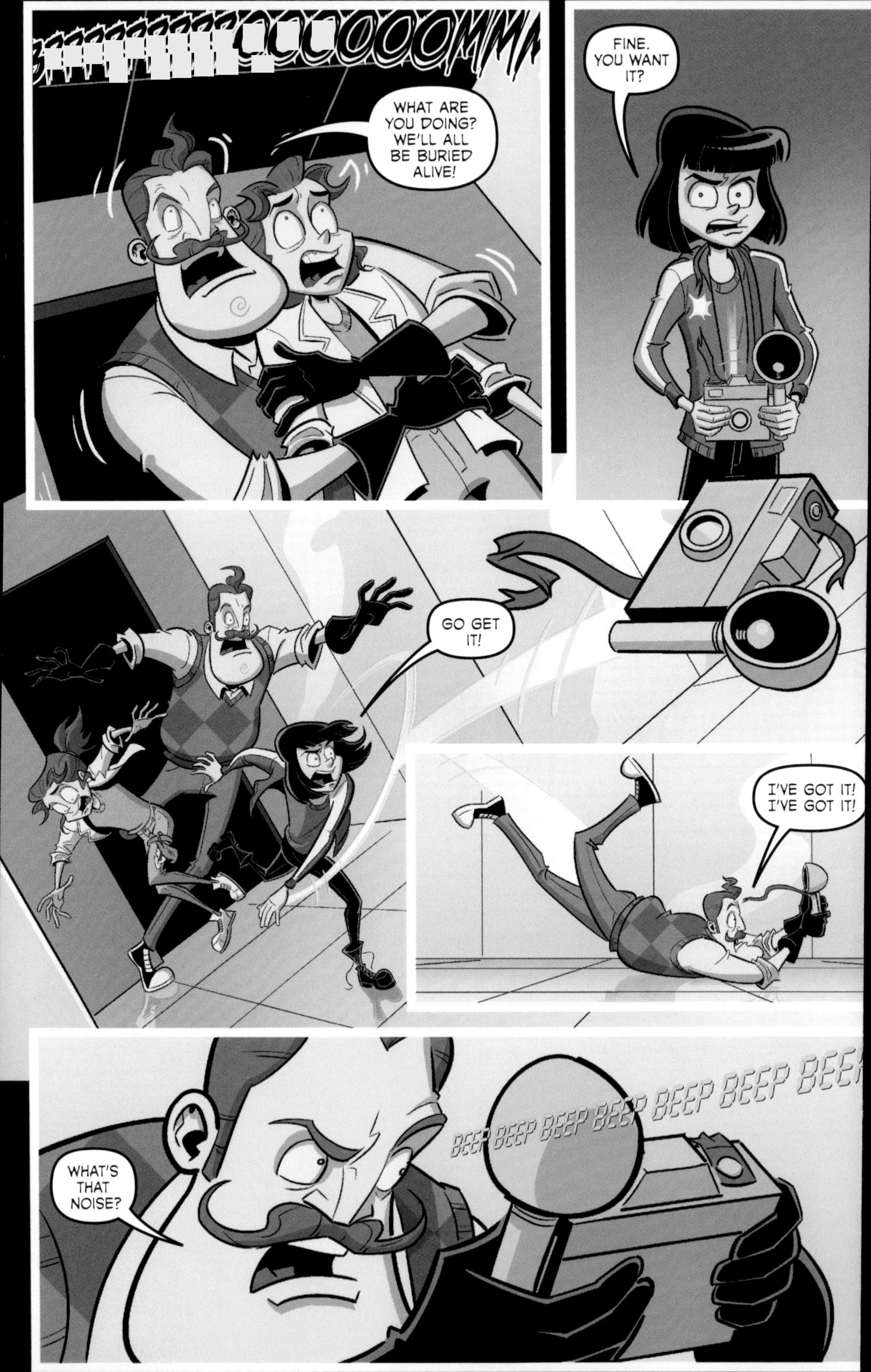
WHAT ARE YOU DOING? WE'LL ALL BE BURIED ALIVE!
FINE. YOU WANT IT?
GO GET IT!
I'VE GOT IT! I'VE GOT IT!
BEEP BEEP BEEP BEEP BEEP BEEP
WHAT'S THAT NOISE?

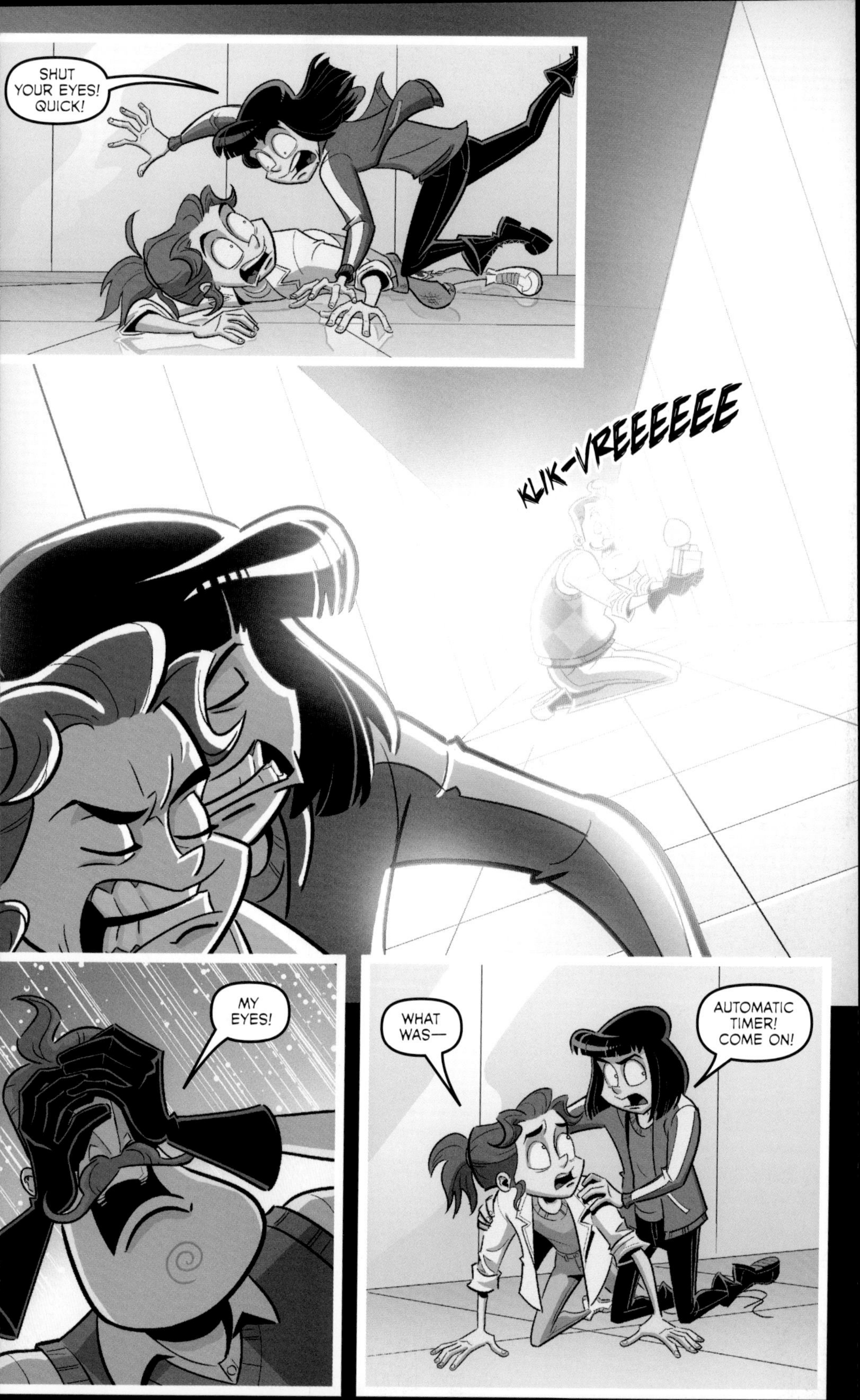
SHUT YOUR EYES! QUICK!
KLIK-VREEEEEEE
MY EYES!
WHAT WAS—
AUTOMATIC TIMER! COME ON!

BRRRRRRRRRROOOOOOOOO

THE FILM! IT'S GONE!

GET BACK HERE!

ALLIE! HURRY!

MY LEG! I CAN'T!

COME ON!

I CAN'T!

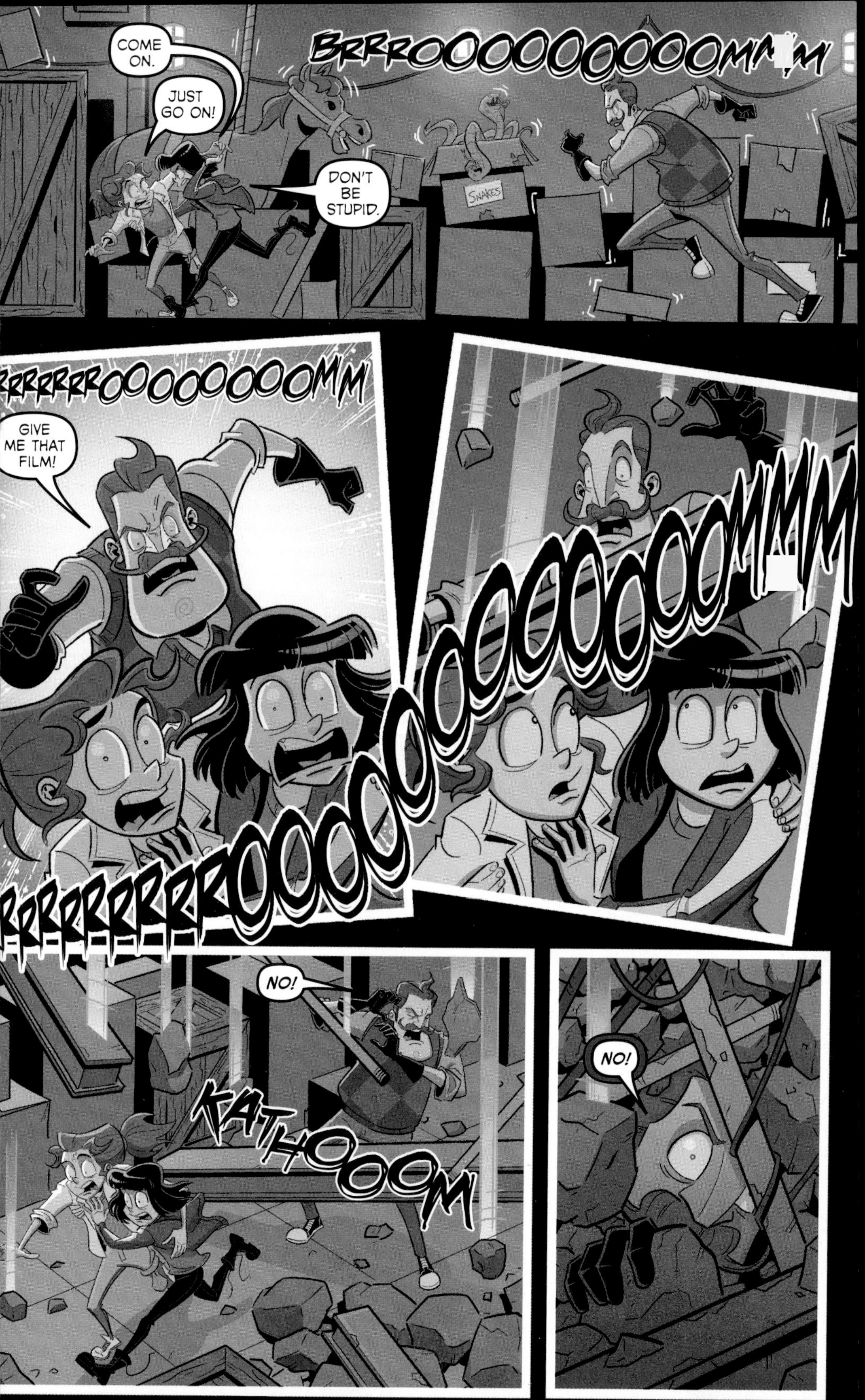
COME ON.
BRRROOOOOOOOOOMMM
JUST GO ON!
DON'T BE STUPID.
SNAKES
RRRRRRROOOOOOOOOMM
GIVE ME THAT FILM!
RRRRRRRRROOOOOOOOOOOOOOOOMMMM
NO!
KATHOOOM
NO!

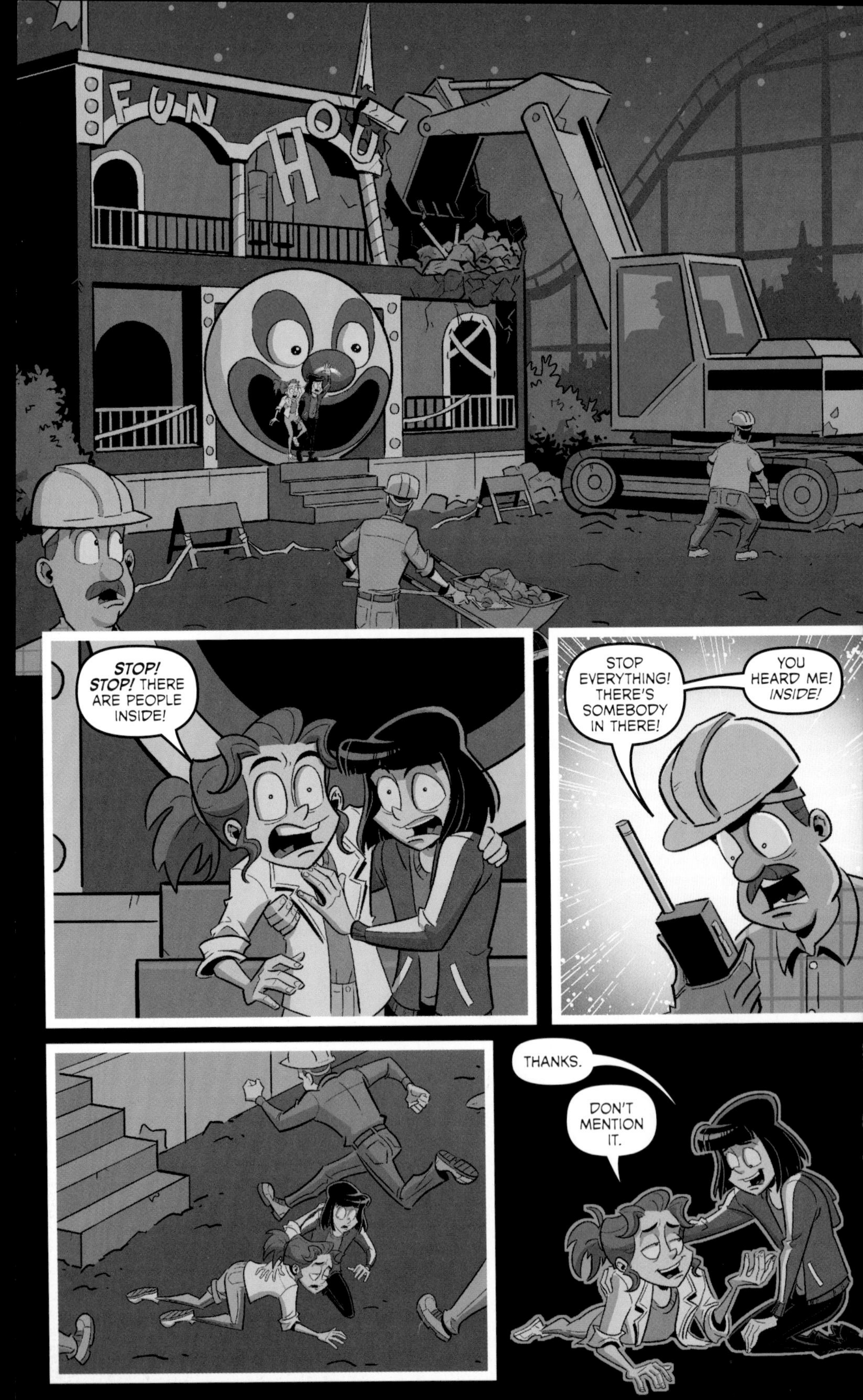
FUN HOU
STOP! STOP! THERE ARE PEOPLE INSIDE!
STOP EVERYTHING! THERE'S SOMEBODY IN THERE!
YOU HEARD ME! INSIDE!
THANKS.
DON'T MENTION IT.

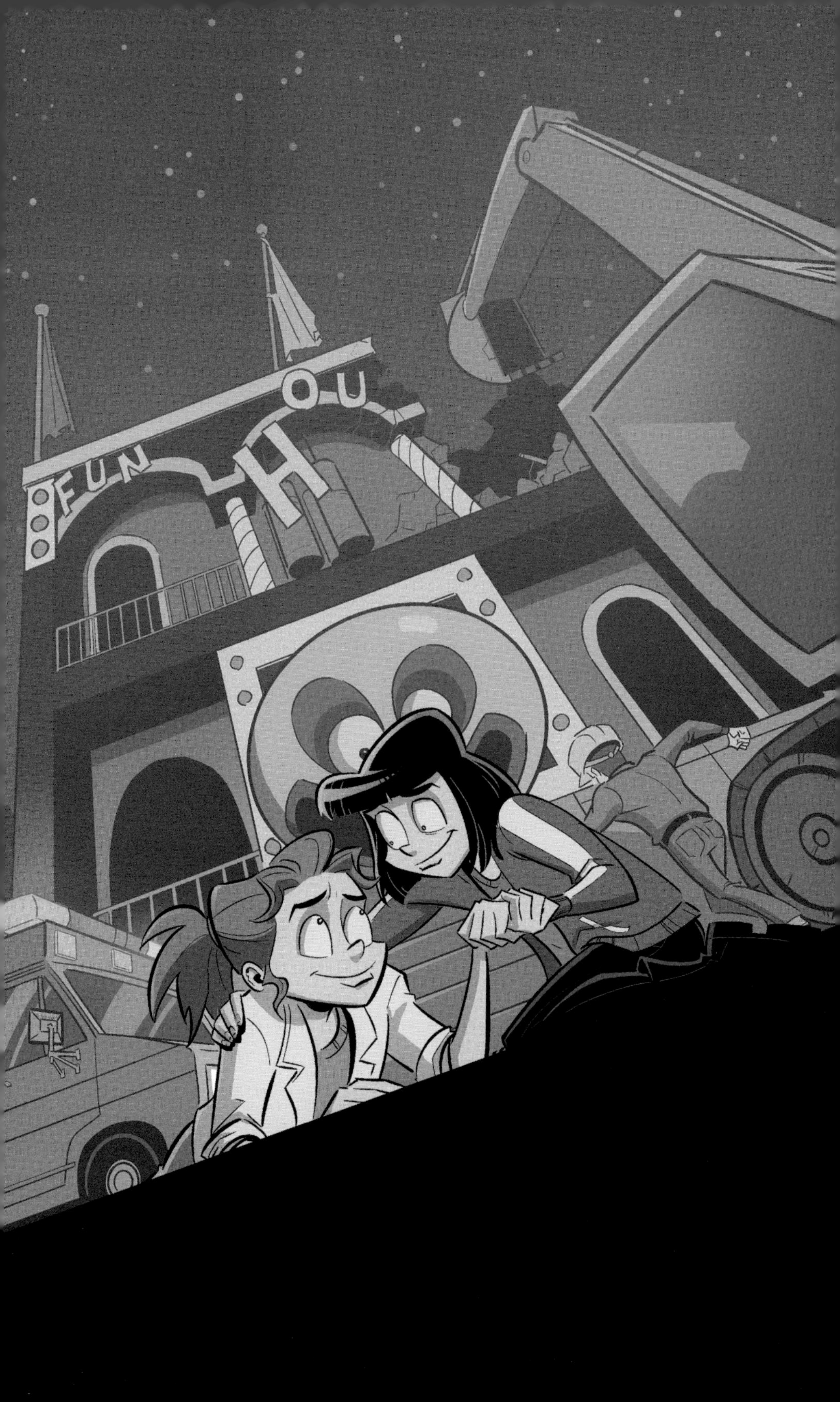
FUN
H
OU

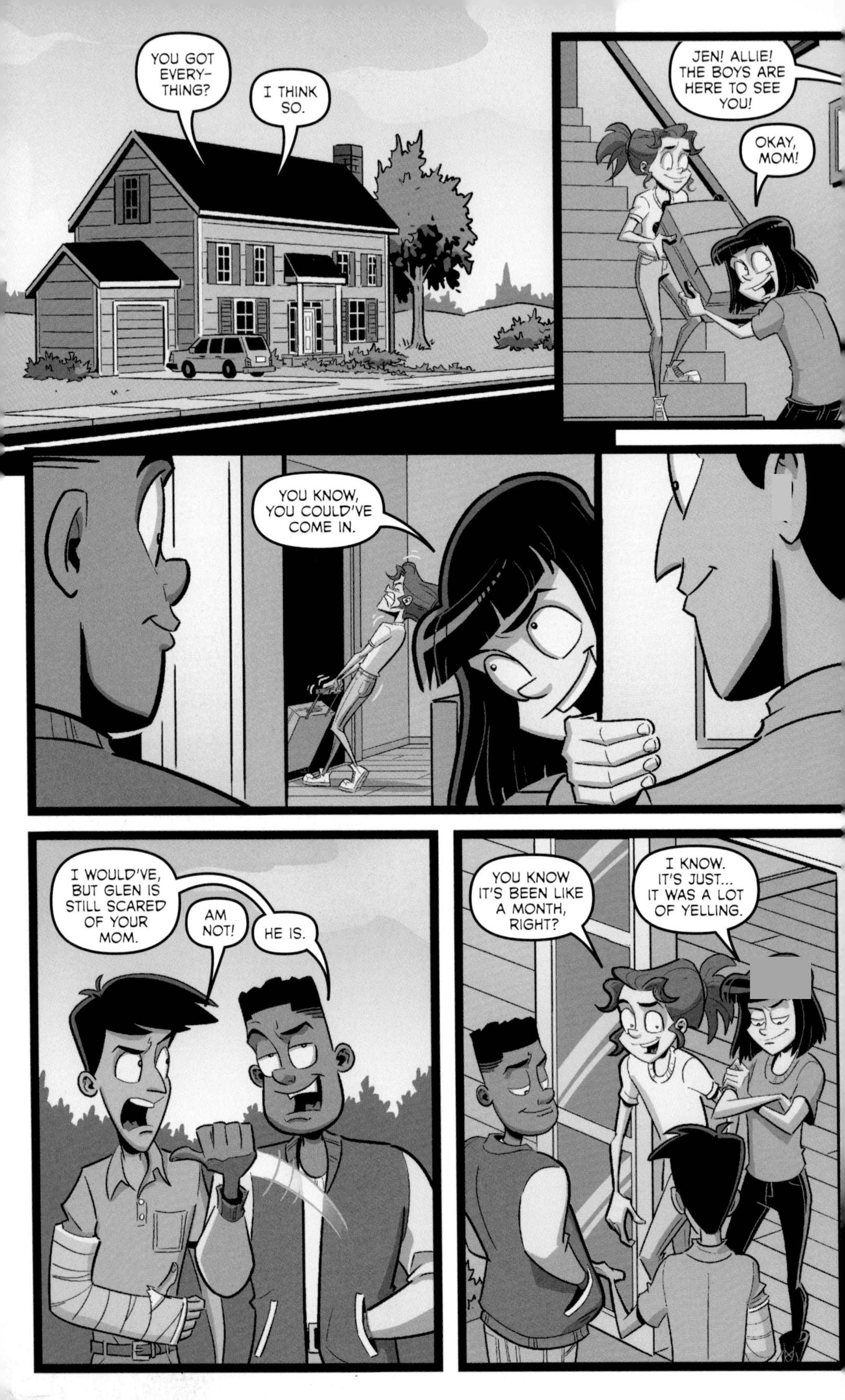
YOU GOT EVERY-THING?
I THINK SO.
JEN! ALLIE! THE BOYS ARE HERE TO SEE YOU!
OKAY, MOM!
YOU KNOW, YOU COULD'VE COME IN.
I WOULD'VE, BUT GLEN IS STILL SCARED OF YOUR MOM.
AM NOT!
HE IS.
YOU KNOW IT'S BEEN LIKE A MONTH, RIGHT?
I KNOW. IT'S JUST... IT WAS A LOT OF YELLING.

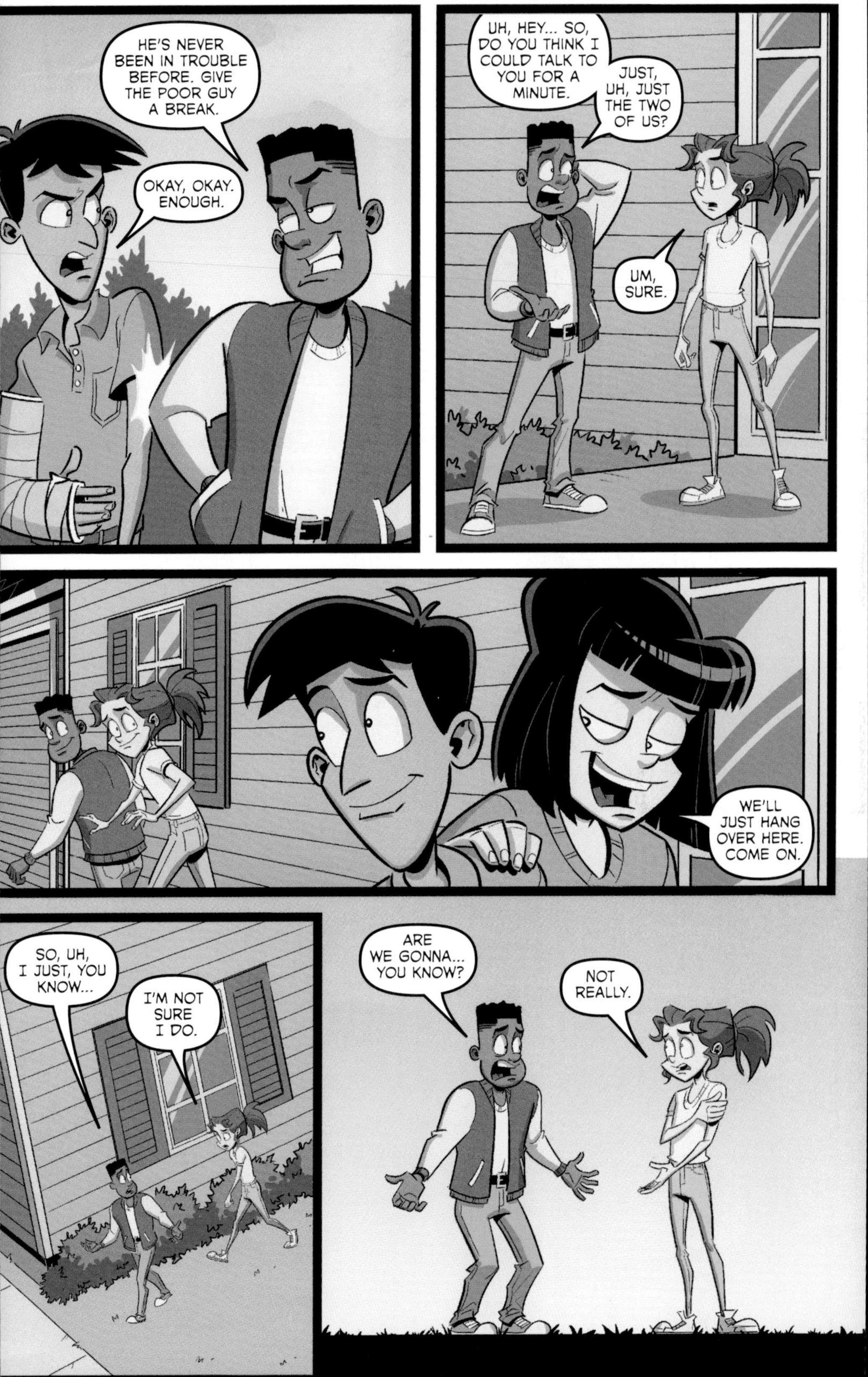
HE'S NEVER BEEN IN TROUBLE BEFORE. GIVE THE POOR GUY A BREAK.
OKAY, OKAY. ENOUGH.
UH, HEY... SO, DO YOU THINK I COULD TALK TO YOU FOR A MINUTE.
JUST, UH, JUST THE TWO OF US?
UM, SURE.
WE'LL JUST HANG OVER HERE. COME ON.
SO, UH, I JUST, YOU KNOW...
I'M NOT SURE I DO.
ARE WE GONNA... YOU KNOW?
NOT REALLY.

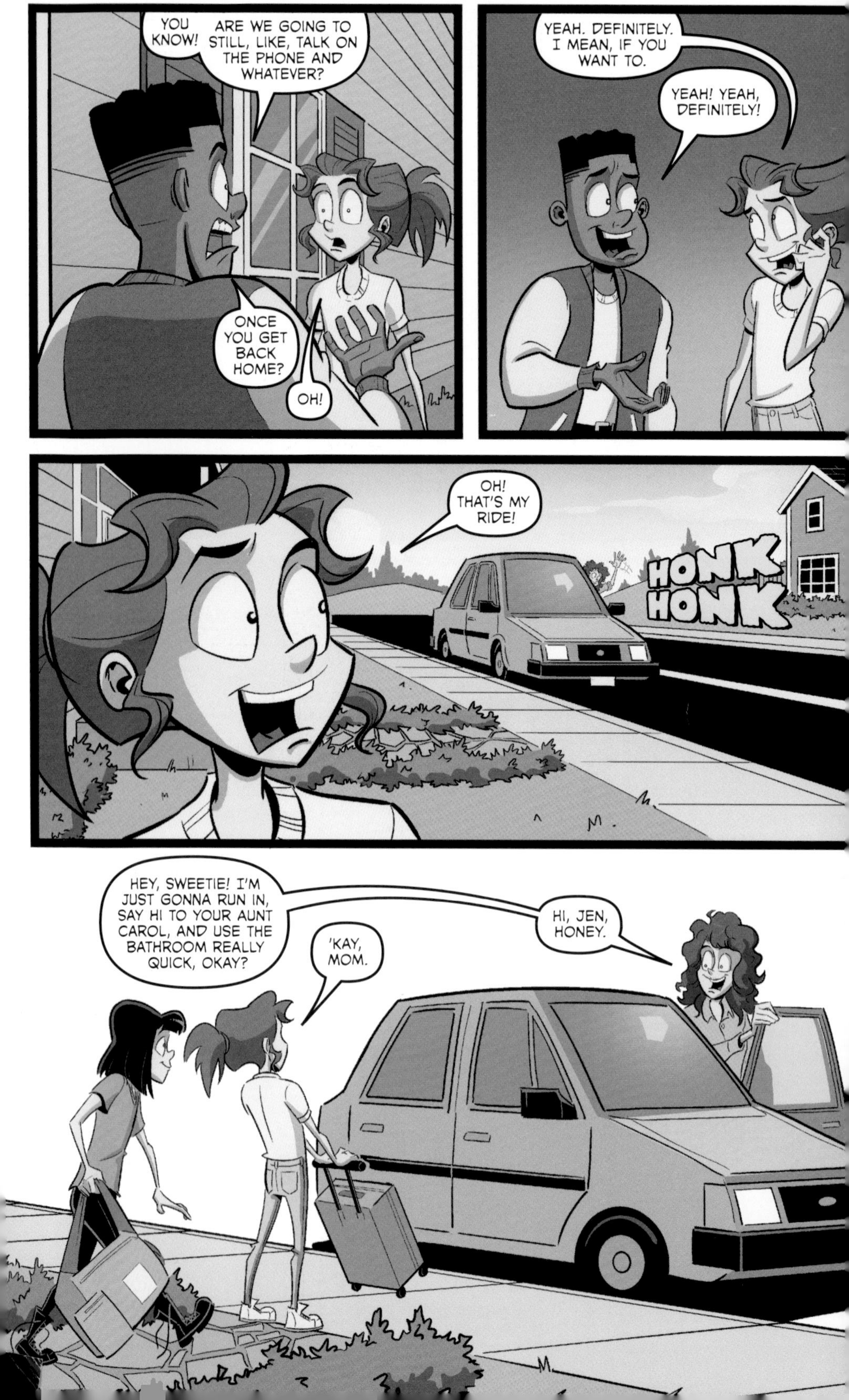
YOU KNOW!
ARE WE GOING TO STILL, LIKE, TALK ON THE PHONE AND WHATEVER?
ONCE YOU GET BACK HOME?
OH!
YEAH. DEFINITELY. I MEAN, IF YOU WANT TO.
YEAH! YEAH, DEFINITELY!
OH! THAT'S MY RIDE!
HONK HONK
HEY, SWEETIE! I'M JUST GONNA RUN IN, SAY HI TO YOUR AUNT CAROL, AND USE THE BATHROOM REALLY QUICK, OKAY?
HI, JEN, HONEY.
'KAY, MOM.

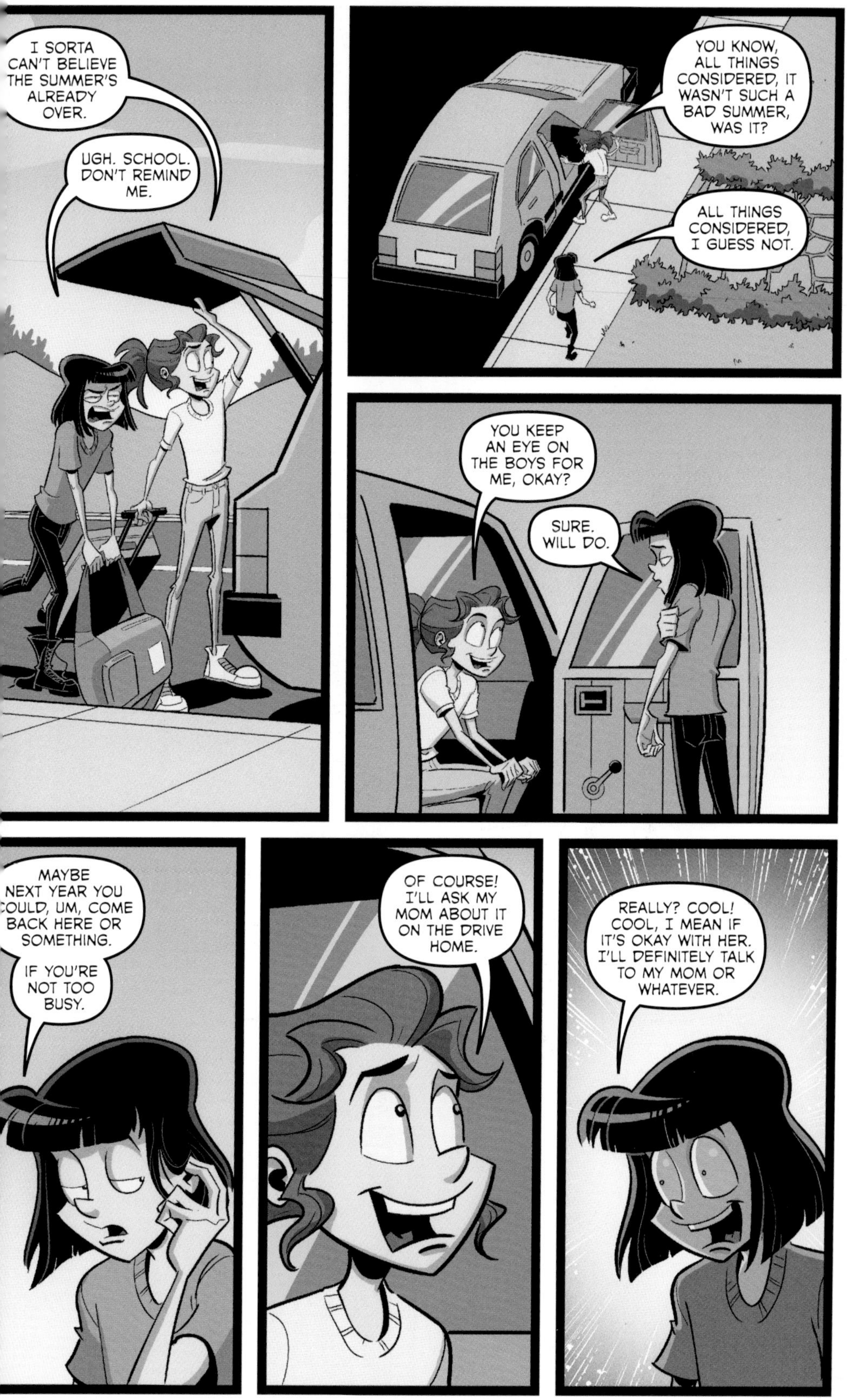
I SORTA CAN'T BELIEVE THE SUMMER'S ALREADY OVER.
UGH. SCHOOL. DON'T REMIND ME.
YOU KNOW, ALL THINGS CONSIDERED, IT WASN'T SUCH A BAD SUMMER, WAS IT?
ALL THINGS CONSIDERED, I GUESS NOT.
YOU KEEP AN EYE ON THE BOYS FOR ME, OKAY?
SURE. WILL DO.
MAYBE NEXT YEAR YOU COULD, UM, COME BACK HERE OR SOMETHING.
IF YOU'RE NOT TOO BUSY.
OF COURSE! I'LL ASK MY MOM ABOUT IT ON THE DRIVE HOME.
REALLY? COOL! COOL, I MEAN IF IT'S OKAY WITH HER. I'LL DEFINITELY TALK TO MY MOM OR WHATEVER.

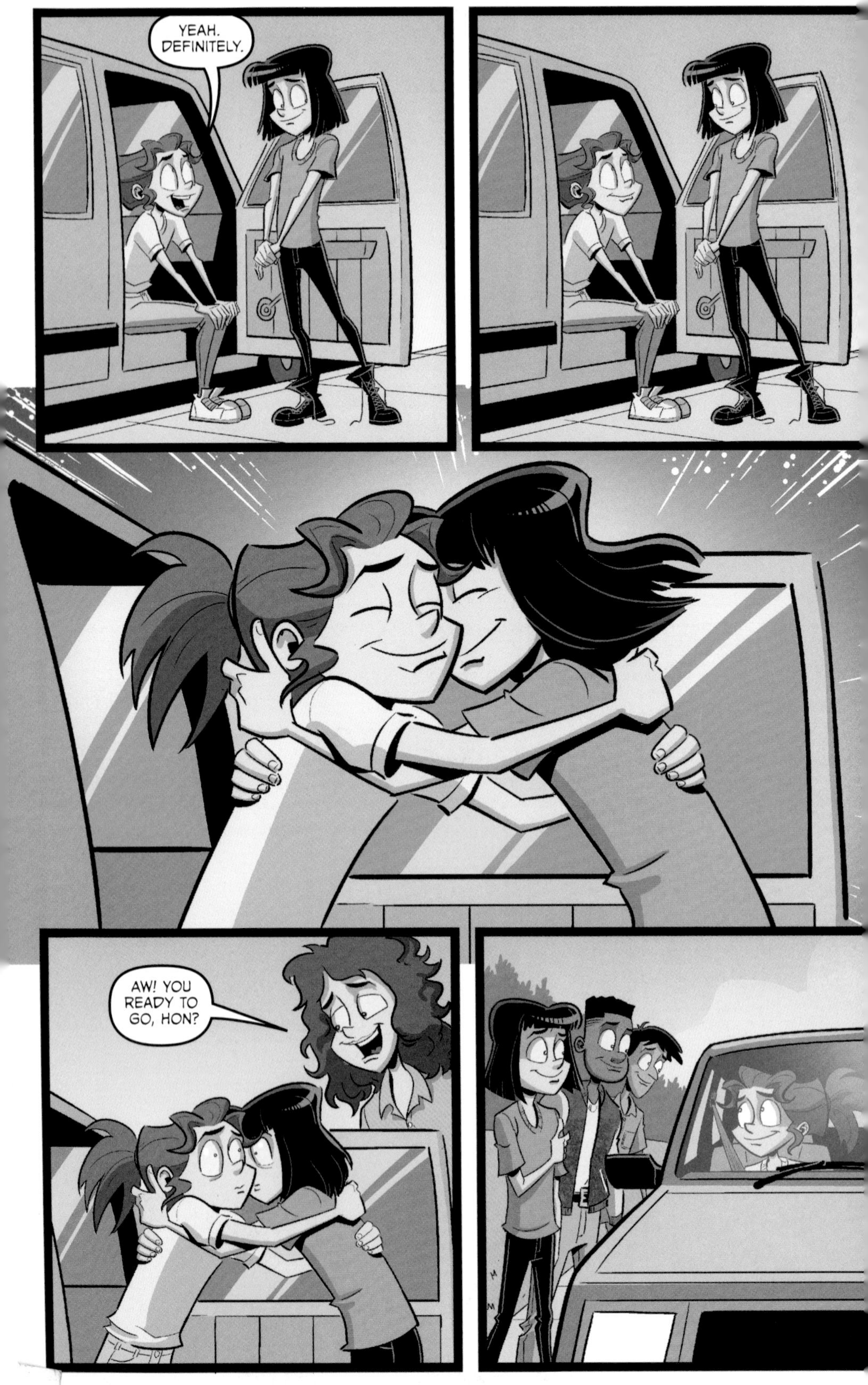
YEAH.
DEFINITELY.
AW! YOU
READY TO
GO, HON?

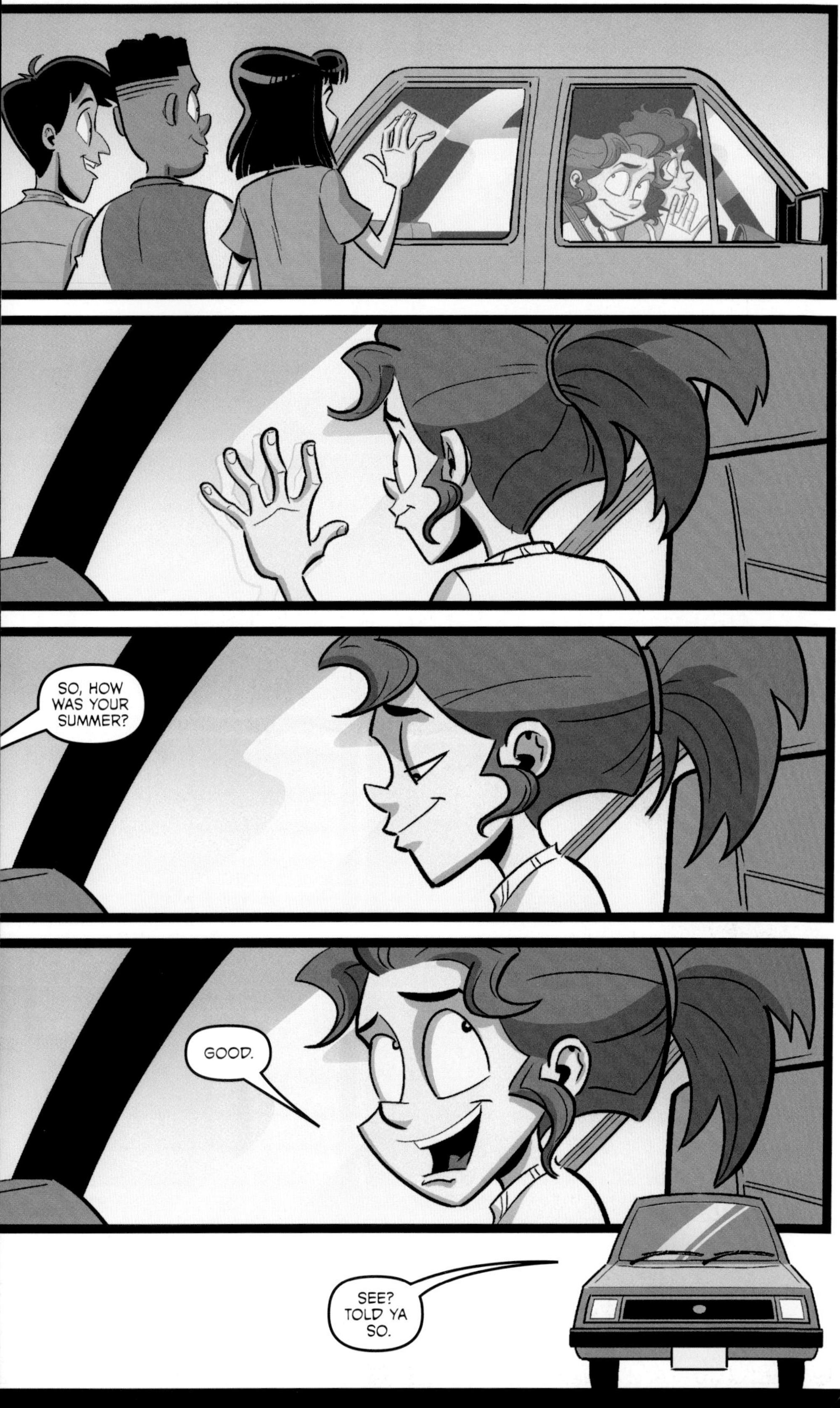
SO, HOW WAS YOUR SUMMER?
GOOD.
SEE? TOLD YA SO.

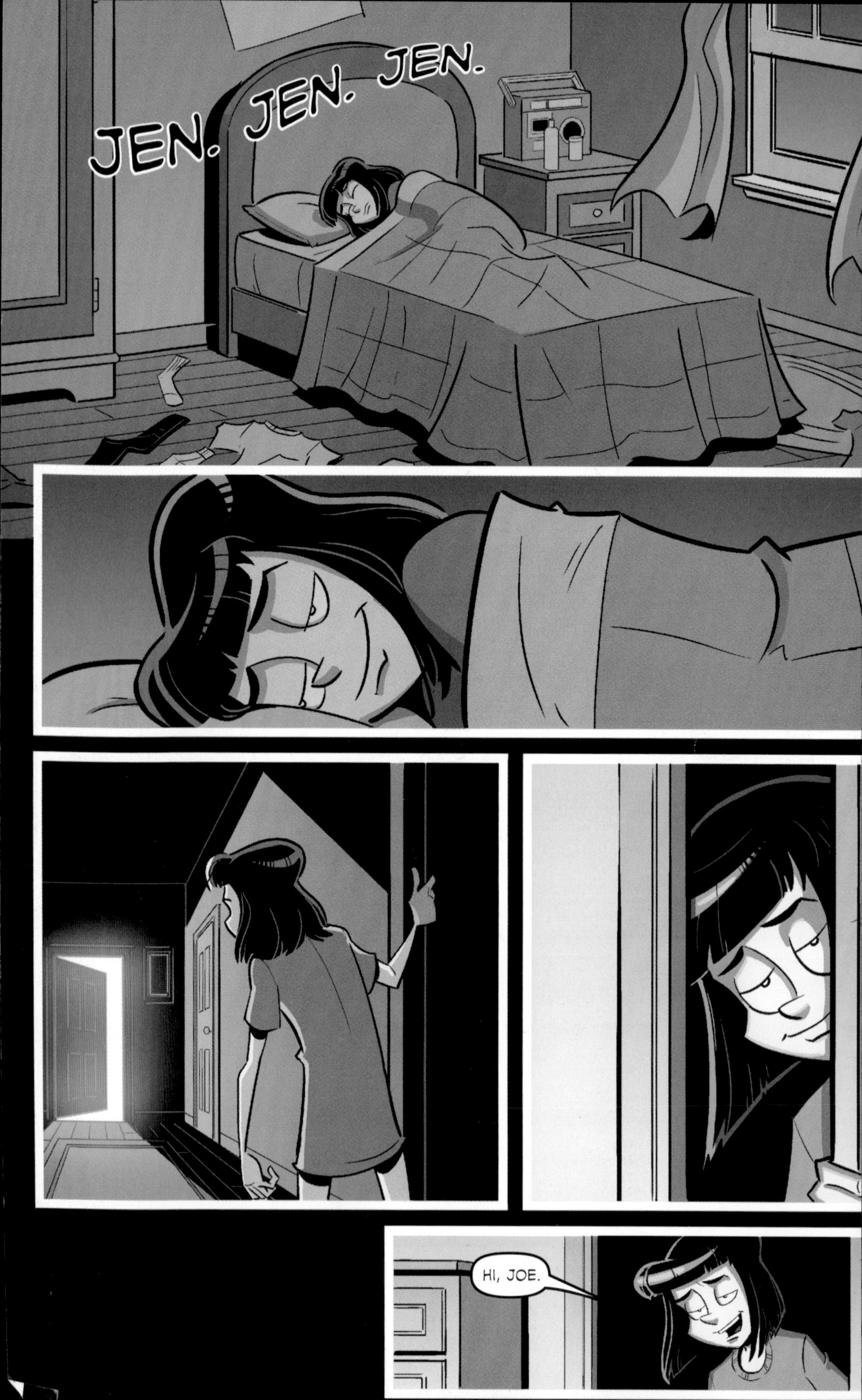
JEN. JEN. JEN.
HI, JOE.

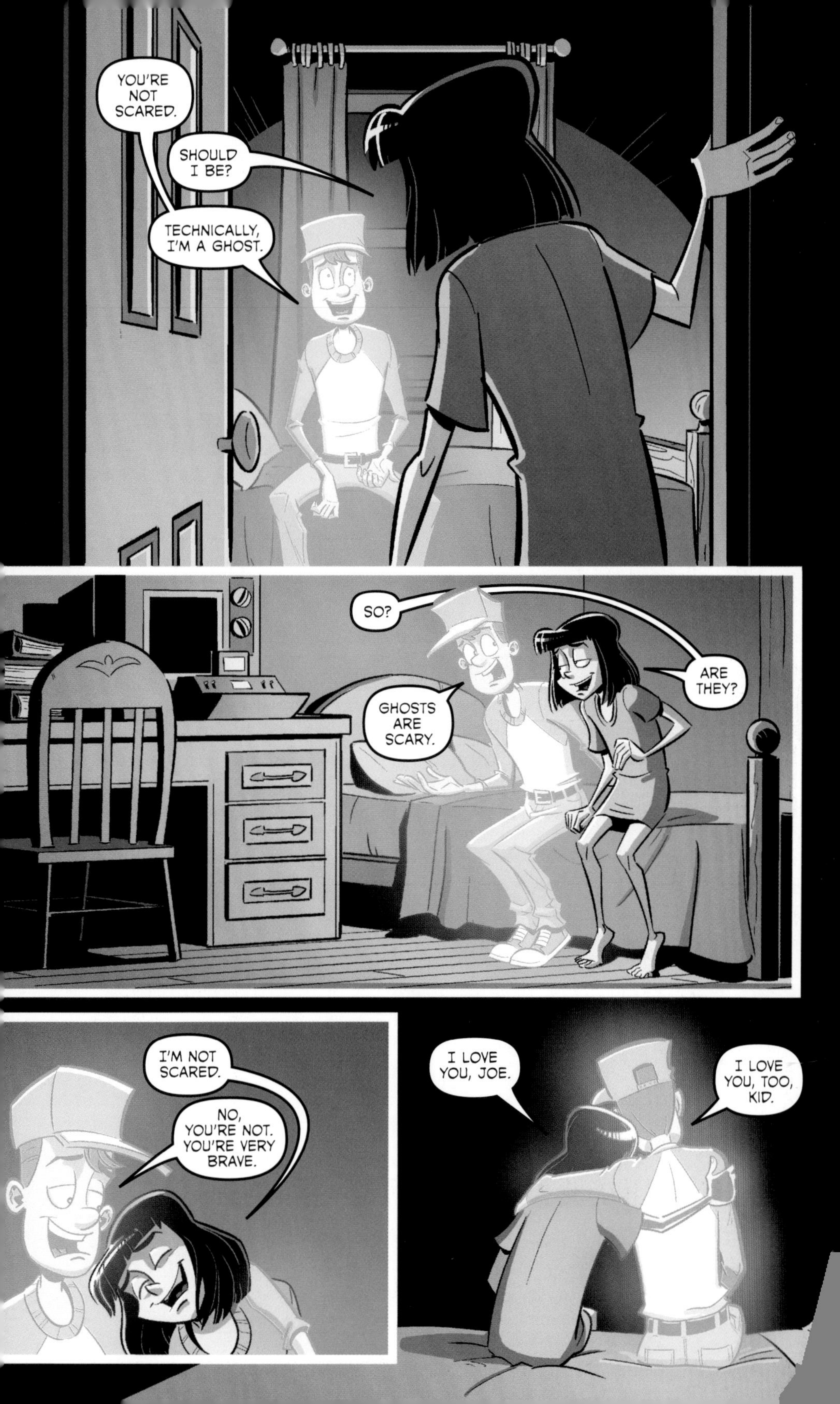
YOU'RE NOT SCARED.
SHOULD I BE?
TECHNICALLY, I'M A GHOST.
SO?
GHOSTS ARE SCARY.
ARE THEY?
I'M NOT SCARED.
NO, YOU'RE NOT. YOU'RE VERY BRAVE.
I LOVE YOU, JOE.
I LOVE YOU, TOO, KID.

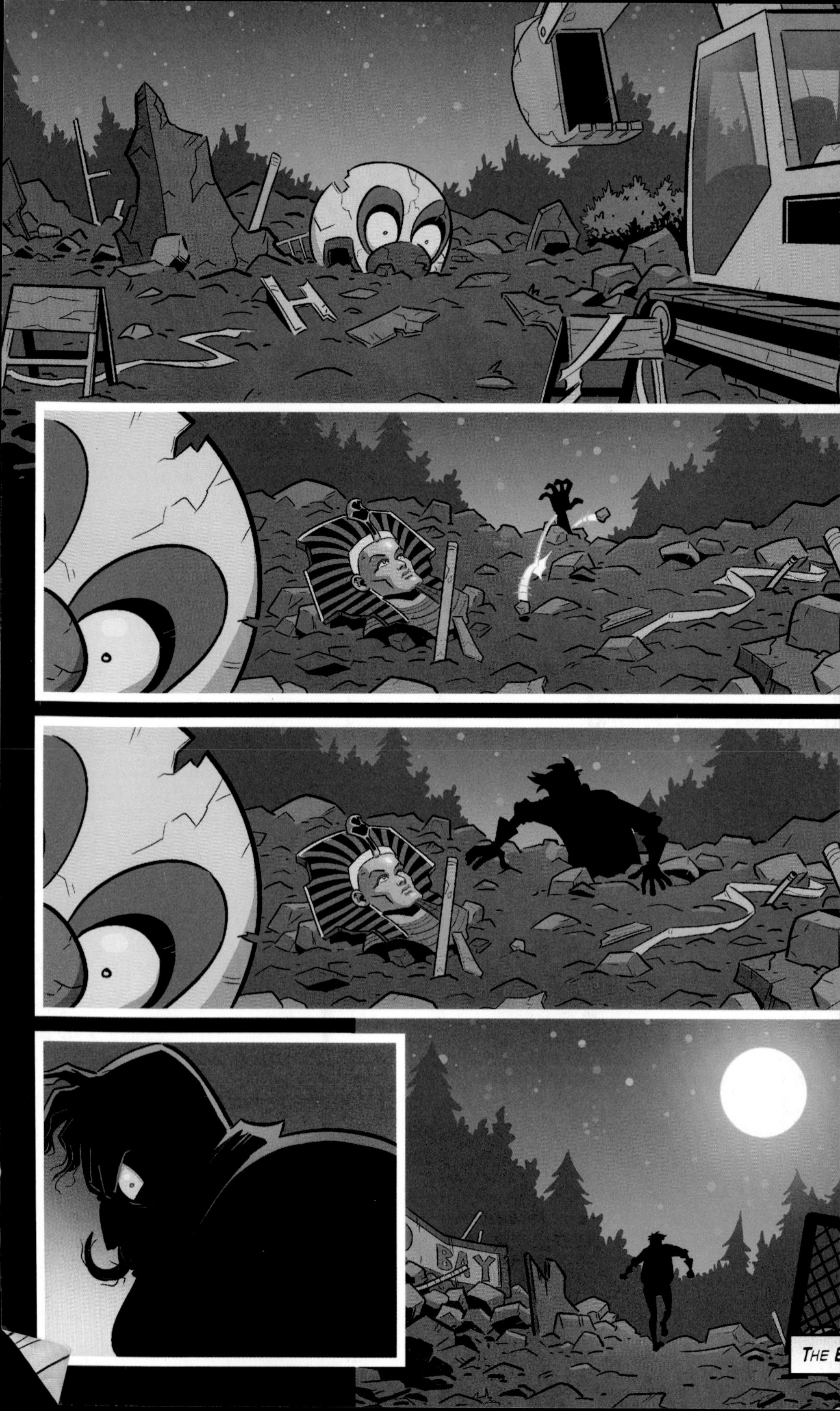
BAY
THE